DUNGEON DELVER

DUNGEON DELVER

VICTOR OF TUCSON ‡ BOOK TWO

PLUM PARROT

Podium

To Paksennarion,
a true paragon of heroism
and the namesake for my best companion

Cover design by Podium Publishing

ISBN: 978-1-0394-2590-3

Published in 2023 by Podium Publishing, ULC
www.podiumaudio.com
Podium

DUNGEON DELVER

1

DEATH AND BONES

Victor felt as if he were being sucked down a cold whirlpool as the portal drew him in. The sensation was panic-inducing, but just as his mind began to run away from him, it was over. The foot he'd stepped into the portal with was suddenly making contact with a hard surface, and then he was standing in a brightly lit stone room with an exquisitely detailed, shiny gold or brass leaf ceiling. Thayla was next to him, and he realized the bright light was coming from his orb that had made the journey through the portal with them.

"This isn't in my records, Victor," Gorz said in his mind.

"What do you mean? Didn't Reevus have to come through here?" Victor asked aloud, and Thayla gave him a raised eyebrow. He motioned to his necklace while he waited for Gorz's answer.

"One would think so, but I don't recognize this location," Gorz replied.

"He doesn't recognize this area, even though his old owner came through this dungeon."

"Maybe it changes over time or as people enter it?" Thayla leaned against her spear, peering around. "Look at the ceiling in here! Have you ever seen something so fancy?"

"Only on VR."

"VR?"

"Um, I mean like not in person—in pictures, sort of." Victor walked around the square room, pausing at the strange, smooth, round door. He couldn't see any hinges, and the pale, maple-hued wood was without feature. "You ever been in a dungeon, Thayla?"

"No. Adventurers and fortune seekers go to dungeons; I never had that kind of confidence or ambition in my old life."

"Really?" Victor looked at the tall, black-braided woman with her strong shoulders, fierce expression, and leopard-like grace. "You never struck me as anything other than confident."

"I had other priorities before I was sentenced to the mines. We adjust as we must, right?" She walked forward with her spear and tapped the sharp point against the wooden door. "Do you see a way to open this?"

"Are we ready? I have some ideas." When Thayla nodded, crouching and pointing her spear at the closed portal, Victor stepped forward and gave it a shove with one hand, his axe gripped in the other. Just as he'd hoped, the door moved easily, receding into the wall an inch and then rolling to the right, disappearing into the hollow stone. A corridor crossed in front of their room, built from the same stone with the same fancy gilt ceiling. "Just a sec," he said, willing his globe of inspiration Energy to float to the back corner of the room, then he poked his head out into the corridor and looked both ways.

Outside of the pool of illumination coming from the doorway, the corridor was utterly dark. Victor looked to his globe and willed it to come closer and, again, was surprised by how easily it floated toward him. "This globe is a lot easier to control than before. Do you think it's the improved spell, or am I getting better at it?"

"Probably both." Thayla shrugged. "Anything out there?"

"Darkness. Well, there's no going back." He gestured to the lack of any other exit, then he moved into the corridor and, trusting his gut, turned right. Victor could feel Thayla's presence behind him, and he started advancing, his bright light following along with him. After about twenty paces, he saw a T-junction ahead and slowly moved toward it. As he drew close and peered both ways, seeing nothing but long, stretching corridors disappearing into darkness in both directions, he noticed, in the light of his globe, a jagged hairline crack in the wall at the junction.

He stretched out a hand and ran it along the crack, tracing its length from the top of the wall all the way to the ground. "What is it?" Thayla asked.

"There's a weird line or crack here." He took a step back and ran his eyes over the wall, and then he saw a tiny, shallow depression near the top of it. He wouldn't have seen it if his light hadn't cast the smallest of shadows into the depression. Again, he stretched out his hand and pushed his fingertips into the depression, and with a click, the stone moved under his touch; the wall separated a couple of inches along the crack he'd seen.

"Whoa!" Thayla backed up as the stone moved, but as they both stood ready with their weapons, they realized it wouldn't open further on its own.

"I'll pull it open. Ready?" She grunted assent, and he hooked Lifedrinker into his belt, reaching out to pull apart the stone halves of the wall. At first, they didn't want to move, but they inched apart a tiny amount as he strained. He realized it was just a matter of muscle, so he flooded his arms with strength using Sovereign Will and heaved. The walls slid roughly apart with a deep grind, and when he had a gap big enough to slip through, he backed up and grabbed up his axe.

"Wow, here just a few minutes, and you already found a secret passage?" Thayla clapped him on the shoulder, peering into the revealed space.

The light exposed another passage, narrower and with a regular stone ceiling. Victor ducked through the narrow gap and started walking forward, Thayla and his light just behind. The floor of this passage had a layer of dust on it, which made him realize the other hallway hadn't. He didn't know if that was a significant clue as to traffic or just how the dungeon worked, but he appreciated being able to tell that nothing had moved through this corridor ahead of them. A few more minutes of walking brought an ordinary wooden door into view. It was made of vertical slats, and Victor could see it had a black metal latch and hinges.

"That door's in good shape," Thayla whispered.

"Yeah, let's see if it's locked." Victor padded forward and reached out the latch. When he tried to depress it, it wouldn't move. He whispered, "Should I try to bash it? I could also use the ring we found."

"Might as well use the ring; no sense waking up the whole dungeon until we have to."

"Right." Victor lifted his left hand with the Ring of the Guest and gently knocked on the door. A raspy click sounded from the metal plate around the latch, and Victor whistled appreciatively before he could catch himself. He clapped his hand to his mouth and winced toward Thayla, but she just shrugged. Once again, he pushed down on the latch, which depressed with a click, opening the door toward them.

Victor stepped back and pulled the door open, and his light revealed the creepiest thing he'd ever seen: a throng of naked, hairless, pale creatures were packed together in the center of the room. They stood with their arms down, swaying and pressing into each other as they stared up at an orb of pulsing, radiating blue-white Energy. They were anatomically similar to humans with all the proper parts, and the way they pressed and hissed at each other through wide, thin-lipped mouths was strangely and disturbingly sexual. When the light from Victor's orb touched them, they jerked their heads away from the ceiling, staring at the duo standing in the doorway.

They didn't scream or growl, but they hissed and gnashed their teeth. For a moment, they stood as if stunned, but then something broke, and they lifted their claw-tipped arms and charged. Victor immediately cast Project Spirit, hoping to drive them mad with his rage-attuned Energy as he had the rats, and it worked, partially. Some of the ghoulish figures paused in their wild charge, others began to hiss and snap their teeth more frenziedly, and still others started to thrash about with their claws, heedless of the damage they inflicted on their own kind. Before they could regain their composure, Victor stepped forward and started to hack Lifedrinker about.

The axe bit deeply into the naked monsters, but not as easily as Victor had anticipated; their skin was tough like old leather, and their bones a lot harder than those of the cultists outside the dungeon. He failed to remove any limbs, though black blood showered the room from his wide cleaves. Thayla, too, delivered a half dozen terrible stabs to the creatures before they managed to shake off Victor's spell and redouble their efforts to claw the two adventurers apart.

They seemed to hate Victor's light, and Victor had to believe that the white-gold glare was counteracting whatever effect the blue orb in the room might have had on himself and Thayla. The ghouls were strong, though, and Victor was having a hard time knocking away all the claws and gnashing teeth, and he accumulated a lot of painful gashes along his arms and legs, despite the carnage he was dishing out with Lifedrinker. He heard Thayla grunt in pain more than once and knew some of their claws were also getting past her guard. "Come on! Fucking kill them!" he screamed, more at himself than Thayla, and he flooded his arms and axe with rage Energy, cast Sovereign Will to improve his agility, and activated Inspiring Presence. The room lit up even more brightly in his vision; the ghoul-like monsters seemed smaller, weaker, and slower, and Lifedrinker blurred in the air as he began to weave her between their grasping claws, striking terrible wounds to necks, bellies, and joints.

Thayla made a sound like a cross between a growl and a howl and began to drive her spear into eyes and mouths, pushing the ghouls back and sending them flopping on the ground. Between her improved accuracy and Victor's sudden show of speed and skill, they had most of the creatures down in a matter of seconds. Still, they thrashed and writhed and tried to stand and attack them. Not one of them was entirely "dead" yet.

Victor growled and stepped forward, bringing Lifedrinker down on one flopping, prone ghoul's neck with all of his might. With a loud cracking snap, her edge bit through its sturdy spine and clicked against the stone floor. As the monster's head rolled away, the body stopped thrashing, and the clacking jaws ceased their movement. After that, Victor and Thayla knew what to do, and they systematically began to relieve the ghouls of their heads. Thayla kept them down while Victor moved among them, powering through their necks with Lifedrinker's keen, hungry edge.

"Thirteen," Thayla counted as he finally severed the last ghoul's head.

"Those fucking things were tough," Victor said, looking at the carnage. His arms and legs were burning from all the gashes he'd received, and now that his Inspiring Presence had faded, he was feeling exhausted and drained. He was about to suggest a rest when motes of Energy began to gather above the fallen creatures, and every single one was tinged with purple. "This is going to be a big one!" he crowed, bracing himself. Just as he'd predicted, the surge of Energy that flooded into him and Thayla was enormous, lifting them both off the ground.

*****Congratulations! You have achieved Level 24 Herald of Carnage, gained 10 will and 8 strength, and have 10 attribute points to allocate.*****

*****Congratulations! You have learned the spell: Channel Spirit, Improved.*****

*****Channel Spirit, Improved: Apply your Core's Energy to your physical attacks, manifesting your attuned Energy as a destructive force that scales based on the amount of Energy you channel. This skill will bypass the usual effect spirit affinities have on the cultivator's emotional state. Energy Cost: Variable. Cooldown: Minimal.*****

"I leveled!" Thayla said, a look of surprise on her face. "That's fast, Victor!"

"Yeah, well, that was a lot of Energy. I leveled too, by the way."

"Victor, do you feel that?"

"What?"

"The orb there, the blue one, I can feel it in my Core. It's like my Core is hungry for it. Does that make sense?"

"I guess? I don't know—I don't feel anything from it." Victor looked to the pale blue orb, unable to shake the notion that its light was sickly somehow, especially after watching those creepy ghoul assholes basking in it. "Hold on," he said, then canceled his Globe of Insight. Suddenly the room was bathed in the pale blue glow of the other orb, and Victor felt its chill seeping into his bones. It was an unpleasant chill that brought to mind hunger, despair, and finality. "I don't like it."

"It's Energy, Victor, and my Core is practically salivating for it. I think I could gain something if I try to cultivate it."

"Well, you know more about this stuff than I do. Can we take it with us? This room is disgusting." It was true; the square room was like a scene from a nightmare, with ghoul bodies and their heads scattered around in big dark smears all over the stone floor. The walls were splashed with black fluid, and the smell was ripe, though the cold air emanating from the orb seemed to dampen the stench. "What is it, anyway? Ice-attuned?"

"I don't know, not till I try it, and no, I don't think we can move it." She looked around and then started shoving the bodies away from the center of the room. She motioned to the door. "Can you watch my back while I try to cultivate it?"

"Um, hold on. You sure you want to mess with that?"

"There's a reason this was kept behind a secret door, Victor; I really think it will upgrade my Core."

"I'll guard you, then." Victor resummoned his Globe of Insight, sighing as the cold pressure of the other orb was pushed back, then he pushed the door closed and stood in front of it, with Lifedrinker, watching Thayla. She sat down with her back to Victor, her legs crossed, and her hands on her knees, just as Yrella had taught Victor to sit when he cultivated. While he watched her, he took another look at his attributes:

Strength:	**82**	**Vitality:**	**90**
Dexterity:	**40**	**Agility:**	**48**
Intelligence:	**32**	**Will:**	**123**
Points Available:	**10**		

Victor knew that, logically, there had to be a perfect way to distribute attribute points, but he kept reminding himself that more than one person had told him how rare it was to have unbound points to spend. That meant that a class usually defined a person, which meant that he had a rather uncommon chance to define himself, at least to some degree. Sure, he was forced to fight savagely for his survival at this time, but did he always want to live that way? Maybe he'd be forced to, but would it hurt to plan for a bit more diversity in his skill set? He felt good, using his free points to keep his minor attributes from lagging too far behind, even if pumping up his strength and vitality might make his current situation more bearable. "But I could pump up lots of attributes with Sovereign Will," he muttered, careful not to bother Thayla.

"Victor, could I be of some help?"

"I'm struggling with how to spend my extra attribute points. How rare a skill is Sovereign Will? It seems pretty great that I could pump up my strength one minute and then my agility or vitality the next."

"That's beyond my scope of knowledge, Victor. I can say that Reevus did not have a similar ability."

"Hold on," Victor paused to really consider the problem. Will was important for a number of factors: according to Yrella, it increased his maximum Energy, his Energy regeneration, and his mental fortitude for both resisting effects and forcing them upon his foes, and in his seemingly rare case, it allowed him to boost any other physical attribute. *"I'm going to keep improving my will for now."* He explained his logic to Gorz, and the spirit indicated that it couldn't find fault with it.

"With one hundred thirty-three will, I can boost any of my stats by over forty points now!"

"It seems quite significant, Victor."

He was looking at his Energy numbers, happy to see he had over fifteen hundred maximum when the orb Thayla was studying suddenly flared. A stream of blue Energy with a sickly white undertone started streaming into her, just below her breastbone. *"That's going to her Core, right, Gorz?"*

"Yes, Victor, and it is not water-attuned Energy as you speculated. I've met elementalists while with Reevus, and their signature was quite different."

"Great." Victor watched as Thayla arched her back, and the stream of Energy continued. Her whole body was limned with the cold, blue light now, and he could feel the pressure of it, even with his Globe of Insight floating between him and her. After another moment or two, the stream finally trailed off, and as it was absorbed into Thayla, Victor saw that the orb was gone. He continued to watch her as she seemed to be processing what had happened. Then, finally, she unfolded her legs and stood up. "You okay?" he asked.

"I'm . . ." She looked around, moving her hands and flexing her fingers, then she turned to Victor, and he saw that her dark-irised eyes were now fully black; the whites were gone. "I'm not sure, Victor. I hope I didn't just make a terrible mistake. My Core has changed, and I have a new affinity."

"What changed? What affinity?"

"I used to have a Pearl Class Core—now it's a Whisper Class. Whisper! I've never heard of it, but worse, Victor, the affinity is for death. I have a death affinity and a big pool of death-attuned Energy in my Core."

"Uh, is that bad? It sounds bad."

"I don't know! I feel strange! I feel cold. Victor, take my hand; is it cold?" She stepped forward, reaching out her red fingers, and Victor took them. They didn't feel cold, exactly, but they weren't as warm as he felt they should be.

"Nah, they aren't cold, Thayla. Look, um, I'm going to tell you this because I'd want to know. I'm sure it's nothing, but your eyes are black."

"My eyes? They've always been dark."

"No, I mean all of them. You don't have any white parts. Don't freak out!" Thayla had slapped her hands to her eyes and was pressing her fingers against them as though she could feel what Victor was describing. "They don't look bad, Thayla! I mean, they're kind of intimidating, which can be good, right?"

"Victor! What did I do? Am I still me?"

"Of course you are! You wouldn't be freaking out asking that if you weren't. Come on, there has to be some bright side to this. Did you gain any more Energy? Any new skills?"

"No new skills, but I have a higher affinity with this new Energy than I used to have, and my Core is two levels higher."

"Well, shit! That's something! You might pick up some skills or spells as we go along."

"I might get offered a different class option at thirty, too," she said quietly, her breathing back to normal.

"That's the spirit. You ready to get out of this stinking room?"

"Yes." She stepped forward and opened the door, and Victor couldn't help but notice that her movements seemed different. It took him a minute to put a finger on it, but he realized she didn't turn to look at him as she went by and didn't smile or frown—just pulled the door open and walked through. He hoped it was just the strange experience and that she'd get back to herself soon, but he was worried about her.

They made their way back to the T-junction, and Victor took a left turn, walking ahead of Thayla. The hallway continued for a hundred paces or more, and then Victor saw a flickering blue light ahead. He crouched and moved forward, glancing back to be sure Thayla knew something was up. When he saw a chamber opening up ahead at the end of the tunnel, he tried to creep forward to get a peek at what was in there, but suddenly a blue, whistling ball of flame tore through the darkness toward him. He flattened to his belly, and the flames whistled by, Thayla narrowly dodging to the right.

Figuring stealth was no longer an option, Victor leaped up, lifted Lifedrinker, and focusing Sovereign Will into boosting his agility, he charged into the chamber. Almost without thought, he urged his Globe of Insight to rush along behind him, and when the bright light burst over the larger space, Victor almost stopped in his tracks. Standing before him was a headless skeleton built from thick, gray bones standing nearly nine feet tall. It held a skull in its right hand, though it was much too small and the wrong shade of yellow to be the skeleton's missing head. As Victor registered what he was seeing, the skeleton turned the skull to face him. Blue flames flickered in the eye sockets, and as they caught sight of Victor, they flared brightly, and a ball of blue Energy streaked toward him.

Victor had played baseball every summer, and it was almost a reflex when he stepped to the left and swung Lifedrinker to perfectly bisect the ball of flames. The result wasn't what he'd hoped; rather than knock the ball away, the axe caused it to burst into a conflagration of flames that engulfed Victor and sent him sprawling back to tumble over the gray stones. The flames burned and ignited his clothing, and Victor screamed as he extended his tumble into a log roll, trying to get them out.

By the time the flames stopped licking at his flesh and clothing, Victor was a dozen paces away from the skeleton. When he looked up, he saw Thayla dancing with it, her spear striking out in wicked blue flashes. The skeleton tried to launch fireballs at her, but she moved nimbly, keeping the skull-holding hand awkwardly chasing after her, unable to draw a bead. Victor jumped up, cast Inspiring Presence, used Sovereign Will to boost his strength, and flooded his axe with Energy using Channel Spirit. He pumped nearly half of his rage Energy into Lifedrinker, and she flared with a blazing red aura as he lifted her over his head.

Thayla had the skeleton's attention, so Victor caught it completely unaware as he brought Lifedrinker down on the skeleton's spine. Her shining razor edge tore into the bone, and the rage Energy stored in the weapon surged down, shattering the spine and dozens of attached bones in a shower of splinters and powder. The skeleton collapsed, and its blazing-eyed head rolled away. Victor saw the eyes still burning, and he quickly stepped around so that he could approach the skull from the side. He saw Thayla do the same, and they came to stand over it from opposite sides. "Stand back," Victor said, lifting Lifedrinker.

"Wait!" Thayla said, holding out a hand.

"What? It's still alive."

"I know; I can hear it."

"What, now?"

"It's talking to me, Victor. It says it can teach me things."

"Thayla, fuck that! You saw what this thing did!"

"Victor, what if it can tell me more about my new Core or affinity?"

"I'm sure it can, but can you trust anything it says? It's a fucking skull!"

"It's promising a lot, Victor," Thayla said, her voice rising as her stress elevated.

"Thayla, back up. Trust me, will you? I don't have a skull whispering in my head."

"Victor! You have that amulet talking to you! I didn't try to destroy it, did I?"

"Gorz? Gorz isn't an undead thing."

"Well, Victor, I don't have my memories from my life, but I was once a living thing."

"Not helping, Gorz."

"Victor, this skull won't hurt you. I promise I'll let you chop it to bits if it does anything. You asked me to trust you, but will you trust me?"

"Argh!" Victor growled, backing up a step and letting Lifedrinker hang at his side. "Thayla, I hope you know what you're doing."

"Me too, Victor," she said, kneeling to pick up the old, yellow, humanoid skull. As she lifted it, Victor saw it had a lot more sharp teeth than a human, and the eye sockets weren't round, more angular. They still held flickering flames in them, though they didn't flare at all when Thayla looked into them. "He's offering me a contract, Victor. In exchange for saving him from your axe, he's saying he'll tutor me until I reach Tier Four."

"Then what?"

"Then we will renegotiate." Thayla pulled some strips of leather out of her ring and began to make a harness to hold the skull. "His name is Belikot, and he says this room is safe to rest in if we shut the door to the hallway we came through."

"We really going to listen to a *pinche* skull? All right, Thayla." Victor turned and saw a large black iron door on heavy hinges that he could swing closed, blocking off the hallway. He did it, throwing the bolt home with a satisfying clank. He scanned the room and saw a similar door on the far wall and several trunks and cabinets along the wall to the right, near where he'd destroyed Belikot's skeleton.

"Belikot says you can search those trunks safely; there are books I should study, some ingredients for alchemy, and one of the trunks has more than a thousand Energy beads in it!" Thayla sat down, occupied with her project, pulling strips of leather around the skull and braiding them near the top of the skull. Victor didn't reply to her, still feeling annoyed. He thought about why he was irritated and realized a big part of it was that he'd viscerally wanted to chop Lifedrinker into that skull.

"I'll check it out," he said, trying not to grouse.

"Victor, when you're done, and if we're going to rest here, I think I have an idea that might be promising. I'd like to try to teach you a weave, a way to combine your different affinities into a different end product."

"What? What will that do?" he asked, walking over to the first trunk.

"It will allow you to use the new Energy type in one of your existing spell patterns, creating a new result, just as you did with your inspiration-attuned Energy."

"What do rage and inspiration make when they combine?"

"I'm not sure, Victor; I don't know that exact weave, so we'll need to experiment. I think it will pay off, though."

"All right. Let me get this stuff sorted first." Victor looked around at Thayla and saw that, though she seemed quite focused on the skull, there was a genuine spark in her eyes, and he hoped it was there for good reasons.

2

COURAGE AND TRUST

"Not like that, Victor! You have to build the weave completely in your pathways before letting any of the Energy bleed out."

"I'm trying, Gorz! It keeps coming apart at the start by the time I get to the end, and then I lose track of it while I rush to fix it!"

"I understand, Victor, and I know it's made more complex because I can only describe the weave to you. I think we'll have more luck if you practice writing it a few more times. Ask your friend's skull if you can use some of its parchment."

"I'm not asking that fucking skull anything. Hang on." Victor turned to Thayla, who sat quietly communing with the skull, which was supposedly teaching her a spell that would utilize her death-attuned Energy. "Thayla! Can I use that blank journal? I'm sorry, I need more than just this page." Victor held up the page where he'd already written one rough draft of the Energy weave Gorz was trying to teach him.

"Yes, of course," Thayla replied, throwing the leather-bound sheaf of papers to him. He caught the flapping pages deftly and grunted his thanks. He'd kept one of the enchanted quills they'd found in the skull's trunks, so he set to work on a blank sheet of paper, drawing the weave of Energies again.

"Victor, make them smaller so that you can write more on the same paper."

"Right, right," Victor muttered, concentrating on the drawing. Gorz had explained how he'd come up with the weave through trial and error using the available patterns in his memory. He'd described the rage-attuned Energy as a bold, aggressive Energy requiring a twisting, twinned strand of Energy in a weave. Then he'd said that inspiration-attuned Energy would have to temper the rage, folding back and amplifying at least one of the strands. He'd said that of the forty-seven possible weaves, he'd narrowed it down to three, and the one he was teaching Victor had the best symmetry.

"Good! Do you see how the Inspiration folds between the rage strands? Do you see how it turns it back and amplifies it? That is much like a weave between fury and hope, a weave that gave me great insight into what you're attempting."

"Mmhmm, you already told me that." Victor tuned out Gorz and concentrated, drawing the weave over and over. After a few minutes, he looked at his paper and the twenty perfect copies of the weave. He'd used a dashed line for the rage-attuned Energy and a solid line for the inspiration. The complicated loops and folds were pretty damn impressive to look at. "If I do say so myself! You know, I'm a way better damn artist than I was back on Earth. Is it my dexterity?"

"I'd say it's a combination of your dexterity and intelligence, Victor."

"All right, I'm going to try again. I'm a lot faster at drawing this weave now." Victor turned his mind inward, looking to the twin stars of his Core, the pulsing, glowering red rage-attuned orb and its white-gold steadily radiating counterpart of pure inspiration Energy. Focusing his will, he teased out a strand of each type of Energy and brought them together in his broadest pathway near his Core.

Now that he had the two strands of his different Energies ready, working as quickly as he could, he began to weave the two threads together in the pattern that Gorz had taught him and that he'd just practiced on the paper. He almost got to the end before the starting point began to unravel, and he growled, "Fuck!" Victor released the threads and took several calming breaths, shaking out his hands as though he were weaving with his fingers.

"I almost got it," he said, closing his eyes and refocusing on his Core.

"Victor! Be sure to have a spell in mind to push the completed weave into," Gorz said shrilly. Victor grunted in reply, but the spirit had a point; he mentally readied himself to cast his light orb spell and then grabbed up his threads of Energy. He took three quick breaths as he'd do while waiting for the buzzer to start a match, then he launched into the weave, pulling and tugging the threads into the pattern. When he finished, he knew he'd done it right because the twisted threads flared for a moment, then the red and white-gold energies combined to form a warm, red-gold Energy strand.

Victor immediately cast his light spell, clamping down on his Core and pushing the thread of new Energy into the spell's pattern. Suddenly a warm golden ray of light shone down from the ceiling, illuminating the area where Victor and Thayla sat. It held a deep, rich undertone of red, and as it flared brightly and the light fell upon him, the doubts in Victor's heart and mind fled, and he felt sure and confident, ready to challenge whatever came next.

*****Congratulations! You have learned the spell: Dauntless Radiance, Basic.*****

*****Dauntless Radiance, Basic: You create a ray of courage-attuned Energy that will help those within its radiance ignore their fears and doubts, finding the bravery to face what challenges them. Energy Cost: 100. Cooldown: Minimal.*****

As Energy surged into Victor, his reward from the System for creating a new spell, Thayla exclaimed, "Victor, that's amazing! I was so worried about this new affinity, but I can see how silly I was being—this is truly a great opportunity!"

"You did it, Victor! What Energy-attunement is this? I can read hints of your inspiration and rage affinities in it, but it's a wholly different signature." Gorz's strange, hollow, tinny voice was squealing with excitement.

"According to the spell description, it's courage-attuned Energy." Victor looked at the beam of light, wondering if it was coming out of the stone or just originating near it. Why was it a different shape than the other light spells? Was it moveable? He stood up and tried to will the beam to move, but it wouldn't budge. "Gorz, why's it shaped differently from the other light spells? I can't move it."

"Most likely because it was cast with a weave of Energy, thereby altering the spell's pattern. I imagine other spells you cast with this weave will be functionally different as well."

"Huh," Victor grunted, looking at Thayla and her blue-flame-eyed skull. "What about you? That thing teach you anything?"

"I'm learning some basics; he says it'll be a while before I'm ready for a full spell pattern."

"Maybe I can help," Victor said, casting Globe of Insight and charging the bright, white-gold light until the shadows in the room were banished. He noticed that his Dauntless Radiance spell faded away nearly as soon as his other light was fully formed. He felt his doubts return and even a niggling fear that he'd almost tricked himself into ignoring—a worry that Thayla was being corrupted. With that realization came another: he'd cast such a bright Globe of Insight in the hopes that it would irritate her skull.

"What's his name again?" He gestured to the yellowed skull sitting on her lap.

"Belikot."

"Right. Why doesn't he teach you one of the spells in that book we found?"

"He says he will. I'm just not ready yet."

"All right, but remember: he's not in charge. You are."

Thayla gave him a long, searching look, her black eyes squinting in the bright light. "You really hate that I wanted to keep him, don't you?"

"I'm just worried about you." Victor huffed out his air and plopped back down, sitting in front of Thayla. "I think I'm struggling with the idea that some fucking skull that was shooting fireballs at us became your loyal tutor the second I had my axe ready to strike. Promise me you will be cautious with him."

"I promise, Victor. Now, come on, let it go. If this skull tells me to kill you in your sleep, I'll ignore it, all right?"

"What the fuck? I hadn't even thought of that!" Thayla laughed at Victor's outrage, and he had to admit, the laugh, with a tinge of wickedness, sounded good—like her old self.

"So that light you made, it was courage? I heard you talking to your necklace."

"Yeah, I guess so. I don't really get it. Well, I take that back. I get it, but it's strange to me that I can make another attuned Energy, even though I don't have that affinity. I wonder if someone could have just a normal courage affinity, with courage Energy in their Core."

"I wonder." Thayla squinted her eyes, thinking.

"It's possible, Victor. It may be possible for you to gain this affinity as well, though I'm not versed in the methods. As with everything I don't have direct experience with, though, I'm not certain—I don't have an exhaustive list of spirit affinities, and my library on the subject of Spirit Cores is quite limited."

"Gorz doesn't know," Victor said to Thayla.

"That's funny; Belikot was just telling me that your affinities were a good counter to some of the undead creatures in this dungeon. He says he hasn't met a 'spirit caster' with an aura as strong as yours."

"Tell him flattery won't win me over." Victor frowned at the skull.

"He can hear you." Thayla shrugged and stood up, tying the cord she'd hung around the skull to her belt. "Ready to get moving?"

"Yeah, I want to try this new Energy with other spells, but I'm not sure this is a good place to try it with Berserk, and to be honest, I'm nervous about sitting in one place too long while we're in here." He stood up and picked up Lifedrinker from where he'd left her leaning against the wall. "So, we're going through the other door?"

"Yes, Belikot doesn't know any other parts of the dungeon, but he knows there are ghouls, like the ones we fought in the secret room, a short way up that passage. He says that if he didn't keep the door closed, they'd wander in here from time to time."

"Oh really?" Victor looked at the large, heavy iron door. "Shall we open it and wait for some to wander in? It might make our next encounter more manageable."

"Yes!" Thayla grinned, gripping her spear and nodding to the door. Victor smiled and motioned to one side of the door; Thayla got the hint and moved to stand there, back to the wall, spear ready. Then he unlatched the door and swung it wide, the thick iron hinges grinding and squealing. When it was resting against the stone wall, Victor stood with his shoulder to it, facing the opening, with Lifedrinker ready to swing.

At first, nothing happened, but Victor held still, figuring everything within a few hundred yards had to have heard that door opening. Surely the ghouls down that dark hallway would want to check it out. His Globe of Insight hung in the center of the room, brightly shining, and he wondered if the ghouls would be drawn to it to investigate or reluctant to enter its radiance. After several more heartbeats, he heard a scuffling sound coming from the hallway and then the strange hissing sound of ghouls communicating. Suddenly Thayla held up a hand with four fingers splayed out and pointed to her skull. So, Belikot was telling her there were four ghouls?

Victor cast Sovereign Will, boosting his strength, remembering how strong the ghouls' bones were, and the surge of Energy entering his muscles made him feel swollen; he yearned for an outlet. Just as he heard the scrapes reach the threshold, he also cast Channel Spirit, flooding Lifedrinker with rage-attuned Energy, and then, as the first ghoul showed itself, he stepped and swung for the fences. Lifedrinker arced through the air in a red streak, and when her edge bit into the bridge of the ghoul's nose, she drove through, shaving the top third of the monster's head off in a spray of black gore. It fell, utterly destroyed, and then Victor backed up, waiting for the others to charge.

Thanks to how he greeted the first one, Victor knew he had the ghouls' attention, so he used that to give Thayla an opening, drawing the crowd of hissing, clawing, pale-skinned, naked creatures forward into the room. He swung Lifedrinker in broad, cleaving arcs, keeping them at bay, and when he saw Thayla getting ready to pounce, he cast Inspiring Presence. Thayla's dark eyes sparkled in the light as she spread her lips into a hungry grin, then she sprang to attack, driving her spear through the back of one of the ghoul's necks, perfectly severing its spinal column. The creature collapsed, drawing her spear down with it, and while she worked to free it, Victor deftly sidestepped a claw, cleaving another ghoul's head from its shoulders.

The monsters were probably only around a hundred pounds each, thin and short but very wiry and quick. Victor couldn't help himself, distracted by his dislike of Thayla's skull, and shouted, "There were fucking five of them!"

"He was guessing based on their hissing! He's not psychic!" Thayla said, jerking her spear and stumbling back a few paces.

As the final two tried to flank him, pushing him back with their wild claw swipes, Victor switched his Sovereign Will's boost to his agility, and with Inspiration flooding his mind, he began to weave a dance between the hacking claws. He thrust Lifedrinker through openings, severing muscles and tendons, crunching partially through a knee, and all the while, he blocked their jagged claws with her haft and axe-head.

As he backed away from the two ghouls, leaving a wake of black blood and hunks of flesh, Thayla came in from behind again and drove her spear into one of the monsters, pushing it against a wall and pinning it. No longer having to worry about two fronts, Victor went on the offensive, and soon Lifedrinker was crunching through the skull of his final assailant. Wrenching the axe free, he turned to Thayla's pinned target and cleaved into its head, grinding through the bone and spraying the wall with black gore.

After they'd received their flood of Energy from the conquest, Victor smiled at Thayla and said, "Let's go see where these creeps came from."

"Yes," she said with a quick nod.

"You all right?"

"Yes, sorry. I'm just preoccupied because Belikot is talking to me. He's trying to explain how the death Energy suffusing these creatures worked."

"Oh really? Is that why they're so fucking hard to kill?"

"Not exactly—they aren't really alive. You know what undead means, right?"

"Yeah, zombies and shit."

"Not just what creatures are undead, but what it actually means?"

"Not alive, not dead?" Victor shrugged.

"Good enough, I guess. Anyway, these creatures were warped by death Energy to the point where they'd be dead without it, but they aren't completely alive even with it. Their hearts and blood don't do anything, but they still need brains to function. If you destroy the brain or its connection to the greater whole, the death Energy will dissipate, and the monster will 'die.'"

"So is that what Belikot's teaching you? To make things like this?" Victor gestured with Lifedrinker.

"No, not yet. He's trying to teach me to control death-attuned Energy so that I can disrupt it in monsters like this."

"Fair enough. If you ever did make a monster like this, would you be able to control it?"

"I think . . ." Her face grew slack, and she stared into the distance for a moment, then Thayla continued. "He says I will eventually. Creatures that are autonomous and strong like these are far beyond my skill, but he says their creation would have been trivial for him when he was alive."

"What the hell? He used to be alive?"

"What did you think? He wasn't born as a skull."

"Yeah, but he's a fucking monster. In a dungeon. I don't know what I thought, but I never considered all these things came from out there." He gestured vaguely to indicate outside the dungeon. "How long has he been trapped in here?"

"He wasn't trapped. The System offered him quests and rewards for inhabiting this place."

"I . . ." Victor shook his head, lost for words. He hadn't had much to do with the System other than his skills and levels, but it seemed to him that it was playing people against each other. "Well, maybe not people," he amended, shaking his head at the skull swinging from Thayla's belt.

"Huh?"

"Just thinking aloud." He gestured to the door. "Let's go."

Thayla nodded, and together they explored down the open corridor. They ended up fighting another handful of ghouls in a small chamber, and then, after opening another door, they cleared several more short hallways of the creatures. He hadn't leveled again yet, but Victor knew he was coming close. After killing a final trio of ghouls at the end of their fourth long hallway, they arrived at something different: an enormous, round, bronze door with ornately inscribed runes around its perimeter and a strange set of dials at its center.

"Gorz, can you read that?" Victor softly asked, looking at the thousands of tiny carved symbols. The dials looked as if they were used to unlock the door—like an elaborate combination lock.

"No, Victor, it's not a language I'm familiar with."

"He said no. What about you guys?" Victor asked Thayla, glancing at the skull on her belt. She got quiet for a moment, and Victor assumed she was talking to Belikot.

"Belikot says he knows how to open it. We need to channel Energy into the dials and turn them until the correct runes are ignited."

"You trust it?" Victor looked at the skull again, remembering how it had hurled balls of blue Energy at them.

"Him. I don't exactly trust him, but do we have another option?"

"I don't know." Victor reached forward and tried to spin one of the dials; it didn't move.

"He says it requires death-attuned Energy."

"Seems kind of convenient," Victor groused, looking around. He felt as if something was creeping up on him, but the hallway was empty, and the three dead ghouls were still broken and headless.

"Well, do I try it?" Thayla raised an eyebrow at him, her dark, bottomless eyes boring into his.

"I guess," Victor said, shrugging and gripping Lifedrinker more tightly. Thayla nodded and stretched out a hand, lightly placing her long red fingers around one of the dials. Victor noticed her other hand resting on the skull hanging by her belt, and then the door took his attention.

With a loud *click*, the dial started to turn, and he saw runes along the edge start to glow with blue, wispy light. As Thayla spun the dial, different runes lit up. After a few spins, she moved to the next dial, and again, the dial clicked, and some runes closer to the center of the door began to glow. She spun it for a few moments, then seemingly satisfied, she moved to the last dial.

Victor watched as the last dial clicked, and Thayla spun it, igniting a third row of runes. She slowly turned the dial, and with each click, different runes lit up, until with a satisfying *thunk* all the lit runes flashed red. Victor opened his mouth to ask if it was unlocked when the floor fell away beneath him.

As he tumbled into darkness, he heard Thayla shout, "What? No!" Then, she was gone, and Victor was speeding through thick black air, his Globe of Insight snuffed out by his sudden departure. Just as Victor's reeling mind started to put together what had happened, and he began to concentrate on calling up a new light, he smashed into a hard surface with a terrible crack, and his consciousness slipped away.

Victor woke in utter darkness, in air thick, moist, and frigid. When he tried to shift his weight to feel his surroundings, he was stunned to breathlessness by a blinding pain coming from his left arm, which was pinned beneath him. He panted for a few seconds, holding completely still, and when the pain faded to a horrible ache, he took long, deep breaths and listened. Somewhere not far away, he heard a drip, a slow, steady drip that was as regular as his racing heartbeat: *thump*, *thump*, *thump*, *thump*, *drip*; *thump*, *thump*, *thump*, *thump*, *drip*.

He didn't hear another sound, so he decided to risk some light. He closed his eyes and cast Globe of Insight, just trickling the smallest possible amount of Energy into it. His right arm was splayed out in front of him, and that's where the little golf ball-sized ball of Energy coalesced—over his outstretched hand. The light flared to life, and in its warm white-gold glow, he felt his heartbeat slow, and his racing mind start to calm.

Blinking, he took in his surroundings; he was lying on a stone floor, one sheeted in ice with strange black fungus growing in mottled patches. Not four feet from his head and to his left were two stone walls also sheeted in fungus-patched ice. Victor craned his neck, trying not to move his body, to look down toward his feet, and he saw a rose-red piece of splintered wood next to his belt, his left elbow jutting out and up, and his feet nearly touching a third wall. "Oh fuck, Lifedrinker," he groaned as he realized the origin of the wood.

"Victor! I'm glad to hear your voice," Gorz said, his tinny voice sending sharp pangs through Victor's aching head.

"Thank you, Gorz."

"You fell nearly fifty meters, Victor. I was fearing the worst." Victor thought about that. Fifty meters was a long way to fall onto a stone floor—he really was lucky to be alive, though he figured he was a hell of a lot more durable than the average human. His vitality and racial enhancements had to have played a factor. Still, something was very wrong with his arm.

"Time to yank off the Band-Aid," Victor grunted, bracing the palm of his right hand on the stone near his head, then he pushed himself up to a sitting position. Again, he was nearly blinded by the white flare of pain that shot from his arm, and when he steeled himself to look at the limb, he felt nausea roil in his gut. His two wrist bones were both broken, with sharp shards of splintered bone piercing out of his skin. His hand was bent at a crazy angle, and the whole limb was swollen and purple. "Oh, fuck me. Goddamn it, Thayla!"

Victor looked up, not because he expected to see her coming down to help him, but because when he thought of her, he remembered how he'd fallen.

There was no square of light above him—whatever trap he'd fallen through had closed. Before he confronted himself with his mangled arm again, he finished his survey of his surroundings. There, lying against the fourth wall of his prison, was what was left of Lifedrinker. Her proud, bearded axe-head was still intact, with about a foot of polished haft jutting out, ending in jagged splinters. "Did I fall on you, beautiful? I'm sorry."

Victor carefully scooted his knees underneath himself, trying to jostle his arm as little as possible, then he stood up. A wave of blackness rolled over his vision but quickly passed, leaving tiny winking stars in its wake. He shook his head, then leaned back against one of the stone walls, the icy surface radiating into his shoulders. "It's fucking freezing in here, Gorz."

"I'm not able to discern temperature. I'm sorry, Victor."

"Gorz, I'm about to do something a little nuts. Now's your chance to talk me out of it."

"Don't you think I should know more about your plan in order to develop a proper argument?"

"No, Gorz. I don't want to think about this more than I have to."

"Then I'm afraid I cannot talk you out of it."

"Perfect," Victor grunted, then he used his right hand to yank his left wrist straight, pulling the bones into alignment. At the same time, he cast Berserk, and the blinding pain gave way to the red of primal rage.

3

SEEING THROUGH

Victor screamed and kicked at the walls, his mind lost to the frenzied rage that had overcome him. Perhaps it was the combination of the vomit-inducing pain when he'd straightened his arm and the effects of the Berserk spell, but any semblance of cognition was gone.

He screamed and frothed at the mouth, kicking, clawing, and punching at the unyielding blocks. When the stone wouldn't bend to his violence, he turned to the black fungus, tearing it off the walls and clawing at the patches on the floor. In his red haze of madness, he didn't note the fine black dust billowing up into the air as he terrorized the space.

Only when he started to hack and cough, struggling to breathe, did the rage start to fade. When the madness slipped away and the constriction of his lungs really set in, he collapsed to the cold floor, writhing in torment, trying to force air through his tight windpipe.

Feeling the panic overtake his mind, Victor growled, gritting his teeth and forcing himself to be still for a moment. That's when he noticed the black dust in the air and realized that each breath he dragged through his windpipe made things worse. He reached with his right hand, ripped the sleeve away from his left arm, shook it out, and then tied it around his face, covering his mouth and nose.

Forcing himself to breathe slowly, he gently pulled a thin stream of air through the cloth into his constricted airway. When he felt that expansion of his lungs, it did wonders for his rattled mind. Before taking another breath, he looked at his Globe of Insight and concentrated, pushing a massive amount of Energy into it until it expanded to the size of a basketball and blazed like a flood lamp. To his wonder and pleasure, he saw the black spores in the air drift away from the light. They gathered in a layer of fine dust as they came to the walls and slowly sifted downward to collect in piles.

"Are you all right, Victor?"

"Give me a few, Gorz! I can't breathe and talk right now."

"Of course, Victor. My apologies."

While he watched the spores, Victor forced himself to very slowly, very steadily take deep breaths. When he couldn't stand it any longer, he filled his lungs to bursting, pulled away his makeshift mask, and coughed. He hacked until he was purple in the face with spittle dripping from his lips, and finally, after several minutes, Victor felt he could breathe without constriction. He had no idea what sort of infection he might be in for with the spores that had invaded his lungs, but he hoped that his Energy levels and racial advancements would help him stave it off.

Finally able to calm down and take stock of himself, Victor looked at his arm. He was happy to see that it was straight and without pain, though his wrist was a bit thicker. When he ran his fingers over the mended bones, there were some knobby spots that should have been smooth, and Victor figured it was because the bone splinters hadn't been perfectly aligned when the Berserk spell caused him to heal. Nonetheless, it felt fine, and all of his fingers worked, so he wasn't going to complain.

Kneeling there, at the center of the stone shaft under his blazing light, Victor turned his eyes upon the shattered remnants of Lifedrinker's haft and on the axe itself. He knew the haft had been incredibly tough, so the fall must have pinned it just right under his weight when he hit the ground.

He reached over, picked up the axe, and said, "I'm sorry. We'll get you fixed up one of these days. For now, I'm going to need you to muscle through." It might have been his imagination or wishful thinking, but Victor swore he felt the axe vibrate eagerly in his hand.

"All right, let's see here," he said, looking at the splintered end of the haft. Several long, jagged pieces were jutting forth, and he used his thumb and finger to snap them off. He wondered at that—was the magic gone now that it had broken? Would this piece of haft shatter at the first powerful strike? "Or did you just let me break those off?" He grinned and stood, then summoned his baton out of his ring and held it in his left hand.

Victor looked around at the four walls, baton in one hand, Lifedrinker in the other. He slowly spun in a circle, scrutinizing every stone block. "C'mon, I know there has to be a way. Where's your secret?" He'd already fed his Globe of Insight nearly five hundred Energy, so he was pretty sure he was getting as much benefit from it as possible as he looked for whatever secrets might be hidden.

When his careful inspection failed to reveal anything in the walls, he turned his eye to the ground, and that's when he noticed a very peculiar detail—the fungus only grew on certain blocks, never crossing the mortar.

"Gorz, can you see that fungus only grows on certain stones?"

"Victor! I'm glad you've recovered."

"Yeah, sorry, Gorz. I've been preoccupied as hell. The fungus?"

"Yes, Victor, I can see the strange fungal growth pattern. It extends to the walls, as well."

"Gorz, I have a question: how the fuck do you see anything?"

"Part of this amulet's enchantment allows me to perceive things in sort of three-dimensional mesh."

"Oh. For mapping, right?"

"Exactly, Victor. Speaking of which, I can see that the fungal growth only extends to about seven feet on the walls."

"So, within reach?" Victor was starting to have an idea. He set down his weapons, picked up his ripped sleeve, shook it off, and then tied it over his nose and mouth again. Then he took his baton and gently rubbed it through the delicate strands of black fungus sprouting on the stone. The rod scraped uniformly as he moved it up and down until he got to the center of the stone, and the baton dipped into a tiny depression. Victor traced the shape of the depression, then he took out his notebook and quill and copied it. It looked almost like a sideways S with a line through the center.

He moved to the next fungus-covered stone and repeated the process, finding a different shape in the corner of the stone. He copied the shape on his paper, keeping track of the stone's location. Stepping back, he realized he'd need to diagram the room to keep track of all the different stones, so he did so. When he was done with that, he returned to scraping his baton through the fungus.

While he worked, copying down the different symbols he found, his mind drifted to Thayla, and he wondered if she were okay. Part of him wanted to laugh at his naivety—how could she be okay? She was alone in a dungeon full of the undead, and the last time he'd seen her, she'd been partially brainwashed by an evil undead skull. "Hopefully, that fucker can't outright attack her." Victor had a small hope that the skull had only dumped him into this pit because it couldn't hurt Thayla, at least not directly. He didn't know what kind of "contract" they'd made, but he could hope.

By the time he'd finished writing the different symbols he'd found under the fungus, Victor was already starting to guess a pattern. It began when he realized there was only one symbol shaped like a T with a small x underneath it. When he noticed that, he looked through his diagram and saw that only two stone blocks had another symbol and that three blocks held yet another. When he finished scribing the final letter or rune, or whatever they were called, he counted the various instances of each and found that not one of them was repeated the same number of times. "Are you seeing this pattern, Gorz?"

"I believe so, Victor. Are you referring to the fact that each rune is repeated a unique number of times?"

"Yeah." There were twenty-eight stones with fungus growing on them and seven different runes. Looking at his map, he saw that all seven runes appeared only on one of the walls and not the floor. Victor approached the stone with the single instance of the T plus a small x rune and pressed on it with his baton. Nothing happened. He tried pushing it in lots of different ways—in the corners, in the center, from the mortar lines. Nothing worked.

"Are you starting with that stone because it's the only one with that rune?" Gorz asked.

"Yeah, but nothing's working."

"Perhaps you're meant to activate it with Energy."

"Oh, shit." Victor slapped his head. "I'm still not used to everything being magical." Victor carefully wormed a finger through the fungus layer, passing a trickle of Energy into the stone. With a satisfying *snick*, it sank into the wall about an inch. "Hell yes!" Victor looked at his map for the location of one of the stones with the rune that only appeared twice. The stone sank when he channeled Energy into it, just like the first one.

"Victor, how do you know you're supposed to activate the stones in ascending order? Or that you aren't supposed to activate only stones that appear in even or odd numbers?"

"I don't, Gorz! I'm just trying this because it's the most obvious."

"Oh, I see. Well, I hope you don't trigger another trap."

"Damn it, Gorz!" Victor had briefly considered the idea that he was activating a trap, but he'd quickly pushed the worry aside. Now that Gorz had reinforced the concern, he felt as if he had to pause and reconsider. He paced for a moment, trying to think of a clue as to which stones he might be meant to activate first or in what order, but he couldn't think of anything. The most logical, straightforward answer was just doing it in ascending order. "I think the fall and the fungus were meant to be deadly. I don't think activating the stones wrong was part of the trap. I don't know, but I have to try."

"I don't have an alternate solution," Gorz replied in a voice more hushed than usual. Victor moved to activate one of the stones with three repetitions of the same rune, and again it sank into the wall. When he repeated the process for the fourth, fifth, and sixth runes, he stood back and considered the room one more time before activating the final one.

Of all the walls, the one he was looking at was the only one with one occurrence of each rune. The floor only had three runes, one of them appearing four times. The other walls' runes were similarly arrayed. Nodding to himself, Victor stepped up to the last fungus-covered tile on the wall he'd been working with and activated it.

With another *snick*, the block sank in, and then a deeper rumble started to vibrate the room, and dust and mortar began to fall away from the wall. Victor watched, braced for anything, as the wall sank into the floor. When it was halfway down, and Victor saw a larger space beyond it, he grabbed up his weapons and stood ready.

As the wall settled into the floor and the rumbling stopped, Victor peered into the long, dusty hallway that had opened up. His light revealed a good twenty paces before shadows encroached, but all Victor saw were stone walls and dust. Hefting his weapons, he willed his light to follow him, and he started forward. He'd taken one step over the sunken wall when a terrible clatter erupted down the hallway, and a mob of skeletons came charging toward him.

Though their skulls differed from humans', the creatures were humanoid in shape. They wielded rusty swords, broken spears, knives, and all sorts of clubs. Some of them wore pieces of armor—a helmet here, a breastplate there, some old boots or belts. Unable to count them in such a mass, Victor knew they were more than he could easily handle, so he quickly cast Channel Spirit, flooding his weapons with rage-attuned Energy, and then he cast Berserk.

Savagely roaring, Victor dove into the throng of skeletons, swinging his baton and Lifedrinker in a frenzy of smashing chops. If he had been cognizant enough to think about it, Victor would have found it amusing that, in this case, the old adage "the best defense is a good offense" held true. His offensive was so overwhelming, and his weapons so perfectly suited for destroying skeletons, the creatures hardly scored any hits, even though they outnumbered him fifteen to one.

The few cuts and stabs that made it to him were quickly healed by his berserking Energy, and he smashed and shattered his way through line after line of the creatures. By the time his rage wore off, Victor was standing over piles of scattered, broken bones, none of the skeletons still standing. He'd just barely noticed that he was at the end of the hallway, standing next to a sizeable dusty trunk with an iron door to his left, when golden Energy motes gathered around the bones and surged into him.

*****Congratulations! You have achieved Level 25 Herald of Carnage, gained 10 will and 8 strength, and have 10 attribute points to allocate.*****

As good as it felt to dominate his enemies so thoroughly, Victor wondered about it—these skeletons had been much easier to kill than the ghouls he and Thayla had been fighting. Was he in an easier part of the dungeon, or were the monsters just randomly placed? Victor knew he couldn't answer the question yet; he'd need to do some more exploring. For now, he turned to the large dusty trunk.

His experiences so far in this dungeon had made him leery of traps, so he carefully paced around the wooden box, looking for any hint that it might hold some danger. The dust was uniformly thick around it, and he couldn't see any strings or mechanisms around the clasp or hinges. "Nothing. You see anything, Gorz?"

"No, Victor. It appears to be mundane."

"Right," Victor muttered. He held his baton out and carefully flipped up the iron latch. Nothing happened, so he used the baton's tip to lift the wooden top of the trunk. It fell back on its hinges with a clatter and a shower of dust. Victor stepped forward and inspected the contents.

Amid cobwebs and more dust, he saw the gleam of shiny metal. Victor reached into the trunk and lifted out a silver plate, tarnished on much of its surface but still gleaming in spots. "Huh," he said, digging through the trunk's contents. It was full of dusty, tarnished silver plates, cups, and bowls, even a set of knives, forks, and spoons. The silverware was ornate with intricate carvings on the handles and around the edges of the plates. Deciding he could sort it later, Victor simply stored the entire trunk in his ring.

Victor examined the destroyed skeletons and found that none of the armor looked any good. It certainly hadn't protected them from his weapons.

Everything was rusty or bent, threadbare or torn. He collected some of the rusty knives, thinking he could polish them up and use them for cutting food or other small tasks. That got him thinking, and he sifted through the clubs and axes, looking for a handle that might suit Lifedrinker.

Most of the wood was dry, cracked, and not in any way better than the remnant of Lifedrinker's haft, but one cumbersome ball mace had a long, stout, and quite heavy handle. It was round and straight, not elegantly shaped like Lifedrinker's old haft, but it would do for now if he could think of a way to properly fit it to her axe-head. He could see that it sat tightly into the hole at the center of the ball mace and that a large metal pin had been hammered into it to hold it in place. Looking at Lifedrinker, he could see where her old haft was fitted similarly but with a wider, open-center pin.

Victor pulled out one of the pitons and the hammer that Captain Lam had given him, and he went to work, chipping away the wood around the pin in the mace. When he got it free, he was able to twist the mace head around until it slipped off the handle. He'd made a mess of the wood, so he set it on the ground, held it in place with his foot, then hacked off the mangled end with Lifedrinker. She tore through the wood like a cleaver cutting a carrot.

"All right, now I have to remove your old haft. Think I can do that without pissing you off?" To Victor's astonishment, the axe-head began to vibrate. At first, he thought Lifedrinker was just agreeing with him, or maybe disagreeing, but she kept shaking, more and more rapidly, and then he saw that the axe-head was slowly inching up off the haft. She was working her way free of the old broken handle! "Hell yes! I knew you were listening to me all those times!"

Soon the axe-head was free, and he was left holding the old broken haft in one hand and Lifedrinker in the other. He held the new handle up to the hole in the axe-head and saw that he'd need to shave it down a bit to fit. He put the handle against the ground, holding it with his knees, then he carved the section that would fit into the axe-head, pushing Lifedrinker downward against the wood, planing off curls of wood with each stroke. He managed to carve it down to fit snugly within the hole in Lifedrinker's axe-head, stopping to check his progress after each cut.

Victor used a knife he'd scavenged to dig and wriggle the roll pin out of Lifedrinker's old, broken haft. Then he hammered it into her new haft with his baton. He gave her a few practice swings and was pleased with the results. "That's right, *chica*. We're going to absolutely mangle some skeletons now!" She pulsed and jerked in his hand, and he couldn't help laughing at her enthusiasm.

He stowed Lifedrinker's old haft into his ring; Victor had no idea what kind of wood it was and figured he might want to find out when he had a proper handle made for her. He also put away his baton; it was a nice backup weapon, but it couldn't hold a candle to Lifedrinker. Satisfied with his work, Victor turned to his attributes, once again putting his extra points into will. With Sovereign Will, he could now boost his physical attributes by more than fifty points.

Victor approached the door, noting the lack of a handle. It was heavy iron and only slightly rusted around the edges. He figured he could break it open with his tools, given enough time, but he knew it would make a terrible racket. Had it been a day since he had used his ring? He pulled out his pocket watch and checked the time; it said it was a bit past midday or midnight. What time had he last used his ring? He chuckled, realizing he had no idea or even how many days he'd lain unconscious.

He decided to give it a try and knocked. Nothing happened, and he backed up, looking around and wondering if there was another way through the door. He was just about to try jerking on it to see how solid it felt when he heard a scrabbling, clicking sound from the other side.

An unmistakable *click* sounded a moment later, and Victor knew the door had been unlocked. He took a step back, hefted Lifedrinker, and cast Sovereign Will, boosting his agility. Then he cast Channel Spirit, flooding Lifedrinker with rage Energy. A moment later, with a terrible creaking sound, the door began to swing open toward him, and a wave of palpable darkness surged through the opening, pushing back the light from Victor's globe.

When the darkness touched Victor, he was filled with dread, and sweat sprang out on his palms. He felt as though he'd just stepped into a room with a firing squad pointing their guns at him, and every instinct in his body screamed at him to turn and run. Suddenly his concentration wavered, and the Energy filling his limbs, granting him extra agility, drifted away. Lifedrinker trembled in his hands, and the blazing red aura around her started to flicker. Victor took a nervous step back, then two, and the blackness flooded into the hallway, completely engulfing his light, reducing it to a pale glow.

Victor saw the light fade and felt the effects of the darkness on his body, and a part of his mind rebelled. Was he scared of some darkness? Was he scared of some fucking creepy undead monster? He'd killed dozens of the things. Trying to rally himself, he screamed and swung Lifedrinker in a wild cleave through the blackness. The axe didn't connect with anything, but the action served to free up some portion of his panicking mind, and he remembered his other light spell. He took a step back and cast Dauntless Radiance.

He felt the spell's pattern draw forth some of both types of his Energy and instantly twist them into a weave. Courage-attuned Energy flooded into the spell, and a golden crack formed in the darkness spilling red-gold light around Victor in a wide pool. The shadows seethed and hissed as they were pushed back. "Come on!" Victor yelled, suddenly more in control of himself. He felt his grip steady and his shaking muscles calm, and he stared into the darkness outside his ring of golden light.

"A strong will has this one," a raspy, shrill voice said from the darkness, and Victor whirled, trying to place its location.

"Indeed, sister," said another, smoother voice, seemingly echoing from several directions at once.

"Put out your light, child," said the first voice. "Come into our embrace; we'll show you secrets you couldn't have imagined."

"Fuck off, and I won't cut you to pieces," Victor growled.

"Feisty! But why would you cut us? Wouldn't you rather embrace us?" Suddenly a patch of darkness swirled away, giving Victor a glimpse of pale skin, smooth curves, and a seductive, red-lipped smile. He stepped toward it, but the shadows swirled again, and the vision was gone. He took a swing anyway, cutting through the shadows with Lifedrinker, only to have her slice through the air without resistance. Shrill laughter echoed around him. He started to say something, but then a flash of pain erupted from his left hamstring, and he slapped a hand there, feeling a deep, bloody gash.

"Come, sister," said the smooth voice, "let's soften him up. He'll comply more readily once we've taken some of his blood. Won't you, lover?"

Victor didn't answer as he put his hand, now sticky with blood, back on Lifedrinker's haft. He had to do something. His light wasn't enough to reveal them, to drive the shadows entirely away. He thought about casting Berserk, but what if they continued to evade him? They'd just wait out the spell and bleed him dry. Maybe he just had to get lucky. Now that he was in his light, he could concentrate, so he recast Sovereign Will, boosting his agility. Then he started jumping around in his golden island of radiance, slashing Lifedrinker into the shadows randomly.

His efforts were met with more laughter, and several more gashes appeared on his back and on the backs of his legs. He started leaving large droplets and smears of blood on the ground, and his breathing grew ragged with his exertions. The cuts were painful and deep, and Victor felt his mind starting to fray. He wanted to scream and hurl his axe, feeling as though the creatures were just outside his reach. Distantly he was aware of Gorz trying to speak to him, but he couldn't concentrate, and he felt as if his sanity was on the verge of snapping.

Finally, he stopped swinging his axe and stood at the center of the pool of light, panting and sweating and drizzling blood down into a puddle. In the moment of calm, Gorz's voice broke through, and he paid attention. *"Victor! Use the weave! Cast Inspiring Presence or Berserk with the weave!"* Victor's first thought was to wonder why he hadn't cast Inspiring Presence already. His second thought was to ask himself if he could concentrate enough to create the weave of Energy for courage.

"I think he's grown tired, sister. Do you think he's ready to come to us?" Again, the shadows swirled, and Victor saw heavy breasts, a seductive smile with a tongue curling along the lips. Then the shadows were back, and the vision was gone. Victor lowered his axe-head to the ground and leaned against the handle. He took a long, shuddering breath and stared into the darkness.

"If I come to you, will you stop cutting me up?"

"Of course, lover; we only want to teach you our secrets!"

Victor truly was exhausted, but he was only buying time. He leaned into his axe, feigning resignation, and then he closed his eyes, turning his attention to his Core. He took three quick breaths, then he yanked two threads of Energy from each of his attunements and built the weave for courage. The instant he saw the threads pulse with a red-gold hue, he cast Berserk and fed the new Energy to it.

A burning heat spread out from Victor's heart into his limbs and up to his eyes. He stood straight, no longer troubled, and looked into the darkness, laughing as the shadows fell away from his gaze.

*****Congratulations! You have learned the spell: Heroic Heart, Basic.*****

*****Heroic Heart, Basic: Your ability to manifest courage-attuned Energy has allowed you to infuse yourself with its benefits for a short time. While this spell is active, you are immune to fear effects, can shrug off confusion, and cannot be mind-controlled. Energy Cost: 400. Cooldown: Long.*****

Victor saw two gray-skinned hags slinking about near the open iron door. Both had long, greasy white hair, wide, fang-filled mouths, and pupilless white orbs for eyes. They were completely naked, though they each wielded long razor-edged knives. "Hello, ladies," Victor growled, lifting Lifedrinker and stalking forward.

4

MOVING UP

Victor stood over the hewn corpses of the hags, panting and dripping blood. When he felt the encroaching darkness at the edges of his vision, he worried at first that there was a third hag or something worse, but then he realized it was simply his vision darkening from blood loss.

"C'mon," he said, staring at the still, pale flesh. He put Lifedrinker's axehead against the stone floor and leaned heavily on her handle, willing himself to slow his breathing. As he'd hoped, golden motes began to gather on the dead bodies, then a stream of Energy surged into him, spreading through his pathways, into his Core, and then out again to speed the knitting of his flesh and partially renew his depleted blood supply.

Victor straightened and looked around; he still stood at the end of the hallway he'd discovered, but now the heavy iron door was partially open, and the stones at his feet were smeared and painted with dark red and black stains. He took a few deep breaths, stretching his back and flexing his legs, happy to see that most of the deep slashes the hags had delivered were closed up. Some were still stiff and sore, with thick scabs, but he was out of danger when it came to bleeding to death.

"Nasty bitches," he muttered, looking at the broken corpses. He didn't let his eyes linger long, but he took a moment to pick up the long, razor-sharp knives the two hags had used against him. The weapons had a single edge and no point, designed with slashing in mind. They reminded Victor of miniature cleavers; he wondered if there was a proper name for that kind of knife.

Both knives had polished wooden handles made of dozens of different colored woods pressed together, and Victor marveled at the craftsmanship. He saw a few runes along their blades and figured they might have some enchantments. Happy to take something away from the harrowing encounter, he put the two blades into his ring and then summoned forth his Globe of Inspiration, willing it to resume following closely behind him. As the ball of warm white-gold light took shape, the shaft of courage-attuned light that had initially saved him faded away.

Victor moved to the door and pulled it open, Lifedrinker held ready. The open door revealed a continuation of the corridor, and looking down into the shadows, Victor didn't see any other doors. "Gorz, you keep track of our movements?"

"Of course, Victor. I couldn't stop mapping if I wanted to."

"That's kinda shitty. What if you wanted to do something else?"

"No, Victor, you misunderstand; I don't actively map where I've been. It just happens as a function of my enchantments. I don't think about it, really, until there's a reason to review the data."

"Huh, all right. Please let me know if you see any sort of pattern or some hint as to where we are in relation to where Thayla, er, that fucking skull, dumped us."

"I know, spatially, exactly where we are in relation to that location, but I think you mean if I see a passage or stair that might lead that way, correct?"

"Yeah, I can't burrow through stone, so we'll need to find our way through the passages." Victor chuckled at the idea while slowly advancing into the hallway. He noticed that the temperature, while still chilly, was nothing like it had been at the bottom of the pitfall. He wondered if some of those runes that didn't activate the secret door were responsible for dropping the temperature. Was it to preserve fallen, dead adventurers' bodies? Was it meant as some sort of torture? Did the fungus in there require a cold temperature to thrive? "Too many questions."

"Pardon, Victor?"

"Nothing, Gorz, just thinking out loud."

As he walked along the stone corridor, Victor's mind kept returning to the two hags and how they'd manifested that palpable darkness. It had seemed to disperse when he'd cast his new spell, but his spell description didn't say anything about banishing darkness spells. It said it made him immune to fear effects, though, making Victor wonder if the darkness hadn't been tangible but some sort of mental trick or manipulation. He wondered how screwed he'd have been if his will hadn't been so high. What if he'd been unable to shake off the panic enough to cast any spells? "No question about it—I'd be hag food." After a moment, he said, "Just talking to myself, Gorz."

"Thank you, Victor."

After another minute of quiet stalking, he came to a left turn in the corridor, and when Victor peered around the corner, he saw a wooden door. When he approached it, he could tell it was in good repair; no light or shadows stood between the slats, and the hinges and latch seemed to be in good working order. Victor reached forward, pushed down on the crude iron latch, lifting it free of the bracket, and pulled it slowly open. It creaked, but just a little. When it was an inch or two ajar, he peered through the opening.

Another stone block room lay beyond the door, illuminated by half a dozen flickering candles on little tables that reminded Victor of old-fashioned school desks. His globe cast a beam of light through the open door, though, laying a shaft of bright light through the center of the room, over a few of the desks, and alerting the creepy, hooded creatures sitting at them. They lifted their cowled heads, peering toward the light source and hissing. "Shit," Victor grunted, then backed up a step, readying Lifedrinker.

A cold wind whistled through the cracks around the door, and when Victor saw palpable darkness writhing through the opening, pushing against his light, he didn't waste any time and cast Heroic Heart. As the heat spread out from his chest, the wispy darkness seemed to fade away, and the cold wind felt more like a simple breeze. He didn't know how long his new spell would last and decided to go on the offensive, no longer worried about what might be waiting on the other side of the door. He strode forward, pulled it open, and stared into the cloaked figures' hooded, flickering red eyes.

They didn't utter any words or screams, just continued to hiss sibilantly as they swarmed toward him, knives in their hands. Two of the creatures near the back stood stock still, lifting their hands and seeming to manifest blue, swirling Energy between the pale, clawed appendages. Victor surged forward, a choked-up grip on Lifedrinker, unable to make a wide swing in the corridor.

As he chopped at the closest creature, he cast Channel Spirit, filling Lifedrinker with a blazing, red surge of rage-attuned Energy. She ripped forward, her bright blade slicing through the creature's robe and biting into something dense and soft beneath it. She pulled and sank deeply into its flesh, and Victor could almost feel her exult in the Energy she drew from it.

As Victor pulled her back to block an arcing knife swipe, the creatures in the back unleashed their balls of blue fire, sending them swirling through the air, over the heads of their comrades, and right at Victor's face. He crouched and hopped to the side, planting his back against the corridor's stone wall, and the balls of blue flame howled past, smashing into the stone ceiling of the hall a few feet past him. They expanded into a blazing blue inferno, the heat of which singed Victor's eyebrows and caused him to close his eyes in reflex. Deep pain in his thigh and a sharp pain in his abdomen had him blindly cleaving in an arc, trying to knock away the swarming creatures.

When the heat faded, he opened his eyes, and while he continued to hack at the creatures, he saw a knife with a pale hand and arm still attached jutting out of his thigh. Victor screamed, kicking out with his good leg to give himself a bit of space, then he released Lifedrinker with one hand and yanked the knife out. He threw it, arm still grimly hanging on, at the creature in front of him. Its smoldering eyes blinked, and Victor gripped Lifedrinker and made a quick chop at its neck. She sliced through its robe, and Victor felt the blade bite through a stiffly resisting neck, and then the creature fell, flopping, to the ground.

Another blaze of blue light alerted him to danger, and he squatted low. This time, the monster in the back hadn't been so careful of its friends; the fiery blue Energy ball hit one of them in the back and burst into a conflagration. Victor rolled backward away from the explosion, and when he regained his feet, he saw that all three of the robed creatures that had been holding the doorway were aflame, flopping and thrashing on the ground as the fire consumed them. Victor took that opportunity to charge, leaping over their flaming bodies and smashing into one of the desks as he broke into the room.

The two creatures making the fireballs stumbled back, the preparations for their next spells spoiled by his encroachment. Victor charged, growling and swinging Lifedrinker for all he was worth, using the entire length of his improvised axe haft and the larger space in the room to give her a proper, whistling cleave. Her bearded, gleaming edge met the first creature midway between its shoulder and hip, snapping through little bones and splashing through soft flesh and innards. Her arc continued, biting into the shoulder of the second caster, relieving it of its arm.

The first fell, rolling to its side and moaning softly as its life poured out with its glistening entrails. The second hissed more loudly, falling back and clutching at its stump. Not wanting to give it a chance to spring any sort of surprise, Victor pressed the attack and jabbed Lifedrinker into its face, leading with the top, pointed edge of her blade, and he felt her hit bone. He grunted and drove forward, pinning the creature's skull between Lifedrinker's edge and the stone wall and grinding until she broke through, sinking into the meat behind the bone. She surged and pulsed, and Victor saw blue veins of Energy flow through the caster's pale flesh into her blade.

When it ceased twitching and Lifedrinker seemed to relax, Victor yanked her free and looked around the room. The strange desks all had paper on them, and the ones he hadn't knocked over still held little pots of ink with quills sticking forth. Victor examined a couple of the parchments, but the language was indecipherable for him, and Gorz couldn't give any help. Still, he gathered them up and stuffed them into his ring. He was in the process of doing so when the surge of Energy from his kills hit him, and he paused a moment to gather himself.

He felt strong and refreshed, his previous wounds now wholly healed, reduced to white scars. "Two fights and no level. I must be close, eh, Gorz?"

"You seem to gain levels rapidly, but it requires more and more Energy to level as you advance, Victor."

"Right," Victor said with a stretch, looking at the exits to the room. Two doors led out, but he resigned himself to searching through the little robed corpses before trying them out. His job was made easier by the fact that the creatures in the doorway, all four of them, had burned up. Their robes were gone, and their flesh was nothing but blackened char. The stench was unpleasant—nothing like cooked meat. It was more like a mixture of old charcoal and a compost bin, and Victor had to hold his old sleeve-mask over his face as he poked through the remains. Some blackened knife blades were all he could find of interest, so he moved over to the casters.

He kept his nose covered as he rooted around the corpse of the creature he'd eviscerated, checking for rings or a necklace or any sort of pouch. He didn't come up with anything, not even a weapon. The final corpse held a surprise, though. Under its robe was a leather sling with built-in loops holding slender vials of green fluid. Victor wasn't about to taste green liquid found from such a dubious source, but he pulled the bandolier off the monster and stored it in his ring. Maybe he'd meet someone who could tell him what it was someday.

That done, Victor turned to the doors; they were both set into the opposite wall of the one he'd come through. He placed his ear against each door, and neither gave him any clues about what lay beyond. He tried the latch on the right-hand door, and it opened, so he pulled it an inch away from the doorjamb and peered through. A narrow corridor led into darkness. Victor softly closed the door, then tried the other one. It too opened without resistance, revealing a small closet, so he pulled the door wide and studied the contents.

A shelf in the back of the closet was stacked with sheets of blank parchment. A bucket sat in one corner with an old dust-covered mop sitting within, and piles of rags and broken pieces of wood filled most of the space. Victor had no idea how valuable parchment was in this world, but he figured he could always use it for kindling if nothing else, so he put the stacks of thick, yellowed paper into his ring. That done, he studied the walls of the closet in the light of his Orb of Insight but couldn't find anything of interest.

"Onward," he said, moving to the other door and advancing into the dark, narrow corridor. The air was heavy with dust and chilly, and the stone held myriad cobwebs that kept clinging to Victor's face and shoulders. He held Lifedrinker out before himself, forging a path through the clinging webs, but she couldn't catch all of them. He grew so distracted by the challenge of avoiding the tangles that he almost didn't hear the scrape and shudder of something very large moving in the space up ahead. The second time the scraping sound came to him, though, he paused and peered ahead through the gloom and obscuring webs.

It was hard to tell with his limited perspective, but it seemed as if the tunnel got wider, not far from where he stood, and he could see something shifting in the darkness just beyond the reach of his light. Victor focused on his globe of light and willed it to float forward. As it softly flowed past the webs and into uncharted territory, Victor saw the reflected light from the walls grow dimmer.

At first, he thought his globe was fading, but then he realized it had advanced into a more extensive area, and its light was growing more diffuse. He started after it, but then he saw the source of the noise and motion—an enormous skeleton with a broken shackle around its ankle lurked against the chamber's far wall.

When his light fell directly on the colossal skeleton, it lurched into an upright stance, revealing long arms tipped in claws that touched the ground, and a broad skull, featuring dentition more fitting a tiger than a human. Pale blue lights shone in its eye sockets, and the massive mouth yawned open, snapping shut with a loud crack reminiscent of a firework going off.

"Fucking hell, don't let it bite me. Got it." Victor muttered, pushing strength into his limbs with Sovereign Will, and channeling rage Energy into Lifedrinker. The massive skeleton, perhaps twelve feet tall, stomped toward him, its shackle dragging behind it with a bouncing clatter.

Victor cast Inspiring Presence as he came into the larger room, and the shadows grew dim in the bright light of his orb. The skeleton was big but slow, and the swipe it was winding up was horribly projected. Victor slipped under the blow, sidestepping the monstrosity and carving a plate-sized hunk of bone out of the creature's hip with Lifedrinker. She peeled away the bone like a sharp knife whittling balsa wood. The monster spun surprisingly quickly, raking its other long arm in a whistling swipe, but Victor saw it coming and drove Lifedrinker's axe-head into the blow, letting the powerful swipe push him back and away from the skeleton.

Suddenly the skeleton dropped to all fours and lunged, driving its enormous maw forward and snapping at Victor's face. He grunted, ripping Lifedrinker up, so her axe-head's heavy, blunt end smashed into its bony chin. Victor's muscles were surging with swollen strength-Energy and Lifedrinker was pulsing with rage; the blow sounded like a car crash as bones snapped and teeth were knocked out by the impact. Victor rolled with the energy of the skeleton's charge, pulling Lifedrinker along with him as he went over his left shoulder and sprang up five feet away out of the somersault.

"Come on, asshole," Victor growled, passing around the skeleton as it struggled back to its feet. When it whirled to face him, its lower jaw hung unhinged on one side, and Victor barked a short laugh when he saw the gaps in its broken and missing teeth. He lowered his center, ready for a charge, and braced Lifedrinker. The skeleton's eyes blazed with fury, and it lifted a hooked, clawed hand, signaling its intent from a mile away. It stomped forward, arm up, ready to swing, and had Victor been stupid or uninspired, he might have focused on that arm and missed the other arm snaking up and clawing at his guts.

Victor saw it coming, though, and Lifedrinker's gleaming edge bit into the bones of the swiping claw, severing digits and cracking bones. Her blade bit deeply, and he could feel her pulling into the cut, eager for Energy, and had to wrestle her away. "Not yet, *chica*!"

He barely jumped aside, dodging the other swiping blow as he broke Lifedrinker away. Just as the claw swiped by in front of him, he switched his Sovereign Will boost to agility, and with the added speed and his state of inspiration, he deftly dodged around the skeleton, circling around its back. "Now!" he hollered, lifting Lifedrinker into an overhead chop and smashing her down, whooshing through the air into the monster's spine.

This time when Lifedrinker bucked and pulled into the cut, he gave her what she wanted, pushing with his arms and legs, driving the axe into the bone. The skeleton's spine was as thick around as a small tree, and she bit into it about halfway.

Victor again swapped his Sovereign Will boost to strength and pushed with everything he had, driving the massive construct over the ground and into the stone wall. All the while, Lifedrinker surged and shuddered, pulling thick rivulets of black-tinged blue Energy into her blade. The skeleton shook and thrashed, flailing its arms against the stone wall, but it seemed to be growing sluggish. "Drink it up, lady! Drink that fucking Energy!" Victor growled, straining against the skeleton's death throes.

After several moments, Victor felt the skeleton's spasms settle, and it grew still, slumping to the ground against the wall. Lifedrinker stopped surging and shaking, signifying the completion of her meal, so Victor took a step back, pulling the axe out of the skeleton's spine, noting how the bone crumbled and powdered away from her blade. He lifted Lifedrinker up into a heavy chop and hacked into the skeleton's neck. It took him three chops, but the head finally rolled free to clatter and bounce onto the hard stone floor. A moment later, large dense motes of Energy gathered around the bony corpse and flowed into Victor, bringing him closer to his next level.

For the first time, Victor could freely examine the larger room where he'd fought the skeleton. There weren't any doors, but, in one corner, a spiral, iron stairway disappeared through the ceiling into darkness. Sitting at the foot of the stairway was a matching black iron chest. "Gorz, did you notice if that chest and stairway were there the whole time? I feel like I would have noticed it."

"Victor, my initial map of this space did not include a stairway. Perhaps killing the bone colossus was key to revealing the path forward."

"Bone colossus?"

"A name Reevus-dak gave a similar creature that he slew."

"Huh, I guess it fits." Victor approached the stairway and chest. The stairway wasn't very large; perhaps two people could mount it at once, but it would be uncomfortable. The chest was about the size of a big shoebox you might get with a pair of hiking boots. He knelt before it, running his eyes over it in the light of his globe. He didn't see anything strange or suspicious about the black wrought iron. No runes were etched or painted onto the metal, and the clasp was a simple loop hung over an iron peg. He could see where a lock might be placed, but there wasn't one.

Victor stood and walked over to the unmoving bone colossus. He'd noticed that the bones had sagged, their unnatural vigor leaving them when the creature died its true death. Victor grabbed hold of one long femur and yanked on it, bracing his foot on the lower leg. The bone yanked free, and he took the four-foot bone back over to the chest.

He wanted to use the bone to lift the lid open, but the knobby end was too clumsy to lift the latch, so he held it down with his foot and used Lifedrinker to shave a point onto one end. That done, he extended the bone from an outstretched hand and flipped the little catch up. Nothing happened, so he used the bone to flip the lid of the chest open. Again, after the lid flapped and clattered open, nothing else happened.

"Better safe than sorry, I guess." Victor shrugged and stowed the long, sharp bone into his ring. When he looked into the chest, he saw what looked like a folded black metal mesh cloth that winked with a soft luster in the light of his globe. He reached in a hand and felt the black rings of metal, noting their smooth polish—these weren't wrought iron.

He lifted the garment, startled by its dense heaviness. It unfurled as he pulled it from the chest, and he saw that it was a shirt of black, glimmering rings, sewn to a soft, fur-lined leather vest, also stained black. "Nice," Victor said in a hushed voice.

"What did you find, Victor? It seems to be a garment?"

"Yeah, it's some armor. Seems way too big for me, though."

"Bond with it, Victor."

"Ahh, good idea, Gorz." Victor pulled off his torn, stained shirt, laughing at the shredded state of the back, then he shrugged into the heavy, ring-covered leather shirt. It felt like the weighted vest the dentist puts on you when they take X-rays, but the leather lining was soft and comfortable.

Victor looked at the oversized, hanging piece of armor and then at the skeleton, a thought crossing his mind. "Nah, couldn't be; even this big shirt wouldn't fit that thing." He touched a hand to the softly gleaming metal links and channeled some Energy into the shirt. It rustled and clinked as it softly shuddered, shrinking to fit his torso perfectly.

*****Ringed Shirt of the Gloom Warden: Artificed armor. Enchantments: 1. Hardened black lacquer, greatly enhances the durability of natural steel. 2. Form-fitting, self-repairing, self-cleaning.*****

"Hell yes. Some nice armor, Gorz, and best of all, it's self-cleaning."

"Congratulations, Victor!"

"Thanks." Victor stood and flexed his torso and arms about. The sleeves of the chain shirt only fell to his elbows, and his arms moved easily within them. Overall, he was very comfortable and felt much more protected than he ever had in the cheap leather armor he'd bought from the mine's Contribution Store.

Victor looked at the iron stairway and said, "Gorz, this stairway is going up, and we had to kill a big tough guy to reveal it. Do you think we, like, fell to the bottom of the dungeon and need to work our way back up to get to Thayla and maybe the exit?"

"I'm afraid it's all speculation at this point, Victor. We have no idea what that door, where Thayla betrayed you, led to."

"Okay, but she didn't betray me. That fucking skull tricked her."

"Noted, Victor."

Victor hefted Lifedrinker and stepped onto the stairway, slowly making his way upward, accompanied by the creaking joints of the narrow, wrought iron stairway.

5

A GAUNTLET OF BONES

When Victor's head passed into the dark stairwell, he immediately grew uncomfortable; smooth stone walls lined the wrought iron stairway, and no matter how he craned his neck, he couldn't see an end to the narrow shaft or the stairs. What made matters worse was the uncomfortably shallow depth of the steps; he was forced to climb on his toes, most of his feet hanging off the metal steps. Victor's light globe floated just behind him, bathing the shaft in bright light, and he could only imagine how strange and uncomfortable the climb would have been without it.

After what felt like an hour of climbing, Victor couldn't take it anymore, and he leaned against the stone wall and said, "Gorz, how fucking high have we climbed?"

"We've ascended four hundred eighty-two meters."

"What the fuck? So we're way higher than when we fell down the trap?"

"Yes, Victor, close to four hundred thirty meters higher."

"Not the kind of progress I was hoping for," Victor muttered, but then he resumed his climb. Sometime later, he noticed a change in the air; the temperature had risen to the point where he'd no longer characterize it as cold, and more than that, there was a dry, dusty quality to it. He plodded on, and a few steps later, he stumbled onto a flat platform. He reached out to grab the iron railing and took in his surroundings.

He was still in a narrow, circular shaft, but the stairs ended with an iron platform, and a heavy, rusted iron door sat not two feet in front of him.

Victor looked up and saw the stone shaft continue well beyond where his light could reach, though he saw no easy way to ascend it. "Not that I want to keep climbing, I guess." He stepped up to the iron door, noting the thick layer of orange corrosion around its edges and powdering its surface. An iron ring served as the handle, and he pulled on it to see if the door was locked or latched. It didn't budge.

Victor shrugged and knocked on the door, testing to see if his ring was active yet. After his third rap, deep in the innards of the iron door, a grinding *click* sounded. He pulled again on the iron handle, and the door inched open this time, grinding in its metal casing. Enough space had opened for Victor to put his fingers around the edge of the door, so he did and yanked with a bit more enthusiasm. The door pulled open, leaving a trail of broken, rusted bits of iron.

Cold, gray light met his eyes, and he immediately recognized it as sunlight. Was he outside? Squinting into the glare, he saw a dusty stone passage, though this stone was different from the blocks down deep in the dungeon; it was more tan than gray, and the blocks sat upon one another with no mortar in between. The light was coming through the high ceiling, some twenty or thirty feet above, where missing stones made way for glimpses of pale gray-blue sky. Victor could see a few dozen paces down the hallway, where it widened into a much larger space, one less well-lit. Gripping Lifedrinker before him, he started forward.

When he came to the passage's end, he clung to one of the walls and crept forward to peek into the larger area. His eyes were immediately drawn to the right, where a pulsing, shimmering portal stood. It looked remarkably like the one he and Thayla had used to enter the dungeon. He saw that it was resting upon a tan stone dais, and he let his eyes drift away to take in the rest of the room.

The space was the size of an exhibition hall, with high stone walls and massive stone arches holding up a matching ceiling. When he shifted his vision to the left, he saw blue, flaming braziers flanking a wide stairway leading into the ground. Arrayed at the head of the stairs were a dozen armored skeletons wielding wooden spears with broad, bronze, leaf-shaped blades. They stood silently facing the portal.

"Victor! I recognize this space! It's the entrance chamber of the dungeon. At least the one where Reevus came in. He fought a similar group of skeletons and then began his descent via those stairs."

"Oh, great," Victor thought. *"So I could basically get the fuck out of here right now?"*

"It would stand to reason that the portal would take you out, yes."

"Well, I can't just bail until I've figured out what's going on with Thayla."

"Very noble, Victor."

"Thanks, Gorz." Victor tried to inflect his mental words with sarcasm but didn't know if he pulled it off. *"All right, let's see here. Twelve skeletons with spears—sounds bad."*

"Reevus destroyed them with a torrent of fire."

"Not helping, Gorz."

"Apologies, Victor." Victor tried to mentally shrug but mostly tuned Gorz out. He knew he was more than a match for a skeleton or ten, but these were all wearing matching bronze armor and had spears, and their appearance gave him pause. Looking at them more closely, though, he saw that their armor mostly hung loose on their bony frames, and there were many gaps between the various pieces. Lifedrinker would have a field day with that shitty coverage. He could imagine someone with a spear, sword, or dagger struggling against such enemies, but Lifedrinker hit like a wrecking ball and would smash their bones even through those bronze breastplates and flimsy helmets.

The spears were what gave him second thoughts, though. If he used Berserk, he'd be able to heal from all but fatal stabs, but could he brute force his way past a dozen spears? Inspiring Presence and extreme agility might be a better way to go; he'd see gaps in their line and be able to capitalize. Victor stood and watched them for a few more minutes, vacillating on the best strategy to take. He considered luring them to the narrow tunnel at one point but quickly scrapped the idea when he imagined their long spears stabbing at him while he struggled to swing Lifedrinker in the confined space.

Finally, it was frustration at his indecision that pushed him forward. Impulsively, he growled, stepping out of the hallway and using Channel Spirit to flood his pathways and Lifedrinker with inspiration-attuned Energy. Then he used Sovereign Will to boost his agility, and as the skeletons noticed his approach and, as one, turned to face him with spears lowered, he cast Berserk.

He'd never used Channel Spirit to push inspiration-attuned Energy into his weapon or pathways during combat. Even in his red-eyed state of rage, he exulted in how he seemed to anticipate the stabs and maneuvers of his enemies. His face reflected his maniacal thirst for violence—mouth open in a leering grin, saliva flaking his lips as he laughed and roared. He dove between stabs, rolling up behind or beside skeletons, smashing Lifedrinker expertly between armor pieces, shattering spines, knees, necks, and skulls.

He suffered many glancing blows and a few direct stabs from the spears, but most of them slid off the black-lacquered rings of his armor. A few tore into his thighs or hamstrings, but those painful barbs only served to enrage Victor further, and he shattered spears and cleaved skeletons in response. As the skeletons fell, it only became easier for Victor to use the expansive space to his advantage. He'd drive madly into a skeleton, batting its spear aside and smashing it to bits with his axe, all the while pushing forward, forcing the monsters to break their formation to follow him.

The combat was over as abruptly as it began, and Victor found himself standing over a widely scattered field of bones, armor, and spears. He was panting, and his arms were slick with blood from a dozen healed slashes or stabs, but he felt nothing other than triumph, looking around. "That's the way to do it, Gorz!" he grunted.

"Well done, Victor! Though I must say, Reevus-dak's spell destroyed the pack of skeletons far more efficiently."

"Gorz, you realize I can't cast any sort of fiery torrent, right?"

"Oh yes, Victor. The way you use the tools at your disposal is commendable."

"Never mind," Victor said, but before he could say more, a flood of Energy surged into him.

*****Congratulations! You have achieved Level 26 Herald of Carnage, gained 10 will and 8 strength, and have 10 attribute points to allocate.*****

As the euphoria of the Energy faded and Victor recovered his senses, he stretched and once again looked around the battle scene. He decided to collect all the unbroken spears, coming away with nine intact, sharp, bronze-tipped weapons, many of which were coated in his blood. Then he started sifting through the armor.

None of it looked comfortable; the linings of the helmets were all but gone, the breastplates couldn't hold a candle to his ringed shirt, and the other bits and pieces were bent, missing straps, or simply the wrong size for him. Still, Victor collected all the bronze armor, putting it into the storage pouch he'd taken from the cultist. "All right. Going down," he said to no one and marched toward the steps. "At least we know where we are now and can hopefully get back here after we find Thayla."

"Excellent outlook!" Gorz said with an appropriately cheerful, tinny inflection.

The stone of the steps was less weathered than the structure outside and seemed paler. Victor wondered if it was limestone, but he didn't know enough about the subject to be sure. He paused at the top step to consider his attributes.

He'd been getting better and better at swapping his boost from Sovereign Will during combat, and so far, it hadn't done him wrong. It seemed clear to him that he had a unique, or at the very least very uncommon, advantage with that ability, and it made sense to capitalize on it. "I'll keep going to two hundred, then give it another consideration, eh, Gorz?"

"Pardon, Victor?"

"My will. I think I'll keep boosting it until I break two hundred. Is that high for an attribute, or am I still a small fry in the big picture?"

"No! Two hundred is an admirable number. I'll caution you to be aware that your leveling pace is far from common. Some people have lived their whole lives on Reevus's homeworld, never to reach the second tier."

"Really? Because of a low affinity?"

"That, and their reluctance to engage in physical conflict. Attaining levels through non-violent means is possible, though immensely slower. When you consider your leveling speed and the generous attribute points granted by your class, you're in an excellent position, Victor."

"Good," Victor said. He was glad that he was growing more powerful at an accelerated pace—in the short time he'd lived on Fanwath, he'd racked up a significant number of enemies, and he didn't intend to let them ever take him again, not without extracting a heavy fucking toll. He pushed ten more points into will and then started down the steps.

The steps were wide enough that twenty people could walk down them side by side, and they descended for about twenty feet before opening into a long, straight corridor. The corridor had a high ceiling, and everything was constructed of that same pale stone, large square blocks stacked and fitted together expertly, with no mortar in sight. In this new hallway, every twenty paces or so, the space was illuminated by braziers holding red-orange flickering flames that gave off no smoke.

About fifty paces from the foot of the stairs, Victor saw a cluster of objects, almost like a display: on either side of the hallway stood two hulking statues made of yellow-pink stone, and between them rested a stone sarcophagus. The statues depicted humanoid shapes but were built more like gorillas than humans, with faces only featuring wide, open mouths and inset eye sockets. Victor approached cautiously, Lifedrinker held ready.

When he came to the tunnel section with the sarcophagus and statues, he settled his breathing and moved ever so slowly and quietly around the stone coffin, something in his mind screaming at him to be careful. The top of the sarcophagus was carved with unfamiliar letters and symbols, and Victor warred with the part of him that wanted to open it and see what was inside. His better judgment prevailed, and he continued past it. He was two steps beyond the left-hand statue when, with a grinding rumble, the floor ahead of him suddenly rose up, forming a stony wall that impeded his path. Victor grunted in surprise and turned to see a similar wall rising to block his way back toward the stairs.

With a sinking feeling, Victor backed toward the new wall, Lifedrinker in front of him, and he watched the stone coffin, priming his spells for action. He was so intent on the sarcophagus that he almost didn't notice the statues coming to life. They moved with rigid precision, straightening up, taking marching-style steps forward, and then pivoting to face Victor. "Oh, come on!" he growled, flooding his weapon with rage-attuned Energy and boosting his strength. The two statues were each more than ten feet tall and had to weigh thousands of pounds; Victor didn't think he should hold back, so he also cast Inspiring Presence.

Rather than give the statues a chance to double-team him, Victor charged toward the right-hand one, watching as it lifted an arm and swung it with predictable stiffness toward him. He ducked under the blow, flanking the slow automaton. "Sorry, *chica*!" he said, bringing Lifedrinker down in a sideways hack at the statue's knee.

He didn't know how effective the axe would be against stone, and he figured he might have to swap to his baton, but he wanted to give her a chance first. To his surprise, Lifedrinker sank at least two inches into the stone, bucking and pulling, as she hunted for Energy to draw. Victor wanted to give her free rein, but the statue was already pivoting to swing at him again, and he was helpless to hold the axe under the relentless pull of the giant's slow step.

Victor twisted Lifedrinker free, chipping away some stone, then hopped back to avoid a lumbering stomp. The other statue was working its way around the sarcophagus, so Victor ducked and jumped under another swipe and chopped the same knee with Lifedrinker. She smashed loose another big chunk of stone, and now Victor could see the deep V where he'd started cutting into the limb. He pushed even more Energy with Channel Spirit into Lifedrinker, and, as the statue worked to pivot again, he blasted another powerful chop into the knee.

With a surging flash of red Energy, Lifedrinker cleaved the rest of the way through the thick limb, and for just a moment, the statue hung in the air, its arms flailing backward, then it toppled. When it struck the hard stone floor, the entire statue crumbled, pieces of pink and yellow stone scattering all over the ground in piles.

Victor was so surprised by his victory that he almost let the other construct catch up to him. As it approached, though, Victor sprinted around the sarcophagus and came up behind the statue, lifting Lifedrinker high over his head and bringing her down directly in the middle of the statue's back. She bit deeply and immediately pulsed and vibrated, digging for what she wanted. Victor held on, spinning with the statue's movements, easily staying behind it.

Meanwhile, Lifedrinker bucked and throbbed, pulling pulsing, surging streams of green-yellow Energy through the stone and into her blade. "That's it! Fuck yes!" Victor cheered her on, jumping and scrambling as the statue tried to pivot and turn to get at him.

Luckily, while massive, rugged, and strong, the construct was not very intelligent—it never thought to try to back him into a corner and smash him. It simply turned, waving its arms, constantly trying to get at whatever was hurting its back but never able to find it. Slowly, the streams of Energy flowing into Lifedrinker grew thin, then faint, then ceased, and the construct stopped moving mid-turn, utterly inert.

Victor yanked Lifedrinker out of the stone, pulling chips of pink rock out with the blade. He examined her edge, and it still looked razor-sharp. "Nice work, lovely," he said, rubbing some stone chips off the side of her blade. Just then, another grinding sound erupted in the room, and Victor had two thoughts simultaneously: a statue was coming back to life, or the walls were lowering. He was wrong on both counts—the stone sarcophagus was sliding open. Victor backed up a step to better view what was happening, and then he saw a wave of darkness start to roll like fog out of the coffin.

"Hell no," he said, casting Heroic Heart. To his relief, the darkness faded away as the warmth flooding out of his chest reached his head, and he took a deep, steadying breath. Just as his hands steadied on Lifedrinker's haft, with a screaming cackle, a skeleton burst from the sarcophagus. It was clothed in tattered strips of cloth, perhaps once upon a time a robe, and it wore an elaborate headdress. Victor had a hard time looking at its clothes, though, for its eyes were difficult to avoid; flaming red points of light bored into him while that disembodied cackling laugh echoed off the stone walls.

Victor lifted Lifedrinker to attack, and the skeleton held out a hand, firing a bolt of crackling lightning right into Victor's chest. It arced around his ringed shirt, jolting through him. Victor shook as if he were strapped to a jackhammer, and all thoughts fled his mind, replaced by pain and white light exploding in his vision.

As the arc of lightning finally passed through him, he found himself stumbling backward, literal smoke rising from his chest where the bolt had entered his body. His thoughts came to him sluggishly at first, and he almost was blasted again, but a fortuitous stumble on a piece of broken statue sent him tumbling to his butt while the skeleton scorched a black mark into the wall above his head.

Victor grunted, rolling to his left, trying to put the inert construct between him and the skeleton. As he crouched behind it, his mind started to clear, and he reestablished the boost to his agility with Sovereign Will and began to use Channel Spirit to charge Lifedrinker with rage-attuned Energy. He could hear the skeleton clattering as it climbed out of the coffin, and he took that opportunity to charge around the statue, leaping and gliding over the floor with superhuman grace. He slid alongside the stone coffin and ripped Lifedrinker in a sideways hack that caught the skeleton's spine just above its pelvis, cleaving it in twain.

At the end of his slide, Victor leaped to his feet and darted around the sarcophagus, anticipating the bolt of lightning that smashed into the dust where he'd been standing. The monster was down and legless, but it was still dangerous. He could hear it scrabbling over the ground, pulling itself after him. Once again, Victor used the sarcophagus for positioning. Running around it, he saw the tail of the skeleton's spine as it turned the corner, chasing after him. Victor grinned and took two leaping steps, and as he rounded the corner, he smashed his axe into the base of its skull, causing the headdressed head to pop off. Suddenly the echoing cackle ceased.

Victor stood, shaking from adrenaline and, probably, from the electricity that had coursed through him, and looked around. He finally began to relax when large golden motes, some tinged with purple, began to coalesce on the skeleton and around the statues, then flooded into him. As the surge faded, he was relieved to see that his scorched chest had healed and his body felt fine. He'd never had a shock like that, and he'd love to avoid it ever happening again.

"Gorz, is this area familiar?"

"No, Victor. When Reevus descended the stairs, they were steeper and opened into a large square room, not a long hallway."

"Good, because I was about to bitch you out for not warning me about this fucking encounter."

"I'll be sure to speak up if I see something familiar, Victor."

"Thanks. I guess I figured you would."

Victor stepped over to the sarcophagus and looked inside. Glittering metals and gems met his eyes, and his irritation turned to pleasure as he took the sight. "Not too bad!" He picked up a handful of heavy gold coins. "Gorz, do people use gold for money in this world?"

"Not commonly on System worlds, though there are people who buy it for jewelry, artificing, and ornamental crafting."

"Good!" Victor scooped the gold and silver coins into his ring, figuring there were several dozen of each, then he collected the gems, coming up with more than twenty of various types. He wasn't an expert on gemstones, but he thought he had some impressive specimens.

At one end of the sarcophagus, a metal rod stuck up from the stone about six inches. At its base, Victor could see a small hinge. "A lever," he softly said. Then he reached out and pulled it. A moment later, with a deep rumble, the walls that had risen to trap him receded back into the stone floor of the hallway.

Victor continued down the wide hallway, able to see quite a distance thanks to the regular red, flickering braziers. He didn't encounter any more statues or sarcophagi, but after a hundred meters or so, he saw a well-lit square room ahead and, at its center, a massive pit with a ramp descending around its rim. Victor was still a few dozen paces away from the room, looking down through the hallway, and he paused to observe for a few minutes to see if anything moved or changed.

The pit with the stone ramp going down into it reminded Victor a bit of the "well" back in the mines, though on a much smaller scale. He watched, waiting patiently for several long minutes, but his diligence didn't pay off—he never saw anything move or change. Sighing heavily, he stood from the shadow he'd been crouching near and continued forward.

When he got to the mouth of the hallway, he saw that the room didn't just contain the pit. It also had a massively vaulted ceiling, with a dozen or more platforms built into the high walls where, if Victor could believe his eyes, bow-wielding skeletons stood, gazing into the depths. Victor backed up into the tunnel and contemplated.

He could still see a couple of platforms on the far wall from where he stood. Extrapolating their size and position on the wall, he estimated there were eighteen archer skeletons in that room, waiting for him to try to descend into the pit along the ramp. "They'll fucking make a pincushion out of me."

He stared at one of the two skeletons he could see from where he stood. It was naked but for the quiver on its belt and the wooden bow held upright in two bony hands. Victor recognized that it was very large and probably meant to shoot long distances. "Gorz, those skeletons have quivers of arrows. Do you think they're magical? Do you think they'd run out of arrows, or do they have, like, unlimited arrows?"

"It's hard to know, Victor. There are artificed quivers that can contain a nearly limitless supply of arrows, but many lower-tier archers don't have such things."

"These skeletons don't seem like elite enemies to me; I'd be pretty damn surprised if they all had magical quivers." Victor backed up and then turned up the tunnel, breaking into a run. In a matter of moments, he was back at the site of his battle with the skeleton and statues. He walked up to the stone sarcophagus lid and hefted it up in front of him. It had to weigh more than a couple hundred pounds, but he could lift it—awkwardly and with strain, but he could do it. He slipped it into his storage ring, then he jogged back to the skeleton archers.

Victor boosted his strength, then he stepped into the square pit room and shouted, "Hey assholes! Take a shot!" As soon as he saw the skeletons start to move, lifting their bows, he called the sarcophagus lid out of his storage ring, stood it in front of him, and then crouched behind it, letting it lean into him. Seconds later, a rain of arrows started to click and skitter against the stone lid.

Clearly not terribly intelligent creatures, the skeletons continued to fire, even though their arrows simply bounced and clattered off the stone barrier. Victor crouched in the lee of the lid, grinning madly, wondering if they'd run out of ammunition. He didn't have to wait too long to find out; after a dozen or so volleys, the number of arrows in the next wave fell off precipitously, then after two more rounds, no more missiles came. Victor stood and slipped the sarcophagus lid back into his ring. Standing there in the open, he waved to the encircling skeletons, and, to his glee, they began to step off their platforms.

The skeletons on the lower platforms mostly survived their fall unscathed, and they lurched to their feet, awkwardly clattering around the pit's perimeter to get at Victor. The other skeletons from higher platforms broke limbs or completely shattered as they smashed into the stone. Some survived with missing parts and struggled to charge into battle, scrabbling along, limping or dragging themselves toward him. Victor laughed, lifting Lifedrinker and flooding her with rage-attuned Energy; smashing skeletons that couldn't stab him or shoot lightning bolts was just what the doctor ordered.

6

GHOUL PARTY

Victor wound his way down the square shaft that descended into the depths of the limestone pit. He'd made short work of the broken, weaponless skeletons up above, and though it had been an excellent outlet for his frustration, he hadn't gotten much Energy for the victory. Still, he felt good about how he'd defeated the design of the shaft entrance. The skeletons would have done a lot more damage if he hadn't run them out of arrows and changed the engagement parameters.

According to Gorz, he'd descended about seventy-five meters when the bottom of the pit came into view, and he saw four stone statues like the ones he'd destroyed above. They stood against the four walls of the shaft, each guarding a different door. He noticed the ground at the base of the stairs, where the huge statues stood guard, was covered in sand. "Looks suspicious," he muttered. He looked at the ramp he was standing on and chuckled to himself. "Why would I fight four of those guys down in the sand?"

Victor dug around in his ring for one of the rusty knives he'd scavenged earlier, and standing on the ramp, two turns from the bottom of the shaft, he threw it as hard as he could at one of the statues. It whistled as it tumbled through the air, clinked as it hit the statue, and bounced off to skitter into the sand. Nothing happened. "Not that dumb, huh?"

Victor looked over the edge of the ramp, lining himself up with the statue guarding the wall beneath him, then he pulled a rope and piton out of his ring. He placed the piton against the marble wall of the shaft, channeled some Energy into it, and marveled as it began to glow and sink into the stone. Once it was secure, he tied his rope to it and dropped it down next to the statue. Gripping Lifedrinker in one hand, Victor looped the rope around his other wrist and walked down the side of the shaft just a few feet until he was hanging above the statue.

Victor braced his feet in a wide stance against the wall, and then hanging out, holding onto the rope, he channeled rage-attuned Energy into Lifedrinker and brought her smashing down onto the crown of the statue's head. Lifedrinker's gleaming, silvery edge didn't let him down—she bit deeply into the stone and stuck, throbbing and pulsing while she dug for Energy. However, the statue erupted into frenzied movement, and Victor yanked on her handle, saying, "Come on, not yet, let go." Lifedrinker pulled out of the split stone as the statue lurched away, and Victor tossed her onto the ramp, climbing the rope after her—he'd accomplished what he wanted.

When he regained his footing and lifted Lifedrinker, the lumbering statue was already starting its ascent onto the ramp, stomping and rumbling, its long arms and hammer fists pumping before it. None of the other statues had awoken yet, and Victor wondered if he'd broken the encounter. Grinning, he waited for the massive construct, and when it rounded the corner, he went to work. As he charged, Victor cast Sovereign Will to boost his agility, and he cast Channel Spirit to flood his arms and weapon with rage-attuned Energy. He didn't use his Berserk or Inspiring Presence because he was confident in his speed and ability to whittle down one enemy.

The fight went as expected; Victor dodged his way around the statue, using Lifedrinker to hack chunks of stone out of its knees until one of them gave way, and the entire construct toppled off the ramp to crash onto the sandy floor. Its impact gave evidence of the sand's shallow depth because it still sounded like a dump truck unloading a pile of stones onto pavement as it broke apart. The statue's destruction must have triggered something, because the other three came to life, swiveling their lumpy stone heads to find Victor and then moving together to stomp toward the stone ramp.

Victor grinned when he saw the statues couldn't quite fit side by side on the ramp, and they had to advance in a single file. He stood by his rope and hollered at the statues, "C'mon then, you big, slow dummies!" It might have been his imagination, but it seemed as if the stone creatures quickened their grinding strides.

Right before they made the final turn to approach him, Victor stuffed Lifedrinker into his belt and slid down the rope. Then he charged across the sand, pulling Lifedrinker free, and ran up the ramp. Just as he'd hoped, the statues hadn't noticed his movement, and the third one still had its back to him. Victor went to work on its right knee like a lumberjack felling a tree.

He landed three chops before the statue started to turn, and when it twisted on that leg, it crumbled. The construct collapsed onto the ramp, actually toppling into the next statue as it turned to face Victor, knocking it backward. The first statue cracked down the middle and ceased all movement. The second fell more softly, only shattering one arm, but still, it thrashed and fought to rise. Victor capitalized on the sprawled construct's state, jumping forward, nimbly hopping onto the "dead" statue's chest, and brought Lifedrinker down in a massive overhead chop to sink into the stony stomach of the thrashing statue.

While Lifedrinker pulled and dug into the stone of his enemy, Victor watched the final construct manage to complete its about-face. It stood, up the ramp, blocked by the body of the thrashing statue, and seemed frozen in indecision, perhaps struggling for a way to get to Victor without trying to climb over its comrade. Meanwhile, Lifedrinker was pulling rivulets of yellow Energy into her axe-head, sinking ever deeper into the stone. Victor held onto her, riding the thrashing of her victim, as he watched the final construct, ready to pull her away if it figured a way to get to him.

As it turned out, the statue never solved the puzzle of how to approach him, at least not before Lifedrinker finished pulling the Energy out of its fallen brother. When the construct stopped moving, Victor pulled Lifedrinker out, then backed down the ramp. The final stony guardian still stood behind the broken dead constructs, staring at him. It wasn't smart enough to get past the obstruction, but it wasn't stupid enough to jump off the ramp, either. Victor didn't like the idea of leaving it behind, so he crossed the sand to his rope, clambered up, and brought the fight to it. He killed it the same way he had the first—broke one of its knees and sent it toppling to the shaft's floor.

When it was all over, he received his surge of conquest Energy, retrieved his piton and rope, and made his way to the sandy bottom of the shaft. No treasure chest awaited him, but he noticed something he hadn't seen before—in the center of each of the four doors, a strange, squiggly rune was alight, blazing with a yellow glow. "Gorz, which door leads in the direction where we fell down the pit?"

"The one to your right, Victor."

"Thanks." Victor walked over to the door, and hoping the glowing symbol meant it was unlocked now that its guardian was dead, he pulled on the handle. The heavy, carved stone slab slid roughly over the sand, revealing a dark, cramped stone passage with a rather steep downward slope. Cobwebs clung to the corners of the hallway, and a loose, thin layer of sand coated the floor. "We're still higher than where we lost Thayla, right?"

"Yes, by hundreds of meters."

"*Comprendo*," Victor muttered, starting into the descending passage. His globe of inspiration-attuned light still floated behind him, throwing the immediate part of the tunnel into bright light that contrasted with the deep darkness a few dozen feet further on. He walked on undisturbed dust for quite a while, nothing changing in the tunnel other than the gradual lessening of its slope. When it felt as if he was walking on a flat surface again, he took a few steps, and then his light revealed the end of the tunnel and a pale, stone door.

The door appeared to open inward, but Victor couldn't see any sort of handle or latch on it. While feeling around its edges, he had a flashback to standing in front of the puzzle door where Thayla had caused him to fall through the floor. With a sudden shiver, he backed up a few feet and looked closely at the ground in the light of his globe.

He couldn't see anything odd about the stone flooring—the gaps between stones were tiny and filled with sand. He tapped Lifedrinker against each stone, noting the solid *clunk* the axe-head made against the dense blocks. Feeling better, he moved forward again and studied the door more closely.

After a few minutes of feeling for seams, hidden buttons, or secret runes, Victor growled in frustration and just pushed his shoulder into the door, driving with his legs. Nothing happened at first, but then, with a slow, ponderous grinding, the heavy stone door began to slide open. When it wouldn't move any further, Victor willed his light forward a bit to see what sort of space he'd revealed.

The first thing he realized was that the door wasn't hinged. It was simply a foot-wide hunk of stone that had been placed against the doorway. The next thing he noticed was that the chamber he'd walked into was enormous, with black shadows obscuring the ceiling and the perimeter. Finally, he became aware of a sound—sibilant, breathy panting sounds coming from all around him. It sounded as if he were surrounded by a horde of asthmatic dogs trying to recover from being too long in the sun.

Victor held Lifedrinker ready, then he pushed his light out and up, so it hung in front of him, pulsing softly. Then he willed more and more Energy into it, so it grew and blazed brighter, revealing more and more square footage. As the light expanded out to a fifty-foot radius, it started to expose little stone slabs on which gray-skinned, black-taloned, hairless humanoids reclined, breathing fitfully in a restless slumber. "*Madre,*" Victor hissed when his light continued to expand, revealing row after row of the creatures. There had to be more than a hundred, and he hadn't seen the extent of the room yet.

Victor started to turn, not keen on waking hundreds of ghouls, when he felt a vibration and heard a grinding sound. The stone slab, alight with orange runes on the inner surface, was swiftly sliding back into place, sealing off the doorway.

"Oh fuck," Victor growled, putting his back to the door. Suddenly the hissing breathing of the sleeping ghouls took on a different note, and soft growls broke out from the darkness outside his light. Claws clicked on stone, and then, with a hissing, shrieking cacophony, dozens of pale, wiry, naked creatures were racing over the stone floor toward him.

They loped on all fours, their claws clicking and scraping the stone, their hissing growls growing in urgency as they laid their black eyes on him. They were smaller but meaner looking than the ghouls he and Thayla had fought. Wide mouths filled with needlelike teeth spread in feral grins as their long, pointed red tongues darted in and out, tasting the air.

Victor didn't see a way out of this, so he braced himself for combat. He channeled inspiration-attuned Energy into Lifedrinker, saving his rage Energy for an extended Berserk—he had a feeling he'd need to let loose in here. He resolved to hold off on the madness of rage for as long as possible and cast Inspiring Presence to start the fight.

"Did I wake you up? Come on, then!" he cried as his mind filled with all the possibilities around him. The light seemed brighter, and when he backpedaled along the wall, swiping his axe to make some space, he realized a corner of the room was only a couple dozen feet from the door. Chopping in wide arcs, he kept the ghouls back long enough to sidestep his way over to the corner.

Victor laughed as the ghouls continued to gather, a large, gray, hairless crowd of hissing, wiry bodies. They were no bigger than middle schoolers, and now that his back was to the corner, they could only approach from his frontal arc. His axe whistled through the air, daring the front of the mob to make the first move.

The ghouls kept darting back out of Lifedrinker's reach, and Victor felt it would have gone on like that for a long while, perhaps until he tired, but the mass of frenzied undead gathering at the rear began to push the front line of ghouls forward, despite their attempts to scurry back out of the reach of his cleaves. When Victor finally made a solid connection, cleaving through a ghoul's ribs and arm, and black blood sprayed out on the stones, it was as if a switch was flipped.

Suddenly the ghouls grew even more frenzied, and careless for their safety, they leaped at him. Victor went to work with Lifedrinker, batting them aside, hacking through limbs, blocking claws with the haft. His arms began to rack up slashes and cuts, his legs too, but his torso was well protected by his ringed leather shirt.

Each claw that slipped past his guard and tore into his flesh sent a burning shiver of rage through him, and Victor began to lose hold of his Core. After fighting for several minutes and almost losing his axe because his arm was bleeding so badly that his grip had grown slippery, he growled and spat, "Fucking assholes!" Then he let go of his rage Energy, let it flow through him, and cast Berserk.

Suddenly his arms and legs weren't stinging anymore. The flayed skin was just a mild annoyance as scars grew over the missing flesh. His axe felt light in his hand, and his grip was more than strong enough to yank it back from the little creature trying to pull it away. Victor roared at it and kicked out with a boot, knocking it back. What were all these things doing scratching at him? Didn't they know what he could do? He'd have to show them! He screamed, exulting in the frenetic need to smash his enemies.

Lifedrinker arced out, again and again, whipping through the air and gray bodies alike, hardly slowing as she snapped through bones. Black blood sprayed the air in thick gouts and fine mists, and Victor began to laugh, a terrible, guttural laugh, as he drenched himself in the blood of his enemies. He fought for several minutes, his actions more akin to a competitive tree cutter than a person on a battlefield. He strode forward into the mass of gray, naked enemies without regard for his lost defensive position.

When a ghoul leaped on his back and tried to bite into his neck, Victor's left hand snaked out, caught it by the arm, and flung it away into the crowd. Then he whirled and leaped, hacking Lifedrinker with such force that she ravaged several ghouls at once with each swing. When he felt his red-visioned rage start to recede, Victor pumped himself with more rage-attuned Energy, extending the duration of his madness.

He fought his way across the enormous chamber, walking over the vacant slabs where the ghouls had slept, standing on them for better reach. He didn't plan to do so; it just felt good to him when he stood above the scrabbling, pestering enemies and smashed them to pieces with Lifedrinker.

How long he fought like that would never be clear to Victor. He had a lot more rage-attuned Energy than he used to. He probably pushed his body further than he should have, but by the time he finally started to think clearly, and the redness bled from his vision, he found himself standing on a stone dais on the far side of the enormous chamber, with just a few ghouls warily circling him. He was exhausted and drained of rage-attuned Energy, but his body was whole, at least as far as he could tell, under the thick, sticky coating of red-black blood and bits of viscera.

Victor used Sovereign Will to boost his agility, then he chased down the last few ghouls, one by one, dispatching them with quick, precise cleaves to remove heads or smash skulls. His Globe of Inspiration still hung in the air, illuminating much of the hall with its radiance. Victor stood, near the rear section, partially cloaked in shadow, observing the trail of broken gray bodies and black smears of gore that painted a grisly picture of the path he'd taken through the room while under the influence of his Berserk ability.

He set Lifedrinker down, bracing her against the stone floor while he leaned into her handle, breathing deeply and waiting for the surge of Energy that would replenish his stores. It didn't come, however, but a grinding sound behind him heralded something else. Victor straightened and wearily lifted Lifedrinker, turning to face the sound. Another stone slab, like the one blocking the corridor he came through, was alight with orange runes and sliding open. When it had slid forward and to the side, revealing a dark recess, the runes faded away.

Victor breathed deeply and quickly glanced inward at his Core. There, the two suns of his Energy pulsed and blazed, though the red heart of his rage-attuned Energy was dim and shrunken. Victor knew he didn't have what it would take to cast Berserk again, not without resting or a System infusion from his victory. Still, his inspiration-attuned Energy was pulsing brightly and not even half depleted. He quickly looked up when he heard metal scraping on stone.

A shadowy figure stood in the opened alcove, and it stepped forward, dragging something long and metallic behind it. Victor backed up toward his light and watched as the tall, lean figure approached. It took slow, deliberate steps, all the while dragging that metal object along the stone.

When it came out of the shadows enough for Victor to discern its details, he gripped Lifedrinker more fiercely and took a deep breath to steady his nerves. The monster was like a ghoul on steroids or growth hormones. It stood a few inches taller than Victor, had sinewy ropes of corded muscle bulging around its torso and limbs, and wore a pair of ragged leather pants. The item the creature was dragging turned out to be a long-handled curved sword or something like a sword, but the blade was nearly round, so severe was its curve.

As the creature drew nearer, it lifted the weapon into a two-handed grip and smiled, narrowing its baleful red eyes to glare at Victor. Its rubbery gray lips peeled back from rows of needle teeth, and a wet, gurgling laugh rolled up out of its throat. Victor scowled and twisted his white-knuckled grip on Lifedrinker, saying, "You laughing, fucker? Think all your buddies are laughing?" He jerked his head, indicating the scene of his earlier slaughter. The ghoul boss didn't answer; it just lifted its weapon and jumped, bringing it down as if it were trying to split a massive log.

Victor knew an attack was coming, so he wasn't caught flat-footed. Still, the speed of the big creature was surprising, and he barely hopped away from the chop in time. He didn't try to block it; he wasn't confident in Lifedrinker's improvised handle when it came to parrying a blade like that. As he backpedaled to get some room, Victor made sure he was still infusing his agility with Sovereign Will, and then he cast Inspiring Presence, glad that his extended rage had given the ability time to cool down.

In the light of inspiration, the ghoul champion or boss didn't seem so terrible. Sure, it was big and had a massive, sharp sword-sickle thing, but it was only one enemy, and Victor could see it wasn't the most intelligent of creatures. He started to circle the lanky creature, watching it move, and when it came at him with a sideways slash, Victor pushed Lifedrinker's axe-head against the curved blade, shoving it down, then he stepped into the ghoul's reach and smashed the butt of his axe haft into its chin.

The sudden move caught the monster by surprise, and it stumbled back, losing grip with one of its hands on its oversized, curved sword. Victor pressed the attack, continuing his forward momentum, stepping wide with his left foot, then lifting Lifedrinker and pivoting on that forward foot so that he swung her in a huge, whistling arc. The ghoul managed to raise its curved weapon in time to intercept her blade, but Lifedrinker wasn't going to be denied—she bit into the sword's edge, and Victor roared, shifting his Sovereign Will boost to strength and driving her further.

The ghoul was forced to step back, but Victor drove on, and metal screamed as Lifedrinker dug into the sword. Backpedaling, the ghoul champion caught its heel on one of the sleeping platforms and stumbled, and Victor jerked Lifedrinker to the side, yanking the sword from its flailing hand.

The long, curved weapon clattered over the stone floor, and Victor grinned savagely at the ghoul as it scurried away from him on all fours. Not wanting it to regain its weapon, Victor circled to the side, keeping the monster in view, and when he got to the blade, he crouched to touch it, slipping it into his storage ring.

"Come on, then," he said, watching the gray, wiry monster as it circled him, moving about on its knuckles like an enormous, evil chimpanzee. Then it flashed forward, and its left-hand claws flashed out in a blur of black shadow, ripping into Victor's thigh. He'd seen the attack coming and tried to block or counterattack, but the monster had been too fast. He stumbled from the blow, finding that his leg couldn't take his full weight. The claws had ripped his thigh to the bone. The monster was circling him again, and Victor quickly shifted his Sovereign Will boost back to agility and lifted Lifedrinker into a cross-body guard.

The ghoul stepped back, its smile widening, and licked its bloody claws. Victor growled and stepped toward it but nearly stumbled on his wounded leg. His pant leg was soaked with blood, and he felt it running down his calf to pool into his boot. He was thinking about trying to Berserk to see if he'd regained enough Energy when the ghoul launched into another attack. This time Victor was ready, and he was just fast enough to pivot on his good leg and put Lifedrinker's edge in the path of the swiping claws. It all happened in a fraction of a second, but when the ghoul scampered past him, it left behind three long, clawed fingers. "That's gotta hurt, eh, fucker?"

The ghoul whirled and hissed at him as it finished its pass. Victor sidestepped, favoring his hurt leg, blood squelching in his boot. The ghoul circled him, and he had to pivot on his good leg, keeping it in view. Suddenly, it burst into motion, circling him, and Victor stumbled slightly, trying to spin to keep it in sight.

The ghoul capitalized and launched another rushing pass, raking its claws along Victor's back. His armor held, and the claws rang as they slid over the metal, but at the tail end of its swipe, they caught Victor's left forearm, and two of them slid through his flesh, grinding against the bone from his elbow to his wrist.

Victor screamed in agony, and as a thick ribbon of his flesh fell away in a shower of bloody droplets, he let go of Lifedrinker and cradled the wounded limb to his stomach. He lifted Lifedrinker in his right hand, holding her up and out and watching the ghoul as he pressed his ripped arm against himself. He knew he was losing blood and couldn't afford to fight like this much longer. He tried to activate Berserk, but it wouldn't take, and he knew he still didn't have the Energy for it.

In his desperation, a thought occurred to Victor, and while he watched the ghoul warily, he switched his Sovereign Will boost to vitality. As nearly sixty points of vitality flooded his body, Victor felt his weakened, tired muscles pulse with renewed vigor. He felt the searing pain of his wounds start to fade to a dull ache as the vessels scabbed over, and with a grunt of pain, he lifted his wounded arm back to his axe haft. "C'mon, girl, we gotta finish this." He pushed what little rage-attuned Energy he could muster into the axe, causing her to flicker with a baleful red glow, and then, just as he saw the ghoul shifting to attack again, he swapped his boost back to agility.

Victor had braced himself for it, but the renewed pain in his deprived body was nearly enough to throw off his concentration. Still, he held on, and with the boost to his agility and using his full range of movement, he was able to see the ghoul's attack coming, and he stepped out just enough to avoid the worst of the claws, only catching three shallow gouges along his left hip. Meanwhile, he'd brought Lifedrinker down in a savage, lightning-fast cleave that buried her gleaming edge into the monster's forehead. The undead creature, amazingly, continued to struggle. It thrashed and flopped, and Victor held on to Lifedrinker, urging her to dig deeper for the Energy she craved.

He held the ghoul pinned to the stone while it kicked its clawed legs in the air, and Lifedrinker pulled black veins of dark Energy through its pale skin and into her shimmering edge. "Yes! Finish this *pinche cabrón muerto*!" As Lifedrinker shuddered and dug into the creature, its legs stopped kicking and finally flopped to the stone. It lay utterly still, and Victor jerked Lifedrinker out of its skull and glared around, fearing more attackers, but hoping he was finally done with fighting.

Soft golden light started to fill the chamber, and he wondered if he'd triggered something else, but then he realized it was Energy coalescing on all the corpses. Even some purple-tinged motes were forming on the ghoul boss. After a few heartbeats, the glittering mist began to flow toward him, and he welcomed it, desperately anticipating the healing of his aching arm and leg. The Energy surged into him, and as the euphoria filled him, he felt his wounds closing up and his Core burning hot and full once again.

*****Congratulations! You have achieved Level 27 Herald of Carnage, gained 10 will and 8 strength, and have 10 attribute points to allocate.*****

When the high began to fade, and Victor could think clearly again, he wasn't surprised that such a massive battle had leveled him. "I might be close to the next one, too, don't you think, Gorz?"

"Close to Thayla?"

"No, my next level."

"Perhaps, though remember, it does get slower. I'm noticing a new object, Victor. Is that a chest over by the alcove where the huge ghoul emerged?"

Victor pulled his globe of light closer and walked toward where he'd first seen the ghoul champion. Sure enough, sitting right in the center of the stone alcove was a softly shimmering silvery chest about as big as his *tío*'s mechanic's toolbox.

7

BLOODLINE

"Gorz, did the dungeon put this chest here after I killed that big guy?" Victor looked at the chest, leery of touching it after all the tricks and traps he'd found in the dungeon already.

"Yes, Victor, I believe so. I ventured into several dungeons with Reevus-dak, and it was quite commonplace for the System or the spirit remnants that controlled the dungeon and its encounters to reward adventurers after difficult encounters. I believe the chest where you found your armored shirt was also such a reward."

"Spirit remnants?"

"Beings not so different from me, though originating from a greater whole. Powerful Energy users often leave their legacies behind in dungeons, shearing off pieces of their very souls to curate those locations."

"Legacies? Like, so people don't forget about them?"

"That's one motivation, but motivations are myriad. One dungeon Reevus explored was curated by a powerful summoner's soul fragment. She'd signed a contract with one of her patrons to create the dungeon as a learning experience, of sorts."

"So you think it's safe to open this chest?"

"Not necessarily. Part of the challenge may be in surviving or bypassing traps."

"Shit," Victor sighed, squatting to look more closely at the chest. It didn't look dangerous. It had a clasp but no lock, and the silvery metal had an inner glow that wasn't menacing at all. Not seeing any hints of danger and losing his patience, Victor stood and pulled one of the spears he'd looted from the skeletons out of his ring. He stood at the full length of the wooden shaft and used the tip to flip up the latch on the chest. Nothing happened, so he wedged the spearhead under the lid and lifted it open. He was awarded with more shimmering light from the chest's interior but no explosions or pitfalls. "Easy, peasy," he muttered, slipping the spear back into his ring.

He stepped forward and looked into the rectangular interior of the chest. Soft-looking, satiny material lined the silver box, but most of its contents were obscured by a floating, silvery orb flecked with black, swirling motes. It exuded a bright shimmering glow that seemed to mist away from the orb, though if it were a physical mist, it dispersed almost instantly as it radiated. "What am I looking at, Gorz?"

"Victor, that appears to be a Delving Orb! Reevus was ever in search of such items! They're quite rare rewards designed to pull forth hidden aspects of your ancestry and advance your racial bloodline."

"Like the fruit I ate that advanced my race?"

"Similar, but far more sophisticated. This was designed by the System, Victor, and will dig much more deeply than most natural treasures would. What's more, in one of the texts that Reevus had me read, it's implied that these orbs grow more powerful the longer they remain undiscovered."

"What do I do? Pick it up?"

"Yes, it should begin its process immediately upon your touch."

Victor looked around the room. When he ate the fruit, he remembered being completely out of it for several minutes. Would something like that happen with the orb? He lifted Lifedrinker and walked around the room's perimeter, making sure none of the dead ghouls were stirring and that there weren't any newly opened passages where further enemies might emerge. The only exits he found, though, were the one he came through, closed off by the rune-covered limestone block and a stone door inset in the back of the alcove behind the chest.

He walked back over to the chest and sat, legs crossed, in front of it. He didn't know what to expect from the orb, but he figured he should be ready for anything. He placed Lifedrinker across his lap, and then, one hand braced against the stone floor, he reached out with the other and touched the orb. Heat instantly flooded his hand and coursed into his arm, traveling through his Energy pathways. It wasn't unpleasant—sort of like dipping your arm into a hot bath. When the sensation reached his chest, he caught his breath, and then, just an instant later, it came into his mind, and he lost himself.

Victor drifted through darkness, his mind filled with a buzzing, vibrating sensation. He felt as though he were stuck in an instant and in eternity all at once, and if he ever had to explain how long he floated like that, he'd never find the words. Eventually, something resolved in his eyes—a shimmering line of yellow light, dancing and expanding in his vision, as if he were hurtling toward it. As the line of yellow light grew to fill his reality, he realized he was standing in daylight between sparse trees in the warm, comfortable summer heat.

He gripped the hard wooden handle of his macuahuitl, the long, flat blade edged with razor-sharp obsidian that he'd cut for himself to craft the weapon. His brothers and sisters were lined up with him, shoulder to shoulder. He looked up and down the line, pride filling his heart at their mighty host, and then his sisters began their ululating war song, and he knew it was time to drive the invaders from their land. He screamed and stomped his feet, exulting in the strength of his blood. He and his Quinametzin brethren would push the little people from their shores.

Victor—no, not Victor—Tenecoalt drew his macuahuitl over his chest, painting a deep red line that flowed down over his belly, and he screamed, shaking the leaves of the forest, and the host charged. The line of Quinametzin, a hundred strong, broke from the trees, loping down the grassy slope to crash into the army of little invaders. He screamed and swung his weapon, cleaving through the little people, shattering skulls and bones and severing limbs.

His enemies had crafted similar weapons, trying to mimic his great people. Still, their tiny blades served only to anger Tenecoalt and his people, and the rampage continued until thousands of little corpses fed the grass. Tenecoalt knelt next to one of the last thrashing invaders and gripped its small head in his hand. Pulling it close, he said, "What do you call yourselves, little man?"

"Aztec," the small one coughed, then fell silent as Tenecoalt twisted his head, pulling it away from the body, trailing a spinal root. He held the head high over his head and screamed his victory to the sun, and his brethren screamed with him. Not one of his mighty people had fallen to the invaders.

Darkness fell over Victor's vision, and once again, he drifted. He was aware of his body, aware of the buzzing, tingling sensation traversing through his every nerve and cell, but he wasn't able to feel time, and his thoughts were just as amorphous. This time, the darkness wasn't broken by a line of light or any sort of vision. Instead, he opened his eyes and was aware of heavy, cloying air filled with the thick, damp scent of decay. A faint shimmer of silvery light was in the periphery of his vision, and he turned toward it, recognizing the chest.

Victor grunted and sat up, stiff, hungry, and with a mouth utterly devoid of fluid. He tried to lick his lips, but it was like running a rubber eraser over cotton. *"Victor!"* He recognized Gorz's voice and tried to answer but only managed to grunt. With his mind a bit foggy, it took him a moment to think of his ring, but when he did, Victor summoned a wine bottle filled with cool river water and carefully sipped at it until things started to work correctly in his mouth.

"Gorz," he croaked, "what's happened?"

"Victor! You were unconscious for eleven days and four hours."

"*Madre*!" Victor hissed. "Let's put some light on the subject," he said, concentrating and summoning his Globe of Inspiration. The previous light must have faded while he lay unconscious.

The first thing Victor noticed as the light took shape was that his boots were lying discarded a few feet away, as if he'd yanked them off in his sleep. He glanced at the rest of his body, and everything seemed to be in order. While he looked at his forearms and flexed his hands open and closed, he noticed that his myriad scars were gone. Every single white line from healed wounds caused by claws, knives, spears, and everything in between had faded away.

He called up his status sheet and looked at his racial information:

Race:	**Human (Quinametzin Bloodline), Improved 1**

When he saw that word, Quinametzin, his mind filled with the memory of his vision, and his heart started to race. "Gorz, how fucking tall am I?"

"Just under two point one meters."

"Meters? What is that, about eighty-two inches? Fucking six-ten? A little under . . . How tall was I before I touched that thing?"

"Approximately one point nine meters."

"Damn, man! Well, at least I didn't grow as big as those things in my vision—they were, like, twice as tall as the Aztecs."

"Did you have a bloodline vision, Victor? The text I studied mentioned that it's possible."

"I think so. It was like I was in another person's body, but he wasn't exactly a person, more like a *pinche* giant. I mean, he was tough as hell, but I don't want to be twelve feet tall."

"Your bloodline might not manifest into a full physical representation, even as you continue to delve into your racial advancements."

"*May* not?"

"Correct. There are many recorded instances of people manifesting the full physical characteristics of their bloodline."

"Shit, Gorz! Well, maybe I'll lay off the racial advancements if I get a chance at another. I'm already at 'Improved One,' whatever that means."

"What were you before, Victor?"

"Um, 'Base Four,' I think."

"Six ranks is an excellent gain, Victor! This orb must have lain undiscovered for a very long time. You should be happy to have reached such a milestone; most races require an improved status to reach Tier Four."

"Well, that's great, but my feet are too big for my boots," Victor said, holding the sole of one of his boots against the bottom of his foot—they were definitely a couple of sizes too small.

"Ahh, a one-time sizing enchantment? Your artificer must have been parsimonious."

"I bought them from the Contribution Store in the mine."

"Yes, items procured in such a way are often looked down upon by discriminating individuals."

"Whatever," Victor said as he stood up, lifting Lifedrinker from where she'd fallen by the chest. He really didn't feel much different, other than a sense of well-being and strength that eclipsed even his prior feelings of wellness when he'd gained his levels and improved his attributes. He felt that his body was full of potential. Which begged the question: why wasn't he in worse shape?

How long could a person go without food or water? He must have been in some kind of comatose state, or, on the other hand, it may have had to do with his racial advancements and level. His body relied more and more on Energy and required less sleep and food than it used to. Victor shrugged, retrieved a couple of sausages from his storage ring, wolfed them down, then turned back to the chest.

He pulled his light over to shine directly into it and saw that there were other items visible within, now that the glowing silver orb was gone. He saw the glint of a glass bottle and a loop of folded leather. He reached in and lifted out the bottle. It was filled with dark red or black fluid and about twelve ounces in size. A cork stoppered the top, but no label gave hints about its contents. Victor pulled out the cork and sniffed; coppery blood tickled his nostrils, and he jerked it away, stuffing the cork back down.

He put the bottle away in his ring, hoping that someday he'd have someone tell him whether it was worth saving. He picked up the loop of leather and, as he'd suspected, found that it was a nicely crafted belt with a simple bronze buckle. He wondered if it was magical, so he trickled some Energy into it and was rewarded with a System message:

*****Belt of Solid Foundations: Artificed item. Enchantments: 1. Solid footing; the wearer of this belt is difficult to knock down.*****

"That's pretty cool," he said, slipping it through the loops on his black pants. His pants and armored shirt had adjusted nicely to his increased size, so he took a moment to be thankful that he was only shoeless and not completely naked. He briefly considered cutting away part of the tops of his boots but dismissed the idea—he wasn't a cobbler, and he was sure whatever he came up with would make it hard to move with any agility.

"Gorz, I'm worried about Thayla. Eleven days, plus the time I was in the pit—I'm afraid she's either dead or in a bad way."

"It's true, Victor, you've been apart for a lengthy time, but anything is possible. Take heart that you're stronger now and more able to help her."

"Oh, thanks for the reminder! I still have some points to spend." Victor looked at his attributes:

Energy Affinity:	**3.1, Rage 9.1, Inspiration 7.4**	**Energy:**	**1891/1891**
Strength:	**106**	**Vitality:**	**90**
Dexterity:	**40**	**Agility:**	**48**
Intelligence:	**32**	**Will:**	**183**
Points Available:	**10**		

He had intended to keep putting points into will, but his regular level-up points would take it over two hundred, and Victor didn't like how his strength was so far outstripping his agility and dexterity. More so, he worried about his agility; he'd never noticed a problem with dexterity while fighting, and he felt that it was high enough for axe work. Maybe he'd learn differently someday, but he wanted to put more points into agility for now. The fight with the ghoul champion had shown him what it was like to face a truly fast enemy, and he knew there were probably plenty of enemies a lot faster than that ghoul.

Decided, he put ten points into agility, and then, hefting Lifedrinker, he moved past the chest to inspect the stone door. There weren't any handles or hinges, and he felt as if it might be another stone he'd have to slide, so he put his shoulder against the hard surface and drove forward, pushing into the cold floor with his bare feet. It slid surprisingly easily, grinding along the floor, and when Victor got a face full of cool, clean air, he expanded his lungs hugely, glad to be out of the stinky, corpse-filled vault where he'd lain for almost two weeks.

His light revealed a short hallway that ended in a set of steep limestone steps leading downward. "We're still above where we lost Thayla, right?"

"Yes, Victor."

"All right, going down." Victor advanced on the steps and started padding down them, rather pleased by how quiet he was in his bare feet. The stairwell was narrow, and the steps steep, and Victor descended for several minutes until he saw a faint, blue flickering light below. He continued, boosting his agility with Sovereign Will to help his reaction time and flooding Lifedrinker with rage-attuned Energy with Channel Spirit. She pulsed and throbbed with a red luminescence, and he knew she was ready to feast.

Victor stopped his light following him, letting it hang back while he continued down toward the blue glow. When he cleared a dozen more steps, he saw movement in the space at the foot of the stairs, and he realized it was a skeleton wearing tattered robes, much like the one that had blasted him with lighting. He didn't want to give it a chance to react first, so he quickly padded down the steps as it passed by, and when he burst out of the stairwell into the room, he saw the back of the skeleton just a few feet away.

Victor leaped and brought Lifedrinker down on the skeleton's skull, shattering it like an egg, and sending its bones clattering over the floor. It happened so quickly, Lifedrinker didn't even get a chance to pull any Energy. Victor glanced around and saw the light coming from a metal brazier in the center of the room that flickered with blue flames. Dusty candelabrum flanked a wooden table on the far side of the room. The table was strewn with bits of broken pottery, some bones, and a plethora of cobwebs. A wooden door stood to the left of the stairway, and, with nothing left to fight, Victor stalked toward it.

A thin stream of golden Energy flowed into him from the downed skeleton as he reached to open the door. *"This is the correct direction, Victor,"* Gorz said, startling him.

"Right, thanks, Gorz," Victor whispered, tugging on the iron handle of the door and sliding it with soft scrapes over the stone floor. The stones here were darker, more gray than white, and Victor recognized them from when he'd first arrived in the dungeon with Thayla. It seemed as though he'd found his way back to the part of the dungeon where they'd met Belikot, and so Victor began to feel some anticipation and a little hope about finding his friend.

The hallway was long and lined with side passages, and Victor began to methodically explore. He ran into many skeletons over the next hour or two. They were standard skeletons with weapons and sometimes broken rusty armor. Victor easily dispatched them with Lifedrinker; they broke and shattered before his mighty, Energy-charged blows, and his bulk and power made it hard for them to get close enough to retaliate. Even the spear-wielding skeletons were easy for him—they couldn't match his agility, and he'd bat aside their weapons, slipping inside their reach and shattering them with his axe.

He ran into a couple more of the spellcasting wizard-skeletons, one of which he caught by surprise and killed before it had a chance to throw a spell. The second managed to cast a ball of fiery blue Energy at him, but Victor slid under the projectile and smashed it before it could begin another spell.

Meanwhile, thanks to Gorz, Victor mapped out the hallways, discerning their pattern and realizing that they all funneled in one direction. Once he saw the design, Victor stopped searching side passages and worked his way toward the corner of the dungeon where all the winding paths seemed to converge. He found a very wide hallway with a low ceiling and started down it.

A dozen steps into the hallway, he saw that it had a precipitous slope just a few paces ahead, and, as he started down it, with a liquid hiss, black sludge began to seep from the ceiling, splattering upon the gray stones. It ran in viscous rivulets toward Victor, and he immediately realized he'd lose his footing if the stones grew slick. Rather than wait for the liquid to get to him and cause him to slip into the darkness, he strode ahead of the slime, hoping to see a safe place to leap.

As he descended the steep, sloping hallway, black slime creeping after him, Victor saw that it ended in darkness just a dozen feet ahead. He crept to the edge, trying to keep ahead of the black fluid, and couldn't see anything else; the tunnel seemed to open into a black abyss. "Fuck this," Victor said and reached into his ring, pulling out one of his pitons and the rope. He quickly used Energy to sink the piton into the stone of the hallway. Then, after securing the rope, he tossed it into the darkness. He tucked Lifedrinker through his belt, and with her axe-head bumping against his hip, Victor grabbed the rope and started to climb down.

When his light followed him out over the edge, he saw that the tunnel mouth opened into the side of an enormous, cliff-like stone wall. He tried pushing his light out into the darkness, but the space was too large, and when he felt himself losing connection to the globe, he pulled it back. The black slime dripped out of the tunnel mouth and down the stones of the massive wall, but only for a few feet. Victor had outpaced it, and as he descended, he lost sight of the tunnel altogether.

When he reached the end of his rope, Victor was still hanging in the darkness. "Gorz, can you sense the bottom of this fucking wall?"

"Yes, Victor, it's only another twenty feet or so. I'm surprised you can't see it."

"I think this darkness is unnatural." Victor gripped the rope tightly with his left hand, then he lifted Lifedrinker out of his belt with his right hand. He took three quick breaths and let go, falling through the black shadows. His globe of light streaked after him, and when his feet thudded into cold, hard stone, Victor bent his knees to catch his momentum. He looked around, noting scattered bones on gray stonework, then he heard the scrabbling clicking of claws on stone and the growls of hungry creatures.

Victor cast Inspiring Presence because he was still weirded out by the darkness and didn't know what to expect. At the same time, he charged Lifedrinker with Channel Energy and bolstered his agility with Sovereign Will. Moments later, four red-eyed hounds tore out of the darkness at him. They were huge, probably approaching two hundred pounds, covered in sleek, black fur, and sporting razored bone spurs all along their spines. Dagger-like teeth hung from their upper jaws, and saliva dripped from their lolling black tongues to sizzle and spurt against the stone flooring.

Victor hopped back, putting his shoulders to the wall, and waited for them to charge. They paced back and forth in front of him, growling and gnashing their huge teeth. "Come on!" Victor roared, admiring the new, deep rumble in his voice. One of the hounds leaped at him, and Lifedrinker licked out like a terrible serpent's tongue, ripping three inches of gleaming, silvery death through the beast's neck. It gurgled and sprayed hot blood, falling short of its target. It tried to backpedal, scrabbling its weakened, flailing legs. Victor brought Lifedrinker back around and crunched her through the monstrous hound's skull.

The other three hounds charged then, and Victor kicked out and punched with his left hand while he wrestled to bring Lifedrinker back into play. He jerked her handle back and forth twice, finally wrenching her from the skull. After he threw off another leaping hound, he grabbed the handle with his left hand and took a step, swinging her as if he were trying to knock down a building. She ripped through the air in a shrieking arc, cleaving a deep runnel through two of the hounds' chests. They yelped, turning and circling away from him, erupting in cries of despair and growls of agony.

The hound he'd thrown warily stalked toward him, and Victor didn't wait for it—he charged, bringing Lifedrinker up under its chin with an underhanded diagonal slash. After that, it was a matter of putting the beasts out of their misery. When he finished, Victor sighed heavily and looked around. The darkness still clung, crowding at the edges of his globe's light. Holding Lifedrinker ready, he explored the boundaries of the room. He was half done when the Energy influx from the hounds caught up to him, and Victor paused to enjoy the euphoria for a moment before continuing his inspection of the room.

Following the walls with his light, Victor found that he was in a rectangular chamber about a hundred feet by twenty, and there was a rusty iron door midway through the long wall opposite where he'd descended on his rope. He didn't find any treasure in the room and was rather eager to be away from the cloying darkness, so he tried the door. It was locked or stuck, so Victor decided to use his ring. He gently knocked on the metal, and with a grinding click and a shower of rust particles, the door popped open a quarter inch. Victor pulled on the door, and hinges squealing, it revealed another low-roofed, very narrow stone passage.

Victor moved into the cramped tunnel, padding through the darkness with his light trailing behind, and after just a few dozen steps, he came to an equally narrow, cramped stairwell. "Are we anywhere near where we lost Thayla?" he asked Gorz.

"We're quite close, Victor. This stair appears to lead to an area just twenty-three meters west of where the puzzle door was."

"All right, buckle up, Gorz."

"Pardon?"

"Get ready!" Victor said and grinned as Gorz protested his inability to do anything, let alone get ready. Then he started up the steps.

8

HUNTING A BOSS

The narrow, cramped stairwell wound upward, each step annoyingly a different height than the ones around it. When Victor finally pulled himself out of the confines of its stone walls into a small square room, barely large enough to stand in, the effects of the cramped spaces were starting to fray the edges of his sanity.

A black iron lever stuck conspicuously out of the wall to his right, and seeing no other options in the tiny space, he pulled on it. With a loud, rumbling, controlled collapse, the wall in front of him fell into the floor, and a wider hallway was revealed.

"I recognize this location, Victor!" Gorz said.

"All right, direct me back to that damn puzzle door, please."

"Forward seven meters, then take a right."

"Okay," Victor gripped Lifedrinker's haft, holding her crossways in front of him. The handle he'd made for her was notched, bruised, and gouged but still solid. Still, he missed her elegant, tough, cherry-colored handle and hoped he'd be able to do her justice soon. He followed Gorz's instructions, taking two more turns and stepping over the desiccated bodies of the ghouls he and Thayla had killed on their initial exploration of the area. In just a few short minutes, he was standing before the bronze-colored puzzle door.

The square hole in the floor where he'd fallen through was still there, yawning wide as if to invite him back in, but more surprisingly, the puzzle door was ajar. "I guess that skull really did know how to open it. Nice of them to leave it open for me," Victor said, his voice hushed.

"I believe the skull thought you dead."

"Yeah." Victor walked to the right of the pitfall, where Thayla had been standing, and peeked through the door. He'd left his light back a few feet, but enough bled through the opening to reveal the strange chamber. Like the door that opened into it, the room was round. It had a convex ceiling painted pale blue, like a sky, and purple mountains were painted around the edges to give the illusion of a distant horizon. Twin suns hung in the sky, one a smoldering red orb and the other much smaller and bright white. A stone table or altar stood in the center of the room, also round, and resting at the center of the altar was a familiar yellow-white skull.

On the far side of the room, another round door stood ajar. Orange light and shadows flickered from the dark recess it revealed, but Belikot's skull was the only object Victor could see in the room. As he watched it, peering from behind the partially open door, he saw a faint blue flicker in its eye sockets. The straps Thayla had crafted to carry the skull were still fastened around it, and the memory of her braiding the leather cords and carefully attaching them triggered a pulse of hot rage in Victor, and he twisted his hands on Lifedrinker's haft.

Grinding his teeth, Victor slowly channeled Energy into Lifedrinker, causing her to buzz and pulse as a red aura limned her long, bearded blade. Now was his chance. He'd shatter this fucking skull before it could protest or further influence him or, worse, Thayla. He'd worry about finding her after this asshole was out of the picture.

Victor used Sovereign Will to enhance his agility, and he hunched behind the door, veritably vibrating from the urge to jump and tumble. He took three quick breaths, then leaped through the door. Anticipating shrieking blue fireballs, he somersaulted to the left, leaped to his feet, and brought Lifedrinker up over his head in a two-handed chop. *"Victor, no!"* Thayla's scream seemed to echo in his head, loud enough to startle him out of his attack. He ducked to the left, circling behind the skull and looking for Thayla. He didn't see her and wondered if Belikot had tried to trick him somehow. Growling, he lifted the axe again. *"Victor? Victor! Are you still here?"*

"Thayla?" he called softly, turning to glance at the partially open door.

"Victor, I'm in the skull! Don't break it!" Thayla's voice sounded disembodied, almost echoing on itself as it came to him.

"What the fuck?" Victor jerked his gaze back to the skull. Licking his lips nervously, he slowly moved so that he could see the eye sockets again. He still held Lifedrinker ready, his knuckles white as he fought with the urge to smash the skull.

"Thank the Ancestors; you're alive! He tricked me, Victor!" Thayla's voice was full of despair, and the tiny blue flames in the skull's eye sockets flared briefly, then grew dim again.

"Is he in there with you?" Victor tried to imagine what could possibly be going on. Had the skull absorbed her somehow? Was Belikot torturing her?

"No! He stole my body, Victor! He swapped with me! I thought we had a contract, but he tricked me." Thayla's voice seemed to be coming from farther and farther away.

"Fuck, Thayla! What can I do? Where is he?"

"I don't have enough strength to keep talking for long; he's too powerful to fight, Victor. If you killed him, you'd be killing my body. You have to beat him another way. Find his phylactery—he mentioned it . . ." Thayla's voice faded to a whisper, then was gone, and the lights in the skull's eye sockets faded to almost imperceptible pinpricks. Victor looked around, suddenly nervous about being jumped while trying to speak to a skull. Nothing moved around him, though, and he gingerly reached out and touched the smooth, polished bone.

"I'm sorry, Thayla. I'm sorry it took me so long to get back here." He gently patted the skull, then he had an idea. Very slowly, he extended a tiny thread of inspiration-attuned Energy out through his pathways and into the skull. The eyes immediately blazed to life, more white than blue now, and Thayla's triumphant laugh echoed into his mind.

"Thank you, Victor! Oh, Ancestors, that feels good! Your Energy is so good!" Her voice, echoing in his head, was stronger now, and her words more sure. *"Did you hear what I said about his phylactery? He tricked me into this skull, but he really did make a contract to teach me. That's why he didn't destroy me after he took my body. He talked to me a lot while he performed rituals here. He mentioned that someday he'd help me make a phylactery of my own. He said I had a lot of learning to do and that a few decades in this skull would do me good. Oh, Victor, he gripped my soul and pulled me in here, and I felt like a child trying to wrestle a grown man when I fought back!"*

"All right, Thayla. You're good now; I've got you. Did the asshole ever mention where this phylactery was? How can it help us? I've never heard of one."

"It's something he made, like a . . . like a tether for his soul. It's what gives him the ability to move his consciousness around. It holds a lot of his power. If we take control of it, we can force him to get out of my body, I'm sure of it."

"Get the thing, confront the guy in your body, got it. So, where the fuck is it?"

"Belikot wasn't meant to be here, Victor. He's not part of the dungeon; he was adventuring here, trying to gain more knowledge of death magic. The lord of this dungeon beat him; only his undead status saved him, but his old body, the one carrying the phylactery, is still in the lord's lair. I don't know where that is, but I think it's in this area."

"What makes you think he didn't already go and get it?"

"He was scared! He said he had a lot of preparations to do before trying to recover it. He was very talkative after he tricked me, Victor! He gloated and gloated." She sobbed for several seconds, then continued. "He went on and on about what he was going to do with my body."

"Fucking *pendejo*!" Victor growled, "Okay, Thayla, so I need to get hurrying. Let's go!"

"Victor, be careful! The lord of this dungeon must be powerful, but I don't know what sort of creature it is."

"Don't worry," Victor grunted, picking up the skull and tying the cords to his belt. "I've had some practice killing undead shit since we last were together."

"You seem different; your voice is rumbling. I wish I could see normally; being in this skull is like being stuck in a tiny cell of stained glass. Everything is strange looking, and I can't do anything!"

"Hang tight, *chica*; I'm not gonna let that guy get away with this."

"Thank you, Victor! I can't believe you're alive! Belikot was sure he killed you."

"Nah, you know I'm more stubborn than that." Thayla's disembodied laugh brought a smile to his lips, and Victor proceeded to the far door, pulling it open farther to see what hid behind it. A short hallway opened into another round room, much smaller than the previous. Victor walked into it, surveying the mess—scattered papers, broken furniture, piled bones, and smashed glass dominated the space, all illuminated by a flickering orange brazier. Hallways led away into shadows to the right and left. Before moving on, Victor rooted around in the papers for a while. He didn't find anything that looked interesting; nearly all of them were covered with scribbles, stains, or scratched-out runes that he didn't recognize.

He noticed that Thayla had grown quiet in his mind, and he glanced down at the skull and saw that the eyes were very dim again. He channeled more Energy into it, and they flared bright again. *"Thank you, Victor. I'm not sure what I'm doing to expend Energy, but when it fades, it's like my mind drifts, and I start to dream, living in my memories. Just now, I was having a picnic with my baby girl. Oh, Ancestors, why did I say that? Victor, I'm not myself in here!"*

"Chill, it's okay. I'm not judging. Hang on, I need to concentrate, though—let's find this fucking boss." Victor went with his gut and started down the left-hand passage. It was identical to all the other stone corridors in this area, and he knew he'd be lost if he didn't have Gorz to guide him.

He explored dozens of passageways, carefully searching behind the doors he found. He never ran into enemies more dangerous than a few random packs of ghouls and skeletons, and he and Lifedrinker made short work of them. Nor did he find any worthwhile treasure or clues as to where the "dungeon lord" was. After several hours and at Gorz's insistence that he was starting to backtrack, Victor returned to the round room and tried the other passageway.

He immediately noted a downward slope to the hallway and a deeper chill in the air. He advanced more carefully, channeling Energy into Lifedrinker and padding softly near one wall, clinging to the shadows, his light well behind him. The passage started to curve, then the slope grew steeper, and Victor found himself creeping down toward an opening illuminated by silvery-blue, flickering light. He stopped the movement of his own globe of light and continued to pad toward the larger space.

When Victor came to the end of the slope and could see clearly ahead of himself, he saw a substantial domed chamber in which a humanoid being paced, limned in a ghostly, silvery-blue light. The figure was holding a flickering, bright sword with a blade more like a cleaver than what Victor imagined a sword blade should look like.

Victor bolstered his agility and prepared to cast Inspiring Presence, and with Lifedrinker humming and pulsing with rage Energy, he stepped into the room. When the figure whirled to face him, holding its gleaming, flickering sword-cleaver high, Victor said, "Hey, what's up?"

If he were hoping for a conversation instead of a fight, he was quickly disappointed—the specter-like humanoid leaped through the air, covering twenty feet, and chopping down with the blade of its weapon right at Victor's skull. Victor, for his part, didn't stand still; he darted to the side, completely dodging the ghostly hack, and whipped Lifedrinker out in a blur of black metal with a silvery, streaking edge, and she tore through the spectral creature as it landed. Bits of glowing, misty goo flew through the air in her wake, and the figure made its first sound, a wailing shriek that rippled through the air and echoed off the walls.

When the sound bounced around and rang in his ears, Victor felt his arms going slack, and he stumbled back. He shook his head, shrugging off the soporific effect, and cast Inspiring Presence. The shadows retreated, and the creature's movements seemed predictable, and Victor laughed at the notion that he'd almost put Lifedrinker down. "Sorry, my friend, but she's thirsty!" He chuckled again, circling the spirit, waiting for it to perform another obvious attack.

He couldn't see many details on his opponent's face, but the slightly darker line of its mouth turned down in a frown, and the pinpoints of bright blue light that were its eyes blazed more intensely. It lifted its sword and darted to the right, bringing the blade down and to the left, trying to cleave Victor in twain. Victor saw the move as if it were being performed by a lousy stage actor and sidestepped, putting Lifedrinker's edge in the path of the cleaving weapon. When the two edges met, there was a flash of light, then the top half of the cleaver-sword flopped away through the air, dissipating into a shimmering mist before it hit the ground.

Victor pushed even more rage Energy into Lifedrinker, then went on an offensive rampage, hacking in a series of wild-seeming chops that proved too fast and too well-timed for the spirit figure to avoid. He tore huge chunks of its strange jelly-like flesh away with each cleave, and, when he had it backed into a wall and cowering, he buried Lifedrinker into the crook of its neck and let her drink her fill. As she throbbed and pulsed, pulling thick streams of bright, mercurial Energy into her blade, the figure dimmed and shrank, and by the time Lifedrinker relented, there was just a puddle of faintly shimmery matter at his feet.

"Well fought, Victor. I think—it's hard to see details from this skull, and my view keeps jumping around. Did you tie me to your belt?"

"Yeah, and thanks." Victor smiled as he saw the golden motes starting to form over the puddle; they were tinged with purple, which meant the thing was a higher level than some of the other undead creatures he'd fought in the dungeon, but it hadn't been much of a challenge. Maybe he actually would stand a chance against the boss.

Victor took in the surge of Energy, feeling recharged, and looked around the room. Heavy bronze-colored double doors sat closed on the far side of the room. The shadows were deep in the corners, so he pulled his globe of inspiration-attuned light closer and walked around, kicking through the piles of strange junk. Again, there were plenty of broken glass objects, torn papers, and little bits of damaged, bent metal. "It's like it used to be a place for crafting, but either that guy I fought or someone else broke everything."

"Maybe Belikot."

"But why?"

"I don't know, but I heard him smashing things in the room behind where you found me. Maybe he doesn't want others to learn what he found here?"

"Don't things change in dungeons? Like, just because he destroyed this shit, does that mean it will stay destroyed?"

"It depends on how the dungeon is curated. It might regenerate over time or completely change, but it could take years or decades. I really don't know, Victor; I'm just guessing." Thayla's voice was quiet and soft, and he wondered how long she could hold together, living in a disembodied skull.

"Victor, I've grown used to you talking to yourself, but your conversation has grown very one-sided, and I'm having trouble following what you mean," Gorz said, his tinny voice echoing in his mind. Victor slapped his forehead.

"Shit, Gorz! I'm sorry—I should have told you Thayla's spirit is in the skull. Belikot tricked her and took her body."

"Oh, I see. She's been speaking to you in your mind?"

"Right, which begs the question of why I didn't ask you about any of this. Sorry, Gorz. By the way, what do you know about phylacteries?"

"Let me think," Gorz said and paused for a moment. *"I have a text in my memory that mentions the use of phylacteries in rituals to master various undead states of existence."*

"Nothing specific?"

"I'm afraid it wasn't one of Reevus's areas of interest, Victor. The text mentions phylacteries in the context of slaying a lich—you must destroy the phylactery before you can kill the physical manifestation of the creature."

"Right, so if we get the phylactery, we should have a pretty good bargaining chip, right?"

"I would think so, yes."

"Thanks, Gorz."

"Victor, might I ask a rather . . . intrusive question? Please answer me using only your mind."

"What is it?"

"Have you considered that Thayla might still be acting on behalf of Belikot? Are you sure she or he or both of them are not using you to retrieve the phylactery for his benefit?"

"No, I didn't think of that, Gorz! Fuck! I . . . I guess I just want to trust her."

"Understandable, Victor—she's your friend. Still, I would caution you to be wary; a creature capable of creating a phylactery and using it to alter their nature is likely to be quite crafty and duplicitous."

"You can read Energy signatures, Gorz. What are you picking up from the skull?"

"It's definitely different from when you first encountered it, Victor. I believe Thayla is within, but that doesn't mean Belikot doesn't lurk nearby."

"All right, thanks. I'll keep my eyes open." Victor sighed heavily, wishing he could just take things at face value for a change, then he walked toward the bronze doors. They were large, each wide enough to allow four or five people to walk through side by side. Strangely they were barred from this side, with a heavy bronze-tipped wooden beam sitting sideways on thick metal brackets. Victor lifted the beam and tossed it to clatter against the wall to his left. He was tired of sneaking around, and the idea that Thayla might still be deceiving him had put him into a foul mood. If something lurked behind these doors, then it better get ready for a face full of axe.

He pulled at one of the big doors, and it opened with a creaking groan, releasing a heavy waft of stale, cold air. A stone ramp led away from the doors into a dusty, stone passage. It was just like any other stone corridors in this part of the dungeon but broader with a high ceiling. Victor started up the ramp, his agility boosted, Lifedrinker in front of him, and anticipating anything and everything.

He saw a wider part of the corridor about twenty meters ahead, and when he drew near, he saw that the broader, square section was lined with standing marble sarcophagi. When he stepped into the space between the first two sarcophagi, he wasn't really surprised when the lids fell toward him, crashing against the stones and revealing their inhabitants—tall, emaciated ghoul-like corpses with leering, tooth-filled mouths and long, razor-edged black claws extending from their elongated fingers. In a domino-like fashion, the other sarcophagi started to open, their lids crashing to the ground, and before he knew it, Victor was surrounded by a throng of twenty hissing, snapping ghouls.

These creatures moved with more grace and intelligence than the horde he'd killed in the other part of the dungeon, and Victor clenched his jaw, backing up to keep them from surrounding him. He was frustrated, but not really, because yet another group of monsters was challenging him. He was pissed off that Gorz had pointed out that he couldn't trust Thayla, even in her seemingly desperate state. He wouldn't feel good about her until she was back in her own body and Belikot was dead—really dead. The more he thought about it, watching the creatures slowly advance toward him, the more pissed he became, and he found it felt good just to be mad for a change. He allowed his teeth to show, bringing his lips back in a low growl that hinted at red, murderous violence.

Victor let go of his hold on his Core and flooded his pathways with rage-attuned Energy. He found that, with his much more powerful will, he didn't immediately start to lose control of himself as he did way back in the days of the Wagon Wheel when he'd first tried to channel his Energy. No, he felt the fury and saw the red in his vision, but he was still too much in control. He didn't want to be in control; he wanted the release of madness.

He growled again, hunching his broad shoulders, Lifedrinker held crossways in front of him, and used Sovereign Will to boost his strength. He swelled visibly, and a deep, angry laugh started to burble up from his throat as he cast Berserk. In the red haze of madness, Victor exulted in the release of pent-up aggression. He launched himself into the pack of tall, vicious ghouls, and Lifedrinker carved a silvery-edged blur of red destruction among the creatures.

Sometime later, Victor came back to himself. He was sitting on the stone floor, his back to the wall between two of the empty marble coffins. Hunks of gray fleshed ghoul parts were arrayed before him in a crazy scatter of gore and destruction. Lifedrinker was lying on the stone next to his leg, her haft scarred, battered, and drenched with black-red gore but still whole. He picked her up, dragging her toward him, the metal of her axe-head grinding along the stone. Victor grunted as he hefted her up, and his eyes widened when he realized she'd changed.

Before, she'd been a large axe with a long beard, larger than you might use to chop a tree, but not much more so. Now, she was decidedly more warlike in appearance, still bearded, still not ridiculously large, but heavier, and her blunt end had grown to look more like a hammerhead than just the back of an axe. What's more, extending back from her bright heartsilver edge, gleaming, silvery veins flowed like a permanent lightning strike through the black metal.

"Look at you, beautiful! Did you level up?" The axe vibrated in his hands, and he knew she was talking to him. With a wide grin, Victor stood up and rested her against his shoulder. "Don't worry, gorgeous; I've got plans to get you plenty more to drink."

Victor walked back to the center of the passageway, surveying his destruction. Ghoul corpses in various states of dismemberment littered the area.

Some were smashed partway into the open sarcophagi. Some were piled up as if he'd stopped moving for a while and simply hacked them apart as they came upon him. Tired of breathing the wet, putrid stench, Victor looked away and started walking along the corridor again. A short while later, he came upon another set of doors. These were also barred from the near side.

When he drew near, Gorz spoke up in his mind. *"Victor! I sense a powerful death-Energy source behind those doors. It's stronger even than the ghoul champion you faced."*

Victor lifted the skull where Thayla was trapped and looked at the eyes; the light was faint, hardly there, and he knew she couldn't speak at the moment. He decided to keep it that way for now; he could talk to her after he'd dealt with whatever was behind that door.

9

TO A TETHER TIED

Victor paced back and forth in front of the massive bronze doors. He knew he had to go in there. He knew he had to kill the boss, "lord," or whatever, but something kept him from lifting off that bar and pulling the doors open. He looked back down the passageway, then at Lifedrinker, then at the skull bouncing at his belt. Did he really need to go in there? He could just leave. He could just tell Thayla he couldn't do it—try to find Belikot another way. "Then what?" he asked himself. How would he get Belikot to leave Thayla's body? What if he couldn't? What if she died, trapped in that skull, unable to cope?

"Fucking hell," he said, then dimly remembering his vision of the Quinametzin giants, he slapped himself in the face and growled. The sting and ringing in his ears stimulated something in him, and he hit himself again. This time he didn't growl; he roared. He did it again, and he screamed his roar at the door and lifted off the massive beam, barring it shut. It had to weigh four hundred pounds, but he tossed it down the passageway as his old self would have thrown a two-by-four.

Victor flooded his axe with rage-attuned Energy, bolstered his strength with Sovereign Will, and yanked the right-hand door open, sending it to slam into the wall with a protesting squeal of ill-maintained hinges. Darkness rolled out of the space before him, crushing the glimmering light of his Globe of Inspiration and snuffing the spell out. Victor felt a chill enter his heart, and his skin grew cold, and then the red, flickering nimbus of Energy around Lifedrinker faded away.

A horrible hissing, wet exhalation came from deep in the chamber, and when Victor's wide eyes turned toward the sound, his breath coming fast and shallow, he saw two red lanterns gleaming in the deep darkness. Victor's heart started to hammer in his chest. His ears thundered as if he were standing in a tornado, and every fiber of his being urged him to turn and run. Perhaps another person would have done just that. Maybe someone who hadn't prioritized improving their will would have crumbled and failed to mount a defense. Victor, however, didn't turn. He didn't flee, and, in fact, he forcibly steadied his breathing and growled, "You'll have to do better than that, asshole."

Victor cast Heroic Heart, and, as the hot, pleasant surge of courage-attuned Energy flooded through him, he took a step forward. When the heat spread into his head and eyes, some clinging, cloying shadows fell away, dissipating into mist, but he still couldn't see his enemy clearly. Victor concentrated on the two hovering red lights, and he cast Dauntless Radiance. A beam of golden light cut through the darkness like a spear thrown from heaven. It illuminated a wide circle in front of him, blasting the shadows away like truth exposing liars. Uncovered, the monstrous Dungeon Lord screamed and advanced.

The lord of the dungeon was not shaped like a man. Victor had imagined a terrible vampire, a powerful lich, or even some sort of super ghoul. However, the creature that stalked toward him through his light spell was shaped like a gigantic skeletal serpent with three sets of long, razor-clawed legs. Red lights shaped like dinner plates filled the black hollows of its skull, and twelve-inch fangs dripping green, acidic venom hung from its bony jaw. Shadows roiled off the bones of its frame, only to evaporate in the light of his Dauntless Radiance.

Victor renewed his Channel Spirit spell, charging Lifedrinker with a red surge of Energy, then lunged forward to meet the serpent. The monstrous skeleton was thirty or more feet in length, and when he met its charge with a powerful overhead chop, it felt as if he were trying to stop a speeding car. Lifedrinker didn't disappoint, however, smashing into its bony snout and biting deep. The concussion from the impact was enough to snap his improvised axe handle and knock Victor sprawling.

Victor rolled to his feet, already summoning his baton, ready for an attack. The serpent, however, was thrashing its long body and clawing at its snout with one of its front limbs—it was trying to dig Lifedrinker's axe-head out of its skull, but she was surging and vibrating, digging herself further into the bone. "Fuck yes! Get him, *chica*!"

Victor ran forward, boosting his strength so that his shoulders swelled, and his arms felt like tree trunks. When he got near the thrashing, kicking monstrosity, he began to lay into it with his baton. Each blow was like a gunshot going off—bones chipped and cracked, and the enchanted baton proved its worth by withstanding tremendous forces. He began to do so much damage that the distracted horror stopped clawing at its nose and turned its baleful gaze upon him. Meanwhile, Lifedrinker sank a little deeper, and Victor could see streams of red-black Energy coursing through the bone into her.

"You're fucked, asshole! She won't let go until you're done!" Like a launched torpedo, the bone serpent answered his taunt by striking out at him. If Victor had been bolstering his agility, he might have dodged, but as it was, the massive head smashed into him, driving him back until he crashed into something heavy built from stone. Victor wrestled with the horror, one fist clutching his baton and thrusting it into its mouth, the other hand pushing down on the jaw, trying to keep it from clamping onto him. Meanwhile, the six huge legs scrabbled against stone, driving him into the hard surface until he felt sharp pains along his ribs as they began to crack.

His baton suddenly slipped off whatever edge of bone it was pushing against, and his arm shot forward into the creature's maw. He managed to muscle down on its lower jaw to keep it from clamping on his arm, but he still felt a terrible searing rip along his forearm as one of the snake's fangs dug a runnel through his flesh.

It felt as if someone had taken a welding torch to his arm, blasting through his flesh and bone. Victor screamed, and with a panicked surge of adrenaline, he threw the snake to the side. He glanced at his forearm and felt the blood drain from his face, and a chill entered his heart when he saw the long jagged wound slowly expanding from the acidic venom.

Victor backed up, holding his baton ready in his right hand; his other arm hung by his side, twitching. He needed to heal, or at least resist the venom better, so Victor switched his Sovereign Will boost to vitality. He immediately felt better as his attribute jumped from ninety to over a hundred fifty. His heart rate slowed, his breathing settled, and the pain in his arm grew less sharp. He could feel his flesh fighting the venom and saw the green fluid bubbling and dripping out of the wound as though it couldn't find purchase.

The dungeon boss had grown distracted by the terrible thorn Lifedrinker had become in its head. She was drawing more and more Energy from the creature, and it desperately clawed at itself with its two front legs, completely ignoring Victor. Victor cast Channel Spirit, flooding his baton with hundreds of points' worth of rage-attuned Energy, then he leaped at the rear left side of the monster, smashing the baton down on its long, winding spine.

With a tremendous crack, the massive vertebrae split with shards of bone exploding away from the enchanted baton's impact. Amazingly, the monster's limbs adhered to the rules of physiology, and the skeleton's rear two legs and tail fell limp. Its collapsing weight pulled the skeleton snake toward the stone floor. It stopped scratching at its snout long enough to whirl and try to snap at Victor, but its damaged spine tripped it up, and Victor hopped back out of striking distance.

Victor circled back to his stationary light, standing in its bright glow. He watched as the snake-like skeleton scrabbled along the floor toward him, but before it could get halfway, it stopped to start digging at the axe buried in its snout. Victor watched as the black and red Energy lines continued to flow toward Lifedrinker and then looked at his arm. The flesh had stopped dissolving, and the bleeding nearly stopped, so he switched his boost back to strength, renewed his Channel Spirit into his baton, and charged forward, aiming at the long bone coming out of the monster's left shoulder; he wanted to deprive it of one of its scratching limbs.

He closed the distance, the skeleton either unaware or uncaring of his intent, and his baton smashed into the bone with an echoing snap, completely shattering it. As its left forelimb fell away, the monster toppled toward him, using its working set of legs to try to bowl him over. Victor tried to roll out, but he was so close, and the creature lurched so suddenly that it fell upon him, and one of its long fangs sank into his right thigh. Once again, blazing pain shot through Victor like a lightning bolt, and he roared and screamed as he thrashed in a panic.

The monster worried and pulled at his leg, whatever semblance of cunning it once had long destroyed by the maddening torture Lifedrinker was inflicting. Victor fought against the snake's movements, flexing his leg and pushing with his hands, fighting to keep the mouth parted. The fang kept slipping partly out of his leg, distributing more and more venom into the flesh, and as it tore into his skin and muscle and bone, a red haze descended on Victor's mind, and he let go of every impulse save one: rage.

Victor didn't remember casting Berserk, but something must have triggered it because deep in his chest, his mighty heart started to quicken and thump, and red, scalding Energy flooded his pathways. Victor's arms suddenly steadied, holding onto the two halves of the giant snake skeleton's jaws. He thrust them apart with a furious roar, ripping the fang from his leg.

Victor stood, still holding onto the snake's jaws, and suddenly it didn't seem so large. He loomed over the twisted, flailing monster and screamed into its dimming red eyes, wrenching with titanic strength. The snake's jaws cracked and tore, and then he pulled the lower half off and threw it, whirling into the darkness. Then Victor, in a mad, psychotic rampage, began to rip the skeleton apart, bone by bone.

Long after the skeleton stopped thrashing and fighting back, the fury started to fade, and Victor's vision returned to normal, and he found himself holding onto a huge rib bone that refused to break away in his hands. He shook his head wearily and let go of the bone. He stepped back to see the half dismantled skeleton lying in the faint gray light that suffused the room. The cloying unnatural shadows were gone, and diffuse light seeped between loose stones in the high ceiling of the chamber.

He limped back another step as hundreds of purple-tinged golden orbs of Energy began to gather on the ruined creature. Victor stood straight, breathing deeply, heavy with relief at being done with the fight. The Energy gathered and coursed into him, and Victor was lifted from his feet, immobilized by the flood of euphoria, healing, and Energy pouring into his Core. When he fell to the ground, he was bombarded by System messages.

*****Congratulations! You have achieved Level 28 Herald of Carnage, gained 10 will and 8 strength, and have 10 attribute points to allocate.*****

*****Congratulations! You have learned the skill: Grappling, Advanced.*****

*****Congratulations! You have gained a new feat: Titanic Rage.*****

*****Titanic Rage: In your veins flows the blood of Giantkind, and your struggles have unlocked some of its potential. Abilities that cause you to Berserk will unleash your giantish heritage, doubling the usual strength benefit and enlarging your physical form for the duration.*****

"Ungh," Victor grunted as he read the notifications. "Well, that's pretty badass." Suddenly he remembered Lifedrinker, and he walked around to the snake's head, or what was left of it, and there she was, lying on the stone next to the broken skull. Either she'd come loose when he was destroying the skeleton or worked herself free when the thing died. Only an inch or two of haft jutted out from beneath her black metal, and Victor noticed that the veins of heartsilver running from her edge had grown thicker and had more branches. "Great damn work, beautiful! I'm going to get you a fantastic new handle. I promise."

He tucked her into his belt, then Victor summoned his Globe of Inspiration, brightening the space and shedding light on the darker corners. Statues abounded in the high, square hall. Broken and whole, they sat at odd angles to each other—leering, monstrous faces gazing around the lair. It was against one of the statues that Victor had been pinned, breaking his ribs.

Victor stretched and twisted, ensuring that the Energy he'd absorbed had repaired the bones, and they felt fine. He lifted his left arm and rubbed at the dark, jagged scar that ran from his wrist to his elbow; the venom-ruined flesh had healed, but not without leaving a souvenir. He was sure his thigh would be similarly scarred, but his pants had already mended themselves, and he didn't feel like dropping his drawers just then.

Victor started walking around the statues, peering into the shadows, looking for treasure, lurking enemies, or something that looked like a phylactery. Some statues were broken, and hunks of marble carved into monstrous faces or taloned limbs were scattered here and there between their pedestals. More than that, bits of rubble, apparently fallen from the roof, and broken timbers created more obstacles to circumnavigate and search beneath. He found several corpses—desiccated, stripped bare, and missing body parts. Bones clattered as he kicked his way farther into the lair, and then he saw the pile.

Behind a statue of a two-headed cat-lizard, Victor spotted a large faintly glimmering chest and, piled around it, various objects of questionable value. As he approached, he saw rusty weapons, packs, piles of dented or broken armor, silverware of all types, and even a few cups that seemed to be made of gold.

Victor decided to deal with the loose pile of stuff before messing with the chest, so he picked up one of the backpacks. It was old and dusty, the canvas material stiff and unyielding. He pulled it open to find a blanket, some stained clothing, a cloth napkin wrapped around a petrified loaf of bread, and some other camping supplies, including a spark striker. He tossed most of it aside but kept some of the camping gear.

The next pack he searched gave up even less of value, but the third, a supple leather satchel still slick from the wax its owner had rubbed it with, contained something very interesting, indeed. *"Victor! I sense a powerful death aura from that object, and I can see its tether winding away like a thread! Can you hold me closer?"* Gorz was talking about a metal cylinder about the size of a very skinny wine bottle. When Victor lifted it out of the satchel, he was surprised by its weight and density; was that metal pewter? Hundreds or thousands of runes were carved into its surface and filled with shiny gold-colored metal. Was it gold?

Victor lifted Gorz from behind his black ringmail vest and held the cylinder close to him. *"Yes! This is the phylactery, I'm certain. Its aura resonates with the same pattern as Belikot's. Victor, I believe I could follow that tether to him. Imagine you saw a bright string leading through a room. That's what it's like for me!"*

"That's great, Gorz. I'll give Thayla the good news in a few minutes. Let me keep going through this shit. But, Gorz, if you see any sign that Belikot is listening or coming back toward us, speak up, eh?"

"Of course, Victor."

Victor slung the satchel over his shoulder after dumping out some old clothes, a shaving kit, and a pair of boots that wouldn't have fit him anytime after seventh grade. Then he grabbed one of the discarded cloaks and wrapped it around the phylactery, stuffing it into the satchel. Victor stowed away all the silverware and the gold cups in his ring. Digging through the other packs, he found a few pouches of Energy beads and added them to his other plundered beads. Finally, he picked out a baker's dozen swords and knives that looked halfway decent and put them into the dimensional container. Done with the piled loot, Victor turned to the chest and stood before it. It reminded him a lot of the shimmering silver chest he'd gotten after killing the ghoul champion. This one was a little bigger and had a slightly brighter tint to its shimmer.

The other chests in the dungeon hadn't been trapped, but he figured he shouldn't take chances, so Victor pulled one of his spears from his ring and used it the same way he had before. Again, nothing bad happened when he flipped the chest open, and a shimmering glow erupted from within, so Victor stowed the spear and looked inside at his haul.

The light was coming from a pale blue crystal necklace. It was shaped almost like a choker, and the seven crystals evenly spaced around its silver frame pulsed with a soft, pale light. Victor reached in and picked it up, noting the cold that bled into his fingers from the sharp facets. When he held it up at eye level, he could see that each crystal was shaped into a rune. Unable to read it, Victor decided to put it away for now; he'd try to find someone who could inspect it without risking an evil spirit possession.

Once he'd put the necklace away, his globe shed light on the other objects in the chest—a hunk of shimmering orange-silver metal that reminded Victor of what gold ingots looked like in VR games and a pale white dagger with a silver hilt. When Victor picked it up, he saw a drop of green liquid glinting at its tip, and he realized it wasn't a dagger but a fang, like those on the monster he'd fought. He shuddered, remembering the acid's bite, and slipped the fang-dagger into his ring. Finally, Victor picked up the ingot, marveling at its weight and the deep resonance of Energy within it. "Gorz, any idea what kind of metal this is?"

"It appears to be very pure amber ore, Victor. Reevus would have been quite pleased with such a find."

"All right, now another question, Gorz: should I wake up Thayla and tell her about the phylactery, or should we hunt down that asshole before waking her, just in case he's using her somehow?"

"Oh, dear. I'm not qualified for such decisions, Victor. I know I cautioned you about Thayla's motives, but I don't know what state she's in. Perhaps languishing without Energy is causing her harm."

"I didn't think of that. All right, I'll wake her up for a bit and see what's up. Keep an eye on her Energy and on that tether."

"I will!"

Victor touched a hand to the smooth skull hanging from his belt and channeled a tiny amount of inspiration-attuned Energy into it. *"Victor! Are you still with me? Oh, of course, you are; your Energy is unmistakable. Thank you, Victor."*

"You're welcome, Thayla. Hey, are you doing okay? Do you suffer when your Energy runs low? Am I going to lose you?"

"No, I don't think so, Victor. When I don't do anything, my own Energy slowly builds up. After a few days or weeks, I'd be able to speak again for a little while. When it's low, I just live in my memories."

"Oh, well, that's a relief. Well, any idea what Belikot's phylactery looks like?"

"No, I'm sorry. Did you kill the Dungeon Lord?"

"Yep! I'll hunt for the phylactery, then work on tracking Belikot and your body, okay? I'll wake you if there are any developments." Victor had already moved his hand away, and Thayla's voice grew fainter with each passing second.

"I can help, Victor—let me help you look for the phylactery. Could you point the skull around so I can see better?"

"You'll be fine, Thayla. Just go back to sleep for a little while; I'm going to find that guy, I promise."

"Victor? Are you shutting me out? I know I messed up with Belikot, but you can still trust me!" Thayla's voice sounded increasingly desperate as it grew fainter and fainter.

"I know, *chica*. I know you're still you. I'm going to make sure that fucker doesn't use you somehow, though. Just go to sleep, and next thing you know, you're going to be back in your own skin." Her reply came to him as a faint whispery breath—no words he could make out. *"Gorz,"* he thought, just in case Thayla could still hear him, *"anything happen with the tether or the phylactery?"*

"I sensed a faint pulse along the tether while you were talking to Thayla, Victor. It came from far away, though, not from Thayla. If Belikot is linked to her somehow, I don't think she knows it."

"Okay, thanks. Let's follow it, Gorz; lead me to that asshole."

Victor followed Gorz's directions back out the way he'd come and then through passage after passage that he frequently recognized as having been through before. After a long while, he came to the round rooms behind the bronze puzzle door. When Victor opened the puzzle door and moved out of the room, Gorz spoke up again, *"Victor! The tether goes down the pit where you fell!"*

"Oh? That's pretty damn strange." Victor retrieved a piton from his pack along with his last length of rope. He sank the piton in the stone next to the pitfall, tied off the rope, and dropped into the shaft, falling very differently from his first visit. He descended the shaft, feet bouncing off the sheer stone walls. When he reached the rope's end, he dropped the last dozen feet or so to land in the cold fungus-covered pit. Victor was glad to see the secret door was still open, so he followed the passageway to the site of his battle with the skeletons and hags. Gorz guided him, saying the tether still ran far into the distance, so he needn't fear ambush.

Victor stalked over his old footsteps, padding lightly on the cold stone with his baton clenched in his right fist. It wasn't long before he found himself standing over the bones of the skeletal colossus he'd slain so long ago. Gorz said the tether ran up the steps, so once again, Victor began the seemingly interminable climb up the uncomfortable, cramped shaft. "It's leading us to the entrance, Gorz."

"Yes, I concur."

"Did that fucker leave the dungeon? Without his phylactery? How long ago?"

"He could be waiting above, Victor, and I'm sorry, but I don't have a way of measuring the time since he passed."

"Right," Victor grumbled, tired of the annoying, shallow steps. After a seeming eternity, Victor finally exited the stairwell into the high, bright corridor of pale limestone and followed it to the entrance room of the dungeon. The skeletons still lay smashed around the room, exactly as he'd left them, and the portal still spun and pulsed on the far end.

"I'm afraid the tether leads directly into the portal, Victor. He's left the dungeon."

"Aw, man! Why can't anything ever be easy?" Victor strode through the vast entrance hall of the dungeon to the portal, looking around and furiously thinking. Had he done everything he needed to in the dungeon? Was he being an idiot following Belikot out? Should he wake up Thayla and ask her what she thought? What if Belikot was linked to her and could hear her thoughts or something? He growled and shook his head in frustration. He was sick of this dungeon, and Thayla needed her body—that meant it was time to leave.

10

STEAMPOOL VALE

The portal's cold pull lasted only a second or two, and then Victor stepped onto a dusty, rubble-strewn stone floor. The portal swirled behind him, throwing his shadow onto broken stonework in a constantly shifting pattern, almost as if he were dancing. In its green and blue light, he saw that he was inside a collapsed stone building. "Well, partially collapsed," he said, looking up at the high ceiling. It was as if the room he was standing in had once been a cave, but someone had built stone block walls inside it.

A very faint pale glimmer of light came through a crack in the collapsed rubble to his left, and Victor went over there to investigate. Sure enough, the remains of a heavy wooden door jutted out from some piled stones, and he figured that was the way out. Up near the top of the pile, the light was seeping through gaps in the fallen stone, mortar, and dirt. Victor took hold of the door's top edge and gave it a pull. He planned to slide the door toward him, dragging a lot of the broken stones with it, and create a space he could crawl through.

It was heavier than he'd anticipated, and he ended up having to boost his strength with Sovereign Will before he could get the petrified, solid plank moving. His idea worked, though; as he dragged the door toward him, a heavy pile of loose blocks, rocks, and dirt slid with it, and a broad shaft of sunlight fell into the chamber.

Victor mounted the pile and worked his way through the gap, his back brushing against the original cave's ceiling. When he slid down the far side of the rubble, he found himself standing near an opening that gave a dizzying view down into a rocky valley. He stepped toward the cave mouth and looked down over the rocky slope. If his eyes weren't deceiving him, it looked as if a dirt road wound between the high hills. "Gorz, does this look familiar?"

"Yes, though when Reevus came here, a path led up the side of this hill to the structure where the portal rests, and it wasn't in ruins."

"Didn't you say a village was nearby?"

"Yes, if you descend this slope to the south and turn to the west, you should reach a village called Steampool Vale in less than a day. Coincidentally, I can see Belikot's tether stretching away to the southwest."

"Down we go, then," Victor said, starting out into the gray daylight. He wasn't sure if it was morning or late afternoon, but then he recalled Gorz said he was going south, so he looked for the sun. There it was, just a bit over the hills to his left, and he smiled as its warmth fell full on his face. "Morning time still," he said, soaking it up for a few minutes. "God, it feels good to be out of the dark for a change." He took a deep breath, savoring the clean, brisk air.

The bristly yellow grass that grew between the stones on the hillside provided uncomfortable footholds but better than the sharp, loose rocks. Victor sorely missed his sturdy boots for the first time. Sure, the gore and filth of the dungeon had been uncomfortable between his toes, but climbing down the rocky hillside was a new level of unpleasantness. He tried to avoid sharp rocks, but, even so, by the time he made it to the road, he was leaving bloody spots on the flat stones he tried to hop between.

Sitting on a large, flat rock near the roadside, he took a few minutes to channel Sovereign Will into his vitality and waited while his boosted constitution brought thick scabs to the cuts on his feet. He found that his body was tougher and more resilient than ever, even without the boost; his improved race and overall higher attributes were starting to make a clear impact. He decided to keep enhancing his vitality while traveling and turned to the west, jogging down the road.

He supposed "road" was being rather generous—it was more like a pair of trails with yellow grass growing between them. As he loped along the right-hand rut, Victor became increasingly aware of his improved stamina. He felt as if he could run like that forever; his breath hardly quickened, and his muscles didn't complain in the slightest. Lifedrinker grew uncomfortable stuffed into his belt, though, so he carried the heavy axe-head while running. "Maybe I can get a proper sling or something made for you when I get you a new handle," he said, swapping her into his left hand for a while.

"Victor, the tether is still stretching away into the distance, though according to my map, we should be drawing near Steampool Vale."

"Has it been that long? You said a day's travel."

"I said less than a day, and you're traveling at a faster rate than Reevus. He wasn't as physically adept as you."

"Gotcha." Victor slowed down, and when he glanced at the sun, he saw it was high overhead. He'd been jogging for a few hours and still felt fine. He pulled one of his water-filled wine bottles out of his ring, drank it down, then took in his surroundings. Rocky hills still rose on both sides of the road. Sparse yellow grass and thin, twisted little pine trees dotted some of the slopes. Despite the high, bright sun, the air was cool, and Victor figured the road must be at a significant elevation. "Unless it's wintertime or something."

Not far ahead, the overgrown road bent to the south, and Victor couldn't see what lay around the bend. He continued walking, still holding Lifedrinker, and when he rounded the bend, a long deep valley opened up before him. The rutted track continued down the hillside to join a wider, flatter gravel road. When Victor gazed along the length of the gray-brown roadway to the south, he saw farmland, animal pens, big farmhouses with high, sloped roofs, and a wooden palisade toward the distant southern end of the valley, stretching around tall, peaked roofs. "Steampool Vale?" he asked, nudging his necklace.

"Yes, Victor. At the far end of this valley. Belikot's tether stretches south and west from here; I think he's gone beyond the town."

"What the fuck? Didn't he care about his phylactery? He's just bolting off into the world?"

"I don't know, Victor. Perhaps there's a way for him to sever his connection to it? Maybe he intends to create a new one."

"Is that possible?"

"I'm sorry, I have no information on the subject. I'm only speculating."

"Right," Victor sighed and started trudging down toward the gravel road. Belikot was a problem, for sure, and he felt some urgency about finding him, but he also needed to deal with more immediate concerns like getting some damn boots. He saw a lot of animals out in the fields and pens. Most of them reminded him a lot of sheep, though their wool had more variety in color, they had longer necks, and were taller. As he started passing by the cultivated lands, an occasional field worker would look up, and when Victor waved, they returned the greeting. All of them were red-skinned Shadeni.

When the tall wooden palisade was only half a mile distant, he passed close by a man wearing a straw hat riding on the back of a plow attached to two giant birds. His fence wasn't far from the road, and he hopped off the plow to approach as Victor drew near. "Hello, stranger!" he called.

"Hello," Victor said back, moving toward the fence.

"Where you coming from?" the man asked, spitting some brown saliva into the grass near his feet.

"Oh, quite a ways off. From the northeast."

"That so? What town, friend?"

"Well, I'm from Tucson." Victor shrugged.

"Must be pretty distant! I haven't heard of it."

"Oh yeah, it's a long way off." Victor saw the man looking at his bare feet, and he sighed heavily, saying, "Ran into some trouble, broke my axe, and lost my boots." He held up Lifedrinker.

"Quite a blade there! Well, old Arlf in town can fix ya up. He's been working wood since before I was born. Plenty of boots to be had in Steampool, too, provided you've the means to pay." The man spat into the grass again, his tone suddenly dismissive. Victor began to wonder if he was being judged or subtly insulted.

"I have the means, don't worry." Victor chuckled and waved, adding, "I didn't get robbed; I ruined them in a dungeon." Then he started down the road again. When the man called after him, he just waved and kept walking. Victor felt a sense of confidence and sureness of purpose that felt strange but liberating. What was that farmer going to do, chase him down and demand he spill his life story? He'd just been through a literal nightmare; he'd fought dozens, no, hundreds of monsters and come out on top. He didn't have to sit through some curmudgeon's interrogation.

As the open gates in the palisade drew near, he passed a few more people on the road. He smiled at a little girl with a basket of flowers and nodded to the woman who glanced at him sidelong as he strode by. His legs were long, and he ate up the distance effortlessly; before he knew it, he was walking through the gate and a Shadeni man wearing a food-stained white and red uniform and leaning on a long spear asked him to stop. "Yeah?" he asked, towering over the guard.

"Your business?" The man scowled up at him; he looked to be in his twenties, and his eyes indicated severe boredom.

"Boots," Victor said, gesturing to his feet. "And, I'm looking for a friend—a tall Shadeni woman with long black braids. She might have been carrying a nice spear. You seen her?"

"Nope. Doesn't sound familiar." The man's eyes tilted to the side, and he shifted, surreptitiously holding out a hand. Was he asking for a bribe? Victor had never dealt with someone like that, but he'd seen plenty of movies. He scanned through his ring, found his pile of Energy beads, and pulled out five. He held them out to the guard. His eyes grew wide, and he stepped close, snatching them. "Not so obvious, man! You trying to get me fired?"

"I don't give a shit." Victor shrugged. "So, you saw my friend?"

"Yeah, that cold bitch came through here. Wouldn't even look at me." He backed up as Victor's chest started to rumble with an involuntary growl.

"When?" he asked gruffly, taking a deep breath and reminding himself it wasn't Thayla—just her body.

"Three days ago. Didn't even stop in town. In this gate and then out the other, at least my friend Moss said so. He followed her through town. Something was off about her, and I'm not trying to be rude, all right?" He stood against the wall under the gate, his spear angled in front of him.

"Yeah, fine. Thanks," Victor said and continued into the town. Most of the people on the busy street were Shadeni, though he saw other races here and there, even a dark-furred Cadwalli who suddenly made him think of Vullu. As Victor moved to the wooden walkway running along the storefronts, people cleared out of his path, his size and strange appearance acting as a physical buffer. The buildings were tall and narrow, most sporting high gabled roofs, and Victor got the impression that shopkeepers in this town lived in the upper parts of their shops. He figured regular dwellings were on streets further back, away from the main thoroughfare.

"Mister, you're even bigger than my dad!" A tug at his pant leg brought his attention down to a little black-haired boy with wide, pinkish-red eyes. He couldn't help the smile stretching his cheeks as he leaned down and tousled his hair.

"Hey, *niñito*. Yeah, that's 'cause my *abuela* always made me eat my veggies."

"Sorry, sir," a woman said and reached down to grab the boy's hand. "Come on, Ryld!" She yanked his arm and started hurrying away.

"It's not a problem," Victor called after her retreating back. She didn't turn, though, and he sighed, straightened up, and looked around at the nearby shops. He saw a glass blower, a bakery, a shop with some dresses on display in the window, and, across the street, a curio shop and a furniture store. The wooden planks of the walkways under the awnings were in good repair, and Victor thought the town seemed rather idyllic. People were clean, the gravel streets were dry and even, and the bright paint on the tall buildings gave it a festive sort of feel. Maybe he was just used to the ramshackle, dingy, depressing mine.

"You looking for something, big man?" Victor looked down to see the source of the voice. A gray-haired, stooped, blue-skinned Ardeni looked up at him with bright yellow eyes. The constant references to his size and the fact that no one was calling him kid or idiot gave him a funny feeling in his chest. He realized he was still smiling from the encounter with the little boy, and he drew his lips back to reveal his teeth in a broad grin and reached out a hand to the older man.

"Hey. Yeah, actually, I am. I need some new boots. Name's Victor."

"Good to meet you!" the man said, grabbing Victor's hand. His knobby, lean fingers had a surprisingly firm grip. "Uld ap'Nar."

"I also need to find someone who can fix my axe," Victor said, letting go of the man's hand.

"I can help you, adventurer." The man reached up to rest a blue hand on Victor's shoulder, then pointed with the other up the street. "Head that way until you get to the corner. Turn right, walk past two buildings, and you'll be in front of woodworker Teng-dak's shop. He can fix that axe right up."

"Not, uh, what was it?" Victor snapped his fingers, then asked in his mind, *"Gorz, who did that farmer say could fix Lifedrinker?"*

"Arlf."

"Not Arlf?" he asked Uld.

"Oh, Ancestors! I wouldn't go to him; he crafts farm equipment."

"Oh? Interesting," Victor didn't know if the cranky old farmer had been trying to throw business to a friend or if this guy was getting some sort of commission. He didn't care as long as Lifedrinker got a good haft. "What about boots, Uld?"

"Well, Victor." The old man smiled when he used his name, leaning in closer and giving his shoulder a comradely jostle. "I know just the lady for you! Miss ap'Larl is a fantastic cobbler, and you'll find her in the opposite direction of Teng-dak at the next corner, just one shop down on the left."

"Thanks for all your help, Uld. Can I do anything to repay you?" Victor had no idea where his sudden manners or friendliness were coming from, but he was soaking in the positive vibes from the older man and didn't want to sour things by bolting off in a selfish rush.

"Oh, what a fine specimen of the younger generation! What manners! Let me ask you, Victor, was I right in calling you an adventurer?" Uld had slowly moved to the side, so they were out of the center of the walkway, and Victor leaned against the wooden wall of the bakery they stood before. He nodded, deciding that adventurer was a fine way to be described.

"Yeah, I think that's pretty spot-on, Uld."

"Well, then, I do have a way you could help me, Victor. How about meeting me at the tavern tonight? Let me buy you dinner, and you can have a talk with my grandson. He's got his heart set on seeking glory, and I was hoping you could give him either a few pointers or some serious warnings, depending on what you thought of him."

"You're leaving it to me?"

"Why not? You're the expert! Take a look at him, hear him out, and then you can decide if you want to encourage or frighten him. What do you say?"

"Well, I'm kinda in a hurry, but I haven't had a good meal in a while. I think I could spare an hour or two for dinner. Where's the tavern?"

"If you follow this road through town to the other gate, the tavern is there, just inside the wall on this side of the street. It's called The Laughing Roladii."

"Sounds good, Uld. I'll see you in a few hours." Victor started to leave, but Uld held out his hand again, and Victor shook it, giving it a good squeeze. Then he strode away, toward the intersection at the end of the block. "What a good old guy," he said, smiling at the lady sweeping the walkway in front of the dress shop.

"Buy a dress for your sweet?" she asked as he stepped around her pile of dust.

"Oh, I don't know her size," he said.

"Well, I have some artificed dresses that will fit her for sure!"

"Well, I don't know what colors she likes," Victor said, grinning and stepping closer to her shop.

"Really? What colors have you seen her wearing?"

"I have to confess; I haven't seen her wearing any colors. I haven't met her yet!" Victor laughed and winked at the woman, then continued to the corner, taking a left. Her chuckle followed after him. "*Un hombre suave*," he said, grinning.

He passed by a weaver's shop, and then he was standing in front of a display window filled with boots and shoes. Some were sleek and elegant, and others looked built for work on a farm. He opened the door and, accompanied by the jingling of a little bell, entered the shop.

It didn't look so different from a modern American shoe store, the significant differences being that the shelving looked handcrafted from polished hardwoods, and the smell of leather and natural oils filled the air. A small Shadeni woman with short black hair sat on a stool behind a counter, and she jumped up, putting her thumbs behind the straps of her yellow overalls as she walked toward him. "Oh, my goodness! Here's a man in need of some big shoes!"

"Oh, hey. Yeah, my old boots are deep underground. You got any boots that self-clean, resize, and can take some rough use?" Victor lifted one of his feet as if to illustrate the pains his new footwear would have to endure.

"Hmm, I sure have some boots that might suit you. What are your thoughts on fashion? Looking at you, I can't get a good feel for your tastes. Let's see, a beautiful, shiny, armored vest. Those pants look well made, a supple leather belt, and an old but nicely made satchel. Everything looks good except your axe sticking out of your belt there. Hard on your tools, hmm? Your hair looks a bit ragged and unkempt. Aren't you interested in fashion at all?"

Suddenly self-conscious, Victor put a hand to his head and felt at his unruly black hair. "Lady, I've been through hell for the last couple of months. You're lucky these pants and this vest clean themselves, or you'd be opening all the windows in here."

"Well, I was going to mention the grime on your neck and arms, but I thought that might be too forward." The young woman's orange eyes crinkled in amusement, and Victor smiled.

"Yeah, I know, I know. I need a bath. Right now, I'm going to have to settle for new boots, though, because I have a friend I've gotta help."

"Oh? That's a shame; I was going to offer you a discount at my sister's inn!"

"I guess it's not my lucky day. Maybe if I can catch up to her and help her out fast enough, I could come back here to spend a little more time visiting." Victor sat on one of the wooden benches near the center of the shop. "My name's Victor. I'm looking for something sturdy but comfortable, and I'll let you pick the style." He grinned, putting one hand on the bench and leaning into it.

"All right, well, are you fond of those pants? Do you wear them a lot?"

"Yeah, they're my only pair."

"Oh. Now I see why you're happy they're artificed." She wrinkled her nose.

"Exactly. I used to have a matching shirt, but it got stolen. I've got this nice armored shirt now, though." Victor ran his knuckles over the black lacquered rings, making them clink against each other.

"Well, anyway, I've got just the boots for you. Their uppers will fit nicely under the cuffs of those pants." She went to the display case behind Victor and picked up a pair of boots, holding them out for him to inspect. They looked almost like square-toed cowboy boots. They were stained black and had a sturdy multilayered leather and wood sole, and the uppers looked like they'd come to about mid-shin. Best of all, they had shiny, steel-cased toes.

"They look great. You have any socks?"

"Of course! Let's talk price, then I can get you set up with a few pairs, and you can bond with these boots."

"Oh, right. How much are we talking?"

She looked at him quizzically for a moment, then her impish smile returned, and she said, "Twenty standard beads for the boots, and I'll throw in the socks." Victor smiled, but his mind started racing as he realized he had no idea the value of an Energy bead. He'd tossed five at the guard, but only because he had more than a thousand in his ring. Some of those were rightfully Thayla's, but she couldn't exactly spend them right now.

"Help me out, *chica*. Is that a lot of money?"

"Oh, please don't call me girl—my name's Sceffi. What do you mean, 'is that a lot?'"

"All right, I don't buy nice boots often. Are those expensive? Is that something a rich guy would buy, or, you know, average Joe the farmer?"

"You're an odd fellow, and it's not just your looks." She softened the blow of her words with a crooked smile. "These boots are expensive because of their quality. They have enchantments for unlimited sizing, scuff repair, and stain and odor removal. I have shoes that look nicer but aren't nearly as well-made. Rich, lazy people would buy those, not these fantastic boots."

"All right, sheesh. Sounds fair, um, Sefi, was it?"

"Almost. Sceffi. Hear the slight 'k' sound after the s?"

"Um, not really, but I'll try. Sceffi?"

"Really close; thanks for trying!" Her grin widened, then she held out a hand, palm up.

"Oh, right." Victor scanned through his ring and pulled out twenty Energy beads. Most of them were pale blue, but a few had red swirls in them. He held out his large hand, the pile of beads glittering in his palm.

Sceffi looked at the pile of Energy beads and said, "Victor, those are attuned Energy beads." She picked up one of the multi-colored ones and said, "This is dual-attuned. They're all worth more than standard Energy beads."

"Really? Shit, well, can you just take what you need out of that?" He nodded to the pile of beads, and Sceffi shrugged. She plucked out ten of the pale blue beads.

"That'll cover it." She handed the boots to Victor. "They're too small; just put your toes into one and bond with it. They'll resize, but wait, and I'll get you socks. Sit tight." Victor nodded, admiring the sturdy thick soles on the boots. The ones he'd bought in the mine had just had a couple of thick, stiff leather layers sewn to the uppers. These were on another level with their craftsmanship. Sceffi returned with several pairs of long gray socks. Victor took the one she held out and admired its soft, durable material.

"What are they made of?"

"Wool, of course."

"Wool? You have sheep here?"

"Sheep?"

"Yeah, the animal," Victor couldn't help a little exasperation slipping into his voice; it was one thing for people to constantly ask him to repeat himself when he was being a goof, but he was just trying to speak normally now.

"I'm not familiar. These are made from holbyis wool."

"Right. Those are the fluffy, long-necked animals out in the valley, right?"

"Right! Where are you from, Victor?" She put a hand on her overall strap, tugging at it absently while watching him put his socks on.

"Yeah, I'm from far away." Victor was tempted to say he was from another world, but then he thought about how dangerous people were looking for him, and he figured that sort of detail was better kept to himself. The socks felt good, and when he pulled a boot partially onto his foot and then bonded with it, the leather stretched and molded to his foot. Soon he was standing in his new boots, walking back and forth, admiring the *clonk* sound they made on the wooden floors. They perfectly hugged his feet, as if he'd spent weeks hiking to break them in. "Very nice, Sceffi. I'll try to return for my next pair!"

"Will you be in town much longer?" she asked, still watching him walk back and forth.

"Not this time, I'm afraid. Like I said, a friend needs help." He looked at her, made eye contact, and said, "Seriously, thanks. I'll see you again, I hope." Then he turned and, with a jingle of the little bell, stepped out the door. Feeling much more secure now that his toes were protected under a hard layer of steel, Victor strode toward Teng-dak's shop—time to get Lifedrinker a new haft.

11

AN EVENING OUT

The woodworker's shop smelled like sawdust and varnish, and Victor was struck by memories of his *abuelo* when he stepped through the door. He remembered his grandpa's bald, wrinkled head bent over his table saw, carefully cutting through planks to make a bookcase or a box to hold his tools. He'd treated Victor like his shop assistant, showing him how to sweep up sawdust, asking him to fetch tools, and most meaningfully, letting him help with the nailing or sanding.

"Hello, warrior. Here for a new rocking chair?" Victor jerked out of his reverie and met eyes with the man sitting on a stool to his left. He was short for a Shadeni and wore a spotted apron over a bare chest. His exposed skin was alive with wild, colorful tattoos—some were strange glyphs or letters that Victor couldn't read, but others were exotic animals, beautiful women's faces, or images of stars and moons. His black hair was long and wispy, and so were his mustache and beard. He favored Victor with a sardonic grin and raised an eyebrow as if to indicate he was waiting for an answer.

Victor didn't answer right away; instead, he took a slow, deliberate look around the shop. Furniture took up most of the space—chairs of all types, bureaus, trunks, shelves. If you looked, though, other objects spoke to broader areas of expertise—carved animals and busts of people, a rack of beautiful composite bows, another stand stuffed with staves of all kinds, and a display case overflowing with wooden curios. Victor brought his gaze back to the man whom he presumed was Teng-dak. "Hello, sir. I was told you're the man to talk to about getting my axe fixed up."

"An axe, eh? I'm assuming you mean the handle, not the blade?"

"Right." Victor pulled Lifedrinker's broad, dark blade from his belt, her gleaming edge winking in the bright Energy sconces lining the walls.

"Oh, now that's a lovely piece of work!" Teng-dak set down the varnish rag he'd been rubbing along the length of a table leg. "Let me get a closer look. Come on over; pull up a stool." He gestured to one of the other stools scattered around his broad workbench. Victor nodded, strode over to the man, gently set Lifedrinker onto his table, and sat down facing the woodworker, the axe between them.

"First of all, she's alive, so treat her like it," Victor said, nodding to the axe, eyes steady on Teng-dak's face.

"Oh? A conscious weapon, hmm? Well, now I'm even more intrigued. What's . . . she, was it? What's she made of?" Teng-dak gingerly picked up Lifedrinker, turning her around, and snorting as he took in the splintered haft sticking out of the axe-head's eye.

"I'm not sure about the black metal, but the bright blade and those veins are heartsilver."

"My, my. Sharp, too, isn't she?" He held Lifedrinker up and eyed along her cutting edge.

"Very." Victor retrieved the piece of her old cherry-colored haft and set it on the workbench. "This was her handle when I first got her. I'm not sure what wood it is, but it held up pretty well until I fell down a deep stone pit."

"Oh, aye, that's Tevellian mahogany. See the darker veins in the red-toned wood? It's quite distinctive and a very lovely hardwood. I'm not surprised it was sturdy to the point of shattering. I'm not feeling any enchantments, either. I'd bet this handle was a replacement—why would someone go to the trouble of making an intelligent, enchanted axe and not artifice the handle?"

"I'm not sure. The previous owner had it for a long time. Maybe she meant to get the new handle enchanted and never did?" Victor shrugged.

"Well, what's her name?" Teng-dak stood up and moved to rummage through a wooden tool rack.

"Lifedrinker." Victor imagined he might have been chagrined to say his axe was named Lifedrinker back in his old life, but he'd seen what she could do and wasn't embarrassed in the least about her somewhat edgy name.

"Oh, my, my. Has she lived up to the name? No, don't tell me. I can see you're a warrior forged by mortal contests. I'm not one to judge, but I'm not eager to learn of her dark history if there is one."

"What do you mean? Oh, are you implying that the axe and I go around killing everyone we meet? No, man, she's a killer, but she and I mostly fight monsters. Any person Lifedrinker kills will have it coming."

"Fair enough," the woodworker said, stepping back to the workbench with a slender wood chisel and a hammer. "Let's get this old wood out first. While I'm working, talk to me about your budget. I have some wood for special projects, but some are costly."

"Well." Victor knew better than to reveal how much money he had. He didn't know exactly how much his Energy beads were worth, but he had a better idea after buying his boots. He also had plenty of other goods—gems, gold, silver, even a big chunk of amber ore. "How about this: tell me about your best three options from least expensive to most expensive."

"Ahh, not a bad idea." Teng-dak lifted Lifedrinker into a large metal vise attached to his workbench. The vise's teeth were padded with leather, and he carefully tightened them along Lifedrinker's blade so he could chisel out the old haft. "By the way, I know your axe's name, but not yours. I'm Teng-dak."

"Victor." Victor nodded, leaning against the workbench and watching Teng-dak work.

"Well, Victor, for thirty standard Energy beads, I could fit a lovely oak handle to Lifedrinker, and I could artifice it for strength, making it incredibly durable. That would be my good but affordable option."

"Oh, you do your own enchanting?"

"I do! I'm Tier Two, and my first class was Woodworker, but I was offered Artificer on my refinement. I'm looking forward to Tier Three."

"Oh, that's cool. Um, that's interesting; I don't know much about crafting classes and whatnot."

"Well, I've learned quite a few nice enchantments to complement my woodworking. You're in good hands. Want to hear about option two?"

"Yeah, of course." Victor tapped the table absently while the pieces of the old mace handle fell away from Lifedrinker.

"Well, I have a few pieces of Umbrilak wood. Umbrilak can hold more than one enchantment, and I'd be able to enchant it for durability and self-repair."

"How much?"

"Well, Umbrilak is difficult to obtain and hard to work. I'd need two hundred standard beads." The woodworker pulled the last bit of wood from Lifedrinker's eye and worked on removing the roll pin from the old wood.

"Hmm, all right, and your third option?"

"Well, the final option is, of course, some sort of living hardwood." Tengdak shrugged as though he was stating the obvious.

"Living?"

"Yes, I've learned to coax specially prepared, living wood into a shape, provided I'm making something small enough for my meager Energy levels. I think I could pull off an axe haft."

"Will it still be alive when you're done?"

"Yes, though not conscious. It will become dependent on Energy after I'm done working it. Provided you never enter some sort of Energy void, like the inside of a dimensional container, it will stay healthy. I'll work it and enchant it to bond with the axe. It'll be able to heal and grow to suit Lifedrinker." He patted the darkly glinting metal in his vise.

"Well, I like the idea of giving her a living handle. What kinda money are we talking about?"

"This is where things get complicated, Victor. You see, the preparations you have to go through to make wood ready to convert to an Energy subsistence are time-consuming and expensive. I've made a bit of a name for myself and have some clients in Gelica; otherwise, I wouldn't have any wood ready for such a project. The wood I do have, though, isn't cheap. No one wants to do this sort of work with a piece of oak or mahogany. No, I have a piece of Star Birch—too soft and flexible for your axe—and a length of hickory from the Coruscating Vale. Now, if I were going to make the haft for myself, that's what I'd use. It's absolutely perfect for what you need. It's harder than any other wood I have; it's beautiful, with dark, rich grain and the telltale glitters from its environment, and capable of containing several enchantments."

"Well, you've got my interest. What's the catch?"

"The catch is that it's the most expensive piece of wood I own, and I'd have to charge you nearly two thousand standard Energy beads for it."

"Mmhmm, and do you ever do any trades? You know, take payment other than Energy beads?" Victor drummed his fingers on the workbench again, gazing into his storage space and trying to appear unperturbed.

"Well, what did you have in mind?"

"I have this." Victor produced his large ingot of amber ore. He knew it was a lot purer than the alloy he and Thayla had found for Captain Lam.

Lam had been excited about the idea of amber ore, so he knew it was valuable. He set it on the workbench with a thud.

"Is that amber ore?" Teng-dak picked up the ore with a grunt. "Heavier than it looks! My, this is very pure, isn't it? I can feel the Energy thrumming within. You're making me wish I was a metal worker!" Teng-dak contemplated the ore for a few moments, then set it down. "You know, a weaponsmith would probably pay you to let them craft a weapon from that ore—a new axe that might be sharper and harder than your Lifedrinker here. Not to mention capable of holding powerful enchantments."

"Sure, but I'm kind of attached to Lifedrinker. She and I have been through a lot, and I wouldn't trust another axe to fucking fight like she does. Um, excuse my language. She, well, she has spirit. You know what I mean?"

"Oh, sure. I know exactly what you mean. I have tools that could be replaced, but I've grown used to their feel and their quirks. Well, Victor, this much pure amber ore would fetch a tidy price in a city like Gelica. I don't think any of the smiths here in Steampool could afford it. I'll tell you what, since I'll need to broker its sale if I take it from you, and I don't know exactly how much it's worth, I'll give you fifteen hundred in credit for it. Can you work with that?"

"Sure. How about the ore and, oh, two hundred fifty attuned Energy beads?" Victor did his best to seem bored.

"Sounds perfect! I'll be going to Gelica next week anyway. This'll give me an excuse to visit an old friend—Teya ap'Horl, by the way, if you ever need an expert metalworker."

"All right, good to know. Hey, that brings up a good question: how far is Gelica from here?"

"Oh, if you follow the western road, you'll be there in a week by foot."

"And Greatbone Mine?"

"The mine's about a day to the west and then half a day to the north. Are you going there?"

"Nah, I don't think so. I just heard about it and was curious. I heard it stretches underground for miles and miles. That true?"

"Yes, it sure is. I think they hire adventurers to protect their crews—might be a good job for you and your axe."

"Maybe, but I'm pretty busy right now. So, how about this: I'll give you the beads up front and the ore when you're done. How long will it take?"

"Ahh, straight to business. Hmm, that sounds fair, but I'll hold onto the axe until you pay up! The great thing about working with living wood is that

I just need to write out the correct spell pattern and then apply the runes. Once that's done, the shaping takes mere moments. I should have it ready in a couple of hours. Of course, I'm supposed to be refinishing this table for old Indrol . . ." he trailed off, looking at the table leg he'd been staining.

"How much was he paying you?"

"Ten beads."

"Yeah, all right, I'll toss in another ten beads to cover his job. Tell him it'll be late but free. That okay?"

"Yes, I think he'll go for that."

"Deal, then." Victor counted out the Energy beads, then stowed his ingot of amber ore. He nodded to the axe and said, "I'll be back for her in a couple of hours."

"See you then," Teng-dak said, moving to the door with Victor. "I'm going to close up while I work—don't want any interruptions."

"Right." Victor waved, then turned back to the main street. He figured he had just enough time for a relaxed dinner with the old man and his kid, then he could head back and pick up Lifedrinker. He felt good; the handle was expensive, but it sounded like the perfect match for Lifedrinker, and as far as he was concerned, she deserved it. The way he saw it, she did as much to earn that ingot as he had—without her drawing that skeleton snake's Energy for the whole battle, things might have gone very differently.

While he strolled through town, the shadows starting to grow long as the sun descended in the west, he nodded and smiled at the people that met his gaze. A lot of the citizens of Steampool seemed busy and preoccupied, but many were openly cheery, waving and saying things like, "Hello, stranger!" or "Welcome to Steampool!" A few shopkeeps invited him in as he walked by, but he just smiled and said he was on his way to meet someone. He was tempted by the barber, who shook his head and tsked when he saw Victor, simply saying, "You need a haircut."

"I sure do." Victor shrugged but kept walking. On a whim, he turned and added, "If I have time after dinner, I'll come by. Or are you closing soon?"

"Nah, I live here. Just ring the bell, and I'll let ya in."

"Thanks!" Victor turned and hurried down the street. It didn't take long to find the tavern. When he rounded the corner and started toward the distant southern gate, he saw the lights and activity around the long, single-story building and knew it was his destination. When he walked up the wood plank sidewalk, drawing near the small crowd of laughing, talking people standing outside, he saw Uld immediately. He stood to the left of the door, talking to a stocky young Ardeni man with bright red hair and eyes.

"Victor! You came!" Uld said as he approached.

"Hey, sure I did." Victor nodded, stepping close.

"This is my grandson, Kenno. Kenno, meet Victor, the adventurer I told you about."

"Oh, hi, Victor! Thanks for coming to meet us!" Kenno had an exuberance to his voice, sounding both awed and excited, even though Victor hadn't done anything impressive.

"Hey, Kenno. Good to meet you. So, we waiting for a table or something?" He looked around at the other people standing on the wooden planks outside the tavern.

"Oh, no, we're early still. We can go sit down. I just didn't want you to have to find us inside."

"What's with all these people?" Victor nodded to the crowd.

"Well, the weather's nice, and people are getting done with work, so they're just catching up. I'm sure they'll come in soon." Uld turned and pulled the door to the tavern open, and Victor followed him in, Kenno close behind. He instantly started to salivate as the aromas of cooking meat and baked bread filled his nostrils. He suddenly realized that he'd never been to an eating establishment in this world, and the meals he'd been served weren't exactly fine dining.

"*Chingado*, that smells good!" He glanced around to see if anyone had heard his outburst, but the tavern was noisy, and there were a lot of people laughing and drinking, and he realized he was probably safe to relax his tongue. He followed Uld to a round wooden table near the window on the left, and he saw some people setting up instruments on a small stage. "Music?" he asked as he sat down.

"Yes! Ynaila will be singing tonight! She's a popular bard in Steampool," Kenno said, also sitting so he could see the stage. Victor nodded and looked around at the tavern. It was an impressive building, boasting a few dozen tables, the stage, and a long wooden bar running along the far wall. A large stone mantle and fireplace dominated the opposite side of the room, but it wasn't alight; the weather wasn't cool enough, apparently. Only about half the tables were occupied, but still, the buzz of conversation and laughter filled the air, and Victor started to truly relax as he sat back in his comfortable wooden chair.

"Three of Barstrum's honey ales!" Uld called to the Shadeni youth wearing an apron that walked by. He glanced at Uld, then nodded, hustling back behind the bar. "You're going to love it, Victor! Best ale of the season!"

"All right, I'll take your word for it."

"Victor, have you ever been in a dungeon?" Kenno asked suddenly.

"Kenno! Relax! Let Victor get his drink before you start to pester him."

"It's fine. Yeah, Kenno, I have."

"What's it like? What kind of monsters did you fight? Did the System give you treasures? I heard dungeons could reset, and monsters could appear out of nowhere. Is that true?"

"Whoa, easy," Victor said, taking a big breath. How old was this kid? He didn't seem much younger than Victor, but he acted as if he'd never spoken to an adult before. Is this how people saw him? Was he like this when he first came here? Nah, he'd never been an eager type of person. While he considered his answer, the Shadeni kid returned with three large mugs of dark, foamy ale. Victor took a deep drink of his and sighed heavily in satisfaction after swallowing. It was crisp, smooth, and had a slightly sweet aftertaste. Best of all, it was chilled. "Man, that's good!"

"I told you!" Uld said, licking the foam off his upper lip.

"Well, let's see here. The dungeon I was in was full of undead. Yes, I got some treasure, and no, it never reset on me."

"Do you think I could handle it?" Kenno asked.

"Well, it was filled with ghouls and other monsters around Tier Three. I think the boss was higher—closer to Tier Four. You ever done any fighting?" Victor eyed Kenno, whose face had grown more sober as Victor spoke. He slumped down in his chair a bit.

"Kenno's still Tier One, Victor."

"Then you don't want to go to the dungeon I'm talking about, Kenno. Not for a while. How about my other question?"

"I've done plenty of sparring with people here in town," Kenno said eagerly.

"Ever had your life on the line?"

"No, not really," Kenno said, his frown deepening. "How could I? Steampool's too safe!"

"Imagine! Complaining that your town is too safe?" Uld scoffed. Victor took another long pull of his ale, savoring the cool, crisp liquid. Just then, a strummed chord caught his attention, and he looked to the stage. Two musicians had sat down, one with a sizeable stringed instrument braced on the floor, the other with a smaller one shaped like a fiddle. A third woman was pacing back and forth on the little stage, clearly getting herself pumped up for the show. When Kenno saw Victor watching, he relented and looked at the stage, eyes eager.

After another minute or two, the two instrument players started with a lively tune that reminded Victor of something he might consider folk music. The slender, small Shadeni woman began to sing then, and her high soprano seemed to fill the room's air, bringing chills to Victor's neck and sending his mind wandering over imagined valleys and through wooded dales. He felt so relaxed and happy from the music that he forgot about Kenno and Uld for a long while.

When the woman stopped singing to take a break, Victor finally returned to himself and smiled when he saw similar looks of glassy daydreaming on his companions' faces. He laughed and cleared his throat. "Kenno, I wouldn't start with a dungeon. You know, actually, I might have an idea for you, but I don't want your grandpa to get mad at me." Victor glanced at Uld and raised an eyebrow in question.

"Go ahead, Victor—Kenno's been threatening to run away for two summers now. I'd rather he had a good idea from you than some half-baked scheme of his own."

"Well, you're pretty close to Greatbone Mine here, right? Why not go there and volunteer to protect miners for a while? I've heard they even have a place called 'the well' where you can fight waves of monsters with other fighters. I think they let people volunteer there, but I'm not certain."

"Oh, the mine is always hiring," Uld said, nodding. "Do you think he'd be safe, Victor? Have you worked there?"

"Well, not exactly." Victor decided he'd already said more about himself than he wanted. "I was thinking about checking it out, but something came up, and I need to go somewhere else to help a friend."

"What do you say, Grandfather? Can I have your blessing?" Kenno's smile had grown the whole time Victor spoke about the mine.

"I'd feel better if Victor evaluated your fighting skills a little," Uld said, then drank from his mug.

"Uh, I'm not looking to spar right now. Just tell me about yourself, Kenno. What kind of skills do you have? What's your class?" Just then, a different tavern worker approached. She was a thin Ardeni woman with short yellow hair and a much cleaner apron with embroidered flowers along its hem.

"You three having dinner?" she asked, eyeing Uld.

"Yes, Glinna, what's on the menu?"

"Uncle Tam's pot roast, fresh sourdough, and rillberry pies."

"Sounds good," Victor said, his tongue loosened by the ale and music. "Another ale for us all, too, please!"

"Yes, yes," Uld said, nodding along with Victor.

"Right, be back in a minute," Glinna said, moving to another table.

"Anyway, tell me what you've got, Kenno," Victor said, draining the last drops of his ale.

"I'm a Fighter. I have basic melee weapon mastery, but my spear mastery is up to improved."

"Any Energy attacks? Can you channel Energy into your weapon?"

"I have Bolstered Charge. I can close distance with it, and it boosts my vitality for a short while."

"Anything else?"

"No, not yet." Kenno looked down, clearly crestfallen that Victor didn't seem impressed.

"I think you have what it takes to fight at the well, but only at the top with plenty of other fighters. Do you understand me? I've heard some people try to go deeper into the well, but lots of people die that way. I think you should concentrate on fighting at the top until you get some more levels and some more Energy abilities." Victor nodded as though he'd just explained a complicated equation and smiled as he saw Glinna returning with their drinks.

"Are you sure he'll be all right, Victor?" Uld asked.

"Uld, I can't be sure, no. What if some asshole pushes him into the well? What if a swarm of something really nasty comes up, and he doesn't flee? There aren't any guarantees, but I can tell you something a person I sort of admire told me. Everyone has challenges in their lives, and if you don't let them fight them, they'll never grow. Well, it was something like that—it sounded smarter coming from her."

Uld nodded and drank his ale solemnly, studying his grandson. As the music started again, Kenno pestered Victor with more questions about fighting and dungeons, and soon their food arrived. Victor couldn't hold back and dug in like a starved man. The pot roast was delicious, and the root vegetables were hot and flavorful. When he bit into the thick hunk of buttery bread, he felt as if he were in heaven, and he used the crust to mop up every last drop of the juices in his bowl.

"If you like that, wait until you taste the pie," Kenno said, also wolfing down his food. It turned out that Kenno knew what he was talking about. The pie was delicious—fresh-baked and served in a bowl with a drizzle of cream on top, and Victor found the berries tasted much like blueberries. When he finished, he sat back and rubbed his belly.

"I haven't eaten that well in a long time, Uld. Thanks for talking me into coming to dinner. I hate eating and running, but I've gotta get my axe."

"That's fine, Victor! Thank you for talking to Kenno; you've given us a lot to talk about."

"Well, at least let me pay for our drinks before I go," Victor said, fishing in his ring for his Energy beads.

"No, no! I wouldn't hear of it. You see that, Kenno? That's the way a man acts." Uld looked at Kenno with a scowl, and Victor realized there was more going on between the two than just Kenno wanting to be an adventurer.

"Grandfather, how can I offer to pay when I'm not allowed to go into the world and make my fortune?"

"There's money to be made in town without challenging monsters, boy!" Uld's face had lost its cheery demeanor, and his cheeks were flushed from the ale.

"Sure, well, I'm sorry, but I do need to be going," Victor said, scooting his chair back. "I'll see you again, I'm sure. You have a nice town here, Uld. Nice to meet you, Kenno!" Victor pushed his chair in and turned to go.

"Thank you again, Victor!" Uld called. Kenno didn't say anything; he'd slumped into his chair, scowling so profoundly that the line between his eyes looked like a canyon. Victor brushed past the people crowding near the door and pushed his way into the cool night air. Uld was a nice old guy, but Victor felt he'd been privy to more of Kenno and Uld's business than he wanted.

He turned back toward the town center and made his way toward Tengdak's shop. On his way, though, he passed by the barber's shop and saw that the old barber had left the light on. "How long could a haircut take?" Victor said, then walked up to the door and pulled the chain hanging next to the door. A bell rang inside the door, and a few moments later, Victor saw the barber descending the steps at the back of the shop. He smiled as he opened the door.

"You came back after all!"

"I did! Think you could give me a haircut?"

"Of course! Come in, come in." He gestured to the wooden barber's chair, and Victor sat himself down. The barber shook out a pale blue sheet and wrapped it around Victor's neck, then, humming to himself, proceeded to get to work with his scissors.

Victor had had plenty of haircuts, but this was a new experience. He could feel the warm pulse of Energy coming out of the man's fingers as he snipped the scissors through his hair, and it was only a few minutes later when the barber put the scissors down on the counter and picked up a straight razor. He didn't ask for permission or if Victor wanted a shave; he just reached into a jar on his counter, withdrew a handful of cream, and rubbed the warm, citrus-smelling lather all over Victor's face and neck. Then he smoothly, quickly, and with a hint of Energy, shaved Victor without a single nick.

"Do you have a barber class or something?"

"'Course I do! You think I'm a charlatan or something?" the old guy asked, setting down his razor and pulling a steaming cloth out of a little basket next to the counter. He rubbed the warm, damp fabric on Victor's face, neck, and ears, wiping away the cream and all the grime he'd accumulated. "I'll need to burn this cloth! Good Ancestors, man! What've you been up to?"

"Sorry! I've been adventuring." Victor shrugged.

"Well, you're looking a lot better. Hope you have someone to appreciate it," the barber said with a wink. Then he held up a mirror, and Victor saw himself clearly for the first time in a long while. His hair was nicely trimmed and combed back. His face was clean and free of any sparse whiskers he might have grown—he'd never really had to shave in his old life. Those facts aside, Victor didn't recognize himself. His head looked too big, his brows too dark and heavy, his eyes too bright and angry. His lips were too full, and his jaw and cheekbones too pronounced. He looked like a professional athlete—a man grown. "You all right? Don't like something?"

"I'm good. You did a good job; I just haven't seen myself in a while."

"Aye, time in the wilderness will change a man."

"Well, thanks, sir. What do I owe you?" Victor stood up from the chair and rummaged in his ring for his Energy beads.

"Just five seeds."

"Seeds? You mean beads?"

"Ha, no. Just seeds."

"Gorz, what's he talking about?" Victor thought.

"People can make tiny beads that are used for small transactions. They take about one tenth the Energy of a normal bead. I think he's referring to those."

"Oh, right, seeds," Victor said aloud. "I appreciate you staying open. Here." Victor handed him one of the attuned beads from the dungeon.

"Good lad! Thank you!" The barber moved over to his door and pulled it open, apparently ready to call it a night.

"Yep. See you around," Victor said, stepping back into the cool evening air. Not sure how long he'd been, mostly because he kept forgetting to look at his watch and had no idea what time he'd left the woodworker's shop, Victor jogged the rest of the way. He was pleased to see the light still on in the window, and when he knocked on the door, Teng-dak was quick to open up for him.

"I'm glad you made it back! I was starting to wonder if I should go look for you."

"You finished?"

"Aye, a little while ago. What a beauty she turned out to be!" Teng-dak moved over to his workbench, where a leather-wrapped bundle sat waiting.

"Is that her?"

"Yes, sir! Let me take this leather off," he said, reaching forward and unwrapping the axe. Victor caught his breath. There she was, her black and silvery head freshly oiled and gleaming. The new haft was dark and elegant, and when Teng-dak picked it up, Victor saw flecks of something glittering in the wood. He couldn't tell if it reflected the light or came from within the grain. Best of all, the handle was elegantly curved and properly designed for an axe, not a clumsy old ball mace.

"Oh God, Lifedrinker, you're beautiful," Victor said, stepping closer.

"Ahem, yes, she is, but there's the matter of payment?" Teng-dak said, stepping back with the axe.

"Oh, yeah, of course. Don't worry." Victor couldn't help glowering a little at the implication, but he reached into his ring and pulled out the amber ore. He set it on the workbench with a thud.

"Excellent! Take note." Teng-dak showed Victor the top of Lifedrinker's head where the wood was flush with the metal. "There's no pin—it's not necessary with the living wood; the handle won't let go of the head. It would take enormous power to separate them. And look here." The woodworker pointed to a line of runes along the back of the handle. "These are the enchantments worked into the living wood. It won't break easily; it heals from damage and will be tough to remove from your hands by force." He held out the handle to Victor.

"Thanks, Teng-dak," Victor said, taking Lifedrinker and hefting her in both hands. "How do you feel, beautiful? You ready to hunt down a runaway asshole?"

12

A STRANGER AT THE FIRE

Under the light of the two moons, Victor ran down the dirt, sometimes gravel, road. One of the moons had rings, and Victor wondered how that worked—did moons have rings or was there another planet so close it looked like a moon? He wasn't an astronomy expert, so he figured he'd just accept the locals' assurance that they were moons. The guard at the gate had said he'd have good light from the "the sisters" while traveling.

He'd been sorely tempted to take a room at the inn and get a good night's sleep, but he couldn't bear the thought of comfortably sleeping while Thayla languished in an old skull in his satchel. He didn't feel sleepy and felt that his desire to get a good night's rest was more habit than need. Since he'd improved his race so much, he didn't know how much sleep he required, but he felt pretty damn outstanding as he jogged through the night. "Not only that," he said to the axe he carried sideways in front of him, "but Thayla's body will need rest. We're gonna catch that creep!"

He'd asked Gorz to keep a close eye on the tether and to let him know if it deviated from the road, but so far, it looked as if Belikot's path coincided with the route toward Gelica. Sometime after midnight, Victor passed the turn-off to Greatbone Mine, and he'd had a twinge in his gut as he ran by. He wondered how Edeya and Heng and all the others were doing. He wondered about Captain Lam; had she had any run-ins with the mine operators? Had they come looking for Victor and found Edeya? He'd just have to trust that Lam had gotten her away for now. Someday, maybe he'd get a chance to come back to the mine and make things right, as least as much as he could.

Victor didn't mind running with Lifedrinker in his hands; she fit snugly in against his palms and was long enough that he could still maintain a normal gait while holding onto her with a wide grip. He had a loop on his belt he could put her haft through, letting her head rest against his hip, but it annoyed him when he ran to have the long wooden handle slapping his calf and knee. No, while running, he'd hold her, and then he'd be ready to fight if something came out of the darkness, a prospect that seemed more and more likely the farther he got away from the town, mine, and all the farms that had dotted the valleys.

Night on Fanwath was very different from night on Earth, even out in the desert near Tucson. First of all, the stars were bright and filled the sky so immensely that it took Victor a while of staring before he could get his mind back on the task at hand. The depth and variety of the star field was something that couldn't be understood by looking at a photo or video—standing under that expanse made him realize why primitive humans had been so in awe of the planets and stars. Secondly, the sounds made it abundantly clear that he wasn't running through the Sonoran Desert—yelps, screeches, barks, howls, growls, buzzing, flapping, and scurrying noises abounded. He felt as if he were surrounded by all the wildlife known to humankind.

Amazingly, nothing bothered him throughout the night, and when the sky started to lighten, he slowed to take in the sunrise and get a look at his surroundings. He stepped off the road and climbed up the side of a gently sloping hill, scrabbling over tufts of hard yellow grass. When he got to the top of the hill, the eastern sky was pale gray, and he could see for miles and miles in that direction. Hills rolled away, covered in the same kind of grass as the one he was on, and eventually came up against the starkly jutting, jagged mountains he'd just run down from. He had no idea he'd lost so much elevation through the night.

Slowly spinning in a circle, he saw the hills falling away to the east, replaced by endless expanses of yellow grassland. A bit to the south, he thought he could see the shadowy blur of a forest on the horizon. "Or maybe an ocean," he admitted—he didn't know what either would look like from a distance. More hills and mountains lay to the north. "Gorz, what way does the tether go?"

"From here, Victor, primarily west and very slightly to the south."

"So, still on the road. I wish you could tell if we were gaining ground."

"As do I. If only you knew a locating or scrying spell. Perhaps you'll meet someone who does."

"Uh, there might have been someone in that town! Let me add this to the list of things you should have mentioned to me, Gorz. Like, oh, I don't know, hundreds of ghouls sleeping in the room I was standing in."

"Victor, I've told you that the physical world slips from my conscious perception when I'm not actively trying to concentrate on something. Time moves quickly, and I'm unaware of your every move. My apologies!"

"It's all right, Gorz; I'm just busting your balls."

"Pardon me?"

"Never mind." Victor shook his head wryly and pulled out a jug of watery wine Captain Lam had given him. He drank thirstily, stretched his legs out, and started running again. The sun was well on its way up the eastern sky when Victor noticed something off to his left. He slowed to look again and saw a rolling cloud of dust coming toward him over the plains. Instinctively, he ducked down, reducing his silhouette, then crouching in the grass, he watched the dust, looking for the source.

It wasn't long before he could make out the dark shapes at the head of the dust cloud. In just a few minutes, they resolved into riders—humanoid figures atop leaping, two-legged mounts. "What the fuck? Are those ostriches?" The riders were streaming over the grassland toward the road, and as they got closer, Victor could see that the mounts were definitely not ostriches; they were larger and thicker, and their feathers were a lot brighter. Moreover, they had a lot of gray skin that wasn't feathered.

Victor counted nine riders, and he watched them, crouched on top of the hill, expecting them to pass by to the road. They were about a quarter mile distant when they slowed and veered directly toward him, which made him urgently reassess his visibility. "Shit!" He didn't fancy running away from giant bird monsters and their riders, so figuring his position was blown, he stood up straight, Lifedrinker gripped before him.

The riders slowed when he stood up but continued their approach to his hill. Victor stood near the crest; if they wanted to fight, he'd make them work to get near him. Lifedrinker buzzed in his hand, and he knew she was anxious for action. He still held out hope that these riders didn't mean him harm, but he was glad to have her ready. When the riders were only a hundred yards or so away, Victor cast Heroic Heart because he didn't know what to expect, and he liked that the spell protected him from mental manipulation.

As always, he felt the heat flood out from his chest, and then the gray light of early morning seemed more golden, and the riders less a threat and more a curiosity. A broad smile displayed his even, white teeth, and he took a step forward, Lifedrinker light and easy in his hands. "Hello, riders!" he called out, pulling the words from deep in his gut, a heavy timbre rolling out over the grass.

A large Shadeni man, riding toward the middle of the group, held up a hand, and they all came to a halt near the bottom of the hill. The man glanced from side to side, his braided black beard clacking with beads and bones, then he rode forward about halfway between Victor and his fellows. "Hail, warrior! We have no ill intent—I am Tellen, Ban-tok of this tribe, and we are hunters."

"Hello." Victor's bolstered confidence didn't really allow him to pause or be cautious; he stepped toward the hunter, releasing Lifedrinker with one hand, so he held her down by his side. "I'm Victor, a traveling adventurer." Victor had a vague recollection of Belsa talking about being in a tribe, so he knew some Shadeni lived that way. They looked rough and travel-worn, their clothes mainly leather, decorated with beads and tassels. They all had long black hair, and most wore it braided like their leader.

Victor had seen a lot of Shadeni in his time on Fanwath, but here, arrayed before him in the bright morning light, the hunters' different eye colors were especially striking. Most were some shade of red or pink, but he saw a pair of yellow-green eyes, and Tellen's eyes were a luminous, bright purple.

"Well met, then, Victor. We're returning from a long hunt, and we thought we should investigate when we saw you on this hill. We're a long way between civilized places here, and we wanted to see that you weren't in need of help or any sort of danger to our clan."

"I'm no danger to good people," Victor said, still grinning broadly.

"It is good, then, that my people aren't bandits." The Ban-tok spoke frankly, taking Victor's words at face value. "Do you mind me asking your destination?"

"I'm traveling toward Gelica, looking for a friend." Victor gestured vaguely to the west.

"Ahh, well, you're still many days from Gelica. Our camp lies between here and there, a day or so further west, in the plains north of this road. You'll see our fires as you go by. You have my invitation if you'd care to stop for a meal and a safe night's rest."

"Thanks! I might take you up on that offer." Victor nodded. The man was silent for a moment, and Victor felt awkward, as though he'd failed to say the right words. "I'm sorry, um, Ban-tok, but I'm not familiar with your customs," he added.

"All is well, Victor. I'm merely debating if we should offer you transport, but our roladii are weary, and you're a large man." He patted the shoulder of his strange mount.

"Nah, that's fine. Thank you for the consideration, but I'll make my own way. Good to meet you, Ban-tok."

"Thank you for your respect, Victor, but you may call me Tellen. Good journey to you; I hope we'll see you in a day or two." He clicked his tongue sharply, and his mount turned around and started moving back to the other riders. "All's well!" he called out, then waved a hand in the air in a tight circle, and the hunters all turned and charged off, skirting the hill and thundering away down the road.

"Gorz, that's still the direction the tether is pointing, right?"

"It is, Victor, though as we travel west, it seems to be veering farther south of the road's path. I think you've gained ground running through the night."

"I hope so! I might need less sleep than a normal human, but I'm thinking I'll need to rest sooner or later."

"Yes, you will require rest at some point, Victor. Even people with advanced racial status must sleep from time to time."

Victor sat down on the side of the hill, watching the retreating dust cloud thrown by the riders while he ate the last of the sausages Lam had given him and Thayla. It felt as if years had passed since he'd stood in that back room of Lam's barracks and confessed, hoping for her to help. He tried to count how many actual days had passed since then, but he lost track when he considered the number of days he'd spent unconscious. Something around three weeks, he figured. "Feels a lot longer," he grunted, throwing a loose stone down toward the road.

After another drink of watery wine, Victor stood and resumed his jog, following the road and the long dispersed cloud of dust the hunters had left in their wake. The morning stretched into midday and then into the afternoon, and Victor came upon the first fellow traveler he'd met on the trail. As he rounded a slight bend in the long, dusty road, he saw a shape up ahead and, after some scrutiny, decided it was a wagon. It wasn't coming toward him—rather, he was coming up behind it.

The wagon was a dilapidated affair, tall and gray, the wood warped with age and weather. Painted on the back in faded, crumbling red paint was the word "Tinker." Victor rapidly gained on the slowly moving, swaying conveyance, marveling at its strange design. It was taller than it was long, like a vertical rectangle of old, creaking wood. Little shutters squeaked and flapped with each jolting bump in the road, and, when Victor examined the tall wooden wheels, he saw giant, coiled springs sitting over the axles on which the whole wagon frame bounced and jostled.

When Victor jogged past the front left wheel and finally could see around the side of the vehicle, he saw an unusually short Vodkin sitting on a metal chair affixed to a wooden beam. He held the reins of a plodding, hissing lizard that would have given an elephant a run for its money, size wise. The driver didn't notice him at first, and Victor called up, "Hello there!" The furry man nearly fell out of his seat in surprise, his large belly jiggling as he jolted up from his slouch and hastily looked around for the speaker. When his eyes fell on Victor, striding next to the wagon with his axe in his hands, he hesitantly held up a hand.

"Hail trav'ler!" He turned to his giant lizard and pulled on the thick leather rein. "Whoa, Grella, whoa!" The plodding beast stopped immediately, perhaps happy to not be moving. It lazily swung its long gray neck back and forth while its thick, red ribbon of a tongue flicked in and out of its mouth. "Not lookin' for trouble, are ya? I'm jus' a poor tinker, nothin' much ta offer."

"No, no trouble. I'm just traveling, looking for a friend. You seen a tall Shadeni woman pass by? Black eyes, long black braids? Maybe carrying a nice-looking spear?"

"Oh, aye. Passed me a day out of Steampool. I wa' camped aside the road, fixin' a loose hub. She give me the impression she din't wan' ta visit. I try to greet her, offer a spot by the fire, but she jus' glare and kept walkin'."

"This was when?"

"Night afore last," he said, hawking a large brown glob of saliva down to the road near his lizard's rear foot.

"She was alone? Still had her spear?"

"Aye."

"Thanks for the information, tinker. Good luck," Victor said and started into a jog. He heard the man call after him, saying something about safe travels. Victor's heart had sped up a bit as he realized he was gaining on Thayla. At the rate he was going, if he hustled through the night, he might catch her the next day. "Him. I might catch up to him," he said, trying to keep in mind that it was Belikot driving Thayla's body around. He sure hoped the phylactery would work when he confronted him.

As he ran, Victor tried to think of a plan. He wanted to wake Thayla and tell her his progress, but he felt that he had the element of surprise at the moment, and waking Thayla might blow it. As he thought about that, he started thinking about the phylactery and the tether, then he slowed his run and slapped himself on the head. "Gorz. Don't you think Belikot can feel this phylactery coming closer?"

"I would say that there's an excellent chance that Belikot is aware of his phylactery and can feel this tether just as I can see it."

"Goddamn it! That's probably something I should have thought of sooner, but you could have mentioned it, too."

"I'm sorry! I don't function well in terms of creativity, or should I say I'm not good at thinking outside the constraints of my directives."

"You don't think outside the box?" Victor snorted. "All right, don't worry. At least I figured this out before walking into whatever trap he's laying. I think I have an idea to turn the tables, in fact."

"Excellent!"

Victor started running down the road again, this time keeping an eye peeled toward the plains on the right, hoping to catch sight of the Shadeni hunters' camp. He figured he might be getting close because he'd been traveling all day, and his pace was probably faster than what the Shadeni had expected. "Keep me posted as the tether leads away from the road. Is it still following it pretty closely?"

"Yes, but its angle away from the road toward the south slowly widens as you continue west."

"Good," Victor said. The afternoon slipped away into the evening, and still, Victor didn't slow, steadily eating up the miles as he jogged along. He drank on the run, but only when he truly felt thirsty, which wasn't very often. As the sun settled beneath the western horizon and the sisters brightened the night sky, he kept on, pushing into the night. A few hours after dark, two things happened almost simultaneously: he saw some flickering orange lights off to his right, and Gorz said, *"Victor, the tether is much more south than east from you now; if you keep going much farther, you'll pass Belikot by."*

"What's south of here?"

"Nothing that I've mapped. I'm sorry, but Reevus never visited that area of the world."

"And he didn't have you memorize any maps?"

"He would have, but remember, he was not raised on Fanwath. We hadn't visited a major city in this world yet when he perished."

"How did he come here, anyway?"

"His parents were born on this world, and he petitioned his master to open a portal for him to come and visit this world. He wanted to learn about his ancestry. Unfortunately, he came to believe he was on the wrong continent and was exploring for a city when he found the dungeon leading into the mine."

"Well, annoying, but I'll find you some maps to read next time we're in a town or city. It seems kind of coincidental that Belikot turned south near the hunters' camp, don't you think? No worries, I'll get to the bottom of this shit." Victor turned toward the fires he'd seen on the plains to the north and started jogging again. He'd covered about half the distance when a bright light flared to life in the darkness before him, and he stopped, holding Lifedrinker down by his side and shading his eyes with his other hand.

"Declare your intent!" a deep, hoarse woman's voice called.

"I'm Victor! A traveler that met your Ban-tok. He invited me to visit your camp."

"Come forward, then, Victor. But know: other eyes than mine are on you." The light pointed away from his eyes, and Victor lowered his hand and strode toward the woman's silhouette. While he walked, he slipped Lifedrinker's haft into the loop at his belt and let her hang there at his hip.

"Hey," he said, as he stepped up to the woman. Her light was pointed at the ground, revealing her in a kind of twilight grayscale. She was thin and wore leather, and the way her braids hung down, he thought she looked a lot like Thayla, at least in the poor lighting.

"Well met; I'm Chandri."

"Cool, um, great. Nice to meet you. Should I just keep going? Or?"

"No, I'll walk you in. We don't want my unruly sister or her boyfriend to fill you with arrows, do we?"

"Uh, no. Definitely not."

"Well, she's on the close watch string and is too hasty to shoot, so best you follow me." A white gleam in the moonlight told Victor she was smiling, so he chuckled. He followed her as she walked toward the fires. Silhouettes of tents started to resolve in the darkness, and Victor was aware of a large mass of shadows moving not far to the north; as he stared in the moonlight, he realized it was a large herd of the bird-lizard things.

"Roladii, right?"

"Yes, those are our roladii." As she spoke, a shrill whistle called out from the tall grass to their left, and Chandri nimbly darted to Victor's side, blocking him from the source of the whistle. "Chala! He's a guest of the Ban-tok. Calm yourself!"

"Bah, are you sure? Perhaps I should just wound him a little to keep him from causing trouble?" The voice coming out of the shadows sounded like a very young woman, and Victor couldn't help smiling at the idea of some kid wanting to put an arrow in his knee so he'd behave.

"I'll behave!" he called. "No need to test your arrows." He laughed when Chandri giggled in her husky, scratchy voice.

"Chala, you've been warned! Be calm, or the Ban-tok will hear!" After she spoke, Chandri motioned for Victor to follow and continued walking toward the camp. Victor waved to the darkness, then followed. Shadeni came into view, sitting around the fires or walking between the tents, and when they saw Victor walking with Chandri, most of them called out greetings. Chandri led the way past a couple of fires, then toward another firepit outside a darkly colored tent, larger than most of the others. Several Shadeni sat around the fire on furs or woven rugs, and Victor saw Tellen the Ban-tok lounging back, his head on the lap of a muscular Shadeni woman.

"Ban-tok, this man says he met you on the road," Chandri said, stepping into the man's line of sight. He sat up then, a broad smile on his face.

"Who's this, then? Victor? You made good time for a walker."

"Hello." Victor glanced around at the crowd of Shadeni watching him and thought about his words before continuing. "Ban-tok. Thank you for the invitation. Do you mind if I spend some time at your camp?"

"Of course not, Victor, provided your intentions haven't changed since our last meeting."

"Not at all; I have no ill intent." It was like a switch flipped, and suddenly everyone was talking again, and some of the younger Shadeni approached, all smiles and questions.

"What race are you?" one little boy asked.

"How tall are you?" another shouted.

"Can I see your axe?" This question came from a teenage girl as she pushed aside the smaller kids.

"Enough!" Tellen shouted. "Give him some room, and perhaps he'll entertain your questions after a meal and a sleep. Go on! Go on, or my switch will speak for him!" At his last words, the kids squealed and dispersed into the shadows, giggling into the night as they moved on to some other game. "Come, Victor, sit by my side here." Tellen patted the woven mat next to him, and Victor nodded, folding his legs and sitting down in front of the fire.

Most of the logs were burned down to embers, but the firepit gave off a lot of heat, and it felt good basking in it out under the stars with darkness all around. The other Shadeni around the fire introduced themselves and greeted Victor, and he nodded, glad to have Gorz memorizing those little details. "I've already eaten, Victor, but we had a large roast with plenty left over. Beln, will you get Victor a plate of meat?" The large man across the fire from Victor stood up and walked away, and Victor hoped he wasn't irritated about having to get him food.

"Thanks," he said to Tellen, then he looked around at the others nearby and repeated it. "Thanks, everyone. I appreciate your hospitality." Goddamn! Why couldn't he talk like that back when he lived in Tucson? He'd have made a lot more friends, that's for sure.

"Victor, have you ever had cheb-cheb?"

"Cheb-cheb?"

"Aha!" Tellen slapped his knee and smiled hugely. "It's a liquor made from the seeds of the chebli flower. Not very common this far east, but I traded for a case when we last passed Gelica." Like magic, two glasses appeared in the Bantok's hand, then he produced a dark brown bottle, about the size and shape of a gourd with a long neck. He pulled the cork with his teeth and poured a generous amount into the glasses in his other fist. The liquid was amber and reflected the flickering orange of the firepit in the oily sheen of its surface.

Tellen handed one glass to Victor then held his out to the fire and said, "To hunters and travelers!"

Victor got the idea, held out his glass, and said, "To sharing a fire with strangers." Everyone around the fire made enthusiastic sounds of approval, Tellen's smile widened, and he took a big drink from his glass. Victor did likewise and was pleasantly surprised by the smooth warmth of the alcohol sliding down his throat to sit like a pool of hot honey in his belly.

They sat in comfortable silence for a while, sipping their drinks, and by the time Beln arrived with a wooden platter of sliced, rare, but heavily seasoned meat, Victor had a nice buzz going. He figured this must be excellent alcohol, indeed, to affect him so much. He'd drunk an entire bottle of Thayla's wine and not gotten as drunk, and that was before his latest racial advancements. After eating most of the meat and finishing his drink, he sat back, leaning on his elbows, and looked up at the stars.

"Wondrous, aren't they?" Tellen asked, leaning back beside him.

"They sure are. I feel like I need to tell you something, Tellen." Victor spoke softly, as if he didn't want to disturb the things out in the dark.

"What's that, Victor?" Tellen took a sip from his second or third glass of cheb-cheb.

"There's a real evil asshole not far from your camp, and I was wondering if I could get a little help tricking him. My friend's life depends on it."

13

JUGGLING SPIRITS

"You're saying all I need to do is ride for a day to the west?" Tellen asked Victor in the sober light of morning, contemplating the strange cylinder on the mat between them.

"Yes. The way I see it, Belikot saw to it that I learned about this phylactery and then trusted my bull-headed nature to charge after him with it. He's set up somewhere south of here, probably a strategic location for him, and he knows I'm drawing near because, let's be honest, it's obvious that he would be able to sense his phylactery."

"Not a day's ride to the south lie the remains of Gel Harra—a crossroads town killed by a plague during the Steppe War." Tellen frowned. "What will it accomplish for me to lead this death sorcerer away?"

"Well, so far, I've been running directly toward him. When he sees the phylactery continue away, toward Gelica, he'll begin to have doubts: was I coming toward him all this time, or just heading to Gelica? Was I unable to follow the phylactery's tether to him, after all? Am I going to the city to sell it or have it evaluated? Would he want to risk someone who knew what to do with it getting their hands on it? These thoughts will torment him, forcing him to give chase."

"And why can't you just carry it toward Gelica?"

"Well, that's the second part of the trick. Belikot will be ready for action as he nears the phylactery, but if I'm lying in wait somewhere between the phylactery and him, I can get the element of surprise. Maybe disable him without harming my friend's body."

"How will you do so?"

"That's a good question. I have some collars that the mine uses to control people, but I don't have a control rod. Honestly, I'd hate to use them, anyway—bad memories. Do your people have a way to disable strong Energy users?"

"It depends on their strength and their will. Some sedatives would work if you could manage to apply them."

"Her body hasn't had any racial improvements, and I'm pretty sure Belikot is less than Tier Three. He'd have gotten his own phylactery out of that dungeon if he were powerful enough. No, I'm sure I can beat him. I just don't want to hurt my friend in the process. If you have a strong sedative, I'll try to disable him temporarily and then force it down his throat."

"Mmhmm, and how will I know you've finished your task?"

"I'll come here and have one of your hunters ride to get you. Also, if someone approaches and it's not me or one of your hunters, you should haul ass away. That's why I want you to hold the phylactery, and I'm not just planting it somewhere—in case he tricks me and gets around my ambush."

"Yes . . . 'haul ass!'" Tellen laughed. "So, I understand your plan, but why would I put my people at risk helping you with this problem?"

"I mean, do you think it's good to have this *pendejo* wandering around?"

"It seems this wizard, evil though he may be, has other things to preoccupy him than bothering my people." Tellen shrugged, lifting his steaming tea to his lips. Victor copied him and took a sip of the pungent, bitter brew.

"Okay, then I could give you something. How about this?" Victor took out the spearhead he'd looted from the guts of the giant tentacle-slug back in the depths. "I've seen a lot of your people using spears. This was looted from a very powerful monster." He held out the spearhead, glinting in the morning light. Tellen took it and examined all of its angles.

"A valuable weapon." He nodded, looking satisfied. "This is good payment for a day or two of riding. Should you fail, and should this death caster come my way, I will try to evade him, but if things look hopeless, I will throw this phylactery away and leave him to his own devices." He nodded to the heavy cylinder and its cold, sinister aura.

"That's enough for me. Thank you, Ban-tok."

"You're welcome, warrior." Tellen held out a hand, and Victor took it, returning the firm but warm grip.

"Can we start soon? I fear for my friend's mind with each minute that passes."

"We can start now. Go to the road, Victor, and I'll talk to my people. When I'm ready, I'll come gather the phylactery from you." Tellen stood and held a hand out to help Victor to his feet.

"Thanks. Sounds good, then. See you in a few minutes." Victor turned and started walking across the half-mile or so of grassland toward the brown ribbon of the roadway. He'd only gone a few paces past the last tent when he heard footsteps running toward him. He turned to the sound and saw Chandri jogging his way. She smiled as she drew near, offering a short wave.

"Victor! Leaving already?"

"Yeah, I've gotta help a friend. Nice camp, though," he said, gesturing to the tents and campfires arrayed behind her.

"Well, thanks for stopping; it gave us something to talk about last night." She fell into step with him, and they continued toward the road.

"Sure. You don't get a lot of visitors?"

"No, most of the trade wagons or caravans that come through this way want nothing to do with us."

"Afraid you're bandits?" Victor guessed.

"How'd you know?" She scowled at him, but he saw she was teasing as her black-stained lips turned up in a grin.

"Ha, well, to be honest, I used to be a pit fighter—not by choice—and there was a girl in my cell from a Shadeni tribe; she said her people got caught raiding a village."

"Yes, some clans practice the old ways, though it's perilous to do so close to the cities of the empire. We're happy to hunt, and if we need to raid, there are lands not far away which aren't part of Ridonne." That caught Victor by surprise. So just because they were ostensibly hunters, these people weren't ashamed to admit raiding outside the empire.

"Old ways? So, it's a tradition?"

"Our people existed for millennia as nomads—hunters and raiders. When we were forced into this world with so many other races, some clans settled, others found different ways to fit in, and still others refuse to bend, though their numbers grow scarce. What about you, Victor? Where are your people?"

"My people aren't in this world. I was transported here by magic—summoned before I had the strength to resist."

"That's . . . hard." She reached up a hand to squeeze his shoulder. "I'd be lost without my clan. I hope you can find people here, Victor, or a way to your home."

"Thanks, Chandri. Yeah, I try not to think about my family because it brings me down. I've met some good people here, though, and I have plans to help some of them that need it."

"That's good, Victor. We could all sense your strength. I'm glad that you're a friend to our clan. The Ban-tok asked me to give you a gift, even though he said he was coming to help you with a task. Perhaps he didn't want it to seem part of any bargain you made with him," she said, holding up a large, bulbous brown bottle with a wax-sealed cork. Victor assumed she'd had it in a storage device because her hands had been empty up to that moment.

"What's this?" he asked, taking the heavy bottle, though he had a good idea of its contents.

"Cheb-cheb! It's from the Ban-tok's personal supply—I think it's a valuable bottle!" They'd just reached the dirt road when Victor put the bottle into his ring and turned to face Chandri.

"That's awesome! Thanks again; I wish I had something good to give as a gift, but I've been living off really bad travel rations and watery wine for the last month or so."

"A gift requires no payment, Victor. Perhaps you'll bring something next time you pass through," she said, smiling. Looking at her face without the distraction of walking, Victor noticed that she had tiny, black tattoos of animals and arrows at the backs of her cheeks, running down her jawline, neck, and back along her hairline.

"What do your tattoos mean, Chandri?"

"The animals are from hunts I've participated in, and the arrows are for kills." Victor noticed she didn't mention if the kills referred to animals or people.

"Right, cool." Victor glanced toward the camp and saw that Tellen had started toward them, walking with his roladii following behind on a leather lead.

"You don't keep track of your kills, Victor?" Chandri asked, bringing his attention back to her.

"Um, no. To be honest, I've lost count. Kind of sad, huh? I'm sure if I thought about it, I could figure out how many people there were, but there's no way I could count the monsters." Victor shrugged. Chandri's smile had faded, though, and she took a step back.

"Well, I hope you stop by again, Victor. I should go before Tellen scolds me for shirking my duties. Safe travels!" She turned and started jogging back toward the camp, and Victor watched her retreating figure, wondering if he'd said something stupid again.

"Victor," Tellen called as he came near, "did Chandri try to talk you into helping her run away?" He laughed, so Victor figured the question wasn't serious.

"Yeah, but she had second thoughts when I told her about my cooking skills."

"Oh? Ha!" Tellen laughed, and Victor smiled, resting his hand on Lifedrinker's head, waiting for him to close the distance. "Well, I think we should move a bit west before separating. I know a good spot for you to lie in ambush. I think your friend won't want to approach the road this close to my camp, anyway."

"Yeah, that's a good point, but, please, he's not my friend. That motherfucker has caused me a lot of grief." Victor couldn't help the growl that entered his voice as he spoke, and Tellen gave him a second, appraising look.

"I don't envy the creature should you get him out of your friend's body."

"Yeah," Victor grunted, and the two of them started walking westward on the road.

"To that end, I have this sleeping draught. Our clan's Blood Healer prepared it. She says anyone under Tier Four will sleep at least for several hours, given the full dose."

"Thank you, Tellen," Victor said, tucking the small glass bottle into his ring.

They walked for a while in silence, then Tellen started filling the void with stories of hunts. He had a story for every sort of game animal, and Victor laughed as he spun one outlandish tale after another. Tellen had just finished recounting how his father had made him hide in a blind, covered in cooked entrails, to lure out a particularly skittish scavenger called a gythalii when he stopped walking, gestured to the left, and said, "This is it."

Victor saw more grasslands over gentle hills and shrugged, saying, "I don't see it."

"No, you wouldn't. If you go much farther south, though, there's a narrow, high-walled gorge splitting the plains for a dozen miles. If your enemy is coming from the south, toward this road, they'll need to skirt this way unless they can fly."

"All right, sounds good. You ready?" Victor took Thayla's skull out of the satchel, tied it to his belt, then handed the bag, with nothing but the phylactery inside, over to Tellen.

"Aye, a few hard days in the saddle is nothing new to me, or Hukka, here." He reached up and patted the roladii's thick gray skin just under its mane of feathers.

"Those are some cool mounts, that's for sure," Victor nodded. "Cool, so, just head west on the road for half a day or so, then keep your eyes peeled. Don't let this asshole sneak up on you!"

"I've not been ambushed since I was a child. Fear not, Victor." He slung the satchel over his shoulder and then smoothly mounted the roladii. He waved and clicked his tongue, and soon he was just a blur of dust in the distance.

"All right, Gorz. I need you to wake up and keep alert for a while. Can you do that?"

"Yes, Victor, I did listen to your conversation with Tellen and assumed I'd need to be on high alert soon."

"I'm guessing you can still see the tether as long as I stay between the phylactery and Belikot, right?"

"Yes, it's steadily stretching away to the southwest from here and then disappears into the distance, parallel to the road."

"Perfect." Victor moved off the road to the south, climbed the first rolling hill, then dug through his ring for one of the bronze spears he'd looted in the dungeon. Using the spear and bolstering his strength with Sovereign Will, he started to dig into the dirt between clumps of tall, yellow grass. With each scrape of the spear, he pulled away significant troughs of soil, his muscles more than a match for the loose, soft ground. Soon he had a trench dug with a loose pile of dirt around it. He put the spear away, then went to the far side of the hill and started pulling up clumps of grass, carrying them back to his trench and piling them around it, obscuring the hole and the loose, dark soil.

When he finished, Victor dropped into his trench and said, "It's on you now, Gorz. Keep me updated on the tether every two minutes, and be sure to let me know if you see any Energy signatures coming my way."

"I will. Thank you for the clear instructions. It will help me stay focused on the physical world."

Victor nodded, unsure if Gorz could see such communication but not in the mood to speak more. Sitting in his hole, he closed his eyes and listened with every fiber of his being. He primarily heard the wind rustling through the grass, but he heard bird calls now and then, and, very occasionally, he heard the thump and scurry of little animals running through the grass. He sat like that, lost in the whisper of the wind for hours, and the sun was well past noon when Gorz said, *"Victor! The tether has shifted! The thread leading away to the south has moved northward."*

"Oh, sweet!" Victor said, suddenly aware of the weight he'd been carrying, worrying that his plan was fatally flawed by some aspect he hadn't thought of. "I think Belikot is on the move. Keep alert!"

Gorz notified Victor several more times throughout the afternoon as the line of death Energy moved this way or that. As the sun started to sink toward the horizon, he said the tether was beginning to grow thicker, as if its source was drawing nearer. As the sun began to sink beneath the western horizon, Gorz said, *"Victor, I'm sensing twenty or more weak Energy signatures. They're reminiscent of the ghouls you slew in the dungeon and are coming along the road at a rapid pace."*

"No sign of Belikot?" Victor thought.

"No, the tether continues beyond the signatures. Perhaps they're moving at a faster pace than Belikot can maintain."

"Right." Victor stayed still, slowly drawing a deep breath and holding it. It wasn't long before he heard the ghouls' grunting wheeze and scrabbling steps as they ran by on the dirt road. They didn't pause as they went by, and Victor didn't move, not wanting to lose his advantage of surprise.

The ghouls were gone about ten minutes when Gorz practically shrieked in his mind, *"Victor! I see the end of the tether and Belikot's death-attuned Energy! He's coming up the road, moving right down the middle of it!"*

"Okay, chill. I'm going to let him get past. Keep an eye on him and say something if he stops or turns."

Gorz was silent, which Victor took to mean nothing was going wrong, and he watched the road, holding his breath, peering between stalks of grass. He ran over his plan a hundred times, imagining how he would move, what he would do first, and how he would react given any scenario he could imagine. At last, after holding his breath for several minutes, he saw the tall, lithe silhouette that had to belong to Thayla's body. She was walking, but, as Victor watched, she broke into a jog for a short while and started walking again. Belikot was pushing her body hard, trying to hurry, but Victor knew she had to be exhausted. "You motherfucker," he whispered soundlessly.

Soon, Belikot had walked-run past his position, and Victor channeled his Sovereign Will boost into agility, effortlessly and noiselessly hopping out of his hole. He could see Thayla's shadowy outline moving away down the road, and as he started to stalk through the grass, he cast Inspiring Presence. The twilight of early evening suddenly glowed with potential—the stars were bright, the moons vibrant and encouraging, and the shadows fled the roadway and Thayla's body. She walked forward, clear as day, and Victor saw her ripped clothes, muddy boots, and the way her braids had come loose and grown tattered.

Concentrating on being quiet, he found the spots on the road free of loose gravel and moved like a ghost through the space between himself and Belikot. Victor found joy in perfectly placing his feet and silently slipping through the night, and when he saw Thayla's head start to turn, it was a trivial effort to concentrate and push some inspiration-attuned Energy out with Project Spirit. Of course, the spell twisted the Energy, causing despair and doubt in Belikot. He felt the death caster's will struggle with his spell, but Victor just doubled down with his prodigious attribute and crushed the resistance, and Belikot turned away, trying to move into a faster run.

Victor was on him in a flash, snaking an arm around Thayla's neck in a chokehold, falling back, and wrapping his legs around her legs and waist, pinning her in place. Belikot, in Thayla's body, gasped and thrashed, and Victor felt his cold death Energy begin to surge. Victor grunted and bore down with his will, pushing inspiration Energy into his pathways until he veritably hummed with it. All the while, he worked with his free hand to pop the cork out of his sleeping potion, and as Thayla's body writhed and twisted, he got ready to pour it into her mouth.

He knew that if he held her long enough, she'd eventually choke out. Even enhanced by Energy, people needed to breathe, but he feared Belikot would work some sort of spell given enough time. As soon as his free hand was ready with the potion, Victor let go of her neck and grabbed her jaw with his hand, driving his powerful thumb and fingers into her cheeks, forcing her lips apart. Then he dumped the potion into her mouth and slapped his hand over her lips. He felt terrible, being so rough with Thayla's body, but as her legs bucked and kicked, he felt a slight twinge of pleasure, knowing it was Belikot who was panicking in her mind.

When Thayla's body fell limp, Victor slid out from beneath her, pulled the mine employee's shackles from his ring, and bound Thayla's feet and hands behind her back. Then he took a scrap of leather, rolled it up, and stuffed it in her mouth. He used another scrap to tie around her head, holding it in place. He'd just finished when Gorz screamed, *"Victor! The ghouls' Energy signatures are coming back this way!"*

"Thanks for being so alert, Gorz." Victor smiled, still under the influence of inspiration, and hoisted Lifedrinker into his hands. Standing over Thayla's body, he waited for the monsters. They slinked down the street, surely thinking they had the benefit of the obscurement of shadows, but Victor saw them from a long way off. Even without inspiration, he felt he'd have seen them coming, what with the bright moons and the stars. They lurched and dragged their limbs, and Victor knew these ghouls were subpar creations compared to those in the dungeon.

The undead creatures launched themselves at him with no thought of strategy, coming singly, in pairs, and, in one case, a trio. Lifedrinker met them all and tore them asunder with ease. Victor moved so quickly with his agility boosted, and he was at such a level disparity with the monsters that the fight felt more like swinging his axe at targets than actually fighting. When nothing but twitching body parts and broken corpses lay around him, he stooped, hoisted Thayla's body to his shoulder, and started to jog toward the Shadeni hunter camp, a thin stream of conquered Energy chasing him into the night.

He covered the ground much faster than when he and Tellen had strolled to his ambush site. Soon the campfires came into view, and he cut through the grassland toward them, braced for the inevitable challenge from the watch. He didn't have to wait long before a husky voice shouted, "Stop! Who comes running?" Victor slowed, put Lifedrinker into his belt loop, then held up his free hand, his other still holding onto Thayla.

"Victor! I was here last night! Someone needs to ride toward Gelica to get your Ban-tok. Did he tell you to expect me?"

"Yes, Victor. Come forward," the voice said, and Victor kept walking. A shadow rose from behind a clump of grass, and Victor recognized one of the men that had been sitting around Tellen's fire the night before.

"Was your mission successful, then?" he asked, eyeing Thayla's unconscious form.

"Yes, but I might need help dealing with her. There's an evil spirit inside her. I, um, I didn't plan this far ahead."

"A spirit? Come, let's see Oynalla—she's our spirit caster."

"Oh, you guys have a spirit caster?"

"Of course," the man snorted and turned to walk toward the camp. He waved his hand into the shadows, and Victor figured he was signaling other watchers. They'd only gone a few steps when he heard the sound of a roladii running away toward the road.

"That the rider going to get Tellen?"

"Aye." The man wasn't talkative, and he silently led Victor into the camp and past several tents before stopping before a small, blue canvas one with an eye painted on the flap in yellow dye. "Oynalla," he called, though not loudly.

"Send them in," a dry, rough woman's voice replied. The man shrugged and gestured to the flap. Victor nodded and pulled it aside, ducking through the opening, carefully squatting low enough to get Thayla through. The tent was small, maybe ten feet across, and he immediately faced a woman sitting on piled furs. She nodded to the hides to her left, and Victor carefully lifted Thayla from his shoulder and laid her down. "And you too, warrior. Sit before me."

The tent smelled of incense and spices, and Victor saw a small pot bubbling on a brass stove, seemingly powered by Energy. When he sat in front of her, Victor still towered over the woman, driving home just how small she was. She had braided gray hair, and her red skin was folded with hundreds of wrinkles and marked by dozens of old, faded tattoos. "Thank you for seeing me."

"Of course! I felt you coming all the way from the road. Such a strong Spirit Core. I'm not sure what you want from me—I can't match your strength."

"Oh, um, it's my friend, she . . ."

"Oh, this one with the death Core? What can I do for one such as this?"

"She's not in there. She's in this skull." Victor untied Thayla's skull and set it on the fur in front of him. "A spirit that had been in this skull switched places with her."

"Oh! Aha! Yes, now I feel her in there—so very weak! So, you need to push him out of her and let her go back in! You have more than enough strength for the task, but I can guide you."

"Really? There's not some ritual or spell I need?" Victor studied the old woman, wondering what her role in the hunter community was. What attunements did she have?

"No. This is a matter of will. Your friend was displaced because she came into contact with the skull and the spirit's will was stronger than hers. You'll have to aid her. Give her some strength, and then push against this invading spirit. Drive it forth so that she can move back in."

"What about his phylactery? I was under the impression I'd need it to force him to leave."

"Oh, a phylactery, hmm? Well, that's neither here nor there. Indeed, the spirit will want it, and perhaps you could use it as leverage, but this can be done without it. I'd caution you not to let the spirit gain control of the phylactery when you're done."

"Right. Okay, where do I begin?"

"Begin by giving me a gift!" the old woman cackled, and Victor couldn't tell if she was joking or just a touch insane. He decided not to risk offending her, so he reached into his ring and looked through his treasure. He found a particularly lovely red gemstone and took it out, holding it in his palm toward the woman. "Oh? A ruby for me? Good boy!" She snatched it, and it was gone in a flash. "Now! Wake up your friend and give her some Energy!"

"All right," Victor said. He put his hand on the skull and channeled some inspiration-attuned Energy into it, much more than he had given Thayla before.

"Victor! Thank you! That feels wonderful," Thayla said in his head. *"Where are we? How are things going? Did you find the phylactery?"*

"Yeah, Thayla. Not only that, but I got your body. We're going to get you back into it now. Are you ready to fight for it?"

"Yes! What do I need to do, Victor?"

"Just wait, and I'll give you instructions. This woman, Oynalla, is helping." Victor pointed the skull's eyes at Oynalla, and the older woman cackled again.

"I'm ready, Victor! Just tell me what to do," Thayla said again, her voice earnest and excited.

"She's ready," Victor said to Oynalla.

"Good! You'll be the bridge, Victor. Your Core and pathways are used to channeling spirit Energy, yes?"

"Yeah, I'd say so."

"Good! So, to protect your friend's spirit from the malignant spirit in her body, you'll pull her from the skull to rest in your pathways. Then you can pull the other spirit out and push it into the skull. Be sure to keep them apart in your pathways."

"You want me to take them into me?" Victor's eyes had grown wide, and his voice strained.

"Oh, come, boy. You've got a powerful will, or you wouldn't have such a brilliant Core of spirit Energy. Show that death caster what a spirit caster can do!"

"Okay, hold on." Victor straightened his back, took a few steadying breaths, and cast Heroic Heart. He wasn't sure he shouldn't go with Inspiring Presence, but he wanted the confidence and resilience of courage-attuned Energy coursing through him at that moment. As the hot, red-gold Energy flooded out of his chest into the rest of him, a smile spread on his lips, and the old woman cackled, watching him.

"That's it, boy! That death trickster will flee before you!" The woman's words bolstered his confidence even more, and Victor slapped his palm on the skull, reaching out with his senses for the spirit within. When he felt the cool tickle of Thayla's spirit, he suddenly could smell her and feel her as if she was in the room with him.

"Come on, *mija*; come with me. I'll keep him off you," he said aloud.

"*Victor*?" Thayla said in his mind.

"Trust me. Come out of the skull; I have to hold onto you for a minute." He tugged at the Energy of Thayla's spirit again, and he felt her let go and start to flow into his pathway. He smiled and stopped pulling at her when she was resting in the pathways of his right hand. There was more than enough space for her. The old woman had been right about that—the amount of Energy he could channel dwarfed Thayla's little signature. Victor smiled and opened his eyes, looking at Oynalla. "Got her."

"Good! The skull is a vessel designed to hold a spirit. Pull the one from your friend's body and put it in there. He'll resist, but you're stronger, aren't you?"

"Damn right," Victor said, resting his left hand on Thayla's breastbone and reaching forth with his mind. With red-gold courage flowing through his pathways, Victor reached out, feeling for some sort of spirit Energy in Thayla's body. He immediately felt her pathways, small and narrow compared to his, and, lurking like a miasmic fog, he felt the cold, slippery presence of Belikot. "Come out, fucker!" he growled and latched onto him with his will, tugging him toward the bridge between his hand and Thayla's chest.

"Fool! I knew I should have dropped feeders down after you!"

"Quiet!" Victor growled and pulled, ripping the spirit toward him. Thayla's body was utterly motionless, still under the soporific effects of the potion. Belikot railed and screamed in Victor's mind, but it was ineffectual, and Victor relentlessly pulled. When the first part of the cold, slippery Energy entered Victor's pathways, he cringed, feeling as if he'd just stuck his hand into a latrine, but he doggedly kept on, pulling and tugging, until every last scrap of the spirit was resting in his left arm.

When he'd finished the extraction, he felt Belikot make a mad rush along his pathway, trying to charge into his mind, and Victor laughed. With Heroic Heart active and his will at nearly two hundred, Victor yanked the spirit back down to his hand and held it pinned there, pressing it into a ball and squeezing with all his might. The spirit thrashed and quailed, and remembering all the problems Belikot had caused and the hell he'd put Thayla through, Victor relished in its throes.

"Careful, spirit warrior!" the old woman suddenly said. "Don't destroy the spirit within yourself unless you want to absorb some aspects of it." Oynalla's words brought Victor back to himself, and he stopped crushing Belikot's spirit. The last thing he wanted was to absorb some element of this asshole. Sighing heavily, he put his hand on the skull and pushed Belikot into its artificial pathways. As soon as the eyes flared with blue flames, Victor snatched the skull into his dimensional ring.

Oynalla cackled again, "Oh, child! So cruel! Existence in a dimensional container will drive any spirit mad!"

"Good. Fuck that guy," Victor said, then he put his other hand on Thayla's chest and gently nudged her spirit out and into her body, pushing her forth and urging her toward the place where he instinctively knew her spirit should dwell, up the pathway deep into her skull. Thayla's breathing quickened momentarily, then steadied. Her face relaxed, and Victor knew she was where she was supposed to be—now he just had to wait for her to wake up.

14

RECUPERATION

Victor removed the shackles and gag from Thayla and folded a soft fur Oynalla had given him under her head. He sighed and sat back, watching her breath steadily with a smooth, peaceful expression on her face. The old woman watched him with a crooked grin, sipping from a cup of steaming liquid.

"You look weary, warrior. How long since you slept?"

"I don't know. A long time." As if on cue, Victor yawned hugely.

"Sleep then. Your work is done—your friend is safe. I'll wake you if anything happens." Victor looked around the cozy little space and then back at Oynalla.

"Here?"

"Yes, lumbering oaf! I would say so if I wanted you out!" She laughed in a high-pitched giggle again.

"All right. Well, thanks," Victor yawned again, then stretched out, perpendicular to Thayla, his head near her ankles. The furs were soft, and the room warm, and he was so exhausted that oblivion took him almost immediately. He must have slept for a long time without any dreams because when they came, they were wild and vibrant, the kinds of dreams you have when you've slept well and are deep into REM.

He dreamed of school, being in class, and laughing with his friends. Mrs. Lopez was trying to teach them about Shakespeare, about why his plays were important, and Marcos made a crack about how important it was to know

Hamlet when you got drafted into one of the militias. Victor laughed along with his friends. In the dream, though, something happened that had never happened in reality, he looked at Mrs. Lopez's face and saw the care and sadness, and he suddenly didn't think things were very funny.

Victor dreamed he was walking in the desert. He didn't know why he was there, but he felt as though he was looking for something. Cicadas buzzed, and the smell of creosote was thick in the air. The breeze felt hot, as usual, but slightly moist, and he wondered if it was monsoon season. He could tell he was in the foothills of the Catalinas, and when he turned around to look downhill, he could see Tucson spreading out through the valley. He turned back to the slope he was climbing and was surprised to see Thayla standing under a palo verde tree at the top of the hill.

In his dream, Victor walked to Thayla, but she was talking to someone. It seemed to take forever to get to them, but he heard their murmuring voices while approaching, indistinct but still buzzing in his head. When he finally got there and reached out to Thayla's shoulder to say hello, she turned, and it wasn't her face that greeted him but a laughing, yellowed skull, cackling with the voice of an old woman.

Victor's eyes shot open, and he was disoriented, not recognizing his surroundings. He kept trying to see his old room in his *abuela's* house, but the walls were canvas, and he was lying on furs, not his old bed. Slowly things clicked into place, and he remembered where he was, and then he heard Oynalla laughing again and Thayla's sharp voice saying something about the mines. Victor jerked his head up and looked around, and sure enough, Thayla was sitting cross-legged facing Oynalla and sipping from a steaming cup. "Thayla," he said, voice croaking with disuse.

"Victor!" she said, setting down her cup and crawling close enough to grab his head in her arms and pull his face into her chest. "Thank you, thank you, thank you! Victor, you did it! You beat him! I'm free!" Victor spluttered, aware that she was pressing his face into her breasts while she squeezed his head, but he was unwilling to ruin her innocent joy by thinking about it or attempting to savor the experience. He grunted, pushing Thayla back with one hand and pushing himself to a sitting position with the other.

"Hey, we're a team. No way I was letting that dickhead take your body."

She laughed and squeezed his shoulder, and Victor was relieved to see that her eyes were no longer purely black. The pupils and irises bled together in darkness, but the whites of her eyes were back, and she looked happy and normal, though dirty and unkempt. "Your eyes. Do you still have the death affinity?"

"I do! But, Victor, something happened when you took me into yourself—when you pushed me into my body, some of your Energy came with me, and I gained an affinity for courage! Courage, Victor! It feels amazing! There's a thin band of it circling my Core, and Oynalla says I can learn to do some spirit magic now. My affinity is low, but it's there. Thank you so much, Victor. For everything. I owe you my life, my soul—everything."

"All right, all right. First of all, you don't owe me shit. I helped you because you're my friend and it was the right thing to do. Don't go falling over yourself trying to pay me back, okay?" Thayla just smiled at him and squeezed his shoulder. "Are my words coming through?" He laughed and shrugged.

"Clever way to help her balance the death Energy," Oynalla said, chasing her words with her usual cackle.

"What do you mean?" Victor asked.

"Hmm? Oh, you didn't do it on purpose? When you pushed so much of your courage-attuned Energy into her, wrapping her soul in it, you changed her—gave her this new affinity. Her Core is a novel thing now. The academics would fall over themselves to hear of this. Those stodgy fools! As if they'd have the guts to try something like that!" She cackled again.

"Oynalla!" Victor recognized Tellen's voice calling from outside the tent, "Oynalla! I hear you cackling in there! Is our guest awake? I need to speak with him."

"We'll talk more about this," Victor said to Thayla, then he stood, stooping, and lifted the tent flap. "Tellen!" he said with a grin, holding out a hand. The wiry Shadeni smiled and took it, gripping firmly.

"We were successful, then?" Tellen asked, and Victor saw his satchel was looped over the Ban-tok's shoulder.

"We were. Thank you, Tellen. Thayla! Come here, Thayla. Tellen helped me to trick Belikot so I could catch him by surprise." Victor stepped out, making space, and held the flap as Thayla emerged into the morning light.

"Thank you, Tellen," Thayla said, warmly grasping the other man by the shoulders and looking into his face. "I owe you a great debt."

"Nonsense. Victor has paid your debt. I'm glad you're well, and that demon is dealt with." He shrugged the satchel off and held it out to Victor. "I think this should be destroyed. I was pursued in the night by apparitions and strange creatures. I felt this pulling toward the southeast, and, I'll be honest, I nearly threw it off at one point." Victor took the satchel with the phylactery.

"I can settle that," he said, trying to put the satchel into the dimensional storage bag he'd taken from the cult leader—he didn't want it in the ring with Belikot's skull. He felt resistance, though, and the satchel disappeared into the pouch, but the phylactery fell to the grass with a thud. "Huh. I can't put it into my storage bag?" Thayla reached for it, but Victor put a foot on it and held her shoulder, pulling her back. "I'd rather you didn't touch it, Thayla. I'm sorry, but that thing is evil as hell, and I don't know if you're more susceptible because of, you know, everything."

Thayla stood up and scowled at him, but then she nodded. "You're right. Best to be careful until I've learned more."

"If it won't go into your container, that means it's a dimensional container itself," Tellen said with certainty.

"Oh. You can't put a dimensional container into another one?" Victor asked.

"Not usually. Some buildings have their interiors enhanced with dimensional magic, and you can bring containers into them, but that's uncommon and requires powerful enchantments. We don't worry about such things out here on the plains." Tellen chuckled.

"Victor, might I add something?" Gorz suddenly asked in his mind.

"Yes, Gorz?"

"I still sense a faint tether stretching away to the south from the phylactery."

"Huh," Victor said, pulling his satchel back out of the pouch and hanging it over his shoulder. He stooped to pick up the phylactery and put it into the leather bag. "My companion spirit says that this thing is still connected to something to the south. Maybe to those ruins where Belikot was hiding?"

"We'll be moving camp in a month, but I hate having something evil lurking so near. Maybe we should move sooner," Tellen said, looking around at the tents and lines of smoke rising into the air from the various fires.

"What if Belikot started a second phylactery? What if part of him is still free?" Thayla asked, her eyes growing with the implications running through her mind.

"Well, shit," Victor said, thinking. "Maybe we should check it out. I'm tempted to take Lifedrinker to this thing right now, but if I'm going to destroy Belikot's phylactery, I'd like to make sure there isn't another one nearby. Let's follow the tether, figure out what it is, and destroy it. Then maybe I'll take that skull out of storage and smash it, too."

"Yes, let's do it, but I'd like to get cleaned up, Victor. I feel . . ." Thayla shook her head, frowning, "I feel wonderful, Victor, but my clothes, my body—I need to get clean."

"Yes! I, too, could use some cleansing heat!" Tellen said. "Come, friends, let's visit the steam lodge." Tellen reached up, grasped Victor's shoulder, and pulled him into a walk with a grin. "Thayla, if you can spare a bead, I bet Chala will scrub your clothes and braid your hair."

"Of course," Thayla said with a sigh of relief. "Is she your daughter?"

"No. Well, sort of. I'm her uncle, but her father is dead. She and her sister are my wards." Tellen meandered through the tents until they passed by a dark red, very large one, and Victor realized it was the tent he and Tellen had sat outside of drinking cheb-cheb the night before last. "Chala," he called through the flap. He waited a moment, then repeated, "Chala! You have work." After another minute, a curly-haired, lean Shadeni teen slipped out of the tent. She was wearing the typical beaded leather of the clan, but hers had a much higher percentage of turquoise, and her face was painted in faded, fierce, black-and-white angled stripes.

"Ban-tok?" she asked with a yawn.

"This is Thayla, and she's an honored guest. She needs her clothes cleaned and her hair washed and braided. Come; we're going to the steam lodge."

"Here," Thayla said, holding out a hand, and the girl accepted something that clicked like marbles with a wide grin.

Tellen led them further into the clustered tents until they approached an earthen dome that seemed to be an extension of the ground. "The first thing we build at a new camp after the latrines—the steam lodge." He walked around the dome until he came to a thick, brown hide and pulled it aside, leading the way into a small room lined with pegs and benches. "It's important to us. We use it for cleanliness, but also for sacred rites and meetings of the elders." Tellen started undressing at one of the benches, hanging his leather vest on the peg and sitting on the bench to remove his boots.

"Uh, are you cool with this, Thayla?" Victor asked, looking around and not seeing any towels or a ladies' room.

"Well, I'm Shadeni, but not from a nomadic clan." She looked around with a skeptical gaze.

"Thayla, come with me; there's another entrance and towels. Tellen should have known!" Chala scolded, then ducked out through the leather flap.

"I'm used to our customs; I'm sorry, Victor," Tellen grunted as he pulled off his boots. "Here," he said, tossing him a large blue towel. It was soft, like cotton, and unlike anything he'd seen in the camp thus far. "I have a few civilized things, and of course that includes a towel or three for my guests." He started laughing, then walked, completely naked, through another leather flap, deeper into the building. He poked his head back out and said, "Just come through here when you're ready. It's dark, steamy, and a perfect place to relax and talk."

Victor shrugged and started hanging his gear next to Tellen's. Most of his valuables were in his ring, and when he took off his pants and ringmail, he slipped them into it as well. Shrugging, he did the same with his boots. He hung his belt up with his storage pouch still attached, then he hoisted the phylactery satchel, about to hang it from a peg. Suddenly he imagined some corrupted clan member snatching the phylactery away and performing some ritual to summon Belikot's soul. "Uh-uh, not on my watch," he said, slinging the satchel over his shoulder.

He took a second look at Lifedrinker leaning against the wall under his belt. It might offend someone, but Victor wasn't leaving her out here. "Nope," he said, and, after he wrapped the towel around his waist, he picked up the axe and slipped under the hide into the hot, steamy, dark interior of the lodge.

"Over here, Victor," Thayla called from his left. There was dim, diffuse, orange lighting in the lodge, and Victor could just make out the beams crisscrossing the ceiling and the woven reed mats on the floor. He walked over the mats toward Thayla's voice and found the woman, a towel much like his wrapped around her body, sitting on a wooden bench. Chala sat behind her, also in a towel, and Victor was relieved to see that it wasn't just outsiders who opted for some modesty.

Chala brushed some glistening concoction into Thayla's hair and hummed a soft, lilting tune. Victor sat next to them, and as his eyes started to adjust, he realized Tellen was seated not far to his right, leaning back against the earthen wall with his eyes closed. The air was stiflingly hot and wet, and Victor was sweating profusely. "Feels good," he grunted, leaning back to close his eyes. He leaned Lifedrinker against the bench between himself and Thayla.

"You brought your axe?" Thayla snorted.

"She didn't want me to leave her alone."

"Oh, Ancestors! You've gotten worse with that thing?"

"What the hell? Don't take out your frustrations on Lifedrinker—she's never done anything against you!" Victor grinned, speaking lazily, enjoying the old banter.

"What about you, Victor? You've changed since I was last . . . present."

"What do you mean?"

"Uh, you're even bigger, for one."

"He is big, isn't he, Miss Thayla?" Chala asked.

"Hey! I'm right here. Chala, you're a lot more polite than I remember. What happened to 'let me put an arrow in him?'" Victor chuckled as he remembered the girl calling her challenge out of the darkness.

"Well, you're friends of the clan now. And Miss Thayla pays very well!" Victor opened his eyes to peek at the girl, and she grinned wickedly.

"Anyway, yeah, I advanced my race some more in that dungeon, Thayla. It took me a while to fight my way back to where you were. I'm sorry about that."

"Don't you dare apologize! I caused that mess by trusting that skull. Not to mention, the whole thing seems like a blurry nightmare now. I'm not sure how long it took you, and that's okay. I'm just glad to be back and that you caught him before he did something terrible to my body."

"Right. Me too, Thayla. Me too."

"So, what's next?"

"Next? Well, let's deal with this phylactery," Victor patted the bag on the bench next to him. "After that, I don't know. Gelica?"

"Yes! We can sell some treasure, do some shopping, and I want to find an old contact, someone who might be able to point me toward my daughter. You haven't heard anything from the, uh, the people who were looking for us?"

"Nah, nothing. I hope they think we're dead. They must think we're dead, right?"

"You have enemies hunting you?" Tellen suddenly asked.

"We did, yes, but it was a long time ago, and they have no reason to believe we're still alive." Victor knocked on the wooden bench, wondering where that old "knock on wood" thing came from.

"I hope you've evaded them, Victor," Tellen said, his voice thick and slurred. Was he falling asleep?

"Anyway, that sounds good, Thayla. I hope we can find her."

"We?" she asked softly.

"Well, yeah. I'm not planning on ditching you as soon as we hit the city. I figure I'll help you, then maybe you can help me with a thing or two. I mean, that's what friends do, right?" Thayla didn't answer, but she reached over and took his hand, squeezing it.

Several minutes passed, and Victor's eyes grew heavy in the steam, then he heard a splash and smelled citrus. He opened his eyes to see Chala rinsing

Thayla's hair from a wooden bowl. She splashed the clean-smelling liquid over her hair three more times, then she started gently wringing it out with a towel. "Chala, you're earning your pay," Thayla purred.

"You have beautiful hair, Miss."

"Thank you." Thayla sighed, closing her eyes. After a minute, she said, "Victor, what will you need my help with?"

"I've told you about my friends in the pit and how that asshole sold me out?"

"Yes." Thayla sighed, her voice heavy and sleepy.

"Well, I think I'd like to see who's still alive and who I can help. If a few people get a taste of justice while I'm at it, that's a bonus."

Thayla squeezed his hand tighter, then she said, her voice small, "Victor, you know my daughter's only six, right?"

"Oh, yeah," suddenly, things clicked for Victor, and he felt like a complete moron. Why would Thayla want to take on slavers and pit fighters when she'd just reunited with her six-year-old daughter? "Listen, I'm an idiot. Of course, you're going to be busy with your daughter. Don't worry about what I said. I still want to help you, and you won't have to worry about following me to Persi Gables or any of that shit."

"I want to help you, you know, Victor," she said, her voice low and subdued.

"Yeah, of course you do. Don't sweat it, Thayla. It's all good. You think I want to be responsible for a kid losing her mom?" He squeezed her hand and chuckled. "Besides, if you're with your daughter, someplace nice, it'll give me a friend to visit. I need more of those in this world."

"You're a good person, Victor," Thayla said wistfully, closing her eyes while Chala braided her hair. Victor smiled, savoring the warmth, both outside from the steam and inside from Thayla's words. They stayed in the steam lodge much longer than would probably have been safe for ordinary people, but with their Energy infused bodies, they were just fine when they finally stumbled out into the late morning light.

Victor blinked rapidly, his body so loose and relaxed that he felt as if he could melt into a puddle. He never washed with soap, but he'd sweat away all the dirt and grime on his body, and when he scrubbed himself dry with the towel, he felt like a new man. Of course, his ringmail shirt and enchanted pants were clean, as usual, which helped. "Feeling good?" he asked, grinning at Thayla.

At some point, while they'd been steaming, Chala or one of her friends had scrubbed and dried Thayla's leather pants and vest, and they'd given her a pale blue, long-sleeved shirt with tiny little pearl snaps up the middle and at the cuffs. "I feel wonderful! Look at this beautiful shirt!"

"Yeah, I like it. Blue's good on you." Thayla smiled at him, and Victor thought she looked younger and less troubled than he had ever seen her. Was it the courage Energy he'd given her? Oynalla had mentioned balance, which he thought was a good descriptor for what he was noticing in her—she seemed more balanced.

"Let's break our fast, and then I'll see you two safely on your way, hmm?" Tellen asked, straightening his leather shirt.

"Yeah, that'd be nice, Tellen, thanks." Victor got the impression Tellen was eager to get them on the road but didn't want to seem rude. "We'll get this phylactery out of here, Tellen, don't worry."

"Perceptive, Victor. Yes, I dread having that near my camp come dark."

"Of course," Thayla added. "We should go now, Victor. We can eat on the trail, and I'd rather handle this problem while the sun is up."

"Yeah, that's not a bad idea. Tellen, thanks for the invitation, but I think we'll get going."

"Hmm." Tellen stroked his chin. "Yes, I should tell you, though; Oynalla wanted me to invite you to stay a while—she thinks she can teach you some things. If you destroy that evil artifact, then I'll extend that invitation. Come back here when you're rid of it."

"Victor, I would like to talk to her some more about my Core. Do you mind?"

"No, I think it's a good idea. All right, Tellen. We'll stop back by after we've dealt with this thing."

"Excellent! Come, follow me." Tellen started walking back through the tents, exchanging greetings with clan members who were much more lively now that it wasn't so early in the morning. As he walked past his big red tent, he hollered for Chandri, and the young woman immediately came out of the tent.

"Yes, Tellen?"

"Go fetch some of old Born's travel bread. I can smell his baking. Bring a few loaves to our friends here; they'll be walking toward the road."

"Oh, thank you," Thayla said, and Victor echoed the sentiment.

"All right. I'll see you in a minute, Victor," she said, grinning at him and giving Thayla a sidelong look as she darted off between two tents.

"Ignore her," Tellen said to Thayla. "Now, you know the way from here, Victor. I hope we see you again before nightfall, but if it's dark when you return, the sentries will know you."

"Thank you again, Tellen. For everything." Victor clasped the man's hand, returning his firm grip. Thayla also shook the Ban-tok's hand and leaned forward to say something that Victor couldn't quite hear. Then Thayla turned and put a hand on Victor's shoulder, and the two of them walked away from the tents, over the grass, and toward the road. Victor glanced back and saw Tellen watching them go, a slight frown on his face. Was he worried? Did he harbor some doubt? He wished he hadn't caught that glimpse of the man.

"What did you say to him?" Victor asked.

"I said he was a good father to those girls and shouldn't tell people he's not their father. He should be proud of what he's done."

"Ahh. Nice of you." Victor nodded. They walked for a few minutes before the thump of feet heralded Chandri's arrival, and they slowed to wait for her.

"Victor! You're lucky! Born just made a batch, and he gave me fresh holbyis butter!" She held out a cloth-wrapped bundle with a little ceramic crock sitting atop it.

"Sheesh, Chandri! You guys are spoiling us." Victor held out his hands to receive the package, and the smell of fresh bread hit his nose like a hammer. "Holy shit, that smells good!"

"Born's the highest level baker on the plains." Chandri shrugged.

"Well, Chandri, do you ever get to go to the city?" Victor asked on a hunch.

"Once or twice a year. Why?"

"Well, let me buy you something next time you go," Victor said, producing a handful of attuned Energy beads. "Your sister already made some profits helping Thayla this morning; this is only fair."

Chandri's smile stretched her cheeks, but she said, "Victor, you aren't trying to pay for a gift, are you?"

"No! This is just a gift. No strings attached." He pushed his fist, clenching the beads toward her, and Chandri held her two hands together. He poured the beads into her much smaller palms and said, "I'm sure we'll see you again, but this is just in case I forget. Thanks again, Chandri!"

"Thank you, Chandri," Thayla said, squeezing the girl's shoulder, then they turned and continued to the road. Victor unwrapped the warm bundle and pulled out one of the three loaves Chandri had given him. It was smaller than a typical loaf of commercial bread on Earth but much heavier. He tore off a hunk and turned to Thayla.

"Hey, open that jar of butter for me. I'm afraid I'm gonna drop something."

"All right, but save some for me,"Thayla said, taking the little ceramic jar and pulling the top off. Victor smeared his hunk of bread through the warm, herbed butter, then took a huge bite, groaning in pleasure. Thayla reached for the bread, but he pulled it away.

"I don't know—I'm so hungry, and it's so good!" He laughed as she reached for it again, and he started running toward the road.

"Victor! Stop! I need food more than you do!"Thayla howled, giving chase.

15

GEL HARRA

"So, it, um, excuse me, *she* is gaining levels or something?" Thayla asked, gesturing to Lifedrinker.

"Yeah. I'm not sure how it works—if she's just changing as she gains consciousness, or if she will continue to grow in power as she drains Energy. Either way, I'm happy." Victor stepped around a large clump of scrub as they climbed the latest "rolling" hill. They'd been walking for several hours at a good pace, and the hills he'd seen in the distance were quite a lot larger up close. Still, it was either climb them or spend extra hours skirting them, so they embraced the effort.

"And you bought that new haft in Steampool? I don't even remember that town! I must have been out of it!"

"Right, it's living wood. It wasn't cheap, but I'm sure happy with it. By the way, I'm still holding onto most of the Energy beads we found. I owe you around five hundred."

"You don't have to . . ."

"Uh uh, none of that! We earned those together, and you'll want some money to get things started with your daughter, right?"

"Right," Thayla huffed, working hard to match Victor's natural pace. He wanted to slow for her, but, more urgently, he wanted to get to wherever the tether led before dark.

"Gorz, any update?" Victor had found that Gorz wasn't lying when he said he had a hard time staying focused on the physical world. His mapping ability seemed to happen automatically, which allowed the spirit's mind to drift easily if he wasn't engaged in conversation.

"The tether continues to stretch to the south, very faintly. It seems like we might be nearing its end, but I can't be sure because it has a much weaker signature than before."

"Thanks." Victor turned to Thayla and added, "He says we're still going in the right direction, and we might be getting close."

Thayla nodded, and they kept climbing, and before long, Victor crested the hilltop and looked out at the plains that continued to stretch away to the horizon. Not so distant, though, was a large copse of twisted, leafless trees, and, from his vantage, Victor could see partially collapsed wooden and stone structures amid the dead-looking trees. "That must be, um, what did Tellen say the town was called, Gorz?"

"Gel Harra, and the tether leads down into those ruins."

"Right, Gel Harra. Ever heard of it, Thayla?"

"Nope," Thayla said, leaning on her knees and catching her breath. "Doesn't look very inviting. Are those trees dead?"

"I think so, and there's no underbrush or grass around them. It's like the soil was poisoned. Tellen told me this town died of a plague during some war. I guess it was probably an intentional attack, right? I mean, you told me people don't really get sick . . ." Victor's words trailed off as he started to imagine the scene—people dying of some horrible disease caused by a spell or potion.

"Yeah, people have done horrible things with spells and alchemy. I've heard of potions that will dissolve a person into dust, let alone make them sick enough to die." Thayla straightened up, and suddenly her spear was in her hand.

"Shit! I forgot to ask about that. He left your spear alone? Any of your other belongings missing?"

"Nothing missing, but plenty of disgusting stuff added," Thayla said, holding up her hand with the storage ring. "Entrails, bottles of gross fluids, even some body parts. From people, I might add." Thayla shivered. "I hope the hunters never look into the latrine where I dumped everything out."

"Oh, sick." Victor repressed a shudder. "All right, let's get going. Gorz, please keep us following that tether."

"I will, Victor."

"He said he will," Victor said for Thayla's benefit, then started jogging down the hill. Thayla didn't have any trouble keeping up going downhill. Soon they were leaping and bounding, making it a contest to see who could get down the hill the fastest. Victor won, but he felt he had to give gravity at least half the credit. As they started jogging over the grass toward the first of the dead trees, Gorz spoke up again. *"The tether is leading a bit to your left, toward the eastern edge of the ruins."*

Victor veered to his left, and as they stepped onto the dusty, barren soil around the dead trees, he slowed, lifting Lifedrinker into his hands. Mist and shadows seemed to lurk among the lifeless branches, and Victor could only see for a few dozen steps in any direction. A shiver ran over his shoulders, and he spun, only to find Thayla looking around warily with her spear held ready. "This place is already giving me the creeps," he said.

"Me too!" Thayla hissed.

"You know, you're lucky to have courage-attuned Energy. I have to make it with a weave of my other Energies. Push some of it into your pathways—you'll feel better. I'll try to ask Gorz if there's a way I can teach you my Heroic Heart spell, though." He looked around and added, "I mean when we have some downtime."

Victor summoned his Globe of Inspiration, urging it to follow him with a nudge of will. Then he cast Heroic Heart—he wasn't going to let some necromancer or something mess with his mind. Heat rushed out of his chest and into his pathways, and he straightened, doubt having fled his mind. The trees looked sad and pathetic, devoid of life but not sinister. The clinging mist he'd perceived before was gone. The shadows were banished by his light or the sun, which Victor could see clearly now, high in the sky.

"That did help," Thayla said. "I just wish I had more of that Energy."

"Something to work on," Victor said, continuing his advance. They passed many trees, never crossing any paths or game trails, but after a few minutes, Victor saw a crumbled stone wall ahead. He nodded to Thayla, and she nodded back, gesturing with her spear. Stalking as quietly as he could, Victor moved to a corner of the wall and peered around. He looked at a dusty expanse of barren land between structures—ancient homes built from stone and wood. The blocks were losing their mortar and crumbling, and the wood was dry, broken, devoid of paint, and sagging under the weight of slowly collapsing roofs.

"The tether leads away to the left, past this building," Gorz said.

Victor motioned for Thayla to follow and then crept around the crumbling wall. As he rounded the corner to the left, he saw a dusty street lined with more crumbling buildings, and at the end, maybe the length of a city block away, sat a squat, half-collapsed building that looked very much like a church to Victor. There weren't any crosses, but at the peak of its roof, a huge window of stained glass, still intact, depicted a Ghelli soaring into the clouds. The figure, armored in silver and with wings trailing sparkles, reminded him of Captain Lam for a moment.

The left side of the building was in ruins, but the big double doors were still in their frame, and the right-hand one was slightly ajar. "That's where the tether leads, I'll bet."

"This was a Ghelli village? These trees must have been a lot different once," Thayla said in a hushed voice, looking around.

"Ghelli like trees?"

"Yes, I've never met a Ghelli that enjoyed living outside one of their forests."

"Huh. Lam must hate it down in the mines."

"Lam's unlike any Ghelli I've ever met," Thayla said with a shrug.

"Good point." Victor started walking down the dusty road toward the strange building. "Is that a church? I've never learned about the Ghelli religion. Is there such a thing?"

"Sure. Like any people, they have different groups that believe different things. Most believe all living things are connected, and they're especially reverent to trees. Some Ghelli cities are built around ancient trees they call 'mother' trees." Thayla shrugged. "Shadeni and Ardeni mostly believe in reincarnation and that our ancestors live through us."

Victor slowed and looked at Thayla. They were about halfway to the church, and he paused to say, "Do you believe that?"

"Sure." She shrugged again. "I've had dreams and memories I can't explain. Maybe it was a past life? What about you? You told me about your bloodline and that vision you had. Isn't it possible that was a past life? Or one of your ancestors that's still alive in your blood?"

"All right, good point. This is interesting shit, Thayla, but we're in the middle of a creepy, dead town, about to follow an evil phylactery to something it's connected to. I guess maybe we should continue this discussion later, eh?"

"Right," Thayla snickered, tightening her grip on her spear and nodding down the road. "Let's get to the bottom of this." Nothing accosted them as they advanced on the large stone building. Victor began to feel a cold, pulsating aura of Energy as they neared, though, and he raised an eyebrow at Thayla, silently asking if she felt it, too. She nodded and gestured toward the gap between the large sagging doors.

Victor moved forward, hooked Lifedrinker's beard on the edge of the open door, and pulled, dragging it roughly over the dirt-covered stone stoop. His orb and the rays of pale sunlight exposed a large hall, much as Victor imagined a medieval church might look. Broken furniture lined the walls, stacked by some person, monster, or force beyond Victor's understanding. In the rainbow light coming through the overlarge stained glass window, Victor saw a greenish-yellow portal swirling near the far wall.

"No!" Thayla hissed.

At the same time, Victor said, "Oh, fuck." He looked at Thayla and confirmed his thinking: "Another dungeon?"

"I fear so," she said.

"Victor, the tether does, indeed, stretch into that portal."

Victor growled and kicked the door wide, striding into the hall. Nothing responded to his presence other than the dust on the walls and beams, which drifted down in a shower of rainbow motes, falling through the light. Victor glanced up at the stained glass, admiring its beauty as the sun's light shone through. Then he walked toward the portal, looking around the corners of the church or meeting hall—whatever it was. The portal was the only thing of note, and the sickly cool aura emanating from it told Victor all he needed to know about what he'd find on the other side. "More undead."

"Probably," Thayla replied, leaning on her spear and staring at the swirling pattern at the portal's center.

"Well, fuck this. Let's smash the phylactery, smash the skull, and say goodbye to this part of the world."

"I can't do that," Thayla said, her voice quiet but resigned.

"What do you mean?"

"Victor, after what that thing did to me, after the connection we made . . ." She paused, her eyes darting around as she searched for the right words. "I can't let him live. I have to see Belikot destroyed, and I think there's something connected to him in that dungeon. If we destroy what we have, I'm afraid this other part will grow stronger and come for us. Or at least for me."

"And you don't want that hanging over your head when you're with your daughter."

"Exactly," Thayla sighed, visibly frustrated.

"Damn it. Fuck it. I've killed plenty of undead; why not some more?"

"You can go, Victor. I won't hold it against you! Go to Gelica; enjoy your life!" Her eyes were earnest, and she reached out to squeeze Victor's shoulder while she spoke, and he couldn't help smiling at her. It felt good to have someone who cared about his happiness.

"C'mon, Thayla. You know me better than that. I couldn't leave if I wanted to. Nope," he said, sighing with mock exhaustion, "time for me to be the hero again." He reached out and put an arm over Thayla's shoulders, leaning heavily on her. "So tiring always having to save the day, you know?" Just as he'd hoped, he got a smile out of her, though she squirmed out from under his arm, turning to face him.

"I'm serious!"

"Yeah, me too. C'mon, it's a dungeon! I'm a warrior adventurer! I should want to go in there, regardless of this tether bullshit."

"Adventurer now, hmm?"

"That's right. Just ask the people in Steampool!" Victor laughed, then picked up a nearly petrified, broken chair and threw it at the portal. To his surprise, it bounced off as if it had hit a stone wall and clattered in broken pieces over the flagstone floor.

"I don't think chairs can enter dungeons by themselves," Thayla snorted.

"Right, right." Victor nodded, moving closer to the portal. "Well? Let's get this shit over with. What do you say?"

"If you're sure," Thayla said.

"One hundred percent." Victor held out a hand, and Thayla took it. "In together, out together, right?" Thayla nodded, squeezing his hand tightly, then Victor walked forward and stepped into the cold, pulsing circle of Energy. He grunted as the icy tendrils pulled him through a dark void, and then he was stumbling over dusty ground illuminated by the pale moonlight. Thayla came through, still gripping his hand, but she stumbled and fell, cussing a word that Victor didn't think he'd ever heard—something like "gakuk!"

Victor reached down to help her up, then in a frenzy of growls and slashing claws, shadows jumped out of the darkness, tearing into them. Most of the ripping claws aimed at Victor slid harmlessly off his armored shirt, but several tore gouges in his arm, and one hooked painfully into the meat of his thigh. He roared, finished yanking Thayla to her feet, and cast Inspiring Presence. The shadows peeled back, and he saw an easy path between the snarling, black-furred, rotting wolf creatures.

He whipped Lifedrinker in a liquid cleave, striding out of the melee in her wake, only to turn and chop at the creatures' flanks. Thayla shouted and rolled, whirling her spear around to create some space, and the fight was truly joined. There had to be a dozen or more of the monsters. They were similar in size and shape to a German shepherd, but their fur was black, matted, and missing in patches. Their exposed flesh was rotten and falling away, especially around their snouts, and cold blue lights shone from their eye sockets.

The zombie wolves were fast, and their claws and teeth were sharp, but they weren't nearly as tough as the ghouls from the other dungeon. As Victor cleaved off limbs and chopped through spines, they fell and were easy to dispatch. Thayla danced among them, using her superior spear skills and speed to drive her weapon's sharp, broad blade through eye sockets in killing blows or into their torsos to hold them down while Victor killed them. The battle was furious and noisy, and Victor and Thayla suffered half a dozen gashes and bites. Still, it was over as fast as it began, and soon they stood panting over the broken corpses of their foes.

"Where are we?" Thayla asked, looking around, particularly gazing up at the moons.

"We're outside, but look." Victor pointed at a nearby tree. It was twisted just like the ones outside the dead village, but this one was decked in black, red-veined leaves. They were broad, shaped somewhat like maple leaves, but they seemed to seethe with shadows. Looking past the tree and the ones behind it, he saw a shadowy cobbled street leading between stone and wood buildings, pale blue streetlights illuminating the scene in pools of soft, cold light.

"Is this Gel Harra? Like a twisted copy of it?" Thayla asked.

"Yeah, I guess so. Nothing says dungeons have to be underground, I guess." Victor sighed with relief as motes of golden Energy flowed into them from the dead wolf creatures. His painful lacerations closed up, and Thayla's looked much better, largely scabbed over. "Gorz? Is the tether visible in here?"

"Yes, Victor, it's rather strong and leads toward those structures in the distance."

"Well, the tether is here. Hang on," Victor said, then he resummoned his Globe of Inspiration, making it large and bright by pushing nearly a thousand Energy into it. "No more ambushes from the shadows, eh?"

"Good!" Thayla said, following close beside him as Victor began walking toward the cobbles ahead. They were only halfway when another pack of the wolf monsters attacked them. This time, in the bright light of inspiration and with Sovereign Will boosting his agility, Victor butchered them without a single injury. Thayla did her part to keep them at bay and drive them off his flanks, but Victor moved like a dancer among them, dealing glittering death with each swing of Lifedrinker.

They paused to take in the Energy of their victory, and not having accumulated any new wounds, Thayla's damaged flesh knitted further. They hurried to the edge of the cobbled road and the first two buildings, and Victor thought they looked like houses. Their lower levels were built from stone blocks, but the second floor was made from masterfully woven wood. The construction was unlike anything he'd ever seen—long solid beams of wood twisted with one another and braided through perpendicular slats. It looked as if the wood had grown into the shape of a house.

"That's how Ghelli build with wood," Thayla said. "They grow it into the shape they want."

"Pretty cool. Did the village outside the dungeon used to look like this, you think?"

"Maybe, but there were still wooden structures standing, and they weren't built this way."

"Yeah, you're right. Maybe the dungeon is more like what it could have been? I don't know. I'm just guessing shit now." Victor shrugged, looking around warily, expecting the next monster to jump them at any second. The air was cold, and the lingering wisps of mist that tried to cling to existence inside his light were palpably damp. Strange hoots and garbled roars started to drift through the night air, and Victor slowly turned in a circle, holding Lifedrinker ready. "I don't know. I'm not sure this is a copy of Gel Harra. Do these streets and buildings match up to the ruins?"

"The buildings are very different, but the layout of the streets seems similar. If we turn to the left, we should see the main road and the Ghelli worship hall at the end." Thayla pointed to the crossroads a short way ahead. Victor nodded and started that way.

He'd just rounded the corner when he heard clanking and the clop of heavy feet rapidly *click-clacking* on the cobbles. He spun to his right and barely had time to react by diving into a roll, narrowly avoiding being smashed by a huge roladii driven by a black-armored warrior. When he rolled back to his feet, he saw Thayla had rushed forward with her spear, menacing the great, armored roladii and its rider as it performed a slow turn to face her and Victor.

The roladii was easily twice as bulky as the ones that Tellen and his people rode. More than just being larger, it was covered in heavy black armor plates. Dark smoke drifted from its smoldering orange eyes, and when Victor's gaze traveled up, past its head to the rider, he saw a similar countenance: a black plate helmet with orange, smoking lights behind the eye slits. Victor sidestepped around Thayla, circling the rider, so he couldn't charge them both at once.

As the rider pulled at the reins and the beast of a mount snorted black clouds of soot, Victor cast Channel Energy, flooding Lifedrinker with rage-attuned

Energy. Sovereign Will was already bolstering his agility, and he thought it wise to stay nimble on his toes. Thayla's spear had a blue nimbus around the blade, and she circled opposite Victor, eyes scowling and lips pressed tight.

"Come on!" Victor roared, trying to taunt the rider into doing something rash. The black-armored roladii stamped and snorted, turning toward Victor, and the rider brandished a smoldering red and black spiked mace. Victor lifted Lifedrinker sideways in front of his chest and nodded, again shouting, "Come on!"

With his agility boosted, Victor was fast, faster than Thayla even, and still, the roladii's charge was a blur to him, a streak of smoking black flesh and metal that tore into him like a comet. He'd just registered the movement and started to step aside when hundreds or thousands of pounds of monster smashed into him with tremendous force, knocking him back as if he'd been hit by a wrecking ball. The impact stunned Victor, driving his axe into his chest and knocking his grip loose. The air was forced from his lungs, and, as he gasped, still struggling to figure out what happened, his back and head cracked into the stone wall of a nearby building.

Stars exploded in Victor's eyes, and unable to breathe, he convulsed on the ground for a few heartbeats before his mind caught up with the events that put him there. Lying on his side, back against the wall, his vision started to clear, and he saw Thayla dancing around the roladii and its rider. She was jabbing her spear in flashes of blue Energy at the haunches of the mount. She leaped to the side, always staying in its blind spot, never giving it a chance to charge her. The rider was roaring, smoke streaming from his black helmet, jerking the reins and swinging his smoldering mace ineffectually at Thayla, unable to match the reach of her spear.

As his chest stopped spasming and he finally sucked in a breath, the black edges of Victor's vision cleared, only to be replaced by a hot, liquid rage. Who was this fucking *pendejo* to throw him like a punk kid against this wall? He saw Lifedrinker lying on the cobbles, and his anger stoked even higher. He knew his rage-attuned Energy was bleeding out of his Core into his pathways, but he didn't try to tamp it down. No, he opened the floodgates, letting it surge and burn. His vision started to tint red, and a low, rolling laugh began to rumble out of his throat. He stood up, a flickering red nimbus rolling along his shoulders, and walked over to Lifedrinker. "Enough dancing!" he barked, changing his Sovereign Will boost to strength.

Victor kept the knight in view as he squatted to pick up Lifedrinker, and when she was resting solidly in both his hands, Victor's laugh rolled out louder. Could he trust himself to keep Thayla safe if he went berserk? Was his will strong enough? He wasn't sure, but he desperately wanted to berserk. His fury at the rider was burning in his blood, and his heart was beating in slow, deep, hateful thuds. He could feel the Quinametzin in his blood, screaming to be let loose. His hands twisted on the wooden haft of his axe, and he looked from Thayla to the rider, watching as she taunted the beast. She was clever, but she wasn't hurting it.

With every ounce of his will, Victor calmed enough to coherently grunt, "Thayla, back off." She glanced at him, carefully hopping to the roladii's blind spot first. When she saw how he stood on the road, red Energy flickering along his silhouette and blazing from his eyes, she nodded and retreated toward him, moving to his left and stepping back out of his view. The rider spun his mount, facing the two of them. Victor laughed at him, a slow, deep chuckle, "Huh, huh, huh," and he beckoned again with his axe. The rider looked at Victor and at Thayla just behind him and nodded, blowing black smoke from beneath his visor.

Victor, enraged though he was, had perfect control of himself, and he watched for the smoke to start to billow from the roladii's snout, and when it did, he cast Berserk. The red of his vision deepened, his breaths pumped like forge bellows, and Victor screamed as pure rage crashed through his pathways, and his bloodline responded like a fuel exposed to flame. The roladii blurred into a black and orange comet, streaking toward Victor, and he caught it on the living wood of Lifedrinker's haft. His huge hands and arms strained as his feet slid backward, and Lifedrinker's handle groaned and strained but held.

The roladii's forehead was pressing into him, trying to drive him back, but its momentum was broken, and Victor roared and pushed. The beast, suddenly not so large at all, gave ground and began to slide to the side, tilting and screaming as Victor drove forward on powerful, massive legs. His feet dug into the cobbles, and red heat steamed off him as he roared and pushed the roladii to the side until it stumbled, and the rider was sent sprawling. Screaming with bloodlust, Victor finished his shove, jerking Lifedrinker to the side and bringing her around in a looping, whistling chop that connected with the back of the roladii's skull, slipping neatly beneath a metal plate and burying her edge up to the haft.

Lifedrinker bucked and surged, digging for Energy, and Victor let her go. The roladii staggered for two steps and then collapsed, the axe still buried in its head. Victor stalked toward the rider, scrabbling to his feet a few paces away. He still held his smoldering mace and spun, swinging it toward Victor's head, but Victor held up a thick forearm and caught the blow. It stung and might have shattered an ordinary man's bones, but Victor shrugged it off, stepped in close, and caught the armored figure in a bear hug.

The knight or warrior, or whatever he was, seemed small and weak, and Victor was furious that he'd tried to stand against him. Who was this worm to challenge the Quinametzin? He grunted and squeezed, feeling the heavy black metal compress under his powerful arms. Victor felt something slapping against his back, and had he been interested in figuring out what it was, he'd have realized the knight was flailing desperately at his back with his mace. The blows were ineffectual, jostling the shiny black rings of his armor but hardly impacting Victor's flesh. It was like a child swatting at a grown man with a broomstick.

Victor squeezed, jerking his arms, savoring the crunch of metal and bones, and when the former rider stopped thrashing, he savagely threw the twitching form to the cobbles with a liquid crunch of meat and armor. He stepped toward the writhing, jerking body and stomped on its steel-encased head, and kept stomping until the orange lights under the bent, twisted helmet stopped glowing. Victor heaved heavy, deep breaths and looked around. In the red blur of his angry eyes, he saw a woman driving a spear into the roladii, slipping it between armored plates. He stepped toward her, a rumbling growl in his chest, but then he caught her eyes, and he knew it was Thayla, a friend, and he forced himself to calm.

Victor stood there, in the middle of the street, staring at Thayla for several heartbeats, and slowly the red nimbus around him started to fade. He seemed to shrink into himself, and a few moments later, he breathed heavily and said, "You all right, Thayla?"

"I'm fine, Victor, but that was crazy! You turned into a giant! You stopped that roladii's charge! You crushed that knight with your bare hands!"

"Yeah, but I didn't attack you. That's good, right?"

16

NAGHELLI

"What do you mean, you didn't attack me? Why would you attack me?" Thayla asked after they'd absorbed the Energy from their battle. She squinted at Victor as she jerked her spear out of the monstrous roladii.

"I mean, I was berserk. I've totally lost myself in the past when I berserk, but I think I'm starting to get some control."

"Oh, right. Well, get your axe. Who knows what's coming next." She gestured to Lifedrinker, still buried in the back of the roladii's skull. He nodded and stepped forward, jerking the handle up and down to break the grip of the bone on her blade.

"You said I 'turned into a giant.' What do you mean, exactly? I know my bloodline does that, but like, when it's happening, I don't really feel how big I get."

"You grew a lot! Like half again as tall as you are now and much bulkier. Not that you're small normally, heh."

"That's so fucking wild." The hoots and growls had died down during their furious melee. Victor and Thayla stood in the quiet misty air, looking up and down the cobbled road. In both directions, it led away into thicker mist and darkness. "This dude was kind of like a boss, don't you think? I didn't level, and I don't see a chest."

"Yeah," Thayla grunted, looking around with a scowl. "Well, levels get slower. I told you that."

"Right. Well, maybe this guy wasn't a boss. Or maybe not all dungeon bosses give a chest. I guess I don't have a ton of experience to draw from."

"More than I do. At least I'm not stuck in a skull this time, hmm?" She punched his shoulder and pointed down the street to their left. "I think that's the way we'd go on the outside to get to the Ghelli worship hall. Odds are that's where we need to go."

"The tether is strongly pulling in that direction, Victor."

"Thanks, Gorz." He looked at Thayla and added, "He says that's the way to go." She nodded in response, and the two of them advanced down the street, Victor's light trailing just slightly behind and both gripping their weapons warily. Victor switched his Sovereign Will boost to his agility again, tensing his muscles in anticipation of another surprise attack.

"Victor, what rank, exactly, have you gotten your race to? I've never seen someone with a bloodline like yours."

"I got boosted up to Improved One. I found this silvery orb with weird flakes of black floating within. Gorz said it was a delving orb or something like that; it digs through your, I dunno, DNA or something, looking for bloodlines."

"DNA?"

"Um, I'm not an expert on the subject, but it's a scientific term for microscopic material in our cells—all our genetic information is stored in it. That's why I figure that's what that orb was 'delving.'"

"That's . . ." Thayla paused and held a finger to her lips. She gestured to a dark alley between two buildings that had come out of the fog on their left. Standing in a cluster, several strange-looking Ghelli were talking in hushed voices. They were tall, thin like most Ghelli, and their dragonfly wings were like black gossamer with streaks and patterns in shades of ochre and red. Victor and Thayla had stopped moving and were quietly staring at the group when one of them turned to regard them with black eyes.

"What the fuck?" Victor's voice was a low whisper.

"Naghelli!" Thayla hissed, "I thought they were all gone!"

"Here are the new guests. What have they done with Garran?" an extremely tall Naghelli said, his long, spindly arms stretching out to gesture and guide his companion's gaze their way. As more and more dark, inky black eyes turned toward them, Victor straightened and moved more to the middle of the street.

"You guys can speak? Nice touch for a dungeon."

"Ha, the brute thinks he's stumbled upon a simple dungeon. What's this, though? Do you feel it, brothers and sisters?"

"I feel it! The master's aura is so strong here. Could it be?" One of the female Naghelli stepped forward, her long, silvery hair glimmering in Victor's light. She wore, like the others, a tightly fitted, lacy black blouse over silky black pants. Her top's open neckline exposed a large swath of alabaster chest, and Victor couldn't help noticing the pulsing red jewel dangling from a chain between her breasts.

While she spoke, the others had begun to fan out in a semicircle, moving slowly toward Victor and Thayla. The tall man, his black, fathomless eyes squinting, held up his hands, making a box with his thumbs and forefingers, and studied Victor and Thayla through the gap. "It's finally happened. The master's phylactery is here. Have you come to join us, then?"

"Join you?" Victor didn't like the looks of things. These creatures, or people, weirded him out. His unease was more because they were weirdly similar to Ghelli than because of how they looked objectively. It also bothered him that they spotted the phylactery so quickly and now mentioned a "master."

"Of course; there will be room for servants in our Twilight Empire." The seven Naghelli had stopped advancing, and though they stood in a loose semicircle in front of Victor and Thayla, none bore weapons. Victor saw jewelry on their fingers, ears, and necks, however, and he knew better than to consider them unarmed.

"Victor, these aren't real people—they must be constructs of the dungeon. Naghelli are extinct, killed off in a great war just after the worlds merged," Thayla said, her eyes jerking from one set of dark eyes to another, her spear pointing out in front of her.

"Extinct? Oh, brothers and sisters! I knew our numbers had dwindled, but is it true? The world thinks we're gone?" A different, shorter woman spoke this time. She had black curly hair, and her voice dripped with venomous anger. The way she clipped off her words made Victor think that if anyone doubted her existence, she was willing to remedy the misconception.

"Nonsense. We aren't the only enclave, and you know this," the tall, original speaker said. He turned to Thayla and continued, "Hiding, regrouping, is not extinct. The time is nearly at hand for us to push forth again. You're lucky—you get to bear witness to our resurgence."

"Mmhmm, and what about Belikot?" Victor asked. The entire group of Naghelli hissed and stared at Victor, exposing their very human-like teeth.

"Do not speak his name so frivolously, knave!" the silver-haired woman hissed, spittle flecking her lips in her vehemence.

"So that is the, um, 'master' you're talking about?" Victor pressed.

"Yes, fool, and you'd rather he didn't wake at the sound of his name in this, his demesne," the tall Naghelli said, craning his neck and tilting an ear toward the darkness down the street. "Your luck holds—he slumbers, yet."

"What do you mean, he slumbers? I've already fought with him outside this dungeon and put his skull someplace very out of reach." The Naghelli looked at each other, amusement lighting their eyes and twisting their lips into grins.

"You faced one of his remnants. A sliver of his soul set loose to scout the world. Should our master wake and face you in his full glory, you'll note the difference. Now that you've brought his phylactery here, he'll wake of his own accord soon and, thus, be less wrathful. One can hope," the silver-haired woman said.

"Victor, we should get out of here," Thayla said in a low whisper.

"Right, well, I think Thayla and I took a wrong turn. We're going to, um, step out." Victor took a step back, keeping the Naghelli in his field of view.

"No, no, large one," said the curly-haired woman, stepping forward, a bright, foot-long, silvery dagger in her hand.

"You have a choice to make!" a different man suddenly spoke up on the left edge of the semicircle. Victor glanced at him and saw his short silver hair, similar black attire, and the thick metal cudgel in his hand.

"What choice?" Victor and Thayla took another step back.

"Choice one: fight with us, lose the phylactery, and die. Or choice two: give us the phylactery and enjoy preeminence among the servants of the Empire."

"That right?" Victor growled, twisting his hands around Lifedrinker's handle. He cast Channel Spirit, flooding Lifedrinker with rage-attuned Energy so that she flared brightly with a crimson halo. "You'll have to try to take it, then." As he spoke, Victor also cast Inspiring Presence.

The Naghelli hissed and started to move, but they seemed to advance in slow motion as inspiration struck Victor. His globe of light was so much brighter in his inspired eyes that the shadows seemed to fall away, and the mystery surrounding the weird Ghelli-like creatures dispersed. In his new clarity of mind, they just seemed like thin, frail people that should know better than to tussle with the likes of Victor Sandoval. He couldn't help it as a chuckle rolled up out of his chest, and he stepped to the right, lifting Lifedrinker in anticipation of the first combatant to come into range.

Victor's perception might have been overly optimistic, though, and while he might have been more than ready for a normal charge, what happened next left him baffled. Each of the Naghelli exploded into a burst of shadowy black smoke, and he was left holding his axe, staring at an empty street. He looked around, confused by their apparent retreat after they'd just threatened him, and that's when he saw them darting through the shadows, just at the extremity of his light. He took a breath to bellow a challenge, but before he could speak, the darkly clad people launched into an attack, darting like liquid smoke and wielding gleaming silvery weapons.

"Victor!" Thayla had time to shout, and then the seven Naghelli were streaking through the air, dashing over the cobbles, and leaping into a furious melee with the two would-be adventurers. Victor blocked one flashing, silver blade, catching it on Lifedrinker's haft, and when the edge caught in her wood, and the Naghelli wielding it was brought up short, Victor kicked out. His boot crunched down on the attacker's thigh, and Victor felt something give. The man yelled out and stumbled back, dropping the shortsword still caught in Lifedrinker's haft.

Thayla yelped in pain, and Victor saw her gripping a wound in her thigh that pulsed thick gouts of blood through her fingers. He tried to spot the Naghelli that had delivered the injury, but suddenly something heavy smashed into his left shoulder blade, knocking him forward. These people were stronger than they looked! While he stumbled forward, he heard Thayla cry out again, and by the time he caught his balance and looked back, she was on her knees, swaying in a daze with blood sheeting down over her face from a deep, wide gash in her forehead.

Suddenly Victor remembered Yrella. He remembered how she lay on the floor of the pit, twitching, dead before her body realized it. Before Victor could think about strategy or formalize a plan, he felt hot rage-attuned Energy flooding his pathways. His heart pounded with a terrific thud that people nearby would have heard, and suddenly he was wielding Lifedrinker in one hand as a normal person would hold a hatchet.

As Thayla toppled to the side, Victor took one step, and he was standing over her fallen form, crouched and ready, staring with red, bloodshot eyes at the darting, flashing shadows that lurked outside the light. He had no words for the emotions roiling in his heart, so he just roared, brandishing Lifedrinker. His scream crashed and echoed off the stone buildings, and the Naghelli laughed in response, mocking, echoing laughter that drifted out of the shadows.

Rage and frustration filled Victor to overflowing, and his body veritably shook with the need to strike something, but deep in the root of his being was the need to stand guard over Thayla, and he refused to leave her vulnerable. He crouched over her, axe held high in his right hand, and waited for one of the mocking, slippery creatures to come within range of it. His desire for contact was answered, but not by one Naghelli. No, all of them struck at once, and suddenly Victor was surrounded by bursts of shadows as they all appeared, driving their silvery weapons at him from every angle.

Victor completely ignored the attacks. Instead, his eyes alighted upon one Naghelli that had appeared perfectly placed in the arc of his axe. While seven blades pierced or slashed him, Victor screamed and brought Lifedrinker down with enough force to shatter a boulder. Her keen, hungry edge cracked through a collarbone and then carved a two-foot trench through the Naghelli's torso. His eyes bugged out in surprise, terror, and the realization that he was dead.

As the split Naghelli fell back, a torrent of red fluid sluicing out over the cobbles, Victor roared again and grabbed hold of a spear that had pierced his abdomen, the narrow tip having slipped just beneath his armored shirt. He jerked the spear forward, driving it through his body and out his back, pulling its wielder within range of Lifedrinker. The woman panicked, let go of the haft, stepped back, and had her arm hacked off at the elbow. She shrieked and fell away, spraying hot blood over Victor's face. Victor roared with guttural laughter.

Most of his wounds were superficial, the spear through his abdomen being an exception. All the other cuts and stabs were rapidly healing in his rage, but still, the Naghelli were fast and skilled, and they kept piling on the wounds. Victor saw the woman with the severed arm kneeling up the street, watching him with hate-filled eyes. If he'd been less enraged, he might have heard her sobs or the cries of terror and horror when Victor split the first Naghelli. As it was, though, Victor saw only red and heard only the thudding of his heart urging him to destroy his enemies.

He crouched, axe lifted high, spear through his gut, and waited for the next attack. He stood that way several long moments before his fury-filled mind realized the wounded Naghelli woman was no longer staring at him, and the shadows had stopped moving. He wanted to dash into the night, hunting his foes, but something kept him still, and when he glanced down, he remembered what it was—Thayla. He had to keep them away from her. He stood, heaving for breath, and, as the immediacy of combat started to fade, he began to feel the discomfort of the length of wood jabbing out of his stomach.

With a grunt and a roar of pain, Victor drove the spear the rest of the way through himself, pulling it out of his back and flinging it to the cobbles. He pressed a hand against his rigid stomach, and as the last vestiges of his rage healed the wound, at least superficially, he fell to a knee next to Thayla and waited. He waited for the madness to leave him, he waited for his enemies to return, and he waited for the vague dread that Thayla was dead to either leave him or be proven true.

Golden motes of Energy rose from the corpse of the fallen Naghelli and surged into him, speeding things along—his rage faded, and Thayla moaned softly as her thin stream of Energy partially healed her head. Victor sighed with relief because he knew the System must consider the fight over if it was giving out Energy. His enemies had truly fled. He was still kneeling next to Thayla, so he turned to regard her. Her face was crusty with dried blood, but her eyes were alert, and she stared at Victor for a moment before comprehension animated her. "We're not dead?"

"No, I think they ran away."

"That doesn't make sense. They really wanted that phylactery. Victor! Where's your satchel?" Victor slapped a hand to his chest, feeling for the strap, and only felt his chain shirt.

"Oh, fuck no! They cut it off? I didn't notice a thing!"

"How long?" Thayla asked, sitting up. She leaned forward and retched as soon as she was upright.

"Easy, you okay?" Victor held her shoulder.

"Things are spinning a little, and my stomach's turning flips. I think it's just the blow to the head—I'll recover. We have to find that phylactery, Victor. You heard what they said!"

"About Beli . . ." He stopped himself and continued, "About, you know, the asshole in the skull? Yeah, I heard them, and then I fought with them, and I think we need to get the fuck out of here. You're not ready for these guys, Thayla." Victor didn't want to call her out like that, but, damn it, she'd been put down in just seconds by those Naghelli shitheads.

"Victor, what if he gets more powerful? What if they come into Fanwath and start another war or something?"

"What if? Look, I'm all for trying to do the right thing, but I'm not going to fucking watch them slit your throat and then have to find your daughter to tell her about her mom. I can't fucking do that, Thayla. Come on; when we get to Gelica, we can tell others about this place. I'll even come back with them. All right?" he added the last as he stood and held out a hand to help her to her feet.

She took it, and once she was on her feet and standing on trembling legs, she nodded. "You're right. I'm not ready to face them again."

"Let's go," Victor said, turning toward where they'd fought the knight and his roladii mount. He held Thayla's wrist with his left hand and Lifedrinker with his right, peering around warily as they progressed.

"Victor, you remember those children's horror stories we talked about back in the mine?"

"Yeah?"

"There are a lot of horrifying stories involving Naghelli. They're not supposed to exist anymore!"

"Well, they're tough and fast, that's for sure. They die good enough, though." Victor shrugged, picking up the pace and tugging on Thayla. They passed to the right of the roladii corpse, turning down the short side street and the forest beyond. They walked past the dead pack of zombie hounds and entered the strange forest with twisted trees and black, feathery leaves. The portal's glimmer was easy to spot in the distance, with no other lights to obscure or drown it out.

Victor hurried even more, still pulling on Thayla's wrist. He refused to let go of her because he could only imagine shadowy, quick Naghelli coming out of the shadows to take her or strike her down. Thayla was keeping up, though her breathing was ragged. Victor jogged around one last tall, looming tree, and then they were in the clearing where they'd slain the first pack of zombie hounds, and the shimmering gateway sat on the other side, between two gnarled tree trunks.

Victor stepped into the clearing, and movement from near the portal brought him up short. He stepped in front of Thayla and watched as the silver-haired female Naghelli moved out of the shadows. "I bear a message, warrior." She had eyes only for Victor, staring at him warily.

"I'm listening."

"I am Vellia, and you've slain my mate, Horol. I know he joined the battle willingly and that you fought fiercely and with honor. I thank you for giving Horol a clean death." She stood straight, pressing both her palms together in front of her chest, and bowed to Victor. Victor wondered what the hell was going on. He looked around, peering into the shadows around the clearing, but he didn't see any other Naghelli.

"Is that all? You're not going to threaten us with your master's vengeance and shit?"

"My master will most likely celebrate you. With his phylactery in hand, he'll be free to leave this realm and begin working toward our great cause again." Victor could feel Thayla growing agitated, and he knew she wanted to say or ask something, but she held herself still. Victor wasn't sure if it was fear, doubt, or respect that kept her quiet, but he knew she was feeling like shit, and he wanted to get her out.

"Sure, Vellia. I'm not cool with you guys jumping me and stealing my stuff, and I'm really not cool with the versions of your master I've met outside this place, so I bet we'll meet again. I gotta get going." Victor started walking toward her, Lifedrinker swinging menacingly in his fist and Thayla trailing behind.

"Can I know your name, warrior?" Vellia asked, stepping to the side, out of his path to the portal.

"His name is Victor, and you should mark it well," Thayla said, suddenly standing up straight.

"Victor. Yes, I agree, little Shadeni. This one is worth taking note of. Until we meet again, then, Victor."

"Yep," Victor said, giving her one last look, taking care to remember the details of her face—her thick silver brows, her long narrow nose, the bluish tint to the skin in the sockets of her dark, black eyes, and the way her lips curled in a slightly crooked smile. Victor nodded at her and then stepped into the portal, still dragging Thayla by the wrist.

Just as before, he felt the portal's cold Energy drawing him through, and then he was stepping into the dusty, ruined worship hall in the desolate village of Gel Harra. Thayla came through right behind him, and they looked at each other for a minute, and she sighed heavily.

"What a disaster. We did the opposite of what we wanted to do!"

"It is what it is, Thayla. Shit, *chica*, at least you aren't dead. I really thought you were dead for a minute!"

"Yeah, thank you, Victor. You saved my life again. I'm sure I'll never repay you, but . . ." she trailed off, her eyes distant as if she was looking for the right way to express herself.

"Hey, I'm not keeping count. What's the difference between saving someone's life once or ten times? Either way, you can't pay it back. You've saved my life a couple of times, so we both owe each other everything. Cool?"

"Cool?" she echoed, but then she smiled and said, "Yeah, cool, Victor. Cool."

"You *do* get me, don't you?" Victor reached out and pulled her into a hug, and she didn't resist at all. She felt much smaller than he'd imagined, and he realized he'd built her up in his mind because of her attitude. "You're all right, Thayla. Let's go give Tellen the bad news, then let's get going to fucking Gelica, eh?"

"Okay, Victor. I'm with you, but only because you promised me you'd deal with Belikot. You are still going to deal with him, right?"

"Yeah, of course. You think I can let some assholes steal my shit and get away with it? No, no. I'll be paying him another visit after you're safe with your kid, cool?"

"Right," she said, standing back from him with a smile. "Let's hurry; I want to see what the hunters are cooking for dinner."

"Now you're talking!" Victor followed her to the crooked door of the partially ruined building, walking through a patch of colorful light cast by the stained glass window. Thayla stepped out, and Victor was right behind her when she fell to a knee, clutching at something in her chest. She tugged at it, and Victor saw the feathers of a tiny, dart-like arrow. Thayla fell to the ground, her legs and arms convulsing as her eyes rolled back in her head.

"Thayla!" Victor cried, diving over her, hoping to protect her from whoever had shot at her. Whistling shrieks heralded the arrival of more arrows and darts, and he felt a sting in his forearm and two more in his thigh. Another hit his calf, and several more sank into his back through the rings of his vest, their narrow, round points easily piercing the armor.

Victor felt as if someone was operating a dimmer switch on the sun as darkness crept into his vision. He felt sluggish and slow, but something was bothering him. What was it? "Oh yeah, some fucking *pendejos* are shooting arrows into me!" he coughed, actually chuckling at how loopy he sounded. No, this wasn't funny—this was bad! Someone was filling him with darts! Someone had shot Thayla! A spark of heat flared in his chest at that thought, and Victor concentrated on it.

With a slow, ponderous buildup, Victor's heart thudded. It sounded like a bass drum, and suddenly his vision flared with a red heat, and the darkness fell back. Victor concentrated on that red, terrible fury in his chest, pushed more rage-attuned Energy out of his Core, and cast Berserk.

"He's not going down!" a gnat's voice called.

"Now! Throw the alchemical canister!" another deeper-voiced gnat hollered.

Victor surged to his feet, but just as he started to look around for the enemies he needed to kill, some sort of fog filled the air around him. His face felt numb, and his legs were like jelly. He sat down on his butt and laughed. What was he so angry about? Hadn't he been shot a bunch of times? Oh, the darts! Victor laughed again, a great, deep belly laugh that shook his shoulders up and down and made it hard to breathe. Why was it so funny? He didn't know, but he couldn't stop laughing, and then the darkness started to creep into his vision again, and he lay back, still chuckling between deep, slow breaths.

17

PRIORITIES

. . . take it and be grateful. You hardly had to do anything," said a gruff, hoarse voice.

"Aye, well, I could use the work if you need a wagon guard wherever you're taking 'em." This voice was wheedling and soft.

"C'mon, Da. He don't need us." A younger voice spoke up from further away. Victor strained, trying to picture where all the speakers were. He'd only been awake a few seconds, and he felt groggy, but he knew he'd been taken. He vaguely remembered the darts and gas, but even if he didn't, his hands being bound behind his back and a dark hood over his head confirmed his predicament.

Victor felt something heavy and cold on his neck, and he knew it was a collar. He felt a strange coldness emanating from it, and it took him a moment to realize it was doing something to his pathways, something to do with his Core. He turned his mind inward to look at the blazing orbs of his Energy, fearful of what he might see.

The voices continued speaking, but Victor tuned them out as he was confronted by a scene at his Core that was more puzzling than disturbing. He could see the cold Energy bands stretching from the collar into his pathways and down into his Core. He could see them wrapped around his rage-attuned Energy, subduing the blazing red sun to a barely smoldering ember. The strange thing, however, was that his inspiration-attuned Energy seemed utterly untouched. It blazed with all of its former glory, pulsing strongly at the center of his being. Could they be so stupid?

Victor grunted and scooted up against whatever they had his hands tied to. He felt bars against his shoulders and figured he was in some sort of cage. "Hey, any asshole out there that can tell me what's up?" He stretched out his legs, feeling for the extremities of his confinement, and that's when he realized his ankles were bound with something heavy that rattled as he moved. Chains?

"Ahh, my guest awakes. No, I can't quibble with you anymore, Turl. Get yourself back to Steampool and spend the coins you just earned, and put me out of your mind." Victor heard grumbling and then the sound of departing feet. A moment later, the gruff voice spoke again, this time much closer, "Not feeling too great, I wager, eh, big fella?"

"I feel pretty okay, to be honest," Victor said, and the words were true. The grogginess had faded, and he felt rather rested, if a bit cramped. He flexed his hands into fists, testing the tightness of the bonds on his wrists. The cold metal bit into his skin, but he heard it creak and strain.

"Now, bravado won't get you anywhere with me, lad. I learned a lot about you after I took the contract, and I had that collar made special. When all that rage gets bottled up, you rage casters aren't so hard to deal with, isn't that right?"

"Rage casters?" Victor's voice was flat as he tried to hold in his emotions, including a slowly building sense of amusement.

"Aye. Old Nareld heard all about your berserking down in them mines. Think you're the first Berserker to break the law? Think you're the first one old Nareld brought in? Nah, boyo. Trust me when I say I intend to get paid back for the expense of hunting you down. Had to pay for five different scryings. Had to pay an alchemist to mix up the sleeping humors. Had to pay all them locals to dose ya. Better believe I'm getting paid." The voice had come much closer, and Victor could smell the man's onion-tainted, hot breath as it permeated the cloth of his hood.

"Hey, since I'm all harmless and shit, can you take this hood off? I'd like to see the face of the man that brought me down."

"Nah, Nareld don't like having his marks know his face. What if you get set free? What if you escape from the fools paying for your capture? Nah, old Nareld don't need you coming looking."

"I mean, you already told me your name. How many bounty hunters go around calling themselves 'old Nareld?'" Victor couldn't help the chuckle that followed his words.

"You're a tough one, ain't ya? Finding humor and laughing with your Core all blocked off? Most people'd be feeling sick as a dog, like yer little friend over there."

"Is Thayla all right? Listen to me, Nareld: if you want any hope of escaping this situation with your limbs attached, you better pray she's all right."

"Oh, making threats? You're hobbled and chained, big boy. I took all your little trinkets, too. Accept your fate, lad. Don't you worry, though—Nareld was contracted to bring you both in alive, and that's what he'll do. The girl's fine, just collared and drugged."

"So, let me get this straight. Instead of putting a general control collar on me, you had one made that suppresses my rage-attuned Energy?"

"Aye, I know how you Berserkers work. It's no wonder you pulled off that mine collar."

"So the mine hired you?"

"Nah. You'll see soon enough. In a week or so, we'll be in Gelica, and I'll hand you off to Lady ap'Yensha's men, much the richer for my trouble."

"Ap'Yensha. They're one of the clans that own the mine, though, right?"

"You might be a brute, but at least you know a thing or two. Aye, that's right. Now, don't you worry; old Nareld treats his prisoners with dignity. I'll be good to you and the lady and feed ya proper. No harm's coming your way while in my care."

"That's very nice, Nareld. Now, I'd like to make a deal with you," Victor said, leaning forward.

"Oh, now, don't try to bribe me, lad. I've got all your belongings, and I'm being paid the full value of everything I turn in to ap'Yensha on top of the bounty."

"No, it's not that kind of deal. I'm going to promise not to kill you in a few minutes as long as you promise to drop this bounty and never mention Thayla or me again."

"What? Boy, I think that alchemist mixed his dose too strong. Is your mind slipping? Can't you feel your Core? The lights on the collar are glowing. I know it's working!"

"Hmm? Oh yeah, I think it works, but Nareld, I don't need rage-attuned Energy to get out of this shit." Victor knew his spells would work as long as he had Energy, and he had plenty of inspiration-attuned Energy at hand. He cast Sovereign Will, boosting his strength, and then Channel Energy, flooding his arms and shoulders with inspiration-attuned Energy.

Victor couldn't see himself, but Nareld could, and when Victor's long, cable-like muscles suddenly swelled, and his arms and shoulders began to flicker with a white-gold radiance, he backed up, gasping. A moment later, Victor jerked his hands apart, and the chain between his manacled wrists simply snapped, one of the iron links having shattered. Victor reached up and pulled the hood off his head.

Sunlight stabbed into Victor's eyes, and as he rapidly blinked his eyes, he saw that they were somewhere out on the grassy plains. Some roladii were staked nearby, munching peacefully at the yellow tufts, and Victor saw a large, gray-furred Vodkin, fumbling with a crossbow and digging around through an overfull quiver, clearly looking for a particular bolt.

The Vodkin's face was panicked, and his breathing was harsh and shallow. Victor didn't waste time, reaching up to his collar and pulling with all his might. It was tougher than the one from the mine, but it still wasn't designed to withstand the kind of force Victor was delivering, and he felt the metal start to give as he twisted.

"Stop whatever you're doing, Nareld. If you shoot me, I'm going to fucking go berserk, and I don't want to kill some old guy just trying to make a buck." Victor growled as he twisted again on the metal, stretching the straining metal another centimeter.

"Huh, huh, how . . ." Nareld was still fumbling with the crossbow, clearly panicked beyond reason. As he pulled and twisted on the collar, Victor saw that he was inside an iron cage on the flatbed of a wagon. Nareld was standing just behind the wagon, and he'd managed to knock a black, barbed bolt to his crossbow and was cranking back the string. Victor grunted and twisted, pulling with all his might, and the metal finally cracked and pulled apart.

Heat surged in his stomach as his rage-attuned Energy was suddenly unbound, and Victor had to strain to hold it back. He dropped the twisted, broken collar and growled, "Nareld. I'm not fucking joking. Put it down, or you're probably gonna die." Victor saw the older man hesitate, and that's when he cast Channel Spirit again, this time driving rage-attuned Energy into his arms and legs. He reached down, gripped the shackles at his ankles, and pulled, shattering the brittle iron chain. Then, he surged to his feet and kicked his cage door open, hopping down with a clatter of loose, broken chains.

"You could earn some points with me by giving me the key. I don't like this look," Victor said, holding up his manacled wrists. Nareld had set the crossbow down and was holding his hands out.

"Easy now, lad. Old Nareld was just doing a job. I didn't hurt ya none."

"So you're willing to take my deal?"

"Um, could ya go over it again? What was it? I, uh, don't try to stop ya, and you don't kill me?" Nareld was backing away, his black otter eyes wide and his catlike whiskers trembling as his lips worked to draw wheezing breaths.

"That's part of it, Nareld. I'd also like you to forget you ever saw us. I don't want more information about me getting back to ap'Yensha." Victor turned around slowly, looking for Thayla, and saw that she was also in the wagon, but further toward the bench, and she wasn't in a cage—just chained to a ring in the corner. "Keys, Nareld. While you're at it, give me my shit. Where's my axe?"

"Yer belongings are all up under the driver's bench."

"Keys?" Victor held out a hand, and Nareld, his furry arm trembling, reached out and deposited a brass key ring into it. There were several keys on the ring—a simple iron one, a many-toothed silvery one, and three different brass-colored ones.

"The, uh, the silver key was for your collar."

"Huh." Victor used the iron key to remove the manacle and shackle cuffs from his wrists and ankles, then he looked at Nareld with a scowl. "Do I need to tie you up or knock you out or something?"

"No! No, Victor. I promise I won't be any trouble. I ain't got the means to fight you without setting a trap. You can see that, right?"

"Hmm. Put your hands on top of your head and follow me." Victor waited for him to comply, and the furry Vodkin, somewhat comically, held his hands on top of his head, still breathing shallowly with wide, spooked eyes. Victor nodded and walked to the front of the wagon where Thayla lay. He held the keyring next to her collar, finding the correct shade of brass, then he unlocked it, slipping it from around her neck.

Victor took the collar and turned to Nareld. "You ever worn one of these? It's not fun, Nareld." He reached out and snapped the collar shut around the Vodkin's thick neck. It had been loose on Thayla, but it squeezed the extra skin and blubber around Nareld's neck, causing it to bunch in a thick roll on top of the collar. Nareld grunted and winced, muttering protestations.

". . . not necessary! I won't cause any trouble." He groaned, and his arms fell limply at his sides as his cheeks drooped and his eyes pooled with tears.

"Sucks having your Energy blocked off, doesn't it? It's even nastier than the control collars they use in the mines."

"Please! I was only working a contract! Don't leave this on me; I'll be helpless." The old hunter's pleas fell on deaf ears as Victor unlocked the chains around Thayla's wrists, lifted her out of the wagon, and set her on the grass. He hopped up to the front of the wagon and opened the top of the driver's bench, and there, beautiful as ever, sat Lifedrinker. Victor lifted her and slipped her through the loop on his belt, then he saw Gorz and pulled the amulet back on over his head.

Gorz started talking immediately, but Victor tuned him out for the moment, digging around until he found a felt pouch that clinked with the telltale sound of jewelry. He opened it and poured his and Thayla's rings into his palm. Victor glanced at Nareld and saw the Vodkin leaning against the wagon, still looking sallow and weak. "If nothing's missing, Nareld, I'll let Thayla decide if you should keep the collar on or not."

Victor slipped his rings on, then he dug around until he found his storage pouch. There were other belongings in the space under the seat, but none of the clothes, bottles, weapons, or packages of food interested Victor, and he thought it sent a clearer message to the old hunter when he left all his stuff intact: Victor didn't need his things, and he wasn't a common bandit. He jumped down from the wagon and walked over to Thayla.

She seemed at peace lying in the sunny grass, and Victor almost hated to bother her. Still, he stooped, slipped her rings onto her fingers, and gently jostled her shoulder. "Thayla. Thayla, wake up."

"Now that you've freed up her Energy, she should wake from the drugs soon." Nareld sounded weak and morose, and Victor found himself feeling sort of sorry for the guy. He shook his head and growled. What the fuck was wrong with him? This asshole was going to sell them back into slavery or, probably, something much worse. Victor sighed and sat down in the grass next to Thayla, keeping Nareld in his line of sight while he soaked in the warm sun.

"When was ap'Yensha expecting you? You have some way of communicating with her?"

"If I tell you, will you take off this damned collar?"

"I told you, that's up to Thayla. I'm sure she'll be nicer if you cooperate."

"When I took the contract, they gave me three message sheets. I already used 'em up, though."

"Message sheets?" Victor took a bottle of water out of his ring and drank it. When he put it back, he glanced through his things, making sure nothing was missing.

"Aye. I could write a message on this paper, and they'd see it. Each sheet only worked once, though." The old Vodkin sank into the grass, leaning against the wagon wheel, looking downright pathetic.

"Let me guess: you announced your success with the last one?"

"Yes. By Vod, yes! All right? Yes, I already told them I caught you. I'm ruined! Everyone will either think me a liar or a fool."

"No, not everyone. Just the assholes that hired you to come after me. Disappear, man. Go somewhere far away. I'll be much less forgiving if you and I cross paths again."

"Ungh," Thayla grunted as she worked her elbows underneath her, lifting her head. "What happened?"

"This guy tried to kidnap us. He's working for some ap'Yensha lady."

"Not just any lady, the head of their clan! Rellia ap'Yensha!" Nareld tried to sound vehement, but his weak, morose voice barely carried over the grass.

"Wow, Victor, what'd you do to that guy?" Thayla scooted up into a sitting position and glanced at him sideways, gently rubbing one of her temples.

"Nothing—just took that collar off you and put it on him."

"He collared me?" Thayla reached up and felt at her neck, a deep scowl furrowing her brow.

"Yeah, they got the drop on us, but I worked around the 'special' collar he'd made for me." Victor shrugged, and Thayla looked at him, raising an eyebrow.

"I'll explain it more when he's not around," Victor said, and Thayla nodded, still looking a bit groggy. "Anyway, he didn't really hurt us, and he's just a bounty hunter. I told him you'd decide if he keeps the collar on or not."

"Yes, he keeps it," Thayla said without hesitation.

"No, please!" The Vodkin begged, still sitting with drooping shoulders next to his wagon.

"Damn your please!" Thayla hissed. "You're part of the whole thing! Capturing and using people—none of you are innocent. I'd like to kill you here, but I know Victor won't let me. No, you can rot here or shuffle your way to a town and beg someone to help you get that off. See what it's like for a while, what you do so flippantly when you capture someone *they* tell you to!" Thayla had clambered to her feet while speaking, and she hissed the last words with pure venom.

Thayla walked over to the big Vodkin and reached out a hand. Victor wondered what she was doing, but he just watched. Nareld hesitantly held out a hand, and Thayla grabbed the wrist, hauling the man to his feet. He stood before her, sallow and sagging, with a questioning look in his big, moist eyes. Thayla didn't say anything. She just walked behind him and shoved him away from the wagon to stumble into the grassy plains.

Victor stood, bemused, watching while Thayla produced a leather flask from her ring and then started sprinkling liquid all over the wagon. "Oh, hey, Thayla, are you sure you wanna do that?" he asked as he realized she was dousing the wooden wagon with oil.

"I sure am, Victor," she growled, then she produced a spark between her thumb and forefinger, and flames started to lick through the oil in an orange-blue ripple.

"No!" Nareld moaned, sitting in the grass and watching his wagon slowly go up in flames.

"Don't whine to me, bounty hunter!" Thayla growled at him. "Do you know what the people who hired you would do to us? You're getting off easy!"

"All right, Thayla," Victor said, walking over to her. He put an arm over her shoulders and steered her toward the north. "Let's get going. This old asshole isn't going to mess with us again."

"I swear, Vodkin," Thayla said, looking back at Nareld, "If we ever meet again, you'll taste my spear." She jerked away from Victor and stalked over to the two roladii tied nearby. Victor sighed and waited while she yanked their leads off the stakes and clicked her tongue, leading them back with her. "Payment for our trouble," she hissed, looking at the collared Vodkin sitting slumped in the grass, watching his wagon burn.

Victor didn't say anything, just started walking, and Thayla followed. As they began their trek toward the road, he had a lot on his mind. What were they going to do about Belikot? His vote was to forget about him for now. Belikot had plenty to deal with—some kind of "great cause," the Naghelli, waking up from some sort of slumber. Surely he didn't have time to mess around with a couple of adventurers busy dealing with a hundred other things.

Aside from Belikot, Victor's mind was trying to wrap around a much more immediate problem: for some reason, the fucking ap'Yensha clan didn't want to let bygones be bygones. Thanks to Nareld's message, they knew Victor and Thayla were alive. Would they be willing to forget about the two of them? It didn't seem likely.

"We have to do something about ap'Yensha," Thayla said.

"Hey, are you able to read minds now?" Victor said with a laugh.

"No, but I'm sick of people treating me like property, and this bitch doesn't want to let us go. We need to deal with her, one way or another, Victor," Thayla spat, and Victor could see just how angry she still was.

"Yeah, I'm with you. I was thinking something similar, Thayla. How can you go be with your daughter if she's hiring assholes like that guy"—Victor jerked his thumb back over his shoulder—"to find you?"

"Exactly!"

"So, we head to Gelica? Is that where they are?"

"I think so—I know those families are in more than one city, but the ones dealing with the mine are probably in Gelica."

"Do we still stop by to let Tellen know about Belikot?" Victor gestured vaguely to the north.

"Yes, I think we owe him that much," Thayla replied. "What do we do about Belikot, anyway?"

"What can we do? He's going on the back burner for now. After we deal with ap'Yensha and get you somewhere safe with your daughter, I'll look into him. All right?"

"Back burner? Like on a stove? I like that one, Victor. Yes, I agree we need to focus on more immediate, more . . . living problems." She smiled, squeezed Victor's shoulder, then turned and clicked her tongue at the two roladii plodding behind her. "They're kind of sweet, the way they just followed along, no questions asked."

"Well, sweet to you, but not their owner. Poor bastard!"

"Don't you dare feel sorry for that man! How many people has he captured for people like ap'Yensha over the years? How many girls has he delivered to the mines? He received more mercy than he deserved!"

"Right, yeah. When you look at it like that, I can see why you burned his wagon." They walked in silence for a while, and suddenly something dawned on Victor, "Hey, it's not noon yet. I guess we were unconscious through the night."

"Yeah, and there's the road," Thayla said, pointing toward the horizon. Victor had to squint against the glare of the bright blue sky, but he saw she was right—a thin ribbon of brown wended across the grassy plains in the distance. They walked for a while more before Victor saw the delicate lines of white smoke rising in the far distance beyond the road, which had grown clear and wide as they drew near.

"Tellen's camp," he said, pointing to the thin, wavy white lines. Thayla nodded, and they continued on. The sun was past midday when they crossed the road, and Victor paused to look for a long while in both directions. He couldn't see any movement or sign of any civilization, and he wondered just how much traffic ever came this way. He wondered if the smart move would be to choose a direction and just keep going until they were so far away that the ap'Yensha clan couldn't be bothered to try to come for them.

"It's quiet out here," Thayla said, as if she was having similar thoughts.

"What if we found your daughter and just made a run for it? It's a big world, isn't it?"

"Yes, very big, but we'd have to travel far, indeed, to escape their reach." Thayla sighed and kicked at the road's dirt. "I'm not sure how we'll even manage this problem. If we killed all the ap'Yensha family in Gelica, there'd still be thousands of them in different towns and cities."

"I guess we need to figure out which members are concerned with us and then see if we can deal with them without getting the entire clan after us." Victor shrugged, not really sure what else to say.

"Deal with them?" Thayla asked, raising an eyebrow.

"Whatever it takes. If we have to fight, we will. If we can strike a bargain, I'll consider that, too. Though I'm not fond of their business practices . . ." Victor stopped, grasping for words, not sure exactly what he was trying to say. Finally, he continued, "Let's cross that bridge when we come to it. First, we get to Gelica, then we get some information, and then we make a plan."

"Sounds like you've already made the start of a plan, Victor." Thayla smiled and started walking over the plains toward the hunters' camp.

"You think they have any more of that bread?" Victor asked, following after her and the two plodding, snuffling roladii.

18

OLD MOTHER

Tellen himself rode out to greet Victor and Thayla as they approached the camp. He pulled up on his roladii, giving them a long, questioning look before returning Victor's called-out greeting. "Well met, Victor and Thayla. I feared something had gone wrong when you didn't return in the night."

"Yeah," Victor said, shading his eyes against the sun as he gazed up at the hunter. "Some things went wrong." Victor saw Tellen glance briefly to the left and right, and that's when he suspected something was very wrong. "What's going on, Tellen?" he asked, putting a hand just beneath Lifedrinker's head, lifting her in the leather loop ever so slightly.

"Oynalla had a vision last night. A dark surge of Energy to the south. We need to make sure you are still you, Victor." He glanced at Thayla and added, "And Thayla."

"Oh." Victor relaxed, letting his hand fall away from Lifedrinker. "That's fine. What do you need? Want us to talk to Oynalla?" Tellen visibly relaxed as he saw Victor release Lifedrinker and whistled and made a gesture with one of his hands. A dozen Shadeni clan members rose up from their hiding places among the grassy tufts and watched the trio warily, arrows nocked in their bows but not drawn back. "Jeez, you really are nervous, eh?"

"I've never seen Oynalla as upset as she was last night, Victor, not to mention the strange lights in the air—evil portents."

"Well, if it helps, I brought you some roladii," Thayla said, finally breaking her silence.

"An interesting gift to bring forth from poisonous ruins." Tellen rode forward, looking more closely at the two stocky roladii. "Bred for draft work. We can find a use for them. Thank you, Thayla."

"Yeah, they weren't from the ruins," Victor chimed in, "but Thayla earned them fair and square."

"Follow me, please, and stay calm, so you don't further alarm my people." Tellen turned and started toward the camp, maintaining a slow walking pace on his mount. He led Victor and Thayla directly to Oynalla's tent, and the old woman was sitting on a stool outside, poking at the coals of her fire. She looked up with squinting, wrinkled eyes and gestured to vacant stools and camp chairs around her firepit.

"Sit down, and Tellen, you can relax; they are themselves."

"Ancestors!" Tellen released an explosive breath and leaped off his mount, striding over to Victor and offering him his hand. "I'm sorry, Victor, but we feared the worst." Victor took his hand firmly and thumped the wiry man on the shoulder.

"Don't worry. After what we saw last night, I understand why you'd be cautious." He nodded to Thayla. "We had an awful experience, and only half of it is due to those ruins and the phylactery we brought into them. Tellen, I've done a lot of boneheaded things in my life, but walking through a mysterious portal with a death caster's phylactery is probably near the top."

"You entered a portal?" Tellen asked.

"A portal?" Oynalla crowed, chasing her words with a short cackle.

"Yeah, let me start at the beginning," Victor said, sitting down next to Thayla. He explained the portal they'd found, the strange, different version of the ruined village, and the conversation with the Naghelli.

"Naghelli?" Tellen asked with a questioning look to Oynalla.

"An ancient bloodline of the Ghelli. They thrived in darkness and fought for control of this continent during the great merging. My grandmother told me they were gone but always to keep a wary eye on the shadows." For the first time Victor could remember, the old woman didn't cackle after she spoke.

"This Belikot," Oynalla continued, "he must be a powerful death caster, indeed, to send shards of himself off in the world. It's not unheard of for powerful Energy users to split their souls in such a way, but for each shard to be so autonomous and powerful . . ." Oynalla trailed off, looking around, then said, "He is not one to be trifled with. We should move to the autumn camp, Tellen."

"Sorry for the bad news, but there's more," Victor said. "Powerful people are hunting us, and I can't stop to help deal with this Naghelli shit right now."

"There's nothing to help with," Tellen said. "We're leaving—this is a problem for the empires and armies of the world. We hunt." He shrugged as if those last two words explained everything.

"Right. I, uh, I guess I was thinking it would be cool if he could be dealt with before it became a matter for armies. You know, to avoid all the death and destruction that comes with warfare." Victor looked at Thayla as he spoke and saw her squint her eyes, but he couldn't tell if she was agreeing with him or not. She saw him looking at her and cleared her throat.

"Belikot needs to be stopped, but it's not something we can handle right now. There might be months, years, or even decades before he makes his next move, Victor. Remember what we talked about? Priorities." Thayla spoke confidently, but she wore a scowl—she wasn't happy about things.

"Yeah, we need to get to Gelica, Tellen. Sorry to dump this all on you, but it sounds like you guys will be moving on, anyway."

"Yes, but I'll post watchers on the ruins, and Oynalla can speak with spirit casters in Gelica. They'll give the word to the council, who can pass the word on to the Imperial Consul. If the Empire takes our warning seriously, they'll no doubt issue a quest for the destruction or capture of the Naghelli lurking in the ruins, Belikot included."

"Really? That makes me feel better about, you know, sort of running away," Victor said. "Hey, Oynalla, can you teach me how you communicate with other spirit casters?"

"Ha!" She cackled again, and Victor was glad to see the genuine amusement on her wrinkled, red face. "Two things you must know: the spell and the spirit caster with whom you wish to speak. I'll teach you the spell, but I can't help with the other part. Ha!"

"What about you? We know you," Thayla said, suddenly leaning forward, eyes hungry at the idea of learning a new spell.

"Oh, the fledgling wants to put her new affinity to use?" She laughed again, rocking back and forth on her stool. "Come," she said at last, gathering her breath, "you'll stay the night, and Oynalla will show you one of her grandmother's patterns. If you can copy it correctly, you'll learn."

"I have many preparations to make," Tellen said. "Victor, Thayla, I'll leave you with Oynalla. If I don't speak to you again tonight, please find me in the morning before we part ways."

"I will, Tellen, thanks." Victor smiled at the angular, lean hunter, feeling a little guilty for the lines of worry and stress that creased the red flesh around his eyes. The hunter nodded and turned, leaving Victor and Thayla with the grinning old woman.

Oynalla was staring into her coals, running her fingers along the little carved bones hanging from her leather vest's tassels. When Tellen had led away the three roladii, and Victor could no longer hear the sounds of their passage, Oynalla looked up, squinting at Victor.

"Do you still have the skull where you trapped that piece of Belikot?"

"Yeah." Victor nodded.

"Don't remove it from that storage device until you are ready to face that problem. No doubt, the greater part of the whole will want all the pieces returned. That shard will be beyond his reach so long as you keep it tucked away—he won't be able to feel it, but if he knows you have it, he might seek you another way."

"Well, that's a problem I'll have to deal with eventually." Victor shrugged. When he saw Thayla's pensive expression, he asked a question he'd been wondering about for a long time. "Is there a way to shield yourself from scrying spells?"

"Of course. You can learn spells to obscure your presence, though they require concentration. I've also seen traveling artificers selling wards, though most were fake or so weak that anyone with any strength could see past their obfuscations."

"Do you know such spells?" Thayla asked.

"Me?" Oynalla laughed again, not really a cackle, more a dry, throaty chuckle. "Oynalla has never worried 'bout people watching her. No, you'll need to seek such protections elsewhere."

"Oynalla, you're the only other spirit caster I've met. Aside from Thayla, now, I guess. Can you teach me, I mean us, about spirit affinities and Cores?"

"Hah! You see what comes of people forgetting the old ways? Each generation, even among the clans, we see fewer and fewer Spirit Cores. More and more of the pearls and gemstones—Oynalla can't teach those! Even my daughter left! Living in Persi Gables, of all places! She'll let things die out; just watch. No daughters, no sons—wasting her talent helping the rich forget their guilt and feel joy for a while."

"It's not that I didn't want to learn, Oynalla," Victor said, trying to soothe her agitation, "I was kidnapped from my world and didn't learn about my Core until I came here. No one I was with knew anything about it."

"Mmhmm, mmhmm, and you've done a nice job building it up! Good lad, you are, Victor. You even gave this one some of the spirit." She poked a bony finger into Thayla's knee. "You're worthy of learning a thing or two!" She punctuated her words with a bark of harsh, high-pitched laughter. "So, you can make courage, eh? I sensed your rage. What's your other affinity, warrior? What do you mix with rage to craft courage, hmm? Is it hope?"

"Hope? No, my other affinity is inspiration."

"Ha!" Oynalla slapped her knee. "What a boon!"

"I only had rage, at first, but some ass . . ." Victor stopped himself, cleared his throat, and continued. "A nasty guy tried to break my Core, but I managed to rebuild it. When I gathered up the fragments, half of them were resistant to my rage affinity, so I had to sort of cultivate them with a different"—he looked to the sky, trying to think of the right word—"aspect of my spirit. That's how I got the inspiration affinity."

"Tribulations like that are how tempered, powerful spirit casters are made. You should find that man and thank him." Oynalla nodded, picking up a long stick to poke around in the ashes of her firepit.

"I had entertained fantasies of finding him, though thanking him wasn't something I'd considered . . ."

"What about me, Oynalla?" Thayla asked after Victor trailed off.

"Hmm? What, girl?"

"My Core is still a Whisper Class Core, but I have a band of courage around the death-attuned Energy at the center."

"Whisper Class, hmm? Yes, not bad! A Core dwelling on the borders of the veil and the spirit. You'll never be as strong with spirit as your friend here, but much more versatile."

"The veil?" Thayla's eyes were wide with interest as she leaned forward toward the old woman, who'd grown quieter as she spoke.

"Death, girl. What did you think when you gathered up that dark Energy? Did you think it would bring you closer to the flowers and trees? To love? No, lass, your Energy is meant to draw forth and compel remnants of spirits before they slip too far away from this plane."

"I wish I'd known . . ."

"You're lucky, though," Oynalla said softly, but her voice was matter-of-fact.

"How so?"

"You've not cultivated that side of your power at all. You've not bargained with any spirits other than the one that tried to dominate you. You can cultivate your courage affinity and learn to use your death affinity for a cleaner purpose—communicating with spirits and putting them to rest, even those in the service of other death casters." As the old woman explained herself, Thayla sat back with a soft exhalation, clearly contemplating her words.

"Oynalla, can I learn other spirit affinities? Can I further split my Core?" Victor asked, filling the silence.

"Of course, but with versatility comes a cost. I can see that your two affinities are balanced nicely but consider: if you hadn't split your Core, you'd have twice as much rage Energy as you do now. If you split your Core again, you'll lose half the potency of whichever part of your Core breaks. Then there's the possibility that you don't have any other strong affinities. I imagine you found your rage easily, hmm? How about your inspiration? Did you have to dig further? There may be others, but I don't know. We have rituals, though; you could seek guidance from powerful spirits."

"Rituals?"

"Yes, boy. Weeks of preparation are required, though, and we're not near one of our places of power. Come visit me in our winter camp, maybe, hmm? Now, you want to learn to walk with your spirit? To talk to others like you?" Oynalla reached a hand to the turquoise and polished bone necklace she wore, and suddenly an ancient-looking, leather-bound sheaf of yellowed papers was in her hand. "You'll need this spell anyway if you ever attempt a spirit quest."

"Spirit. . ." Victor started to ask, but Oynalla held up a hand as if to shush him.

"Let me find this," she muttered, slowly thumbing through the thick, yellowed parchment, squinting carefully at each page as though she were trying to puzzle out a mystery scrawled there. Victor watched for a while and glanced at Thayla to see if she thought the old woman's pursed lips and squinting eyes were as funny as he did, but she was still staring into space, clearly mulling over what Oynalla had said earlier.

"Here!" Oynalla said with a bark of laughter, pulling a sheet of paper out of the leather binder. She smoothed it out atop the binder on her lap. "Pull that stool over here, please, warrior." Victor did as she asked, dragging a stool to act as a table between the three of them. Oynalla put the parchment down and turned it so that he and Thayla could see the intricate pattern depicted in delicate red and black lines.

"This is the spell?" Thayla asked.

"Aye, girl. Do you have things to write with?"

"I do! I have notebooks and a spellbook that belonged to Belikot, or at least the fragment of him that we met in the dungeon."

"You keep that tucked away for now, girl. You should spend your days and nights building up your courage attunement. When it blazes brighter than your death affinity, then you can start to dabble with those magics. Do you hear me?" Oynalla's face lost its nearly ever-present crooked grin, and she stared at Thayla until she nodded her head deeply, almost bowing to the older Shadeni.

"Yes, I understand."

"Good!" she said, and Victor sighed, relieved to see the smile come back on her face as she cackled again. "Give your large friend a notebook; you both should copy this pattern. You'll need to study and practice for a while before this spell will be yours. Might take you a few nights, might take you a year. Ha!"

"Will we know what to do when we finish the pattern? I mean, in our pathways?" Thayla asked.

"No! Start copying, and I'll explain."

"I already have a notebook, Thayla," Victor said, pulling out the one he'd taken back in the dungeon so that he could work on his courage weave. Together, he and Thayla started to scrawl out the pattern for the spell Oynalla had laid out for them. Oynalla cleared her throat and began to explain the magic while they worked.

"You must never practice this magic if you aren't secure. Lock yourself in a hidey-hole, or have a friend watch over you! Tsk! Don't ask why; I'm about to explain! When you cast this spell, your spirit will enter a plane adjacent to this one—the spirit plane. Your body will lie helpless, and you won't be aware of anything happening to it. Do you see the danger? I hope so because if you didn't, Oynalla would be wasting her time on your soft brains."

Victor grunted and kept concentrating on the delicate spiral he was currently drawing. Thayla also made a sound of assent, and Oynalla continued, "Distance on the spirit plane is different from this one. You also won't be bound by the same limits that your physical body endures. You can travel great stretches of space with just a thought, and that's how you can communicate with distant spirit casters; if they expect you or make themselves available at a certain time, you can think about them, think about moving toward them, and your spirit will make the journey in the matter of a few 'steps.'"

"So, we still walk around? As spirits?" Thayla asked.

"Oh yes, your spirit will be bound to a form similar to your physical one, simply because that's the construct your mind will be most familiar with. Experienced spirit walkers can change their form, which brings me to the next part of your lesson: beware of other spirits you meet while spirit walking."

"We might run into others?" Victor took his turn to ask a question.

"Aye, warrior, and your axe won't help you on that plane. You might meet a harmless, lost, wandering soul, or you might meet a predator—a spirit caster that feeds on those weaker than herself." Her laugh sounded ominous, and Victor glanced up from his drawing to see a distant look in her eyes. "One such tried to take me when I was younger. Oynalla bested him, though." Her laughter was deep and husky, and Victor could tell she was reliving a relished memory.

"Well, what do we do if we see someone like that?" Thayla asked.

"Run! Fool girl, hah!" Oynalla reached out and took up one of Thayla's long braids, giving it a gentle tug. "Don't pout; Oynalla is just teasing. This spell is easy to cancel; if you see danger, just end it, and your soul will rush back to your body. You must be quick, though—a true spirit hunter will have ways to bind you if you aren't."

Oynalla spoke for a while longer, but then she returned to her tent to "prepare herbs," and Victor and Thayla kept working on their copies of her ancient spell parchment. Victor was surprised when he finished his copy before Thayla was much further than halfway done. He spoke to Gorz for a while in his head while he waited for Thayla to finish, and Gorz speculated that Victor's intelligence attribute was probably higher than Thayla's.

Victor thought Gorz might be correct, but when he looked at Thayla's copy of the pattern, he saw that she was shading the lines, whorls, and weaves of the pattern far more elegantly than he had, using different colors of ink, and he said, "You're creating a work of art, there."

"Well, it's the first time someone ever let me copy something so precious. Think how old this spell is. Think about the honor of having this Old Mother share it with us. I want to save this in my spellbook for my daughter." The way Thayla said "Old Mother" was heavy with reverence, and Victor looked at his friend for a moment, realizing he'd missed something about her and the way she felt about Oynalla.

"Did you have someone like Oynalla in your family?" he asked.

"My father's mother was sort of like her. Everyone respected her, but none of us could be bothered to learn from her. When she died, a lot of our family history was lost. If I could go back in time, I'd do things differently with her."

"Ahh, yeah, I can see that. Oynalla's story about her daughter hit you kinda hard, huh?"

"I hope my daughter doesn't resent me or refuse to learn what I want to teach her, Victor. I'm afraid the damage is already done, and I've missed too much time. I hope I can help her build a Core that uses this kind of magic—it seems special, Victor. It's not like the cold, callous magic of a Sorcerer or an Elementalist. It's not like the flashy weapon skills used by many Hunters, Warriors, and Skirmishers. Spirit magic is a reflection of the caster; it's a reflection of what they are."

"Yeah, I guess so. What does that say about me, that my strongest affinity is with rage?"

"It means you've had a hard life! Victor, you're so strong—you've shown me what a spirit caster can do, and yet, I've never seen you hurt someone that didn't deserve it. Your second affinity is with inspiration! Think about that! You found inspiration when you were nothing but a slave, beaten down and nearly broken. What does *that* say about you?"

Victor opened his mouth to reply, but he couldn't find the right words, so he just sat back and looked at the pattern Oynalla had shared with them. It was beautiful and complex, and he wanted to start trying to build it with a strand of Energy in his pathways, but he felt he should wait until Oynalla told them to. He decided to sit back, study it, and wait.

Thayla smiled softly at his silence and kept doggedly working at her beautiful copy of the spell. Half an hour later, when she was finishing the last swirl, Oynalla came out of her tent as if on cue, and she carried an ornate silver tray with a pot of steaming tea and three cups. "Good, good, daughter," she said, glancing at Thayla's work. Victor saw Thayla's eyes widen at the old woman's words, and he wondered how she felt. "Daughter" was definitely a loaded term where Thayla was concerned.

Oynalla looked at Victor's copy of the spell and smiled, nodding. "This is clean and simple: a good reflection of your spirit, warrior." She handed the tray to Victor, then reached down and scooped up her spell, clearing the little stool they'd used as a table. She gestured for Victor to set the tea tray on it, and after he'd complied, she said, "Now, we'll try to spirit walk together, hmm? This tea will help focus you, and Tellen will watch over us. This is the best way to learn, children."

"Now?" Victor asked.

"No, no. First, you need to build the pattern in your pathways, and when you feel it's right, when you see your Energy accept it, and the nosy System tells you what you've done, then we'll cast it and meet on the spirit plane."

"So, you were teasing about it taking us a year?" Thayla asked.

"Yes, and I was snooping when you spoke to the warrior here. I want to meet your daughter, Thayla, and I want to help her gain a Spirit Core. Would you like that?"

"I . . ." Thayla opened her mouth to speak but then stopped, clearly at a loss for words. "I think she'd . . ." Again, she stopped, and Victor could hear the thickness in her throat and see that her eyes were welling with tears, and he looked down, self-conscious about staring when she was feeling such raw emotion.

"Hush, tut. Oynalla forgets how sensitive young people can be. Don't worry, daughter. We'll talk many times before you bring her here. I'll meet with your spirit, and we'll make plans. You want to learn, yes?" Thayla only nodded, wiping at her eyes, and Oynalla shuffled over to her and pulled her into a hug. Thayla's head came up to her collarbone, even sitting, and when Victor saw the smile on Oynalla's face and the tears streaming down Thayla's cheeks, his own eyes started to fill, and he rubbed the backs of his knuckles at them, taking a deep breath, happy to see such joy in a world that had, so far, demonstrated a great deal of the opposite.

"Better?" Oynalla asked, stroking Thayla's braids.

"I am, thank you, Old Mother." Thayla sniffed, glancing at Victor and smiling when she saw his watery eyes. "What are you crying about, you softie?"

"What? It's the smoke!" Victor laughed and looked up at the stars, and, for the first time in a long while, he felt lucky to be where he was.

19

A LOT TO LEARN

Victor painstakingly twisted his braid of inspiration Energy into the last loop of the spell pattern. Suddenly the whole thing—all the coils and whorls, all the twists and branches—seemed to solidify and glow with bright, white-gold Energy, and then a System message appeared.

*****Congratulations! You have learned the spell: Spirit Walk, Basic.*****

*****Spirit Walk, Basic: Prerequisite: any spirit-based Energy affinity. Using the fundamental, primal nature of your Energy, you send forth and sustain your soul on its essential plane of existence. The duration of this spell is dependent on your Energy stores, and no protections are granted to your soul or your physical being. Energy Cost: Minimum 50, scalable. Cooldown: Long.*****

When Victor wiped away the message and his eyes fell on his surroundings, he was startled to realize that he was standing in a strange, gray-lit twilight. He, Oynalla, and Thayla stood in a peculiar echo of the plains, with nothing but grass and starlit sky for as far as he could see in any direction. Thayla was smiling hugely, and she shimmered with faint, golden luminescence. She laughed, and her voice seemed to echo out of a deep chasm, coming oddly to Victor's ears.

He turned his gaze to Oynalla and was startled to see she wasn't an old woman any longer. She was still diminutive, but her skin was smooth, and her eyes were bright, glowing with warm, pink Energy. She laughed along with Thayla, and her old woman cackle was gone, replaced by a rich, smooth, mirthful sound that brought joy to Victor's heart.

"Oynalla, you're beautiful!" Thayla said.

"Of course! Wasn't I always?" she asked, still laughing.

"This is weird as hell," Victor said, looking around them and flexing his mouth as his words came to his ears, sounding as if a different person had spoken them.

"This is the spirit plane, and, yes, things are different here. Remnants of things made by people rarely have an echo here, so you see the world as it would be if we hadn't built upon it. No roads, no tents, and even if you stood in the middle of Gelica, only a few things would stand out of the rich, soft grass."

"I feel a cold tugging in my chest," Thayla said, suddenly putting a hand over her heart.

"You don't have enough spirit Energy to keep this spell going long, child. Let's all return—you've seen enough for your first walk, and now you know the spell. More practice will come easily. Just concentrate on the spell and end it, as you would a simple light spell." Thayla nodded, closing her eyes, and then she was gone.

"You have to watch over her, warrior. She's vulnerable while her death Energy so heavily outweighs her spirit Energy. Help her cultivate her courage. Protect her and keep the temptation of her other side at bay until she's grown stronger. Promise me!" Oynalla reached out, and her smooth, strong hands bit into Victor's wrists, where she grasped him.

"I promise, Oynalla. I want her to be safe just as much as you do."

"Good, good. It's time, warrior, let's join her. End your spell." She still held Victor's wrists while she spoke, and he nodded, closed his eyes, and concentrated on his Spirit Walk spell, willing it to end. Suddenly the cool, still air was replaced by the heat of a campfire and smoke, and the sound of camp life crashed in, banishing the silence of the spirit plane.

"That was incredible, wasn't it?" Thayla asked, smiling at him as he rapidly blinked, waving the smoke away from his face.

"Ha, you've barely scratched at the wonder of spirit walking. A good start, though, daughter. A good start." Oynalla laughed and stood, shakily leaning on her walking stick. "Now, this old woman needs some sleep. You two should also sleep, and you're welcome in my home. The dawn will bring the start of a long journey for you."

She didn't wait for them to respond, ducking into her tent, a breathy chuckle accompanying her progress. Victor looked at Thayla as the canvas flaps fell closed and said, "Yeah, it was incredible." He moved a little closer to her and said in a low voice, "Do you know how to cultivate spirit Energy?"

"Oynalla was talking to me about it before you woke up the other day. Something about focusing on the emotion that gives you the same feeling as your affinity and then drawing from the Energy it produces somehow? It seems complicated! For my old Core, I just drew the Energy in the world around me into my pathways and slowly built it up, pushing it into my Core."

"Well, lucky for me, I never learned any other way. When I just had rage-attuned Energy, I learned to focus on the memories that caused me the most anger, and then I'd examine the memory, breaking it down until I'd taken the essence of rage from it, sort of a construct that was separate from the emotion. I could study it, creating a feedback loop of rage that coursed through me, through my pathways, and into my Core. It wasn't pleasant coming up with those constructs, but I think it kind of helped me. I learned a lot about myself in those weeks."

"It sounds hard, Victor. What about your inspiration attunement?" Thayla leaned close, copying Victor's hushed tone.

"That was really different—it was like my introspection about inspiration helped me deal with my current reality. I was new to the mines, and my Core was all fucked up, so I was pretty down. I stumbled on inspiration almost by accident when I started to examine how I felt about Captain Lam. On the surface, I thought she was beautiful, but I was also terrified and in awe of her. I didn't focus on that, though. A certain image kept coming to my mind: Lam gliding down out of the darkness to smash into the beetle horde." Victor paused to gather his thoughts, looking up at the stars.

"I remembered how I'd been pretty sure we were goners. I was on my last shreds of Energy, and my body was exhausted, and then Lam came out of nowhere, crashing into the center of the horde, and I felt like I had to respond; I had to keep trying as long as she was fighting. You know what I mean? I was inspired."

"So, after you realized that, what then? You started making mental constructs about inspiration and focused on them to cultivate?"

"Exactly! I started thinking about people I admired and how they made me feel—coaches, other athletes, friends I made in the pits, but, yeah, Lam was the key."

"This is really helpful, Victor. Oynalla tried to explain this to me, but now it's all starting to make sense." Thayla nodded, her eyes unfocused as if she was picturing something.

"You have any ideas for what you might think about to cultivate courage?"

"Oh." Thayla smiled, sitting up and refocusing on Victor. "I have a few ideas." She reached out, squeezed Victor's hand with both of hers, and continued, "I'm going to work on it for a while. You can turn in if you're tired."

"Not a chance. I'll work on my cultivation drills for a while, too. Let me know if you have any more questions." Victor sat back, took up his lotus position, and began gathering Energy into his pathways, using the drill he taught himself so long ago. He started with rage, and when he felt exhausted and spent, he turned to inspiration, which felt like a vacation after the strain of confronting the demons in his memories, most of which were reflections of himself.

It didn't come as a surprise when he opened his eyes and saw the glimmer of pale light on the eastern horizon. He'd made good progress with his cultivation, and with his improved racial status and high vitality, he felt quite rested, even though he hadn't slept at all. He was happy to see that, at some point, Thayla had curled up on the woven rug and was sound asleep near the now cold firepit. Victor yawned and stood, stretching his arms up into the sky to the accompaniment of pops and cracks from his neck and spine.

"Awake already, warrior?" Oynalla pushed aside her tent flap and stepped out into the dim light, her breath puffing out in a small cloud. The predawn chill was more biting than he remembered it, and Victor, not for the first time, wondered what the seasons were like in this part of the world.

"Yeah," he said. "Oynalla, is summer almost over? What's winter like around here? Any snow?"

"Oh, autumn is upon us, warrior. You should know this, ha! Snow will find us, aye, but we've a cozy winter camp south and west of here, and I think you and Thayla will come to us there. You to visit, and Thayla to stay with her daughter. I've had a good sleep on this, and that's how it should go. Do you understand me?" Victor looked at Thayla's peaceful, sleeping face, and he nodded. She deserved a break, and he'd make sure he got her back to Oynalla.

"Yeah. Didn't you say something about moving to your autumn camp? Is that on the way to your winter camp?"

"Clever warrior! Yes, it is. Don't worry about finding us. Oynalla will look for you in the spirit realm and give you guidance. On the first day of each week, I'll wait for you at midnight—walk your spirit to me, and I can help you."

"Great, thanks, Oynalla. I'll tell Thayla."

"I heard,"Thayla said, grunting as she pushed herself up to a sitting position. "I have to pee. Get the fire going, Victor! I'll be back in a minute."

"Hey, I was about to go . . ." he trailed off as she hurried away. "Oh well. Oynalla, do you have some wood?"

"Yes, boy. Sit down, sit down. Who do you think starts my fire every day? I don't need a traveling warrior to help me with that."

When Thayla returned, Victor took his turn at the latrines, and when he returned to Oynalla's tent, Tellen was sitting across from Thayla, and they were eating some sort of porridge that Oynalla was stirring in a pot. She handed Victor a bowl when he sat down, and he ate it, listening to the conversation already in progress. The warm cereal wasn't sweet as he'd guessed, but rather buttery and salty, and it felt good in his stomach.

"Yes, our autumn camp is closer to Gelica than this one, but the winter camp is a bit further. Both are southwest of here, and the winter camp is near the Blue Deep—a forest that stretches for a thousand miles. We hunt rich game on its edges during the coldest months and never fear hunger."

"I've heard of the Blue Deep!"Thayla said. "Isn't there a Ghelli city there?"

"Oh, aye. Twilight Home, they call it, but it's hundreds of miles from our camp."

They talked for a while more about Tellen's plans, but soon it was time for Oynalla to pack her tent, and several youngsters from the clan came to help her. Victor and Thayla started to feel they were in the way, so they gathered their things, and while Victor shook Tellen's hand and promised to visit again, Thayla hugged Oynalla. He couldn't hear what she said into the old woman's ear, but both of them had tears in their eyes when they parted.

"And you, warrior. You remember what I told you. Take care." She turned, without any laughter, and ducked into her tent.

"Thank you, Tellen,"Thayla said. "We'll see you again soon, I hope."

"I'd offer you mounts, but we've lost some of our best riding roladii in the last months to boyii hounds, and I don't think you'd enjoy trying to ride the stubborn draft bulls we've got, even the ones you brought in."

"Yeah, I don't even know how to ride, to be honest," Victor said. "I suppose I should learn sometime, but I'm good with walking for now."

"We'll be fine,"Thayla said. "Thanks anyway, Tellen." After yet another handshake and goodbye, Victor and Thayla finally began to walk over the grassland toward the road, angling to the west.

"How many days to Gelica?" Victor asked, even though he'd heard it mentioned several times that it was a four- or five-day trip.

"At this pace? Five days, I bet." Thayla said.

"Well, I'm happy to go faster! How long do you think you can keep up with me?" Victor laughed, starting into a jog.

"Ugh! No, Victor! It's too early for a run. Let's walk for a while!" Thayla yelled after him. He laughed and relented, and they walked along the road, steadily putting miles between themselves and the hunters' camp as the sun climbed the eastern sky. They didn't talk much, but their silence was comfortable, and they both seemed to be in good spirits. Sometime past midmorning, Thayla said, "Victor did you sleep last night?"

"Nah, but I made some good progress on my Core. I think I'm near the next rank. Honestly, I feel just as rested from cultivating all night as I used to feel sleeping five or six hours before school."

"You went to a school?"

"Yeah, ha! I know I don't act like it, but in my world, pretty much everyone attends school up to a point."

"Some towns and cities here are like that, but in most of the bigger cities, it's just the wealthy that send their children to school. The rest of us learn from family and then through apprenticeships."

"Well, what about you? I mean, last night; did you make any progress with your courage affinity?"

"Yes!" Thayla said passionately. "Victor, it was so amazing! I did like you said: I searched my memories for emotion and then really got into them, relived them, and then made 'constructs' out of them. It took me a long time to come up with the first one, but then it got easier and easier. I have seven good courage constructs now, and when I'm done cycling through them all, I feel so exhausted but so *good*. Do you know what I mean?"

"I know exactly what you mean. When I go through my rage constructs, I feel utterly spent. My inspiration constructs don't do that, though; I feel the work I'm doing, pushing the Energy through my pathways, but mentally I feel damn good when I'm done."

"I wonder how long till my Core levels," Thayla said, kicking a round stone off the road to bounce and tumble through the yellow grass.

"Can't you feel it? I feel a pressure building and a sense that I'm going to break through."

"Yes, I think I know what you mean, but it's very different from my other Core. You know, my old Pearl Class Core. I never had any experience cultivating when I just had the death Energy, either."

"Well, that's a good thing. You want your courage Energy to outweigh your death Energy, right?"

"Yes," Thayla said, nodding.

"So, it's good you never built it up, then. You gained a lot from that dungeon orb, but I think you'll build up your courage side quickly, then you can stop worrying about what that death Energy will do to you."

"I know the Old Mother asked you to watch out for me. I feel kind of stupid—when we first fled the mine, I thought I'd be the one looking out for you."

"Eh, we look out for each other, right?" Victor shrugged. Thayla opened her mouth to say something but then held up a hand, pointing down the road. Victor followed the line of her finger and saw, far down the dirt-colored ribbon, near the horizon, a tiny black dot under a faint puff of dust that hung in the pale blue sky. "A rider?"

"I think it's a wagon," Thayla said, squinting.

"You've got good eyes," Victor held a hand to his brow, squinting, trying to see what was coming. As he watched, the black dot slowly grew and resolved into the shape of a dark brown wagon being pulled by a large, black animal. "Yeah, you're right." He looked around and saw nothing but grassy plains on either side of the road. "No point hiding, even if we could."

"No, I don't think it's a threat. That's a bundii pulling that wagon—they're strong but slow."

"Bundii? Is it like a big roladii?"

"Not exactly. They're more like birds. I think they are birds—they have dark feathers and taloned feet, but they can't fly. They're huge and strong; one of them can pull as much as three or four roladii."

"Why don't people make enchanted wagons?"

"You mean self-propelling wagons?" When Victor nodded, she continued, "In the cities, you'll see coaches and some wagons that run on Energy, but the enchantments are expensive and difficult for people with low affinity to keep powered up and running."

"Makes sense." They kept walking toward the approaching wagon, and as it drew nearer and nearer, Victor started to make out its details. It was tall, made from dark wood and dull gray metal, and he frowned when he realized there were bars built into the wood. The driver was a Cadwalli, one with long, spiraling horns coming out the sides of his head. "Do all Cadwalli grow horns eventually? I don't remember noticing them."

"No, it depends on their bloodlines and how far they've advanced their race. Looking at his clothes and that wagon, I'd say this is an old, wealthy Cadwalli, indeed." Thayla said, and Victor noticed she was leaning on her spear, holding it like a walking stick.

"You think we're in for trouble?" He loosened Lifedrinker in her loop.

"I don't know," she said with a shrug. The wagon was only about fifty yards distant now, and Victor could see the driver staring at them. He wore a dusty yellow jacket over a blue shirt, and an oversized crossbow with a complicated firing mechanism was mounted next to his seat. The Cadwalli didn't reach for it, but it was menacing, nonetheless. Victor and Thayla stood to the side of the road, and the man waved as he came a bit closer.

"Hail, travelers!" he called out. Thayla lifted a hand to wave, but Victor just watched as the wagon rolled closer, then stopped a good twenty yards away. "How's the road ahead?" The Cadwalli had a gruff, deep voice, and Victor saw he was stouter and taller than other Cadwalli he'd met, much larger than Vullu and even Fenlale. His hands glittered with gold and silver rings, and when he shifted in his seat, Victor noticed a brace of pearl-handled knives under the flap of his dusty coat.

"Road's fine," Thayla said. Victor nodded and started walking toward the wagon.

"Where you headed?" he heard himself ask, almost as if he was observing things from outside his body.

"Greatbone," the driver said.

"Quite a wagon and beast," Victor said, stopping a few feet from the giant bird. It looked very much like an overgrown ostrich. Its bulbous black eyes regarded him placidly before it dipped its head into the feed bag attached to the complicated yoke it wore.

"Thank you, stranger. This is Gzantha." The driver gestured to his enormous bird. "She's my pride and joy."

"What you hauling?" Victor started walking around the side of the bird, and he noticed the driver shift toward the crossbow.

"Criminals. Now, how about you stop acting so threatening, hmm?"

"Criminals?" Victor stopped, still a few feet from the front of the wagon and off to the side of the bird. He glanced back at Thayla, and she met his gaze evenly. He had the impression she was going to follow his lead. "I've heard that before. I suppose you're selling them to the Mining Consortium?"

"No, I don't traffic slaves. I'm selling these criminals' contracts."

"Now that *really* sounds familiar." Victor backed up a few steps so he could see the side of the wagon. It was built very solidly, with small, barred windows spaced evenly on what appeared to be two separate decks. "You mind if I look at the contracts?"

"Who are you, stranger, to ask such a thing? Are you an imperial official? If so, I'd like a look at your seal of office."

"I'm a concerned citizen. I've heard innocent people are being sold into the mines."

"My name is Karth, and I'm a legitimate broker. Mark that name, stranger; I'll not have my reputation impugned!"

"All right, Karth. We're not saying differently, but would you mind letting us see those contracts? For our peace of mind? It's just us out here, and we're not criminals." Thayla had come up behind him and spoke soothingly to the driver, clearly trying to defuse things before they got worse. "My name's Sala, and this is my friend Thengal," she continued, and Victor smiled and nodded. It was smart, he supposed, to use fake names since this guy was heading to Greatbone.

"Your friend has a dangerous look, and I don't like the tone he's taking," Karth said, straightening his jacket and frowning down at Victor.

"Sorry, Karth. I'm not a bandit, okay? Like I said, though, we've had some bad dudes bringing captured people with fake contracts to sell at the mine."

"Do you work for the mine, then?" Karth still looked skeptical, but he leaned away from his big crossbow.

"No, we're out of Steampool Vale. You been there?" Victor asked.

"Once. I usually just head back to Gelica from the mine, though." He sighed heavily, then produced a leather-bound sheaf of papers. "I have eighteen passengers, and all of their contracts are in order." He held the binder out toward Thayla. Thayla, smiling, strode forward to take it, giving the bird a wide berth. Victor watched closely, but Karth didn't do anything threatening, and when Thayla backed away with the contracts, he sat back on his seat and proceeded to file his long, black nails with something that glinted silvery in the bright sun.

Thayla brought the papers over to Victor and started flipping through the contracts. None were as shoddy and full of stricken through lines as Victor's old contract. Many of them were bordered with runes, and Thayla said, "Some of these are binding Energy contracts. Those are expensive, and I see official seals on most of them—imperial prisons." She spoke softly and faced away from Karth while Victor kept an eye on the man.

Victor backed up a few steps, and Thayla followed. In little more than a whisper, he asked her, "Does it say how old the prisoners are? I hate the idea of letting this guy deliver eighteen more victims to the mine, but are we ready to go to war with the mine right now?"

"A few of the contracts mention ages. I don't see any kids, but some only mention names, crimes, and places of origin. And, no, I don't think we're ready to go to war. We're supposed to be coming up with a plan to get the Mining Consortium to forget about us, remember?"

"Yeah." Victor thought about her words. Thayla was trying to get free of trouble so she could get her daughter—it wouldn't be right for him to start making new enemies for her. He took the sheaf of contracts and walked toward Karth. "Hey, I don't see any problems here, but let me ask you: do you have any kids in that wagon? I mean, young people screwed over by circumstance? I'm not going to steal from you, but if you do, I'll buy their contracts."

Karth's face went from a scowl to something more like a smile at Victor's words, and he said, "Lad, I'm coming from Spiral Rock Penitentiary. People don't get sent there if they haven't been mixed up in some bad stuff. You hear how quiet they're being? That's because my wagon is artificed for strength and to silence the occupants—for my protection!" Karth was the first stranger to call Victor a 'lad' or a 'kid' in a while, and it made him wonder how old the man was. If he'd advanced his race a lot, he could be ancient and still look young and healthy, at least according to what people had told Victor.

"Well, Karth. Thanks for humoring us." Victor stepped back next to Thayla and watched as the wagon driver clicked his tongue and the great bird started pulling the huge, creaking wagon down the road. "Eighteen more victims for the mine. I feel like shit not doing something." Victor spat into the dusty road.

"We can't afford the trouble right now, Victor. If you're going to help people caught up in this system, you shouldn't start with those kinds, anyway. People like Edeya I could stick my neck out for, but those in that wagon? Just glancing through the contracts, I saw murder, rape, ensorcellment, really vile stuff."

"Okay, Thayla." Victor sighed and started walking, and she fell into pace beside him. He was frustrated, mainly because he knew the contracts could be full of lies, but he had no way of discerning or proving them. "Let's pick up the pace a while, eh? I need to run off some steam." Victor started down the road at a jog, gradually increasing his pace, and Thayla followed without a word.

He really wanted to do something about the legal system in this world, or at least in Ridonne, but Victor had to admit that he really didn't know shit. What the fuck was ensorcellment? Did people convicted of terrible crimes deserve to work in a place like Greatbone?

He ran harder, pushing to a sprint and leaving Thayla in the dust. He knew for damn sure that injustice was happening—he was a prime example. He slowed, and while he waited for Thayla, he said, "I need to learn more, though. I need to learn about this empire, I need to learn about the laws and prisons, and I need to learn about the corruption. Gorz, will you start making a list of the shit I need to learn? I'm going to lose track."

"Yes, Victor. I will begin a list. Would you like me to populate it with my own observations?"

"Haha, fuck you, Gorz." Victor laughed at the cheeky amulet, and Thayla smiled as she caught up to him.

"Feeling better?"

"I guess, but Gorz just reminded me that I have a lot to learn."

"Well, that's true, but we all knew that, right?"

"*Chingado*! Both of you?"

20

BOUNTY HUNTER

On the third day of travel toward the city of Gelica, the grasslands gradually gave way to cultivated farmland, and travelers and local workers began to share the roadway with them. Victor had no idea what sorts of crops were being grown in the fields they passed through, but he enjoyed the smell of rich, irrigated soil and the blossoms on many of the rows of plants.

They didn't get much conversation from the locals they passed by—usually, just a grunted greeting and then wary glares. Thayla blamed Victor, saying he was large and strange looking to the blue and red-skinned natives, which prompted him to ask, "Why don't we see any Ghelli or Vodkin around? It's mostly Shadeni or Ardeni."

"If you think those are uncommon, good luck trying to find an Ilyathi or Onaghi. Cadwalli, though, they like to farm."

"I have no idea what you're talking about. Other than Cadwalli, I mean."

"Ilyathi and Onaghi have the same origin world as the Ghelli, though some people claim we all came from the same world and had spread to populate the four worlds around our sun. Then the System came and mashed us all back together."

"I don't get it. If the System combined all the worlds, why isn't the gravity smashing us into the ground?"

"Gravity?"

"The force pulling us to the ground . . ." Victor started to explain.

"I know what it is! I was just thinking aloud. It could have something to do with Energy or how the System structured the new world. It is enormous, but who's to say what the System did to the mass under the surface? The short answer is, I don't know."

"Well, if you know about gravity, then I bet there are scholars in this world that have studied the subject."

"Of course, but do you remember what I told you about schools? Well, my parents had other priorities."

"Understood," Victor said, lifting an arm to wave to a woman working in a nearby field. She wore a wide-brimmed hat with silky, turquoise-colored mesh hanging down from the brim. She waved back, and Victor asked, "Is that mesh on her hat to keep bugs off?"

"Yes, and the sun, I would imagine." Thayla held a hand out to block the hot orb as if to illustrate.

"Anyway, you didn't answer my question. Why so many Ardeni and Shadeni?"

"I don't know. We've always been more numerous, but I've heard Gha has many more Ghelli and their relatives living on it."

"Gha?"

"Oh, Ancestors! You know so little! Gha is a continent across the sea from Fala, far to the southeast. Before you ask, yes, Fala is the continent you're standing on."

"How many continents are there? Do you know?"

"Four major continents and many, many islands and archipelagos that are big enough to spend centuries exploring."

"Seems like we ought to be able to lose ourselves in this world if we really tried."

"Oh, I see where this is going. Yes, we might be able to flee our troubles, but we'd never be able to let our guard down. Maybe you could, but I would never feel like my daughter is safe."

"Right, no worries, Thayla. We'll try plan A first—deal with the people hunting us. Running for the hills will be a distant plan B, all right?"

"Sounds fair," she said, taking a big drink of water from one of her containers.

Victor had noticed that the road they'd been following was very gradually losing elevation. They were coming down from some high, dry grasslands into a more fertile, verdant part of the world. Around midmorning, he saw a line of blue-green trees in the distance stretching from left to right perpendicular to the road. At first, it seemed strange, this ribbon of greenery, but then he realized the trees were bordering a river and that the road was approaching a large, wooden bridge that stretched in a broad arch over the water. "Any idea what river this is?"

"No. We'll be crossing a lot of similar rivers, I think. Gelica is surrounded by rich farmland. These rivers are like tiny streams compared to the Rill Catcher—the great river Gelica is built upon."

"Rill Catcher, huh?"

"Yes, it's a river that crosses most of the continent. Many, many rivers and streams feed it."

"Huh." Victor nodded, stewing on what Thayla had told him. The world seemed huge, but he knew from conversations with people in the pits and the mine that there were ways to travel great distances quickly, making it smaller in that regard. Most cities had System Settlement Stones that the citizens had improved to the point that they allowed teleportation for a fee. He'd also heard there were airships and even people who could fly, teleport, and create portals. In other words, taking a boat across the continent didn't necessarily mean it would be difficult for someone to pursue them.

He was lost in his daydreams about flying ships as they started up the wooden bridge, and he gazed over the hand-carved railing, watching the wide river drift lazily by beneath it. They'd just reached the center of the bridge when movement caught his eye, and he looked away from the water to see a stick-thin, blue-robed, and hooded figure step to the center of the bridge, not twenty paces away from them. The person's long arms were outstretched, each holding a curved, naked shortsword.

"Patience seems to have won the day," a man's dry, raspy voice said from within the hood. Victor didn't remember pulling Lifedrinker from her loop, but she was in his hands, and he'd stepped in front of Thayla.

"Fuck off, man," he growled.

"So then. My reward will be greater should you come with me alive, but if I must deliver your heads, no doubt a quicker, quieter journey will offset my loss in revenue."

"Back up, Thayla," Victor said, glancing back the way they'd come. He couldn't believe the guy was challenging them by himself, but there was no sign of anyone else on either side of the bridge.

"No, Victor!" Thayla's spear was pointed at the blue hooded man, and she'd moved to Victor's side.

"Listen, Thayla," Victor said quickly and quietly. "I can't fight my best if I'm worried about you, and damn it, I promised the old lady I'd get you to your daughter. Please!"

"I can hear you, warrior. I like your words. A duel, is it, then? Yes, should you fight me honorably, I'll promise not to harm your friend when I bring her in." The rail-thin, lanky man bowed as he spoke, and Victor saw that his hands, gripping the sword hilts, were smooth and gray. At first, he thought they were blue and that this man was an Ardeni, but he'd never seen an Ardeni so tall, and the shade of his skin was definitely off.

"Thayla, please." Victor stepped forward again, putting Thayla behind him, and he heard her angry huff as she backed up a step.

"This isn't fair, Victor," she muttered, but he could tell she didn't want to distract him further in the face of the stranger. Victor didn't care if she was mad. He'd be damned if he was going to hold her bleeding, limp body again—not when he'd made so many promises to get her out of this mess. As he heard her backing away, he boosted his agility with Sovereign Will and began channeling rage-attuned Energy into Lifedrinker.

"That's quite a weapon, warrior," the man said as Lifedrinker began to hum and glow with a baleful red aura.

"She's thirsty," Victor growled, his throat thick with murderous intent. Hadn't this asshole just said he'd be happy to take their heads? An image of the bounty hunter holding Thayla's head, fingers gripping her hair as blood dripped to the bridge, flashed into his mind, and a deep rumble began to roll up out of Victor's chest.

The bounty hunter sketched another bow. Victor only had time to wonder if he should bow back before, in a streak of blue, flapping robes, he was under attack. Victor wasn't slow, especially with his agility boosted, and he saw the attack coming. He even had time to raise Lifedrinker to intercept one of the blades, but the other slipped under his guard, crashing into his ringed armor. The blade hit him so hard that the impact cracked and echoed over the bridge like a gunshot.

Black flecks of enamel showered up into the air between them, and Victor grunted but didn't flinch. He jerked Lifedrinker down, driving back the blade that had caught in the crook under her head, and trying to muscle her into the lanky fighter now standing right in front of him. While he strained against the other man's surprisingly strong arm, he felt a series of lightning stabs from the other sword, testing his armor and finally slipping between two rings. Liquid fire lanced under his ribs as the blade pierced his abdomen, and Victor roared in pain and fury.

As they stood interlocked, Victor slowly pushed his axe down toward the other man's neck, and the bounty hunter drove and twisted his blade into Victor's guts. Red hot fury began to boil out of Victor's Core, and before he lost himself to it, he channeled it into Project Spirit, and the red waves of his spirit rolled out of him, engulfing his attacker.

The blue-robed man jerked his head back, and his hood flopped back, revealing a strange, smooth, gray face with wide, black eyes devoid of emotion. He had wispy white hair, a flat, almost nonexistent nose, and no ears to speak of. His mouth opened in a strange, silent wail, and then he started thrashing about with his swords, completely dismissing any strategy in favor of an all-out, maniacal attack.

Victor felt better having the sword removed from his guts, but the wild, hacking attacks of the bounty hunter were still difficult to avoid or block. As he backed away, trying to put Lifedrinker between himself and the chopping, slashing shortswords, he took several deep gashes to his forearms. Whipping Lifedrinker in savage arcs to hold the frenzied attacker at bay, he cast Inspiring Presence.

As always, things clarified in his mind when the spell took hold—the swords seemed a lot shorter and their wild, hacking trajectories a lot more predictable. Victor's breathing steadied, and he began to dance with the enraged hunter. He stepped forward as a blade whipped by, snapping Lifedrinker forward to smash her heavy head into the hunter's smooth, gray face. As she cracked into him, the bounty hunter's chin jerked up, and Victor stepped forward with a devastating kick, driving his boot into the blue-robed man's lanky knee.

Victor knew he had to weigh more than three hundred pounds these days, and he could kick harder than probably anyone on Earth. Thus, he wasn't surprised when the sound that followed his boot meeting the man's long, extended leg was a resounding, wet crack. The bounty hunter's scream echoed over the bridge, and his wild, frenzied sword swings came to a halt as he stumbled back and fell to the broad, dry planks.

Victor leaped forward, bringing Lifedrinker down with a two-handed overhead swing, and was utterly stunned when she ripped into the bridge timber, not his opponent. He jerked her out of the wood and spun, looking for the bounty hunter. As he turned toward where Thayla stood, he saw the man, still lying on the bridge, but tipping a small vial to his gray lips.

As Victor charged at him again, the man tossed aside the empty bottle and leaped to his feet, dancing back nimbly from Victor's wild cleave.

"Stronger than the reports indicated, warrior," he rasped, darting in, stabbing at Victor's left flank. Thus far, adrenaline and Energy had kept Victor ignorant of his condition, but he couldn't help noting the thick ribbon of bright red blood that followed him as he danced away from the hunter's attack. The center of the bridge was painted with his blood, and he knew that the stab he'd taken at the outset of the battle had to be taking a toll. Still, he felt strong, and with his agility boosted and Inspiring Presence active, he managed to avoid any significant injuries from the hunter's onslaught.

Vaguely, as he and the hunter danced, stabbing, parrying, hacking, dodging, and even tumbling, Victor was aware of Thayla watching with a worried expression and gripping her spear like a rope keeping her from falling off a cliff. A small corner of Victor's mind, not fully occupied with fighting the bounty hunter, knew she was worried, but he wasn't—not yet. He'd wanted to beat the hunter without going berserk, but he knew he still had that card. Still, he held back; he wanted to see everything this man had before he played his ace. So they danced, and Victor bled, and the man began to grow ever so slightly slower.

"Your vitality must be prodigious, warrior. I didn't want to resort to this, but I fear you were more than I anticipated," the man said, stepping back, holding his blades out in a guard position. Victor didn't reply; he simply strode forward, lifting Lifedrinker for a heavy cleave. His rage Energy was starting to seep into his pathways, and he had only one thought as the man spoke: he'd smash those fucking swords to pieces. Suddenly the man's black eyes flared with red Energy, and matching red coils detached from his outstretched swords, flopping through the air between them and whipping into Victor.

Victor jerked Lifedrinker at the weird ropes of red Energy, trying to knock them aside, but they wrapped around his axe unharmed and rippled up along his arms, and then Victor felt himself being pulled, almost as if he were bound to a rack. His arms were jerked to the side, and though he held onto Lifedrinker with his right hand, he couldn't swing her. He looked to his left and right and saw that those red coils had fully wrapped around his wrists and stretched into the sky as if they were anchored there. He was bound.

"Sorry to resort to spells, warrior, but when I saw that you'd gone berserk, I knew I had to bind you until it wore off," the man said, his raspy voice wheezing from exertion. Victor didn't respond, but Thayla did, barking a short laugh. "Something funny, Shadeni?" the man asked, turning so he could keep Victor and Thayla both in his view. "Will you be laughing when I disembowel your friend here?"

"Actually, yes. You think he's berserk?" Thayla laughed again. The hunter's round, black eyes seemed to grow wider, and he turned away from Thayla, slashing a sword toward Victor's midriff, apparently keen on making good his promise to disembowel him. His response was a second too late, though. Victor had cast Berserk while Thayla was speaking, and as his vision darkened, shading the world in a bloody fog, he dimly felt the hunter's sword cleave into his left hip.

As his flesh knitted and fury filled his mind, he tried to smash the little man in front of him, but his hand wouldn't move. If being cut angered him, having something hold his arm when he was trying to hack at an enemy caused his rage to boil up out of his gut in a wave of hot fury that roiled out of his throat in a terrible, ear-shattering roar. He jerked his arms, and his shoulders bunched with the effort, muscles standing out like cords of knotted cables, and then something gave.

The hunter stumbled to a knee, holding a hand up to his head, and Lifedrinker sang through the air, splitting the top of his head like a cleaver through an apple. Victor tugged the sword, still jutting from his hip bone, and, in his rage, drove it through the bounty hunter's body, pinning it to the bridge. He stood, heaving, hunched over his dead enemy, and glared around.

In his red haze, he saw Thayla, and though a large part of him wanted to leap at her, give her a taste of his fury, another part of him said, "*No! Not this one,*" and he growled and paced in a circle, seeking something else to vent his rage upon. Before he had a chance to act or calm down, though, a surge of Energy entered him, so thick and rich that it lifted him from the bridge and instantly cooled his boiling anger. Euphoria filled him, and System messages came into his vision.

*****Congratulations! You have achieved Level 29 Herald of Carnage, gained 10 will and 8 strength, and have 10 attribute points to allocate.*****

*****Congratulations! You have learned the spell: Berserk, Advanced.*****

*****Berserk, Advanced: Prerequisite: Affinity, Rage. You double your strength and speed for a short while, losing yourself in the glory of combat. Your body becomes more resilient, and you benefit from rapid regeneration during the duration, though you'll lose all sense of self-preservation. Your powerful will and experience with rage allow you to retain some**

self-control while this spell is active. Energy Cost: Minimum 100, scalable. Cooldown: Long.***

When he fell back to the bridge, his thoughts were his own again, and he saw Thayla standing near the corpse of the bounty hunter. She looked at him and frowned. "That wasn't fair to me, Victor." At first, he thought she was talking about how he'd just gained some Energy and a level, but he knew Thayla didn't think that way, so he revised his response.

"I know it's not fair, but Thayla, you realize you can't take the kind of beating I can, right? Look what that asshole did to my armor. Do you think you'd live through a cut like that?" Victor gestured to the rent in his black-ringed armor and all the shiny links that had lost their magical enamel. He hoped the shirt could recover from the damage—it was supposed to be self-repairing.

"No, but I'm not a damsel in distress, either! I deserve to stand up for myself! I have a spear, and I'm fast—he might never have landed a hit!"

"Well." Victor wanted to argue with her. He wanted to tell her he was faster than she was when he boosted his agility, but he decided it wasn't worth "winning" this argument. "Look, I might have been wrong. I don't know. All I know is that when you nearly died to those Naghelli, it wrecked me. I've got too much invested in seeing you back with your daughter. Like I said, I know it's not fair, but if I can help it, I'll never hold your bleeding body while struggling with the idea that I need to find your daughter, alone, to tell her about her mom. Not again. You can hate me for it if you want."

"It's not fair, but I appreciate you, Victor," Thayla said, kneeling to look through the corpse of the bounty hunter. "By the way, this guy was an Ilyathi. If I'm being honest, he would have destroyed me—I think he was around Tier Four; you're overpowered, Victor."

"Overpowered? Is that how you describe my amazing talent?" He stepped closer and watched while Thayla checked the robed man's pockets and slipped an ornate, serpent-shaped ring off his finger. She flicked the ring up to him, and he caught it.

"Sure, you're talented, but you've also got the strongest combination of abilities I've ever seen. Well, maybe other than Lam. Ancestors! You should have seen how you looked when you went berserk—like a hulking titan. That bounty hunter didn't realize what he'd signed up for, that's for sure." She picked up the sword that wasn't jammed a foot into the bridge and examined it. "This is worth a lot of money, Victor. Both of these swords are if we can get the other one free. They'll fetch a pretty price in town if you don't want them. Anything in the ring?"

Victor bonded with the ring and let his inner eye drift to its contents, listing off what he saw to Thayla. "Some food—like a few dozen bowls of soup, lots of wine, water, and bread. Six potion bottles like the one he drank to fix his knee. Um, some more robes in different colors, a pair of boots, a bow with some arrows, and more than a thousand Energy beads." Victor leaned down and yanked the other sword out of the bridge and body. "You keep one of the swords," he said, stowing the one he held into his ring.

"No, they're a set, Victor. You'll get a lot more for them together." She held the other sword out to him, and he took it, figuring he'd share the money with her when he off-loaded them. "I know you've been busy fighting and all, but there's a wagon coming, about a mile up the road."

"Right," Victor said, picking up the bounty hunter's body and tossing it over the bridge.

"Victor!" Thayla said, aghast.

"What?"

"I don't know. I mean . . . oh, never mind. We could have put him in a storage ring and buried him or something." She sighed and started walking down the far side of the bridge.

"Sorry, Thayla. I wasn't thinking." Victor walked beside her, poking at the tear in his chain shirt, pleased to see that it felt a little smaller.

"Oh, it doesn't matter. Fish need to eat, too, right? It's not like he was a friend or even a good guy."

"Yeah, he started it, right?" Victor punched at Thayla's shoulder playfully, trying to get a smile out of her, but she was stoically serious, allowing him to jostle her without a word. "Hey, you still mad I fought him alone?"

"No, I'm just worried. That guy wasn't cheap and wasn't some old, wily hunter trying to catch a big score. That was a real killer." Her eyes were focused down the road on the wagon coming their way. Victor could see it was a farmer; the wagon was piled high with green hay or alfalfa or something.

"Yeah, well, another day, and we'll be in the city. Job one, we'll get something to hide us from scrying spells."

"Right, and then we need to find a place to lay low while I use that stone Lam gave me. She might be able to help us figure out who's responsible for the bounty on our heads. I mean the specific members of the ap'Yensha clan."

Victor snapped his fingers and said, "You've been thinking about this plan without me?" He'd completely forgotten about the stone Lam had given Thayla.

"Not really. I figured that much was common sense." Finally, she looked at him with a smile, and he laughed.

"So, you really think that guy was Tier Four, huh?"

"Well, I'm not sure, but the Energy he gave off was tinged with a lot of purple. That's a pretty good sign." They'd left the bridge behind, and, as the wagon piled with green grass passed them by, she waved at the driver, a short Ardeni woman in a pair of yellow overalls.

"Ho, travelers, how's the road ahead? I've a few miles yet to take this hay!" She had a bright, cheerful voice, and Victor was quick to wave back and reply.

"Pretty smooth back the way we came. How's the road where you came from?"

"Lovely! What a day! Doesn't the sun feel good? Soak it up because autumn's coming fast."

"How far's Gelica?" Thayla asked.

"You could get there tomorrow by the end of the day if you hurry. I'd stop at the Red Roladii, though—you're only an hour or two out, and they have the best brewery this side of the Rill Catcher."

"Oh really?" Victor asked.

"Yep! I stayed there last night—got so drunk I didn't get on the road till noon! My dad's going to have my hide!" She laughed and gave the roladii pulling her wagon a little switch with the reins and started rolling again. "Good travels!" she called as she passed them.

"Well? What do you say? A night at the Red Roladii, then hit Gelica tomorrow?" He draped an arm over Thayla's shoulders and started walking. She leaned into him for a minute but then pushed his arm off.

"You're too damn heavy to be leaning on people, Victor," she said, but her words were softened by the smile on her face and a poke in the ribs with her elbow.

21

THE RED ROLADII

The Red Roladii was a sprawling complex that covered three corners of a crossroads. The tavern sat at the northeast corner. A covered wooden bridge led from it to the three-story inn on the southeast corner, and across the other road was a stable bigger than any of the buildings Victor had seen in Steampool. "Big fuckin' place."

"Yeah, I think this crossroad leads south to Persi Gables and then northeast toward the capital."

"Of Ridonne?"

"Yep." Thayla spat into the dust, and Victor couldn't tell if she was saying something about the empire or if a bug had flown into her mouth.

"Looks busy," Victor said, watching the stable hands rushing around with buckets, rakes, and brushes and the people moving between the various buildings. The surrounding acreage was all farmland, and the air was rich and smelled alternately fresh or like manure, depending on the wind. "Still wanna stay? I could use a hot meal and a shower."

"They probably only have baths," Thayla said. "Yes, I could use a damn break, too. Let's hope we don't have another friend waiting for us here."

"Yeah, I wish I could blend in better." Victor lifted Lifedrinker a couple of inches, then thumped her back down in the leather ring on his belt.

"Not likely someone will outright attack us surrounded by so many people. We'll have a chance to talk or run. The mines won't expect you to be as strong as you are, Victor. That Ilyathi at the bridge . . . he was not expecting to struggle against you, let alone die. What I'm saying is, if some bounty hunters are lurking around this tavern, hopefully we can make them back down."

"Right, well, let's go." Victor started walking again, waving to the field workers tending grapes or something like them on the vines in the nearby field.

"Too bad you're not red," Thayla said suddenly. "No one would mess with a Shadeni your size."

"Yeah, too bad." Victor laughed and continued, "Too bad I'm not furry, then you could say I was an ugly Vodkin."

"Ha!" Thayla burst into laughter, "You would be an ugly Vodkin! Especially your eyes—they're not supposed to be honey-colored. Where are your shiny, black, tearful marbles?"

"Tearful marbles? You should be a poet, Thayla." Victor snorted.

"What makes you think I'm not? I have a journal full of poems."

"Prove it!" Victor said, eyes suddenly wide at the idea. Thayla just snickered, though, and he said, "Tearful marbles! I know a guy named Ponda you should meet. If you told him his eyes were like tearful marbles, he'd probably twist your head off."

"Ponda? Was he in the mine?"

"No, he worked for the asshole that made me fight in the pits. He wasn't really that bad a guy, all things considered. You know, in my memory, he was huge and impossibly tough, but I think he was only Tier Two, maybe Tier Three."

"You've probably changed so much that he wouldn't recognize you," Thayla said.

"We'll see. I'm pretty sure I'm the only human that's been to Persi Gables. When I head back that way, I'll be sure to drop in and say hi."

"Then you can spirit walk to me and let me know if they recognized you," Thayla said with a chuckle. They'd spent a lot of time over the last couple of days talking about how they'd use the Spirit Walk spell to stay in touch. Thayla had been diligently working on cultivating her courage-attuned Energy, and they'd taken turns watching over each other while they practiced the spell each night before sleep.

They'd only spent a few minutes each time in the spirit plane. That was all Thayla could manage anyway, but she had increased the duration of her walk significantly since their first visit with Oynalla. Victor was confident he'd be able to find Thayla on the spirit plane fairly quickly, leaving them plenty of time to gossip.

"Travelers," said an Ardeni man leading a roladii past in the opposite direction. "How's the road ahead?"

"It's calm, sir," Thayla said, nodding.

Victor eyed the man as he went by, suspicious of every traveler, thanks to the bounty hunter on the bridge. The man nodded to him and clicked his tongue, pushing his animal into a faster pace. Thayla gave Victor a sidelong glance.

"You scared that guy," she said.

"Well, it's a dangerous world—he should be a little scared." Victor shrugged and kept walking. Soon they were walking up the wooden steps leading to the deck in front of the inn, elbow to elbow with other travelers, and Victor was forced to relax. However, he still held one hand just under Lifedrinker's axe head, her weight comforting, as he lifted her an inch or so out of her loop, letting her drop back with a satisfying *thunk*. They stepped through the propped open doorway, and Victor took in the common room of the Red Roladii.

A large fireplace dominated one wall, and several groupings of couches and comfortable-looking leather chairs were arrayed around the wide, high-ceilinged space. The front counter was long, and three people stood behind it, seeing to the needs of the guests. The outside of the inn had been weatherworn, perhaps in need of paint or stain, but the inside was clean and the woodwork polished.

Thayla walked to the counter, and Victor followed behind, keeping a wary eye out, watching the other patrons, and trying to guess their intentions. Most of them avoided eye contact with him, and a few even moved a few steps farther away. "We'd like a room," Thayla said when a young Ardeni woman with bright coppery hair greeted her.

"You're in luck! I have a few vacancies. We have beds in the shared dorm for two beads a night, and we have private rooms from four up to our more spacious rooms with bathing facilities for seven."

"It seems really steep, but we'll take one with a bath." Thayla drummed her fingers on the counter, frowning.

"You'll get two meal vouchers for the tavern, and of course, stable fees are included. We also have a laundry service included, though you should know our cleaning staff makes a living from gratuities." The woman seemed a little defensive about the price, and Victor didn't know enough about the economy of this world to know if the price was exorbitant.

"I got it," Victor said, producing a handful of beads. He dropped four attuned beads on the counter. "That cover it?"

"Yes, sir. I have a corner room on the second floor with a sitting area and a bath. Could I get your name?"

"Alia and Tornic of Steampool," Thayla said. Victor managed to keep his face neutral, or at least he thought he did, and he nodded.

"Very good," the young woman said, writing in a leather-bound ledger with a long, faintly shimmering quill. "We'll need you to be out of the room by noon, though if you choose to stay longer, you just need to let me know. Will that be all right?" She turned and opened a cabinet on the wall behind her, withdrawing a large, shiny brass key. She laid it on the counter in front of Thayla.

"Yes, that's fine, thanks." Thayla picked up the key and nodded to Victor, "Come on, Tornic."

"Nice to meet you, miss, um . . ." Victor trailed off, trying to get the woman to tell him her name.

"My apologies! I'm Ulla. Enjoy your stay!" Victor smiled, nodded, and followed after Thayla.

"Really? Tornic?" he asked as they climbed the wooden stairs to the second level.

"What's wrong with Tornic? That's my uncle's name!"

Victor just grunted in response, following Thayla down the hallway to the end. Their room was on the right, and when Thayla opened the door, he saw bright sunlight coming through the west-facing windows. "Nice sunset view," he said. His eyes fell to the rest of the room, and he realized there was just one fairly large bed. "Um . . ."

"What?"

"Well, I mean, there's only one bed. I didn't think about it. Don't worry; I got the floor. It's not like we've had comfortable beds up till now."

"Don't be an idiot. There's plenty of room for us both on that bed. Just keep your hands to yourself." Thayla snorted as she moved to inspect the big brass bathtub. Victor shrugged and moved into the room. Just as the girl had promised, a couch, chair, and table were arranged in front of the window. A big trunk sat at the foot of the bed, and Victor wondered how much use it got, seeing as dimensional containers seemed to be pretty common.

The tub was behind a standing, paneled screen, not in its own room, and as Thayla twisted the tap, he heard water pour forth. "At least we don't have to ask for water to be brought up," she said.

"Cool. We going to get cleaned up before we get some food?"

"I sure am. Um, you sit over there. I'll go first," Thayla said, pointing to the chair by the window. She stepped behind the screen and started pulling off her boots without waiting for Victor to move. He and Thayla had spent a lot of time together over the last weeks, so it wasn't as if Victor hadn't seen her in all sorts of compromising positions, but the idea of seeing her get into a bathtub was different somehow. He quickly stepped over to the window and sat down, his back to the screen hiding the tub, and looked out at the people milling about at the crossroads.

It looked as though people were heading to the tavern from the surrounding countryside—farmers and field workers, he guessed. He thought he could hear music coming from the tavern, and as the sun sank behind the horizon, he saw the bright lights in the windows, and his stomach rumbled. "How much longer you gonna soak in there?" he asked loudly.

"I'm getting out. Relax!" Thayla said.

"I'm hungry. Let's go, and I can clean up when we get back."

"No, Victor! You stink, and I don't want to ruin this wonderful soapy smell by catching a whiff of you every few breaths."

"Oh, jeez! All right, well, come on, get dressed. I want to get going. Victor stood and stared at the partition, waiting for her to emerge. Thayla harumphed and threw a towel over the top, hanging it to dry, then she stepped around, another towel wrapped around her head, and wearing her usual leather pants with a soft blue blouse Victor had never seen. "Where you been hiding that shirt all this time?"

"This is not an adventuring shirt! Why would I wear it out on the road?"

"Huh," Victor said, stepping past her to start undressing for the bath. He could hear it draining, and as soon as it was empty, he closed the stopper and turned on the water again. Then he finished taking off his armored shirt and pants, tossing them atop his boots. "I need to get my socks and underwear cleaned. I mean, my socks are all fucking stiff."

"Not something I wanted to know about you, Victor." Thayla chuckled. "I have some socks you can borrow. My underwear won't fit you, though." She laughed again, louder this time.

"I still have a pair that's, well, mostly clean." Victor laughed too. "I'll just go commando till I get some laundry done."

"Commando?"

"Never mind." Victor sank into the hot water and saw the little shelf of soaps Thayla had been talking about. He started scrubbing himself, washing off a week of grime and road dust. Thayla, to her credit, was a lot more patient with Victor than he had been with her. As soon as he sank into the hot water after rinsing his face and hair off, he felt like dozing, and he might very well have done so because when he sat up, the water was only lukewarm.

Victor stood and dried off, then he put on his pants and armored shirt, still clean and remarkably whole. In Victor's opinion, whoever had enchanted the pants deserved a medal, because he'd taken dozens of cuts and stabs to the legs, liberally soaking them in blood and grime. Yet they still felt whole, and not even an unpleasant odor lingered. "I need to buy some casual shirts, but I guess it's good to wear armor at dinner when people are out for your blood," he said, stepping around the partition.

Thayla didn't respond because she was snoozing on the bed, completely oblivious. Victor walked over to the bed and grabbed Thayla's big toe, giving it a squeeze. Thayla's eyes shot open, and she leaped out of bed with a howl. "What the shit, Victor?"

"I'm hungry! Where're those socks you promised me?" Victor laughed, backing away and holding his hands up in defense.

"You wait till I wake you up next time, my friend." Thayla produced a pair of socks and threw them at him. They were small but made of something like wool and stretched over his big feet passably well. When the two of them had their shoes on, and they'd collected his dirty laundry to drop off for cleaning, they headed downstairs and then out, through the crowd, into the evening air.

They crossed the street to the tavern, and as they walked in, Victor thought it looked like a cross between a cafeteria and a Renaissance festival. Rectangular wooden tables filled the ample space, and most of them had a patron or five sitting at them. A stage dominated one wall, and musicians were setting up to perform while Victor and Thayla looked around for an open pair of seats.

There had to be a dozen tavern hands bustling around the place, all wearing matching red aprons. One, a thin, lanky Shadeni, brushed past Victor with a tray of frothy mugs and said, "Pick a seat, please. Keep the aisles clear!"

"Right," Victor muttered, putting a hand on Thayla's shoulder and leading her over to a table with three dusty field workers already deep into their ale mugs. The table was long and had benches, not chairs, and when Victor sat on the far end of one of the benches, the other end bounced up a bit. The fieldworker sitting down there, mid-drink, sloshed beer onto his face. His friends laughed uproariously, and Thayla snickered at Victor's abashed look.

"Thanks! I meant to wash my face," the man laughed, holding his mug up in salute to Victor.

"My bad," Victor said, relieved at the good humor.

"Relax, Victor," Thayla said. "These people are all drunk and here for a good time. Look at the door and in the corners. See those burly men and women?" Victor followed her gaze, and sure enough, several large, intimidating people stood around, eyeing the crowd carefully. "My guess is that the owner of this place doesn't tolerate violence. Those people are here to keep the peace."

"Bouncers," Victor said.

"Exactly." Thayla waved at one of the servers, and he came over after depositing a bunch of mugs at a nearby table.

"Ale? Something stronger?" he asked as he stepped up.

"Two of those big mugs. You have something cold on tap?" Thayla asked.

"Yeah, a stout and a pale ale."

"The pale, then. We're hungry too," Thayla said, nodding to Victor.

"We've got pork sausages, fried greens, fresh bread, and a potato mash."

"Perfect," Victor said.

"Which part?" The young man asked.

"All of it. We'll take a serving of everything."

"Right, okay, I'll be back soon as I can." He turned and hurried off to another table where a burly Vodkin was hollering for service.

"Pork?" Victor asked, looking at Thayla.

"Yeah?"

"Well, I never asked what kind of meat was in the sausages we got in the mines, but I didn't know there were pigs in this world."

"Oh, definitely! Where do you think bacon comes from?"

"I wouldn't know—they don't generally feed slaves bacon." Victor shrugged. "I guess it's good to know, though. In fact, I'm salivating thinking about it."

"Oh, I thought that was just your usual drool . . ."

"The hell? You're getting meaner the closer we get to civilization!"

"I'm not getting meaner. I'm just getting more comfortable with you; when I insult you, it's a compliment. Haven't you figured that out yet?" Thayla's eyes were bright over her red cheeks, and her smile was infectious.

"All right, well, I like that you're in a good mood." Just then, the band started tuning their instruments, and the crowd got louder, trying to keep their conversations going over the noise. Victor liked the raucous atmosphere, feeling anonymous in the noisy gathering. "You think we'll get to Gelica tomorrow?"

"Yes!" Thayla said, almost shouting to be heard. The server arrived with their mugs of ale, and Victor tossed him an attuned Energy bead. He nodded and stepped away, and Victor picked up his mug—it had to have more than forty ounces of beer in it. He held it out toward Thayla, waiting for her to pick up her own.

"To getting the fuck out of deep pits, dungeons, and collars!"

"To getting out of trouble," Thayla said, grinning and crashing her mug into his. Beer sloshed onto the table, but they both just laughed and took a long pull of the cold, frothy beer.

When the music started, it reminded Victor of the girl who sang at the bar in Steampool, and he wondered if there were genres of music in this world. "There have to be," he said to himself.

"What?"

"This band reminds me of the singer I heard in Steampool. Is there a name for this kind of music?"

"Sha'nel—it's like folk music. Ardeni and Shadeni have a few variations of it, but most of the songs are really old. I'm sure they've changed and evolved over the years, but some of them tell stories of things that happened before the worlds were joined."

"I like it. I like the string instruments, and the lyrics are catchy, even if I have no clue what they're singing about."

"Yeah, people in taverns generally love this kind of music. It evokes a lot of emotion if you let it, but it's also nice in the background if you don't pay attention." Thayla took another long pull of her beer, and the server returned with a tray of steaming food.

Victor understood why the man had been a little surprised by his order—each dish might have fed a large, hungry man. They were given a plump loaf of warm bread that steamed when Thayla pulled off a hunk, a pot of fresh-churned butter, a big bowl of fragrant, garlicky greens with bits of bacon mixed in, a platter of long, plump sausages, still sizzling from the pan, and another bowl of lumpy mashed potatoes with flecks of herbs sprinkled on top.

As he set down the last dish, the server met eyes with Victor and held up two fingers. Victor nodded and handed him three Energy beads. Thayla saw him paying and said, "Hey, don't we get a meal on the house for staying at the inn?"

"Sure, but this is more like four meals," the server replied, shrugging. Thayla laughed and nodded.

"Okay, two more beers when you come back around, please!"

Victor and Thayla ate and drank, listening to music for hours. The road and their troubles were largely forgotten in the pleasant interlude. It took a few big beers before Victor's large, robust body started to feel the effect. A warm buzz suffused him, and he laughed even more easily, clapped along with the songs, and felt genuine, deep pleasure to see Thayla doing the same. He'd grown very fond of her through their struggles and was happy beyond normal reason, at least in his experience, to see her enjoying herself.

"I think this beer is making me mushy," he said during a break between songs.

"What you mean?" Thayla asked, slurring her words slightly.

"I think I'm closer to you than anyone I've known. Except for my *abuelos*."

"What?" Thayla looked alarmed.

"Relax, I'm not trying to hit on you, but I really fucking care about you. You know what I mean?" He leaned forward, trying to display his earnestness.

"Victor, you're drunk. I appreciate the sentiment, though. You know what it tells me, though? You've had a hard life! If I'm that important to you, what does that say about the other people in your life? I don't mean here, but back in your home!"

"My aunties and uncles . . . pfft! They always judged me because of my mom. My cousins weren't close to me, either. My friends were mostly fucking fake. Even my girlfriends—none of those people went through anything *real* with me. You know what I mean?"

"Victor." Thayla reached forward to grab one of his hands in hers. "I know the alcohol is talking, but I also know your words are coming from the heart. You mean a lot to me too, and you better believe I know what you're talking about regarding fake relationships."

Victor felt his eyes start to well from the emotion, and he laughed at himself. "God, I am drunk!"

"Come on, let's get back to the room, but put a meaner face on, please. I don't want anyone getting any ideas." The tavern was still rowdy and loud, and Victor nodded, shaking his head to try to focus.

"I'm good, don't worry," he said, standing up, pushing the entire bench back with three other men sitting on his side. He stood and looked at the others sheepishly. "Sorry, guys." He stretched, getting some blood flowing in muscles that had been hunched over a table for hours, then he started walking for the door. Thayla followed, a hand on his shoulder, so they didn't get jostled apart by the busy room.

When they stepped outside, the cool night air felt as good as dipping his head in a bucket of water for clearing the fogginess out of his brain; his senses sharpened up, and he took a deep, steadying breath, glancing back to see Thayla doing the same. He nodded to her, and they started down the steps, walking under the covered walkway toward the inn. "Hey, is there a second story in the tavern? Holy shit, that place does some serious business," Victor said as he realized he hadn't seen where the walkway led out from the tavern.

"I guess so," Thayla said, glancing up.

"You two staying at the inn?" a third voice asked. Victor followed the sound to see a man standing with several others not far away. He'd noticed them as they left the tavern but thought they were just patrons heading home after a night out.

"Who's asking?" Victor growled reflexively.

"Just making conversation, friend," the man stepped closer, and Victor saw that he was a big Vodkin. The way he walked made Victor think this guy was used to throwing his weight around to get what he wanted. He wore dark leather clothes over his bulky torso, and Victor saw several knife handles protruding from sheaths. His friends hung back, four shadowy figures in heavy coats that didn't fit the pleasant evening.

"We're tired; have a good night," Thayla said, starting to walk toward the tavern again.

"Now, don't be rude, lass. Everyone prefers honey to vinegar," the Vodkin said, taking a step closer, and his words caused a spark to erupt in Victor's Core.

"*Tornic*, no . . ." Thayla started, but it was too late. Victor had released his rage-attuned Energy and used Channel Spirit to fill his imposing frame with it. His entire body surged with power, and a red, flickering aura outlined him from his fists to his shoulder to a spiky crown that leaped and sparked with a life of its own. Victor balled up his fists and stepped up to the man, growling.

"Fuck off," he said, the words coming from deep inside him, guttural and full of intent, and the Vodkin, clearly not used to looking up at the people he spoke to, backed away, his eyes wide with Victor's red aura flickering in their moist, black depths.

"Right, let's go, boys. It's been a long night."

Victor felt Thayla's hand on his forearm as he glared at the retreating figures, and when they'd faded away into the night, he sighed heavily, forcing his Energy back into his Core. "Sorry," he said, turning to look at her.

"No, you're fine. I thought you were going to attack them. I think they were just ruffians, though, and you were a fish bigger than they wanted on their hook."

"All right, it's time for Tornic to get some sleep," Victor said, smiling and looping an arm over Thayla's shoulders. They made their way back to their room, and Victor kicked off his boots and socks, shrugged out of his armored shirt, and collapsed on top of the blanket on one side of the bed. He was asleep before Thayla could say anything, utterly exhausted for the first time in a while.

22

WELCOME TO GELICA

Victor and Thayla saw the walls of Gelica from several miles out. The traffic on the road was heavy, with carts, people, and animals going in both directions in a staggered line, and Victor wondered if it was always so busy or if it was just the hour of the day. The sun was nearing its zenith when they had to slow to a stop and get into line at the gate. A dozen or more carts and groups of people were ahead of them, so they settled in for a bit of a wait.

"I'm hungry," Victor said.

"You're always hungry, though you shouldn't be. It's in your head, you know?" Thayla said, giving him a sidelong glance.

"Doesn't matter; I want some food," Victor said. "You think muscles like these can sustain themselves on thin air?" He flexed his biceps, grinning.

"You're a dolt," Thayla chuckled.

"What should our first stop be?" Victor asked, changing the subject.

"I think we need to find an enchanter, a high-class one. I'm thinking it would be good to not be scried when we're securing a place to stay."

"Yeah, good call. Let's get some protection from that kind of magic, then we'll get a place to stay, then we'll use that thing Lam gave you. Sound good?"

"Yes, but can your stomach wait that long?"

"Oh, I'm sure I'll see a street vendor on the way. I'm assuming Gelica is something like Persi Gables in that regard? When they led us around to different fighting venues, I saw lots of vendors selling food."

"You haven't been to Gelica?" Thayla asked, glancing at the tall, off-white, stone city walls.

"Yeah, I have, but I was unconscious. The guy who wrecked my Core sold me to the mines here, but I was out of it." As Victor spoke, the Ardeni man sitting atop a roladii-drawn cart glanced back at him and quickly looked away when their eyes met.

"Maybe we shouldn't talk so loudly about our plans and problems," Thayla said in a low voice.

"Right." Victor sighed and stretched, looking up and down the line, relieved to move a bit when the guards waved a train of three wagons through the gate. Nearly an hour later, it was finally their turn to face the scrutiny of the guards, who reminded him of road crews back home—one guy was talking to the people coming through the gate while six or seven others leaned against the wall or on their spears, watching.

"Nature of your visit?" the burly Cadwalli asked.

"Shopping and meeting with friends," Thayla said. Victor just stood behind her and nodded.

"You have funds for lodging?"

"Yes," Thayla said.

"Right, well, there's a ten-bead visitor tariff at the moment," the guard said, pointing to a painted wooden placard affixed to the wall behind him.

"So much?" Thayla raised an eyebrow.

"Town's been busy, and we've had too many vagrants in the streets." The guard shrugged, clearly used to the question.

"All right," Victor said, handing the guard ten attuned beads. That should cover the two of us, hmm?"

"Aye, enjoy your stay." The guard nodded, and to his credit, he put the beads into a pouch stamped with the same symbol Victor had seen flying on the flag over the gate—some sort of bird of prey clutching a large fish in its talons. Thayla hurried through the gate, and Victor followed, painfully aware of the guards all staring at him as he passed through. If the people looking for him and Thayla had put the word out to the gate guards, they'd have people on their tail in the city in no time.

"You know where to go?" Victor asked.

"Not exactly, but I know where the wealthier shops are. We should hurry because those guards were staring at you like they'd bought tickets." Thayla put action to her words, lengthening her stride and pushing past the crowds of people in the square near the gate. Victor followed, enjoying the sights and smells of the busy square.

He'd never been to a big city back on Earth. Tucson was pretty good-sized but sprawling and so damn hot that you never met crowds of people walking around. He'd heard stories about how cities smelled like urine or garbage, especially in the past. Still, the only scents in the busy streets of Gelica were the pleasant aromas of food cooking, the various odors of people, and, under everything, the faintly fishy smell of the big river running through the center of the city.

Occasionally Victor would catch a whiff of animal dung, but the roladii were the most common animals, and their droppings came out in dry round balls with no odor that Victor could detect. "They have sewers here?" he asked, leaning forward to Thayla's ear so she could hear him over the shouts of street hawkers and yelling, jostling people.

"Huh? Yeah! The city rulers probably purchased them through the Settlement Stones. You have to upgrade your settlement with certain infrastructure for the Stone to increase in level to a Town and then to a City Stone. I think there are even higher-tier Stones, but I've never seen one. Maybe at the capital."

Thayla was leading the way up the main road that ran into town from the gate square, and they passed another big, busy market before she started up another road that led uphill. The buildings and shops were larger and cleaner on this street, and fewer people were walking about. The farther they pushed their way up the hill, the more affluent things seemed, and soon, Victor was having difficulty distinguishing between homes and places of business because they all looked like little manors to his untrained eye.

The crowds thinned further, and most of the people in the area wore clothing that stood out as tailored and enchanted. A woman strode by with a train of liveried soldiers wearing a silky, pale-blue veil and robes that left a trail of blue mist behind her. "Talk about flashy," Victor said, watching her procession.

"The nobility—always looking for a way to stand out or impress their peers." Thayla shrugged and spat, to the horror of an older Shadeni woman who happened by at that moment. "Apologies, ma'am," Thayla said, her face twisted in embarrassment.

"Come on," Victor laughed, urging her to keep moving.

The road eventually leveled off and came into another market square, but this one was much more subdued than the ones nearer the gate. A white fountain shaped like a howling dog with four bushy tails spouted water into a series of descending basins, and around it, the square spread out in white flagstones. Elegant shops lined the court, and people sedately moved around, murmuring, laughing, and generally showing off their fancy clothing. Thayla approached one of the guards standing around the perimeter. She wore livery that matched the gate guards but was much cleaner and better fitted.

"Hello, do you mind pointing me to the establishment of an enchantment artificer?" Thayla's voice was soft and sweet, unlike anything Victor had heard from her before.

"Hmm? What's that, sweetie? Enchantment?"

"Yes, ma'am," Thayla said, still speaking in a voice an octave higher than Victor was used to.

"Let's see," the guard said, rubbing her blue chin with her fingers. Victor saw that she had painted her nails purple to match her eyes, making him wonder about all the strange fashion possibilities that opened up when people were so colorful. "What sort of enchanting? Are you looking to have a weapon worked on? Or do you want something like a dimensional container?"

"I'm looking for protection enchantments." Thayla clasped her hands in front of her, fidgeting like she was nervous.

"Oh, I see. Even with this brute following you around, hmm?" The guard eyed Victor from under well-maintained brows, her painted yellow lips pursing in amusement.

"I, uh . . ." Victor started, then stopped, unsure what was afoot here.

"Oh, relax, big man. I think you should visit Master Kuth's shop. He's a true artificer, and everyone speaks highly of him. His shop is just up at the next intersection, that way. He's not cheap, though!"

"Oh, well, if he's too expensive, at least it will give us an idea of what's possible. Thank you for your help, ma'am," Thayla said demurely.

"Anytime, sweetie. I work this shift every weekend, if you ever want to chat or have a bite." She reached out a hand to Thayla and continued, "I'm Tella."

Thayla took the hand between hers and said, "I'm Alia." They looked at each other for a moment, then Thayla smiled and said, "Come, Tornic," and walked in the direction the woman had earlier indicated.

"The fuck was that about?" Victor asked as they moved away from the market square.

"Oh, I saw her staring at me the moment we entered the square. I figured I'd flirt a little to get good directions." Thayla shrugged.

"I've never seen you act like that," Victor laughed, remembering Thayla's high, sweet voice.

"What? I can be charming when I want to!" Thayla jabbed at his ribs with her elbow, but all it did was make his ringed shirt jingle and clink. She snorted and walked faster, and soon they were in front of an opulent shop. The window displayed beautiful cloaks and robes sewn from luxurious fabrics in rich deep colors. Hats with feathers and pins, staves, belts, and a rack of glittering jewelry were also on display. Above the door, embedded in the stone facade, were letters crafted from green gemstones that read simply, "Kuth's."

Victor pulled the door open, and they stepped inside. No bell announced their presence, but Victor thought he detected a surge of Energy nearby. He looked around, unable to see its source, but his attention was soon grabbed by all of the display cabinets filled with rings, jewels, necklaces, watches, and baubles of every sort imaginable. Along the right wall hung racks of coats, robes, and cloaks, and along the wall to his left were staves and wands of every shape and size. A man worked at a tall table near the rear of the shop, his gray-haired head down and his hands busy with a brass-colored cube.

"Welcome in. I'll be with you in a moment," the proprietor said with a scratchy voice. Thayla walked toward him, ignoring all the displayed merchandise, and Victor followed. In his opinion, there was simply too much to look at, and he had no idea what did what. He saw that most items had little handwritten labels on them, but he figured he could shop for hours before he found what they were looking for. They stood near the workbench, trying not to loom or intrude on the artificer's concentration.

He ignored them for several minutes, using a tool that seemed to melt the cube's metal as it touched it, allowing him to carve delicate glyphs into the surface. "Just let me finish this enchantment—I'll botch it if I try to stop halfway and finish it later. Five minutes, please." He didn't look up as he spoke, and his tone brooked no argument.

"No worries," Victor said, shrugging to Thayla. She nodded, and they spent a few minutes browsing through the aisles in the shop. Victor thought a lot of the jewelry was beautiful, but he already wore more rings than he ever thought he would and couldn't see himself buying something more unless he really needed it. He saw Thayla holding a pendant with a lustrous, dark blue stone hanging from it and was about to ask her what it was when the shopkeeper cleared his throat.

"Now, thank you for your patience; what brings you into Kuth's?"

Victor and Thayla moved back to the workbench, and Thayla said, "We're shopping for some wards. We need to be protected from scrying attempts."

"Scrying, eh? Jealous lover? Angry employer? No, no, none of Kuth's business. I pride myself on discretion—it comes with the purchase. Do you each need an item? Or just one for the two of you?"

"Each of us," Victor said.

"Any idea how strong it needs to be? What tier are those seeking to spy upon you?"

"We don't know, but better to err on the side of caution," Thayla replied, leaning against the workbench and staring steadily at the Ardeni craftsman. He had goggles on his head with several lenses flipped up out of the frames. Green lenses hid his eyes from view, but his mouth was very expressive, smiling widely with straight, sharp teeth exposed. Victor had assumed he was old because of his white hair, but his face was smooth and unlined, and his fingers drumming on the workbench were long and nimble. His overalls had dozens of pockets along the front, and Victor wondered what could be in them all.

"Well, there's quite a cost differential between Tier One and Tier Four protection. I'm afraid I cannot craft anything portable that would block Tier Five or higher scrying."

"Tier Four, please," Victor said.

"Very well, I have some wards that will suit you. Such protection requires dense metal, a significant amount of it, so I only have wards that powerful in broaches, bracelets, or pendants."

Thayla glanced at Victor, and he tried to shrug with his eyes. She nodded and said, "I think we'd prefer pendants."

"I'm sorry, but I only have one pendant that powerful. I do have a rather manly bracelet if you could see yourself wearing such a thing, sir." Kuth looked at Victor and reached up to flip the green lens away from his right eye, revealing a bright, magenta iris. "I think it would suit you well, warrior."

"Sure, I guess." Victor nodded.

"Excellent. One moment please," Kuth said, then walked over to one of his displays and began running his finger over the contents, humming off-key the whole while. Thayla looked at Victor and raised an eyebrow. He just shrugged and thumped the workbench with his fingers, content to wait.

"I'm hungry. I can't believe I didn't see any good street food on the way over."

"Oh, Ancestors! Again with your hunger?"

"There's a lovely restaurant nearby. My daughter runs it, and I'm sure she'd appreciate the business if you stopped by when you're done here."

"Ardeni food?" Thayla asked.

"Well, southern Ardeni, aye. Spicy sauces over meats and fresh veggies. She serves everything in bowls with a bed of wild rice." Kuth lifted what he was looking for out of the case and then made his way back to the workbench. He set two objects down in front of Thayla and Victor.

"We'll try that restaurant," Victor said, studying the objects. One was a silver chain with a circular pendant about two inches in diameter. It was studded with tiny red gems, and when Victor looked closely, he saw that they were set into a carving that made them look like shooting stars over a mountain range. The bracelet was thick, brass-colored, and, at its center, sported a large, singular amber-colored stone with dark stripes running through it.

"They both have the same enchantment—protection from scrying and, to a lesser extent, protection from mind-altering enchantments. The gemstones on either item will glow briefly if they block hostile Energy workings."

"Great, how much?"

"The pendant has more precious metal and stones, so it sells for two hundred and forty beads. The bracelet sells for one-eighty."

"You take any precious metals or gems in trade?" Victor asked.

"Probably! Show me what you have, sir."

"All right." Victor nodded and started pulling out the silver plates and cutlery he'd found in the dungeon. Then he piled up the silver, gold, and platinum jewelry and the precious gems he'd found. Thayla did the same with her loot. Victor thought for a moment and then snapped his fingers, producing the creepy crown he'd taken from the cultist at the dungeon entrance. He thought about adding the blue crystal choker but then looked at the pile and thought better of it. This wasn't a smart way to negotiate.

"That's quite a collection . . ." Kuth started to say, but Victor cleared his throat and spoke.

"We've heard you have a reputation for being fair, so don't let us down." He allowed a slight growl to enter his voice as he spoke, and Kuth glanced up sharply, his one visible eye widening.

"Of course, of course. Let me get my scale and rate sheet." The artificer lifted a black slate from under the counter, set it on top of his workbench, and produced a thick notebook. He then proceeded to weigh each piece of precious metal and closely examine each gemstone, making notations in his notebook. It took him nearly an hour.

"You've already told us a good place to eat. Do you happen to know anyone looking to rent out some rooms? We'd rather avoid inns," Thayla asked while the man was working.

"That's funny you should ask! My daughter has a merchant friend going out with a caravan. She usually tries to rent her villa while she's gone, and it might still be available. You should ask when you stop by to eat."

"Great, thank you!" Thayla smiled and nodded to Victor. He grinned back encouragingly. It seemed awfully convenient, but he couldn't think of a reason to be suspicious—it wasn't as if this guy had sought them out.

"All right, good news, folks! All of these metals are useful in my business, and some of these stones are quite remarkable. I'd value this haul, minus the crown, at more than seven hundred beads. The crown is a dirty piece of magic—put it on and have a good time battling for your soul with a rather insane spirit. I recommend purging the enchantments, and then I can add another fifty beads to the haul for the materials."

"So we can walk with the two warding items and a few hundred beads?" Victor asked.

"That's right, and it's my pleasure doing business—I'm always happy for a source of materials like these."

Victor and Thayla accepted the deal and took their new warding items. They each bonded with their jewelry, and after getting directions from Kuth to his daughter's restaurant and promising to return if they had more materials to sell, they left the man's shop. The restaurant was nearby, just back to the square and a short distance up a different street. Victor led the way, feeling a lot more secure now that he didn't have to worry about people spying on him magically.

Kuth's daughter was a friendly woman who had inherited her father's magenta eyes and white hair, and her spicy bowls were pretty damn good, in Victor's opinion. After he'd finished more than half of his food, he paused to take a breath and said, "You know, dungeons are pretty good money. Also, killing bounty hunters." He snorted at his gallows humor and took another bite.

"Well, they're dangerous, though. Look what happened to me," Thayla replied, sitting back to let her stomach rest. They were sitting at a two-person table near the front window, and no other patrons were nearby. The restaurant was more like a cafe in Victor's mind, and he could see Kuth's daughter watching them from her counter, waiting to see if they needed anything else. Her business was slow and seemed as though it had been for a while.

"Excuse me," he said, waving to her. She smiled and hurried around the counter, over to their table.

"Yes? Something else I can get you?"

"You can pack me ten of these bowls to go. Do you have containers for takeout? If not, I'll pay for some of these nice wooden bowls."

"Ten?" Her smile brightened, and she continued, "Of course! I don't normally sell food for people to take away, but these wooden bowls aren't costly; I'll just add them to the total."

"No problem, but you should get some paper bowls made. You could make a lot of money selling these to people who are in a hurry. They could take them back to their jobs!" Victor smiled, thinking he'd had a genius idea.

"Oh, thanks for the suggestion! I'll look into it," she said, and Thayla snorted.

When Kuth's daughter left to prepare the bowls, Thayla said, "You think she hasn't thought of that? She obviously wants to have a restaurant, not a street cart."

"Where I come from, plenty of restaurants make a killing doing to-go orders." Victor shrugged. "You gonna finish that?"

"No, I'm stuffed," Thayla replied. Victor pulled her bowl over and proceeded to wolf it down. The meat reminded him of *barbacoa*, and the tangy sauce brought back memories of squeezing lime on his *abuela's* tacos. When Kuth's daughter returned with his order, and he slipped them into his storage ring, he contemplated trying to explain tacos to her but then shook his head. Who was he to try to teach a cook about how to serve food in her home city?

"Hey, I know Kuth is your dad, but I never got your name," Victor said instead. "My name's Tornic, and this is Alia."

"Very pleased to meet you! My name is Yasha." She nodded, her white ponytail bouncing behind her head, and smiled, holding out a hand.

Victor shook her hand and said, "Hey, your dad said you might know someone with a villa to rent? We're looking for a place to stay while we're in the city."

"Really? Yes! My friend, Veysi ap'Narl, has a villa for rent! She had to leave on a caravan for business and couldn't find any renters, so she asked me if I could help out. She won't be back for months!"

"How much is she asking?" Thayla asked.

"Forty a week," she said with a slight frown. "I know it's a lot, but she's got a really nice place right here in the Garnet Quarter."

"You're getting a cut, I hope?" Victor asked.

"Yes! Veysi was so upset that she couldn't find a long-term renter that she promised me a percentage if I figured something out for her."

"All right, sign us up for two weeks, and we can talk after that. We're not sure how long we'll be in town," Victor said, glancing at Thayla for confirmation. She nodded, sitting back and eyeing Yasha through half-closed eyes.

"Wonderful! I'll get the contract, and you can read through it. I have an employee coming in the next half hour—if you're agreeable, I can have him watch the counter while I show you the villa. Does that sound all right?"

"Yeah, sounds good," Victor said, smiling and squashing the urge to wink. Yasha hurried back behind her counter and started rifling through some papers.

"That was pretty convenient," Thayla said.

"Yeah, I had that thought earlier—this all seems so easy and smooth, but we sought out the artificer, and it's not like the gate guards sent us here; it was that random guard lady that had a crush on you." Victor frowned and drummed his fingers on the table.

"Tonight, do you think you can try to spirit walk to Oynalla?"

"I can try, but she'll need to be listening."

"She will be. I'm pretty sure she's been there every night since we left. She's interested in us, Victor, and wants to hear from us. If you can get to her, you can ask her to try scrying us to see if these things really work." Thayla lifted the pendant hanging at her neck.

"Oh. Yeah, that's a good idea. You think she can scry? She said she didn't know any defenses for it."

"I'll be surprised if she can't," Thayla said with a firm, quick nod.

"Right, well, we'll try that tonight. If things check out with our new wards, you can use your stone to contact Lam. Sound all right?"

"Yes. Meanwhile, let's check out Yasha's villa." Thayla nodded to the young woman as she approached, holding a sheet of thick paper covered with dense lines of script.

"The contract," she said cheerily, blowing a strand of loose white hair out of her eyes as she set the paper onto the table.

23

CONTACTS

Victor looked around the pantry space in the basement of the villa they'd rented. Jars of pickled fruits and jams lined one wall, and sacks of flour and sugar and bins of root vegetables lined the other. The pantry door was solid, and with a little bit of work, he and Thayla had secured a thick wooden bar over it. "This should do. Even if this place is a setup, they won't expect us to be hiding in the pantry in the basement, right?"

"Makes sense to me," Thayla replied, giving the door a stiff tug to make sure it wouldn't budge. Victor threw out a couple of blankets and then sat down, Lifedrinker in his lap. It was near midnight—they'd spent the evening visiting with Yasha, taking a tour of the villa, and then shopping for travel supplies from a general store they'd seen near the home.

They'd bought ropes, pitons, blankets, sleeping mats, two tents, cooking supplies, racks of spices, an Energy powered camp stove, glow lanterns, fishing gear, snares, shovels, hammers, pliers, hatchets, and even a massive canvas tarp. Victor figured that as long as he had storage rings with enormous space inside, he might as well be stocked up and ready for anything.

"All right, so you'll wake me at the first hint of any trouble, right?"

"Of course, Victor! I won't leave you helpless." Thayla looked almost irritated by the question.

"I know you won't, but even if you aren't sure, even if it's just a strange noise that you think might be a rat or something, wake me up." He lay back on the blankets, still holding Lifedrinker in his hands—he felt comforted by her handle's warm, vibrant aura.

Thayla put her glow lamp into her ring, and darkness closed in. "I'm here, and my spear's ready."

"Here I go," Victor said, then he closed his eyes, relaxed his body the way Oynalla had taught him, and cast Spirit Walk. He and Thayla had practiced the spell almost every night, and it came quickly to him. He stood up from the ground in a twilit, grass-covered plain. At the very edges of his vision, he thought he saw movement and flashes of color, and he wondered if they were other spirit walkers—the city had a lot of people in it; surely some of them had this ability.

Victor slowly spun in a circle, taking in his surroundings, marveling at the bright, iridescent stars in the black sky. The moons were especially radiant and seemed to pulsate with slightly different shades of white and blue light. Using them as a guide, Victor oriented himself toward the east and thought of Oynalla. He pictured the woman both as she was in reality and how she'd appeared on the spirit plane. He saw her bright, intelligent eyes and remembered her cackle, and suddenly he felt a sensation of movement.

The feeling was almost like sliding over the ground on a pathway, and Victor stepped into it, letting the momentum take him. As he did so, he accelerated, and his surroundings became a blur. He perceived just a few seconds of time passing, then the world stopped blurring by, and he stood on a different grassy plain, one with taller, sporadic clumps of grass, and right in front of him stood the beautiful, youthful version of Oynalla. She clapped her hands and cackled.

"So easily you come to me? Wonderful! Oynalla is still a great teacher!"

"Hello, Oynalla! We've missed you! Thayla wanted to come but was afraid she'd run out of Energy. She's been practicing, though!"

"Yes, warrior, I imagined that was the case. When I saw your smooth face and untroubled brow, I knew she was well."

"Did you worry something was wrong?"

"Not exactly—I've been keeping an eye on you two since you left, and earlier today, I lost track. You found some wards to protect you from prying eyes, hmm?"

"Oh, great! Yes, that's why I came to you tonight—we wanted to see if they worked. Things were going, well, too smoothly, and we started to fear we were being tricked."

"Mmhmm, Oynalla knows the feeling of not believing life can be easy, especially after long, troubling times. Still, sometimes the Ancestors look away from you for a while and stop meddling with your affairs. In those moments, it can be surprising to have things happen exactly as you might hope." She laughed again, but not a cackle, more a warm chuckle that Victor found infectious.

"You think your ancestors are meddlers? Do they ever make things easier?"

"The Ancestors that choose to bide their time nosing about in our affairs rarely concern themselves with our happiness. No, they want to see a particular end and like to treat us as a means to that end."

"So benevolent ancestors are more hands-off? Doesn't seem fair." Victor's words elicited another true cackle from Oynalla, one that lasted a while.

"Imagine believing life is fair! Silly warrior. Do you think your foes feel that things are fair when you refuse to die, refuse to keep bleeding, and rip them limb from limb?"

"Fair point," Victor said with a chagrined smile. Suddenly Oynalla looked away, staring into the horizon behind him.

"Something dark and powerful comes this way. Return to your body, warrior. Come to me at this hour whenever you can, and try to bring my daughter with you!" She reached out and touched Victor's forehead, and then he was blinking his real, physical eyes, staring into the dark pantry.

"Damn, she fucking kicked me out!" he said, his words dry and scratchy, as if he'd been holding his mouth open the whole time he was out.

"Was she mad?" Thayla asked, producing her glow lamp.

"Nah, she said something dark was coming our way and kicked me out. She wants us to visit her again, though. She said this was a good time."

"Us?"

"Yeah, so you better keep working on cultivating that courage-attunement. By the way, she called you 'daughter.'" Victor paused as Thayla looked away for a moment, either embarrassed or ashamed of whatever emotion she was feeling. "Anyway, she said the wards worked—she lost track of us earlier today when we picked them up."

"Oh, good! I like this villa and didn't want to have to move." Thayla said, briefly brushing her eyes. She held out a hand, and Victor took it, pulling himself up to his feet. Thayla grunted and had to hold onto the door handle for balance.

"Don't say it! I am not going on a diet." Victor laughed and lifted the bar from the door, opening up the pantry to the rest of the basement. "Want to contact Lam now or wait for morning?"

"Now! She's likely in her quarters at this hour. Who knows what she'll be doing in the morning."

"Yeah, good point." Victor gestured to the larger basement space, "Since we're sure we're not being scried, no one should know we're here. Let's head upstairs to the sitting room, and you can use the stone in comfort."

"Yep," Thayla said, brushing past him and walking to the stairs. Victor followed her up and then through a short hallway into the villa's sitting room. Wicker chairs with soft pads around a pale green, rag-style rug filled most of the space. Wide, glass-paneled French doors opened onto a stone-flagged courtyard. Victor crossed the room and opened them, letting some night air into the room.

"That's better," he said, taking a deep breath of the cool, jasmine-scented breeze. "Am I smelling jasmine blossoms?"

"Rust orchids."

"Huh, smells like some flowers that grew by my auntie's house." Victor took another big breath, then moved over to one of the wicker couches and sat down, watching Thayla. She took the black stone from her storage container and contemplated it.

"I don't know how this is going to work. Will it just alert her that I used it? Will she be able to see us? Speak to us?"

"No idea. Are you worried about whether we can trust her or not?" Victor frowned.

"Sort of, but I guess that's a little silly—if she'd wanted to double-cross us, why would she help us to slip away? Why give us all these supplies and weapons?" She nodded at the axe hanging from Victor's belt.

"Yeah. Go for it; she's not going to sell us out. She wanted info on that dungeon, anyway, so it's not like she's not motivated."

"Right." Thayla nodded. "Here goes." She lifted the stone in her palm and concentrated for a moment. Victor felt her reach out with a tendril of courage-attuned Energy, and he wondered if he'd have noticed if it had been some other Energy attunement. The thread of courage Energy had a very familiar feel to him, and he smiled at the feelings it triggered: confidence, boldness in action, a warm feeling spreading from his heart.

The stone shifted from black to yellow and then back again to black. It did it again, three seconds later, and then again, three seconds after that. "Does that mean it's working?" Victor asked.

"I don't know! It's getting warm," Thayla said, closing her fist over the stone and releasing it. "It feels nice." Suddenly the stone seemed to burst into a million fragments that hovered in a small cloud in front of Thayla's face. A moment later, they started to swirl around and then condense into a grayscale shape: Lam's face. The representation of Lam blinked a few times, and then she opened her mouth.

"Thayla? You're alive! I'd lost hope of hearing from you, then my stone started to pulse, and I knew someone had the one I gave you."

"Lam? Can you hear me?" Thayla asked, talking to the gray-black face.

"Yes! Be quick, though—these stones are linked but can only maintain a connection for a few moments. How are you? Are you someplace safe? Did Victor survive?"

"We're safe! We're in Gelica, but we have assassins and bounty hunters chasing us. We need to figure out a way to get the Mining Consortium to let things drop."

"Gelica! So, the dungeon was real? Victor found the way in?"

"Yes! Do you think you can help us, Captain?"

"I'm due a visit to the city. I'll come to you, and I'll bring along a friend of yours! She's been driving me crazy with questions about what happened to you both." Victor's cheeks turned up into a smile at the mention—she had to be talking about Edeya!

"Is Edeya well?" Victor asked, but it didn't seem Lam could hear him.

"We can make the journey in two days. I have a close friend that owns a restaurant—Nissa's Small Plates. Talk to Nissa; tell her where I can find you. She won't speak to anyone; you can trust her."

"Okay, thank you. Lam, is there any . . ." Suddenly, the shadowy image of Lam's face fell to the floor—a million particles of inert dust. "Guess it ran out of time."

"That was pretty cool, though!" Victor said, leaning forward to look at the pile of black dust at Thayla's feet.

"Yeah, I didn't expect that! She's bringing Edeya! Aren't you excited to see how she's been?"

"Hell yeah." Victor nodded, clapping his hands together. "Well, shall we get some sleep? Tomorrow we can find Nissa's restaurant."

"Yeah, I'm beat. Lock up the doors, though, please." Thayla gestured to the doors Victor had just opened.

"Right. See you in the morning." He moved to close the doors, and while he was latching the bolt, Thayla moved off toward the bedrooms. They each had a comfortable room, and the villa sported a Roman-style bathing room with a large, perpetually full, steamy bath. Thayla said it wasn't uncommon for wealthier people to have such pools in their homes—Energy powered the heaters and filters.

Thayla didn't avail herself of the bath, heading straight to sleep, but Victor wasn't all that tired, so he spent some time splashing and floating around in the hot water, sampling the soaps and oils that the owner had arrayed in great quantity and variation. After his bath, he went to his room and fell asleep rather quickly, more tired than he'd thought.

He must have slept well because Victor found himself in that cozy half-awake, half-asleep state he sometimes got into when he'd slept through the night. His dreams were vivid, and he was almost lucid in them. One strange scene after another drifted through his mind, and he could feel his face stretching into a smile while he laughed at his friend Paul mimicking their wrestling coach, "Oh, you didn't make weight? When I was your age, I spent half my day wearing three sweat suits and laying under the mats with the heaters cranked up! Get some gum in your mouth and start spitting! You got two hours!"

That strange memory-dream faded away as Victor found himself walking through the desert with his old friend, Anthony, looking for a stick suitable to use as a "sword." Their neighbors, twins named John and Eric, had bullied Anthony on the bus again, and Victor was going to help him get even.

The dream morphed away from memory when he found himself holding an axe, not a stick, standing in a dark hallway made of stone. Victor's heart started to beat faster, and he crept toward an even darker opening ahead, trying not to breathe loudly. He moved into the darkness, unable to see anything, and when he whirled back toward the hallway he'd come from, it was gone, and he stood alone in the fathomless black.

Somewhere in the back of his dream-muddled mind, Victor thought he should be able to produce a light somehow, but he couldn't quite figure out how. His breaths came short and shallow, and his hands gripped the handle of his axe until his knuckles started to hurt, and then a voice came out of the darkness, familiar but different, "Ahh, your spirit wanders wide, warrior."

Victor couldn't quite put a finger on whose voice it was—deep and raspy, echoing strangely, confident, but not demeaning. It was a man's voice, but had he ever heard it before? Why was it familiar? Before he could puzzle out any more, it spoke again, "Nothing to say? You should learn to guard yourself better when you sleep. A spirit as strong as yours can venture to places you aren't ready to see. You need to keep your mind in control of it. Luckily for you, I bear you no ill will. It was irritating that you took my apprentice away, but the service you did far outweighed such an insignificant loss. As a gesture of goodwill, I'll tell you this: I'm not the only one that saw your spirit drifting around this night."

"Apprentice?" Victor managed to say, his mind jumping to every possible conclusion. "Thayla? Are you Belikot?"

"Wake up now! And learn to tether your spirit before you sleep so deeply again." The voice was deep and suggestive, and Victor, worried that he'd done something he shouldn't have, willed himself awake. Gray morning light was filtering through the gauzy drapes on his windows, and his bed felt like a warm nest in the cold morning air. A chilly draft drew his eyes to the windows, and he saw the drapes flutter. Had he opened them last night? He stood and walked over to the window, pulling the fabric aside to look out on the villa's courtyard.

A thin layer of frost lay over the flagstones and the marble fountain. The short shrubs were similarly coated, and Victor shivered, cranking the window closed. "I guess summer's definitely over."

He found Thayla in the kitchen, rooting through the "cold-cabinet," as she'd called it. To Victor, it seemed just like a refrigerator, but it was made of wood strapped with rune-covered bronze. Brightly glowing crystals were inset into the back of the interior, and it felt just as cold as the fridge at his *abuela's* house. "Looking for breakfast?"

"I found sausages, but they were slimy and smelled. There're eggs, though." Thayla turned and set a ceramic bowl filled with eggs on the counter. She looked up at Victor and smiled, "You look like you slept well!" She chuckled and pointedly looked at his hair.

"What? My hair a mess? Damn, but I had some weird dreams." Victor pulled out one of the stools in front of the long kitchen counter and sat down. "Either my subconscious is weirder than I thought, or Belikot spoke to me in my dream."

Thayla dropped the frying pan she'd picked up. It clattered on the tile floor, and she turned to look at him. "Not funny, Victor."

"Yeah, I'm not trying to be funny. He said my spirit was 'wandering' in my sleep. I mean, on the bright side, he didn't act like we were enemies. He even said he wanted to warn me that he wasn't the only one that had noticed my spirit wandering around last night. He said I need to learn to tether myself before I sleep so deeply again. Whatever that means. Ahh, it all sounds stupid when I say it out loud. I probably had a dumb dream."

"I don't know, Victor," Thayla said, stooping to pick up the pan and placing it on the stovetop. "Where would you come up with something like that? I mean, if it was just a dream—your spirit wandering, Belikot warning you. Is that something you'd dream up on your own?"

"Maybe. Oynalla talked about stuff like that, and we've been practicing Spirit Walk. I'm sure Belikot is one of the worries I've got buried in here." Victor thumped his skull.

"Well, just in case, we should see if we can find anything out about keeping your spirit from wandering while you dream."

"All right, add it to the list. Anything good to drink in there?"

"Some juice," Thayla said, pulling a pitcher out of the cold-cabinet and getting him a glass from a nearby cupboard. Victor drank the tangy, sweet juice, and Thayla scrambled up some eggs for them to eat.

"I could go for some toast or bacon. We should go shopping after we find that friend of Captain Lam's."

"Yeah, I had the same thought."

"Well, I'm ready when you are," Victor said, rinsing his plate in the sink.

"Okay, let me go get cleaned up a little bit. I'll meet you in the courtyard." Thayla walked back toward the bedrooms, and Victor stretched, moving out to the courtyard to stand in the morning sun. The frost had already melted away, and though there was still a chill in the air, the sun felt good on his face. Victor could hear the sounds of the city waking up around them and even saw the silhouettes of people walking by through the wrought iron gate. Victor had admired the gate when Yasha had first shown them the villa; it was heavy with a solid feel, and the tiny holes in the metal were nearly impossible to see through, let alone sneak through.

Long metal bolts held the gate shut, and they made quite a racket when you slid them open. Victor thought it was a nice security touch, but he supposed he was still thinking like an earthling—anyone with a decent agility score or some Energy abilities could get over the wall, completely ignoring the heavy gate. Victor walked over to it, pulled the lever, slid the long bolts free, and swung the gate toward him. A woman was walking by on the sidewalk, and he smiled and said, "Good morning."

"And to you," she said, hurrying on her way.

"Trying to flirt with the locals?" Thayla asked, noiselessly walking up behind him.

"Damn, Thayla! Do you have to creep up on me like that?"

"Was I really creeping, or were you just too busy staring at that poor woman to notice me?"

"All right, all right. Where do we go first?"

"First, we should find the source of that smell! She sniffed loudly, her lips turned up in a pleased smile. Victor turned his attention to his nose and took a big whiff; sure enough, the sugary smell of toasted caramel wafted into his nostrils.

"You think it's a pastry shop or something?"

"Yes! And we need to buy a bunch of them!" Thayla started up the street toward the corner, and Victor closed the gate, following behind.

"Did you lock the villa?" he asked as he caught up.

"Sure did." Thayla wore a smug smile and seemed almost bubbling with positive energy, and Victor couldn't quite put a finger on why, but she seemed different.

"What's up with you? You seem happy or something."

"I'm not allowed to be happy? No, no, I'm teasing. I'll tell you what it is: I've thought about what you said, about your conversation with Belikot while you were sleeping. If he really did warn you and said he held no ill will, that's good, right? That's a weight off my mind. I think I've been worried that we'd run into him sooner or later, or at least some Naghelli assassins he might send after me. I think it's like you said all along—he's got bigger problems than you and me, especially if we're not looking to get back at him."

"All right, well, that's cool. I'm glad you're feeling better about that shit . . . Hey! A bakery!" He pointed to the corner shop with a line of patrons coming out the door. The sugar-scented fresh bread odor was coming from within.

He and Thayla joined the queue and talked about mundane things, like finding a store to buy wine and a place to sell some more of the odds and ends Victor had collected in the dungeon, including the various weapons and armor bits. Thayla said she wanted to try to find a clothier to buy some new outfits, and that, of course, reminded Victor that he had a very limited wardrobe.

"No, Angra, I'm not doing this again. You either tell him we're serious and he needs to back off, or I'm done!" A short Ardeni man had suddenly raised his voice and turned to face the large Vodkin behind him.

"Oh, you're done? Maybe I'm done! Did you think a sweet roll would make up for how you spoke to my mother last night? And you referred to my nephews as a litter! A litter of nephews! I'm done with this! I'm going to talk to Drayel, all right, but it's to tell him that you and I are *through*!" The big Vodkin turned on his heel and strode away, jostling Thayla. "I'm sorry, miss!" he said, tears on his fuzzy face.

"Wait! Angra!" the Ardeni called, chasing after him down the sidewalk. Victor looked at Thayla and raised an eyebrow. She suppressed a giggle and turned back toward the bakery counter.

"That's one way to get the line moving faster," Victor said, leaning forward to speak quietly in her ear.

"Hush!" she hissed.

When they finally got a chance to make a purchase, Victor loaded up on all sorts of pastries, creating quite a pile in one of his storage rings. He and Thayla sat at a small table and savored one of their purchases with a warm drink the locals simply called spiced milk. It reminded Victor of a cross between hot chocolate and apple cider, though if someone asked him what the actual flavors were, he'd struggle to describe them. All he knew was that it was delicious and paired perfectly with the buttery fruit-filled pastry he was eating.

When they finished eating, he and Thayla walked toward the nearby market square and started asking friendly-looking people if they knew where they might find Nissa's Small Plates. The first few people they asked didn't have any idea, one suggesting they look around various other city sections. Thayla didn't give up, though, and after a few more attempts, she asked an older, gray-haired Shadeni woman selling carved figurines that looked to be made from something like ivory.

"Oh, Nissa's? Yeah, I've seen it. Not my taste, or my price range, though."

"Could you tell us where it is?" Thayla asked, picking up one of the figurines shaped like a little wolf with three bushy tails.

"Seven Bell Square. On the corner next to the candlemaker. That's how I know it—I buy my wax there." She gestured at the little figurines.

"These are wax?" Victor asked, picking one up. It was hard and lustrous, nothing like a candle, the only object made of wax that Victor could think of.

"Yes, but I treat them with my artisan skills."

"Pretty cool! How much for the one my friend has there?" Victor pointed to the little three-tailed wolf.

"Eight," the woman said, smiling with crinkled eyes. Victor dug in his ring and took out three attuned beads.

"How about this? We got a deal?"

"Sure. Happy to help young love," she said, snatching the beads faster than Victor thought she ought to be able to move.

"We're not in love!" Thayla said, but she pocketed the figurine. "Thanks, Victor."

"Sure," Victor waved to the woman and started walking toward the broad road that led down the hill toward the greater part of the city. "You know where the square she mentioned is?"

"Yeah, it's pretty well-known." She moved to Victor's side and took the lead. They walked in silence for a few minutes, then she said, "I liked the figurine because it reminded me of my daughter—she loved a story about a three-tailed boyii hound that befriended a little boy. Thanks for buying it."

"What's her name?"

"My daughter?"

"Yeah, I'm always thinking of her in those terms. 'Thayla's daughter.' I'm just curious."

"Her name's Deyni." Thayla smiled wistfully as she said the name. "I haven't said it aloud in a while. Victor, can we make a detour when we're done talking to Lam's friend? I want to try to find an old acquaintance who might have an idea where Deyni and my old friend Rhessa might be hiding."

"Fuck yes! We've got a couple of days until Lam gets here; we might as well accomplish something while we wait!"

"Thanks, Victor!" Thayla clapped him on the shoulder, and they continued in silence, walking toward the city center and Seven Bell Square.

24

HEART FINDER

Nissa regarded Victor and Thayla over her wooden chopping block, bits of diced herbs clinging to the knife in her hand. "So, you know Lam, hmm?" They'd knocked on the restaurant door, seeing that a light was on in the kitchen, and when Thayla had mentioned Lam to the grumpy, narrow-faced Ghelli woman, she'd motioned for them to follow her back to the kitchen.

"That's right," Victor said. "She asked us to leave a message for her with you."

"Don't get me wrong, I love Lam, but I need to keep my nose clean. I'm not the same Ghelli she used to run with." She smirked, reliving some private memory, and then went back to dicing herbs.

"This won't get you into any trouble. We're just going to tell you where she can meet us," Thayla said.

"Mmhmm, and I won't have some thugs coming here to torture the information out of me?" The knife beat out a staccato rhythm, faster than Victor's eyes could follow.

"I don't see how—no one knows we have any connection to you. I mean, we don't—Lam does." Thayla pressed.

"All right, then, spit it out. What do you want me to tell her?"

"If you could just tell her to get breakfast at Parlo's Bakery near Boyii Square, we'll look for her there each morning," Thayla said, giving the instructions that she and Victor had decided upon. They knew they could trust Lam, but they didn't know if Nissa was as trustworthy as Lam thought.

"Parlo's. All right, got it. Is that everything?" She scraped her herbs into a pile on the cutting board, then put a bright orange pepper under her knife, "If it is, you might want to leave—scorch peppers aren't fun to be around when they're being chopped."

"One more thing," Victor said, calmly putting one of his large hands over the pepper. "I know you don't know us and don't have a reason to want to help, but we don't have any good contacts here in the city. Do you think you could point us in the direction of a spirit caster? Someone who runs a business, so it won't seem odd, us showing up."

"A spirit caster? What kind? A Fate Teller? A Heart Witch? A Spirit Singer? I know a few." Nissa reached forward and grabbed onto Victor's thumb, trying to lift his hand off her cutting board. "Do you mind?"

"We're looking for someone that might be able to help with some questions about Spirit Cores in general. Someone friendly and knowledgeable." Victor said, still holding his hand over the pepper.

"Well, if you care about discretion and want someone friendly, Ren the Heart Witch is your best bet. People don't go to her for things they want blabbed about, if you know what I mean." She winked at Victor and nodded toward Thayla.

"We aren't interested in love potions," Thayla said, slapping a hand on Victor's shoulder. "Let her have her cutting board back. Even so, Nissa, can you tell us where to find Ren?"

"She's in the shambles down by the docks. I'll have to write you instructions, or you'll be wandering around down there for days." Nissa turned and rummaged through one of her drawers until she pulled out a pencil and a notepad that looked like something a server would write orders on. She wrote several lines of text, even drew a sketch of a map on the paper, then handed it to Thayla. "Here. Now, can you kindly get out so I can prepare for my lunch rush? Use the back door, please." She pointed to a door at the rear of the kitchen.

"Thanks, Nissa," Thayla said, tugging Victor along, "We'll tell Lam how much you helped us."

"Sure, sure," she said, then started chopping the pepper on her cutting board, and even from several feet away, Victor's eyes began to burn. He and Thayla rushed out of the kitchen.

"I get the feeling that she and Lam don't really hang out anymore," Victor said as they walked through the back alley back to the street.

"Yeah, well, at least she helped us out. My contact is down at the docks, so this worked out nicely."

"The one that's going to point us toward your daughter?"

"Hopefully," Thayla said, her face betraying her worry. "Rallo isn't really a friend—more of a mutual acquaintance of mine and Rhessa's. He used to find jobs for us when we 'worked.'"

"What kind of work?" Victor asked, failing to note the inflection Thayla put on the word.

"Oh," she sighed, "no sense trying to keep secrets from you, I guess. I mean, I think you've shown me I can trust you more than anyone else. Rhessa and I used to go to parties thrown by wealthy merchants and nobility. We'd flirt and sometimes more, and when things were in full swing, and people were out of their minds with drink and potions, we'd rob the place, slipping away before anyone knew something had happened."

"Shit, for real?" Victor glanced at Thayla with a raised eyebrow. He'd always assumed she was a victim of circumstances, especially when he'd learned about her daughter.

"Yeah, for real. I tried to straighten up and lead a clean life when I got pregnant, but my past caught up with me. The constable that caught up with me didn't have a warrant for Rhessa, so he let me leave my daughter with her, and she promised me she would disappear with her—keep her safe and raise her away from that kind of life."

"So, you think this guy that used to give you jobs might know where Rhessa ran off to?"

"It's just a hope at this point. I don't know if Rhessa ever had any contact with him. Rallo was good to us, but he was tied to our old lives."

"Okay, so, we seeing him first or the love potion lady?"

"The shambles are on the way to the docks, so let's find Ren first," Thayla said and started walking with purpose toward the city's western side. Victor followed, and soon the jostling crowds and noise and commotion of the streets made conversation difficult, so he let his mind wander.

He thought about all the different threads pulling him in various directions in this world. He wanted to revisit Persi Gables and the Wagon Wheel. He wasn't sure what he'd do there, but he felt some sort of reckoning was in order, even if it was just to see if Belsa was still there. He wanted to look into the noble that had tried to wreck his Core. He wanted to do something about the mines, though one of his motivations for returning there, seeing if he could help Edeya, was being taken care of for him, thanks to Lam. He wanted to find some sort of resolution with Belikot. Most of all, Victor wanted to help Thayla get her daughter and get them safely to Oynalla.

Thoughts of Persi Gables and his time in the pits there naturally brought back memories of how he came into this world. He thought about how he'd been yanked out of his *abuela's* house and confronted with those strange mages that had so effortlessly controlled him. He remembered how they'd dismissed him and sold him into a kind of slavery that, in their minds, would lead to his quick death. He imagined it would be good to do a little investigating into those assholes, too.

"And that's just the tip of the iceberg," Victor said aloud. He thought about all the other little things on his mind—learning more about his Spirit Core, gaining more levels, exploring, and, beneath it all, gaining enough power and influence to do something about the labor system in this world.

Lost in thought, Victor almost tuned out the city, but when they turned down a steep hill leading toward the docks, the smells and scenery intruded on his reverie. He could see the wide, green ribbon of the Rill Catcher stretching north to south in a meandering pathway through the densely packed structures of the docks district. No wall stood on that side of the city, the river itself serving as the defensive barrier. The buildings were lower, more numerous, and built of cheaper stuff than in the other parts of the city. The far side of the river was even worse, with thousands of ramshackle structures vying for space along the muddy, partially graveled roads.

As Victor took in the distinctly fishy smells and the crowds of people battling for space, he said, loudly so Thayla could hear him, "They push all the poor people into this section of the city?"

"Well, it's not like they push them here, but this is where most of the jobs are, and living is cheapest. If you go a bit further south or north, there are nicer homes that overlook the river, but, here in the heart of the city, the docks are important business—everything else is secondary."

"And the shambles? That's these winding streets along the hill, I guess?"

"Yes, and the little shacks people live in." Thayla stepped to the side of the street to look more closely at the directions Nissa had given them. Then, she started walking again, trusting Victor to keep pace. He followed her through a veritable maze of narrow streets with leaning wooden structures built one atop the other. The people in the dingy district were either hurrying to get somewhere or lingering around with their friends, drinking from shared bottles. The clean smell of the upper city was gone, and the tang of urine was heavy in the air.

Thayla had to stop several times to scrutinize the instructions, and twice she backtracked to turn into different alley-like streets. When she'd reached the end of Nissa's written directions, and they still hadn't found Ren's shop, she said, "Ask someone for directions, Victor, and try to look like you mean business."

"All right," Victor said, then he approached a group of Shadeni men sitting around on broken barrels and drinking from brown bottles. "Hey," he growled, speaking from his belly, "Where's Ren's shop?"

One of the men looked at him with bleary eyes, made a circle with a thumb and forefinger, and then jammed his other thumb through it repeatedly. His friends laughed raucously, one falling off his barrel, eliciting more laughter. Victor walked up to the guy who'd made the gesture and channeled some rage into his pathways, repeating his question while leaning very close to the man's face.

"Orl's bones, man!" the drunk said, pulling back, but Victor snaked a hand out to grab his shirt, pulling him close again.

"Where?" he growled.

"Right there! That's her house behind that mean-looking bitch." He gestured toward Thayla.

"Thanks," Victor stood and shrugged. "I guess you found it, after all," he said to Thayla. He strode past her and knocked on the shack-like building's flimsy door. Glancing over his shoulder, he saw Thayla behind him, eyeing the people in the area warily, and he decided to speed things along. He pulled at the door, which opened easily—not even latched. Victor stepped into the dim interior, and Thayla followed. "Hello?" he called out.

"Well, come in then, and close that door," a high-pitched voice said from the shadows to his left, and, as Thayla shut the door and Victor's eyes adjusted, he saw a small Vodkin woman sitting on a couch, smoke spiraling up out of a thin brass pipe held between her thin, black lips. She had sleek white fur with pale brown spots, and her long whiskers twitched while she inhaled the smoke. "What brings you to Ren? Looking for lost love?"

"No, we just need some advice," Thayla said, coming up from behind Victor and ducking to avoid the many strands of beads hanging from the ceiling.

"Oh? I've seen a lot in my years, and I do have some wisdom to share, but your friend seems to be the type to solve problems with his axe." She leaned back, blowing out a long stream of blue-tinged smoke. Her huge, black eyes seemed even more depthless than other Vodkin Victor had met, and he wondered what she saw.

"This problem can't be solved with my axe. I need advice about my spirit."

"Oh?" She leaned forward, this time with genuine interest in her eyes. She closed them for a moment, and Victor was surprised to see how long and thick her lashes were. When she opened them, she smiled and said, "Oh, now I see. You have a strong Spirit Core, warrior! Sit, sit." She gestured to the wicker chairs facing her couch. Thayla had to lift a tattered robe from hers and set it aside on a cluttered table, but the two of them sat down.

"Do you know much about spirit walking?" Victor asked.

"I know how to do it if that's what you mean."

"Not exactly. I know the spell also, but I'm having a problem with my spirit wandering on its own while I sleep—particularly when I sleep deeply and dream."

"Oh? Your mentor didn't teach you to control your spirit?"

"I don't really have a mentor—I guess I kind of met one recently, but my time with her was short."

"Ha! Until you gain more control, I could teach you to tether yourself. I mean to say if your spirit wandering is worrying you. I assume that's why you came, no? The wandering is troubling you somehow? It's the simplest of patterns. I'll show you for a small favor."

"A favor? Ren, we have a lot on our plate, and not much of it is in our control. Couldn't we just pay you?" Thayla interjected.

"Tosh, this is easy," Ren said, and, from somewhere, she produced a jagged, pale crystal. "I just want the warrior here to channel some of his Energy into this crystal. I could work some interesting magics with that rage attunement."

"Oh," Thayla said. "All right, Victor, that's pretty painless."

"Huh," Victor said, reaching out to pick up the crystal. It was heavy and cold. "How much Energy do you want in it?"

"As much as it will hold, silly man."

"First, let me see the spell pattern," Victor said, frowning.

"Fear not, warrior. The pretty mistresses in the upper quarters might frown on Ren's services, but I've never cheated anyone in a bargain. You fill that crystal, and I'll teach you to tether your spirit tight while you dream."

Victor looked at Thayla, and she raised her eyebrows as if to say, "Up to you."

He sighed and said, "All right." Victor turned inward to his Core and pulled a thick band of rage-attuned Energy out into his pathways, pushing it toward the hand that held the crystal. When his fist began to radiate with red light, he pushed the Energy out and into the Crystal. It rapidly soaked it up, turning from pale white to pink, then gradually darkening to red.

As Victor kept pushing Energy out, the red hue deepened and then began to pulse brightly from the Crystal, and within a matter of seconds, he found he couldn't put any more Energy into it. "That's it?" he asked, looking at his status sheet to see he still had more than eighty percent of his total Energy.

"Nicely done, warrior!" Ren said, reaching for the crystal. Victor closed his fingers around it again and grinned.

"The spell?"

"Tosh! Such a lack of trust! Very well," she said, then briefly touched a bug-shaped bronze pin on her maroon blouse. A second later, she held a rolled piece of parchment. "You'll have to learn it now—this pattern page is good for a few uses, and I'd like to keep it for my apprentice. If I ever find one."

"How does it work?" Victor asked.

"Just stare at the symbols for a few seconds," Ren replied as she unrolled the parchment and held it so that the ink-covered side faced Victor.

"It's enchanted parchment, Victor," Thayla said. "It will impart the spell pattern directly into your mind. Some people call them learning scrolls."

"Oh, cool," Victor said, looking at the weird, squiggly symbols all over the paper. As he tried to decipher them, they seemed to move around on the paper, subtly at first but then more obviously. As he traced their movements, some of them seemed to lift off the page and flow toward his eyes. A moment later, dozens of them were streaming into him, and he felt the warmth of Energy in his skull, behind his eyes, and he wondered what it was doing to his brain. As quickly as it started, it stopped, and a System message appeared in his view.

*****Congratulations! You have learned the spell: Tether Spirit, Basic.*****

*****Tether Spirit: Prerequisite: A Spirit Class Core. When you cast this spell, your spirit will be bound to your corporeal form for a period of twelve hours. This will serve to protect you from hostile attempts to sever your spirit and will keep your spirit from drifting while your conscious mind is unable to be vigilant. Energy Cost: 10. Cooldown: Short.*****

Victor looked at the parchment and saw it still had all its markings, but they'd faded somewhat, appearing more gray than black. Ren snatched the paper away and then held her hand out expectantly. Victor nodded and passed her the glowing red crystal. "Fair deal; thanks, Ren."

"You learned it, Victor?" Thayla asked.

"Yeah—it seems pretty basic. I can probably teach it to you after I study the pattern for a while."

"Is that how you thank me? Teaching my secrets to everyone in town?" Ren curled her lips into a frown and tucked her parchment away into her storage device.

"Not everyone in town, just my close friend here. I promise," Victor said, trying to use a soothing tone.

"Tosh, tosh. Do as you will but be careful! See that you show her the exact pattern, or she may be left vulnerable."

"Got it. Thanks, Ren."

"Ren, can you really find lost love?" Thayla asked just as Victor was starting to stand up.

"I can! Love is my affinity. Can't you feel it in your chests?" She hummed a gentle buzzing tune, and suddenly Victor did feel it—warmth in the center of himself, not really his chest, more close to his Core. Images of his mother and *abuela* came into his mind, and, to his dismay, he saw a memory of Thayla smiling and laughing.

"Like a sister, maybe," he said softly. Thayla looked at him sharply, but she smiled, giving him a knowing wink.

"Did you see your missing loved one?" Ren asked Thayla.

"Yes, but just a memory. I need to find her!"

"Do you have anything of hers?" Ren drew a long pull of smoke through her pipe, watching for Thayla's response.

"No." Thayla's eyes welled with tears. "They took everything from me when I was captured."

"Oho! So the imperial masters had business that required you to give up your freedom, hmm?" Ren let out a very unladylike growl that rolled around in her throat, almost like a purr. "Don't worry; Ren can help. Here." She stood and waddled over to a trunk, lifting the lid and rummaging for several minutes. She returned holding a small, polished, pink stone. It was flat on one side and had little lines carved in every direction from a central indentation.

She sat in front of Thayla again and pulled a long, slender needle from her hair. "I need a drop of your blood." Thayla glanced nervously at Victor and then licked her lips, holding out a finger.

"Wait!" Victor said, snatching her hand away. "Ren, Thayla's been through a lot of shit in the last weeks. You better not be trying to mess with her somehow."

"No, warrior. If I do aught to hurt her, you may split me with that terrible axe. I have only good intentions, and we'll seal this bargain with a payment so all parties are satisfied." At her words, Victor reluctantly let go of Thayla's hand and then watched.

Ren, quick as a snake's tongue, pricked the needle into Thayla's finger. Thayla jerked away from reflex, but the damage was done—a thick droplet of blood welled up on her fingertip. "Quick now! Let it drop into the center of the stone." She held the pale pink stone out, and Thayla did as she was told, letting the drop of blood fall into the center. Ren smiled and then hummed again, a soft buzzing sound, and her hand began to glow with violet light. As Victor watched, Thayla's blood sank into the stone and was completely gone.

"What did you do?" Victor asked.

"Just the perfect thing for your friend here." She looked into Thayla's eyes and said, "Hold this in your hand, and when you think of the one you love, your blood will point the way."

"Really?" Thayla asked.

"Yes, truly. Now about my fee," the furry woman said, holding the stone back.

"What do you want?" Thayla asked, desperation in her eyes. Victor put his hand on Lifedrinker's cold metal head, annoyed that this woman seemed to be profiting from Thayla's distress.

"Nothing much! Just another gem filled with the warrior's Energy." She turned to Victor with a narrow-eyed grin.

"What the fuck are you going to do with that rage-attuned Energy? I don't want to be responsible for helping you cause a fight or something."

"Tosh! Is it Ren's fault that you came here with such potent Energy? Perhaps you have something else to offer?"

"I do!" Thayla said, cutting Victor's response off.

"Can it be? Two spirit casters visiting me at once?" Ren studied Thayla for a long moment, then shook her head. "I can't see it—my Discerning Eye isn't what it once was. What attunement do you have, girl?"

"Courage."

"Are you . . . truly?" She quickly tried to compose herself, but the damage had been done—Thayla and Victor had both seen the greed in her eyes.

"I'll give you some, enough to work several spells, but I won't fill a crystal as large as the one Victor did."

"A bargain well-struck, dear." Ren closed her eyes, touching her pin, and a moment later, she held a crystal similar to the one Victor had filled. She handed it to Thayla. "Give me what you can, and the Heart Finder is yours."

"All right," Thayla said, taking the crystal. She closed her eyes, and a few moments later, her hand and the crystal began to glow with red-gold light. She grimaced in concentration, but long before the crystal was full, she stopped and held it up. It pulsed at its center with a dim but warm light.

"No more?" Ren asked, perhaps a bit disappointed.

"It's enough," Victor said, motioning for the woman to hand over the Heart Finder.

"True, a bargain's a bargain!" the little woman said, handing the polished pink stone to Thayla. Thayla quickly handed over the crystal, and then she held the stone in her palm and closed her eyes. A moment later, a thin bead of red filled one of the carved lines on the stone's surface, pointing to, as far as Victor could tell, the south.

"No way to tell distance?" Victor asked.

"Tut! Of course! A bright, thick line means they're very close. A thin red line like this means they're within a few days' travel. If it were thinner still and more pink than red, it would mean they are quite distant." Thayla opened her eyes, looked at the stone, and smiled brightly.

"Thank you, Ren!"

"Yeah, that's pretty cool," Victor added. He stood, and Thayla followed him as he moved to the door, pulling the rickety thing open. "I'll be sure to send business your way, Ren. Thanks for the help."

"Hush now! Don't send any unwanted attention my way!" The Vodkin said, stepping forward and poking Victor in the ribs with her thin, claw-tipped finger.

"Oh, all right. We'll keep this between us!" Victor gave her an exaggerated wink, and she huffed, pushing him further out, toward Thayla and closing the door behind him. Thayla laughed and smiled brightly, tucking the Heart Finder into her storage ring. "Well, that put you in a good mood!"

"Of course! I learned two things—my daughter isn't far away, and you love me! Ha, even if it's like a sister, I can use all the love I can get in this world."

"Come on, just cause that crazy witch made me think about you, my mom, and my *abuelita*? That doesn't mean anything much." Victor looked around the alley, noting that the drunken Shadeni were gone. It seemed awfully quiet. How long had they been in the witch's house?

"Oh, hush! You basically admitted as much the other day when you were drunk," Thayla said, her spirits too high to notice that something was troubling Victor.

Thayla was lifting a finger to poke him in the chest when Victor stepped forward, ripping Lifedrinker from the ring at his belt. Several figures had stepped out from behind broken crates, barrels, and dilapidated buildings. They all wore livery Victor was intimately familiar with—the soldiers that had chained him to a rotating table so a tentacled demon could fuck around with his Core had worn the same—dark maroon with a silver sun and three half-moons at the breast. These were Lord ap'Horrin's men.

"Took us a while to track you down, Victor," said one of the men, a tall Shadeni with long, red horns and heavy black armor. "Lucky for us, Tkelvic took a piece of your Core as a souvenir." He held up a faintly glimmering red gem that dangled from a chain on his wrist. Victor had been counting while he edged in front of Thayla—there were seven of them, including the talkative asshole.

"Only seven? That dickhead, ap'Horrin, must not like you guys." Victor channeled a surge of rage-attuned Energy into Lifedrinker, and she blazed with a red nimbus. "Well? You gonna stand around holding your nuts all night, or are we going to fight?"

25

NO GOING BACK

The horned Shadeni didn't seem pleased by Victor's bravado and scowled, looking left to right as if reassuring himself that he was the one pulling off an ambush. He tucked the chain holding the glimmering shard of Victor's Core into his belt, and then his hands were holding a massive black iron maul. He smirked and said, "Bows!"

Victor saw some of the ambushing party lift heavy, flat crossbows and level them at him. He roared, casting Project Spirit, pouring forth a torrent of negatively attuned inspiration Energy. Sickly yellow waves rolled through the cluttered alley, engulfing most of the attackers, with the three crossbowmen at the center. Their eyes widened, and their fingers fumbled, and Victor charged.

As he covered the dozen feet between himself and the central cluster of ap'Horrin's men, Victor cast Inspiring Presence and boosted his agility with Sovereign Will, then he was among them, capitalizing on their shaken, dismayed state. The leader of the crew seemed least affected by Victor's projected spirit, but even he hesitated for a split second as Victor tore past him, and that was all Victor needed—Lifedrinker fell in three quick, devastating hacks, opening terrible wounds in the crossbowmen, leaving them broken and bleeding as they fell before his onslaught.

By the time he'd finished with the crossbowmen, the horned Shadeni had recovered enough to bring his maul whistling toward Victor's head. Victor's situational awareness had improved a great deal over the course of his many battles, though, and he felt it coming, ducking forward to take the brunt of the blow in the back of his armored shoulder. It hurt and sent him stumbling forward a step, but his size and durability weren't things to be scoffed at, and he mostly shrugged off the blow. He whirled just in time to see Thayla drive her spear through a sword-wielding ambusher's throat.

"Charge him, you cowards!" the black-armored leader shouted, but when he glanced around and realized Thayla was keeping his two remaining minions in check with her long spear, he licked his lips and turned back to Victor, saying, "Come quietly, Victor, and no one else has to die."

Victor could only laugh at the absurdity of the statement. He said, "You come to me with a piece of my Core that was ripped from my guts. You come to me with loaded crossbows, ready to fill me with holes, and now you speak of 'coming quietly?'" He growled and stepped forward, lifting Lifedrinker. "Quit embarrassing yourself." Victor stepped over one of the crossbowmen—a stocky Cadwalli who thrashed weakly as his life's blood pumped out of the ruined stump of his left shoulder where Lifedrinker had sheared away his arm, and continued, "Are you going to lay down your weapon, or do we finish this?"

"You think you can defy ap'Horrin? You think you can defy me, Tazrodak?" He glanced to his left, where Thayla still danced with the other two ap'Horrin soldiers. "Come, then, you won't find me as soft as those whelps!" Victor hadn't been waiting for an invitation and was already moving to strike as Tazro lifted his maul in an awkward parry attempt. He might be a big Shadeni and have some skill in battle, but he wasn't strong enough to wield that maul with the adroitness necessary to counter Victor's lightning cleave with Lifedrinker.

Tazro drove his maul forward in a thrust, trying to catch Lifedrinker on its broad metal head, but Victor angled his swing with such speed, stepping into the blow, that she ripped through the air under the heavy bludgeon, and her blade peeled away a thick curl of the maul's haft as she tore down its length and into the armored fingers of its wielder. Tazro screamed as several of his digits were severed to fall in a splatter of blood to the dirty alley floor.

"Lifedrinker's not impressed with your armor," Victor said as Tazro dropped his maul with a clatter, unable to hold onto the heavy weapon with only a third of his fingers still intact.

"I yield!" Tazro screamed, holding his hands tightly to his chest, blood pumping out of the ruined gauntlets and down his armored chest piece. Victor glanced at Thayla and saw that she held her spear to one soldier's neck while the other stood back, hands empty, his axe and small shield on the ground in front of him.

"You yield?" Victor asked. "Should I show you mercy? I don't feel like you had much mercy in mind for me."

"I can give you your Core fragment! I can give you a key to ap'Horrin's oubliette, where he has several more! You'll never find your way in without my guidance! I swear—let me live, and I'll take these men and disappear for months until you've settled your business with the lord." He'd fallen to his knees and was doing a fine job of looking pathetic.

"Thayla, what do you say?"

"I say we have too many people hunting us and wanting us dead to let these blackguards loose. It's not our fault they came after us with murder in their hearts." Victor looked at the bodies in the alley and at Tazro begging on his knees, and the only emotions he could muster were disgust and anger.

Rather than prolong the miserable situation with more discussion, allowing Tazro to sow further doubt, Victor lifted Lifedrinker, stepped forward, and brought her down at an angle into Tazro's neck, just above the black gorget of his armor. She bit deeply, severing his spine in a spray of dark blood, and would have removed his head if her blade hadn't caught in the metal collar due to the downward angle.

Tazro hadn't had a chance to scream or protest, and when Victor heard footsteps running, he turned to see that Thayla had impaled one of the soldiers with her spear, but the other was running down the alley. He yanked Lifedrinker free and charged after him, and in just a few strides, he caught up with the man and cleaved into his shoulder, ripping a terrible wound and sending him crashing into a pile of broken crates.

Victor hurried back to Thayla and Tazro's corpse, feeling they should make themselves scarce but not wanting to leave behind his Core fragment or any valuable information. Thayla must have had the same thought because she was already rifling through Tazro's belt pouches. She tossed him the chain with the red, pulsing gemstone, and Victor felt his Core throb hungrily when he caught it. Not wanting to take the time to deal with it just yet, he hung it over his head, tucking it under his armored shirt. A surge of Energy almost knocked him over as he bent to help search the corpse.

Thayla grunted beside him and said, "Level!"

"Nice one," Victor said, then bent back to the task. "Where the fuck is this guy's storage device?"

"The fingers!" Thayla said suddenly, looking at the sausage-shaped metal encased digits Victor had severed. They were scattered around the ground, and Victor hurriedly moved to scoop them up.

"You all should get lost," a high-pitched voice called from off to the left and high up. Victor glanced toward the source of the voice and saw a red-headed Ardeni boy leaning out of a second-story window. "The town watch'll be coming soon; Matra the Crone went to fetch 'em when the killin' started."

"Thanks, kid," Victor said, scooping the fingers up and into his pants pocket. "C'mon, Thayla," he said more quietly, and the two of them hurried away down the alley, wending their way through the maze of narrow streets, putting as much distance as possible between themselves and the scene of the ambush.

"Will you be all right?" Thayla asked after a while when they'd finally worked their way back to one of the main roads.

"What do you mean?" Victor looked at her quizzically.

"Well, it's different killing someone in combat than outside of it. We executed those men."

"Yeah, well, they didn't have good intentions for us. If I start to feel guilty, I'll remember those crossbows getting ready to punch holes in us, or I'll remember what ap'Horrin did to me when he had me strapped to a table in his dungeon."

"Fair enough. I guess you have another task to add to your list, though—if he has more fragments of your Core, he'll be able to find you again." Thayla took his elbow and steered him uphill as she spoke.

"Aren't we going down to the docks? To find your old contact?"

"No, I think we should go lay low for a while. I have this now, anyway." She lifted up her Heart Finder, which she held tightly in one fist.

"Well, if you're sure." Victor picked up the pace, quickly climbing away from the shambles and into the city proper. He asked Gorz for directions a couple of times but managed to mostly lead the way back to their villa by memory.

He was feeling particularly paranoid, thanks to the ambush in the shambles, but even as he looked around with suspicion at nearly everyone he passed, he couldn't see anything out of the ordinary. Sure, he drew a few looks, but that was probably because of his stature and the fact that he was the only human in the city. In any event, it wasn't long before they were slipping through the villa's gate and then securely locking themselves inside.

Victor moved into the kitchen and pulled the severed digits out of his pocket, dropping them onto the counter. Thankfully, the blood had mostly dried, so he didn't create much of a mess, but it was still a rather grisly affair, trying to shake and prize the flesh from the gauntlet fingers. Thayla helped him, and it was she, on her second attempt, that fished out a fat finger with a golden ring around it.

"Bingo!" Victor said when Thayla hissed in excitement. "You do the honors." Victor wasn't sure why he wanted Thayla to bond with the ring and search through it. He supposed part of it was that he wanted to show her that she'd earned his complete trust. She looked at him with an arched eyebrow but didn't say anything, pulling the golden band off the pale, dead finger. While she concentrated on bonding with the dimensional device and then the process of searching through it, Victor scooped up the fingers and their metal casings and went out to the courtyard.

He found a spot under a shrub in the corner and dug a small hole, burying them in the soft soil. By the time he'd finished and returned to the kitchen, Thayla had set out a small collection of items for him to go through. A small stack of documents sat next to a heavy, black key. Next to the key was a large leather sack, and next to the sack was a pile of thin rods that looked very much like amber ore. Thayla looked up at him as he arrived and gestured to the collection. "Everything else is just supplies, clothes—stuff like that."

"Did you read any of the documents yet?" Victor asked.

"No. I was about to, though." She picked up the top page, passed it to Victor, and started reading the next one.

Victor looked at his document and saw that it was a letter from ap'Horrin. He skimmed through it, then read the final paragraph aloud, "'Tkelvic is a resource that grows less stable each year, and I cannot count on his abilities to solve every minor problem. The Core fragment he took from your quarry is a boon that you should count yourself very lucky to have. If you lose it or fail to properly make use of it to find your target, you should seek employment elsewhere. House ap'Horrin doesn't have room for incompetence.'"

Thayla set her document down and said, "This is just a copy of a lease for a skyship. Well, if you take that at face value, it sounds like maybe Tazro was lying about ap'Horrin having more of your Core fragments."

"Yeah, hopefully. In any case, I think I'll need to deal with ap'Horrin sooner or later."

"What kind of name is Tkelvic, anyway?" Thayla asked, picking up the next document.

"I'm pretty sure it's the tentacled spider dude that tore apart my Core."

"Tentacled? Spider? Oh, Ancestors! Was he a Yovashi?"

"Yovashi?" Victor looked at her quizzically.

"They're a race of insane cannibalistic monsters. They come from the same origin world as the Ilyathi and Ghelli, but something's wrong with their minds—when I say they're insane, I mean it literally. I've never heard of one working for someone. In fact, I think any civilized person that was working with a Yovashi would face condemnation."

"Well, something tells me ap'Horrin doesn't give a shit what other people think." Victor picked up the last document and glanced over it. It was a requisition for house soldiers and supplies—ap'Horrin had authorized quite an expenditure for Tazro's mission. "You know, they might have really underestimated our ability to fight, but I think the loss of this squad is going to sting ap'Horrin a bit. He spent quite a lot on those soldiers and their transport."

"Good!" Thayla said, putting down her document. "This one is just a recipe for marmalade. What a weird thing to find in a murderous bounty hunter's storage device!"

"Well, what else do we have here? Are those rods amber ore?"

"They are, though not the purest I've seen. The sack is full of attuned Energy beads, at least a few hundred."

"And the key? Do you think it's to the 'oubliette' that *pendejo* was talking about?"

"No idea, but it wouldn't hurt to hang onto it." Thayla scooped the rods, bag of Energy beads, and key toward Victor.

"You don't want any of this?"

"He had two sacks of beads, and I kept one. The other stuff, though—you should keep it. They were hunting you, so I say you should keep the spoils. Besides, you've been more than fair and generous to me."

"Eh, we're a team, *chica.*" Nevertheless, Victor scooped the items into his storage ring. As he tucked away the sack of beads, a thought occurred to him, and he said, "Hey, Thayla, I never got around to learning how to make these beads. Is it very involved?"

"No, it's simple as can be, but it takes time and concentration. Want me to show you?"

"Yeah, we have some time to kill, don't we?"

"Hmm, well, come over to the couch—we might as well get comfortable." Thayla led the way to the sitting room, and the two of them sat side by side on the wicker couch, which creaked in protest to Victor's bulk, but held up gamely. "Now watch; this should really be as easy as rum-sugar cookies for someone with your will." Before Victor could ask about her strange turn of phrase, Thayla held her hands out in front of herself, one with the palm facing up, and the other about four inches above it, palm down.

He could feel her channeling Energy before he saw it, but soon there were two thin streams of red-gold Energy tentatively snaking out of her palms to meet in the air between them. Her face was rigid with concentration as she slowly folded her two streams around each other, rolling them tightly with each fold. After just a few moments, the ball of red-gold Energy snapped into a tiny bead. "This is the smallest form of Energy bead. They're quick to make and are often used for minor transactions. We want a real Energy bead, though, so I'll keep going."

"That's cool," Victor said, leaning close to watch her weave more Energy around the tiny bead. As the minutes stretched into an hour, the process began to lose its novelty, though, and he said, "*Madre*! How long does this take?"

"I'm about halfway done, I think. Some people can do it faster, but most people are considerably slower. I've got a higher than normal will, too, thanks to the courage attunement you gave me and the advice Oynalla gave me—I've been increasing my will at every opportunity."

"Huh," Victor said, sitting back with a sigh.

"If you're that bored, get started on your own bead!" Thayla said, nudging his leg with her knee while she continued to work.

"All right!" Victor mimicked her posture and started trickling out some rage-attuned Energy through each of his hands. Using his will, he forced the threads together, tightly binding them and rolling them together. It seemed pretty easy, so he broadened the threads, pushing out more than double the amount of Energy. Almost immediately, the tiny version of his bead snapped into being, and he smiled, continuing to wrap his Energy threads around it, building layer upon layer of Energy into the nascent bead. "If I finish before you, you have to make dinner!"

"Oh? Cocksure, aren't you?" Thayla laughed, though, and he saw her narrow her eyes in renewed concentration.

As it turned out, Thayla finished her bead before Victor, but only just barely. When she finished, she laughed victoriously and held her gleaming red-gold bead out in front of Victor's face, taunting him. "Hey! Let me finish, at least! Sheesh, I can't even see with that right in my face!"

"Well, it looks like you're making dinner. You know, I don't think I've ever seen you cook, Victor!"

"Well, I'm not much of a cook," Victor said, trying to refocus on his task. "My *abuela* always had beans and tortillas; if I wanted food outside of meal time, that's what I ate." He wrapped a final layer around his bead and sighed happily as the bead flashed and solidified—a balefully pulsing red ball. "You know, that sounds pretty damn good. They have tortillas in this world?"

"Tortillas? Describe them."

"They're usually made from flour or corn. I guess it's like soft, flat bread. Really thin, like this," Victor held his finger and thumb close together to indicate the thickness. "About the size of a plate. We usually eat them with eggs and potatoes or, like I said, refries."

"Refries?"

"Uh, a kind of beans. Refried beans."

"It doesn't sound like it would be hard to make something like that. Someone with some cooking talent could probably do it based on your description, and then you could help them refine it by tasting. I'm not your girl, though—I can make a stew or grill some meat, but I don't know anything about baking bread." Thayla shrugged.

"No worries. I guess I'll just add tortillas to my list of things to figure out, huh?" Victor stood and went to the kitchen, looking in the cold-cabinet. It was pretty well stocked with eggs, lots of vegetables, and even some thickly cut bacon. "How's breakfast for dinner sound? Scrambled eggs and bacon?"

"If I weren't so hungry, I'd tease you for your unoriginal ideas, but at this point, I'll take it." Thayla sat at the kitchen counter and prepared to watch him cook their meal. Victor smiled and got to work. While he cooked, they joked and shared memories of favorite meals, and even though Victor wasn't very talented with a skillet, the food was good. Thayla had encouraged him to add some greens to the scramble, and he'd diced some funny little purple-orange peppers into the mix after sampling their heat—they were a bit milder than jalapenos.

While they ate, Thayla encouraged Victor to try absorbing his Core fragment. He'd almost forgotten about the little red gem, and he had an idea which he quickly dismissed, that he was subconsciously blocking out the whole fight scene in the alley. He pulled the fragment out from under his armored shirt, and again he felt his Core throb hungrily, so he went with it; he reached out to the Energy in the red gem and pulled it toward his Core. It flowed into him effortlessly, and he felt the red, blazing sun of his rage Energy throb and pulse heavily. When he looked at his status sheet, he saw that he'd leveled his Core from Base Five to Base Six.

"What happened?" Thayla asked, seeing the grin on his face.

"My Core leveled. I guess that piece was bigger than it looked."

After the two of them ate, they checked the locks on the windows and doors and called it a night. Victor cast Tether Spirit before he went to sleep, and though he remembered having dreams, they must have been relatively mild because, by the time he stood up from bed and pulled on his pants, he'd forgotten them. He stumbled groggily into his bathroom and decided to take a bath. He set his clothes and armor on the counter next to the sink, leaned Lifedrinker against the tub, and started running the water.

As he stood there, waiting for the water to fill, and his eyes fell on his axe again, he remembered how he'd chopped her silvery edge into Tazro's neck while the man had been on his knees, begging for his life. Suddenly the whole thing seemed surreal, as if it hadn't really happened—as if it couldn't have happened. He felt an unpleasant surge of saliva and swallowed it down, and then nausea gripped him, and he hurried to the toilet, where he vomited his guts out.

What had he become? Could he still be the same kid from Tucson? He glanced at his reflection in the mirror, his face red and lips flecked with spittle from heaving. "I'm a fucking monster," he said when he took in his thick neck, ropy muscles, and massive stature. "I'm a fucking monster that executes people on their knees." He felt dizzy, and vertigo began to grip him, so he grabbed the side of the tub and sank down, naked, to the tile floor.

He sat there, mind reeling, unable to reconcile his current reality with the life he remembered before he'd been summoned to Fanwath. One thought kept coming to him: he could never go home. His family wouldn't even recognize him. How could he ever explain to them what had happened to him? How could he ever explain the things he'd done or the changes he'd gone through? "Is this real?" The question seemed simplistic, but the more he thought about his situation, about how people were hunting him, and he was killing people in the streets, the more he found it implausible.

As he sat there, shaking and confused, his eyes fell on Lifedrinker, and he reached out a hand to her haft and pulled her close. Her wooden, living handle was warm and seemed to pulse softly under his fingers, and he found himself saying, "It's not your fault, *chica*. All you ever do is get me out of trouble."

He rested Lifedrinker's cool, silver-streaked, black metal against his forehead, and he felt a buzzing sensation where they touched. Then a strange, ethereal voice sounded in his mind, *"Not your fault, Victor."* His eyes bulged wide, and he pulled her away from his head, staring at the axe, and, through all his distress, a slow smile spread on his lips.

"Are you talking to me, lovely?" The axe vibrated softly in his hands, and he pulled the metal against his forehead again.

"Not your fault! Those that hunt wolves must beware the fang!" The ethereal, feminine voice rang in his head again, but this time with a sense of finality, and Victor somehow understood that she couldn't speak much without rest, at least not yet. Victor felt tears start to pool in his eyes, and he wiped at them furiously. He didn't know why his axe's approval meant so much to him, but it did, and she'd made a good point: this was a dangerous world, and Tazro had meant to kill him. His master had already done something to him that he'd thought was worse than death. It was no time to be pulling punches.

"Thank you, *chica*," he said, clambering to his feet and leaning her against the tub again. "Time to get cleaned up."

After his bath, Victor still avoided looking at himself in the mirror. He might be able to justify his actions, and Thayla and Lifedrinker might approve of him, but he still felt raw, and seeing his huge, manly physique just drove home the point that there was no going back for him. He'd never be plain old Victor Sandoval again. No, he was a berserker, a warrior, a killer with the blood of titans in his veins. "If I can't go back, then I need to go forward, and I need to make it worth something," he said, shrugging into his armored shirt. He picked up Lifedrinker, gave her warm haft a loving stroke, and slipped her into the ring at his belt.

Victor strode out of his room and called out, "Thayla! We've got a day before Lam gets here! Let's do some shopping—I need more clothes."

26

THE PRICE OF FREEDOM

"There she is!" Victor said, pointing down the street toward the little cafe tables outside the bakery. Sure enough, Lam was sitting at one, sipping at a mug of something steamy. She was impressive, as always, with her wings dropping glittering motes behind her, even at rest. Her attire was notably different here in the city than she wore down in the mines—sleek black leggings, a loosely buttoned, red, silky blouse, and a gleaming silver diadem resting among her platinum curls.

"Edeya's with her," Thayla said, and Victor saw that it was true, though he might not have recognized the younger Ghelli. She sat to Lam's right wearing polished leather armor studded with steel knobs and with a black and gold tabard hanging from a rod jutting up behind her left shoulder.

"What's on that tabard? A broken crown and some feathers?"

"I think it's Lam's sigil. Ha, she's flying Lam's banner wherever they go!" Thayla snorted and started walking down the street, and Victor matched her pace. Lam met their eyes before they were within a hundred feet, and she smiled and waved. They hurried over, and Lam gestured to two chairs at the table, but not before Edeya could squeal and leap to her feet, grabbing first Thayla and then Victor into a tight hug.

"Damn, you've gotten stronger, *chica*!"

"Oh, not that again! You might have grown even more beast-like, but don't think I won't give you a thrashing if you keep calling me girl!"

"Right, sorry, sorry," Victor laughed.

"Should we move somewhere more private, Lam?" Thayla asked, looking around nervously.

"That won't be necessary. You won't need to hide anymore, in fact. Sit down, and I'll explain some things. Order some food first if you want. This revashi root tea is exceptional, and I'm finding it quite stimulating."

"I'll sit first; I'm eager to hear what you have to say," Victor said, pulling out a chair and sitting in it, to the sounds of metal creaking and straining.

"Trees, Victor! I remember I used to tower over you—I think we'd be on a level now."

"He's so much thicker than you, though, Captain! I could barely put my arm around his trunk!" Edeya laughed.

"I literally just got here, and you're attacking me!" Victor feigned dismay, holding a hand toward Edeya, palm out.

"Don't let him fool you—he wants you to think he's being melodramatic, but he's truly quite sensitive. Don't beat up on him so much, Edeya," Thayla said, also laughing wickedly.

"Enough, enough!" Lam said, clearing her throat. "Do you want to know why you don't have to hurry back to your hidey-hole or not?" Thayla and Victor both nodded, and Lam smiled and began her story. "Well, when you reached out with my stone, I knew that Edeya and I could catch the next Consortium airship to Gelica, but I had a day to kill before it left. While we were waiting, I had one of my more brilliant ideas—I went to the mine administration office and looked up your contracts. Yes, you'd killed a member of the ap'Yensha family, and they were hunting you down, but they never bothered to snatch up your contracts. When I asked about them, the administrative clerks looked through their files, and sure enough, they were still there. They hadn't even marked you deceased! Victor, I bought your contract for a ridiculously low price, and Thayla, yours wasn't much more."

"What? You bought our contracts?" Thayla asked. "Are we off the hook?"

"You are! Victor's going to have to jump through a few more hoops, but I managed to secure your indemnification, Thayla."

"Hoops?" Victor asked, frowning.

"Nothing of my doing, I'm afraid. Lady ap'Yensha has a claim against you because the scries of your brutal slaying of her nephew were rather clear. Thayla didn't have a physical role in it, so when I made the claim on her contract, ap'Yensha dropped their grievance against her—for a small donation, of course. I couldn't get them to do the same for you, Victor, but I did come up with a solution: a duel."

"What?" Victor asked.

"A duel?" Thayla said at the same time.

"Oh, come now! You act like this is a bad thing—if I told you yesterday that you could be done with this whole mess for the price of one more fight, wouldn't you have jumped at the chance?"

Victor and Thayla gave each other long, measured looks, and then Victor said, "Yeah, of course. Thayla's good, though? Even if I lose?"

"Thayla's good. Here." Lam produced two sheets of paper, both marked upon with several different inks and seals, but Victor recognized his contract right away due to all the crossed-out lines and scribbles. "My gift to you both. Victor, after you win your duel, you'll be free. You won't have to worry about the mine coming after you, even the ap'Yenshas—I secured their guarantee, witnessed by the ap'Bale representative. If you don't remember, the ap'Bale's are rather hostile to ap'Yensha, and they'll see that no repercussions come your way after your victory."

"Shit! Congrats, Thayla!"

"It doesn't feel right," Thayla said, taking her contract and glancing at it, then back to Victor with worried eyes. "Duels aren't anything to scoff at, and ap'Yensha will have a stable of champions to pick from!"

"Ha! You know the rules—any champion chosen to fight Victor will have to be in the same tier as him. What level are you, Victor?"

"Twenty-nine."

"Gods! He's a natural ringer—I can feel your aura from here, Victor. A Tier Four would struggle with you. I pity whatever jumped-up dandy they put against you."

"Really? So as long as I'm Tier Two, they have to pick a Tier Two to fight me?"

"Those are the rules for champions; she's right," Thayla said. "It's the same rule if you initiate a legal duel—you can't fight someone lower than your own tier, and of course, the challenger may not use a champion."

"Of course, I'm right! If Lady ap'Yensha wants you dead, then she's got to find someone your tier to fight you. Now that you have my legal backing, she can't send bounty hunters after you, at least not if she doesn't want the whole empire to come down on her. I've been building my influence, and I owe you both for a large portion of my wealth. I pay my debts." Lam smiled and winked at Edeya, and the girl giggled. He wondered what inside joke he was missing.

"So what's next? When's the duel?" Victor asked, taking up his contract and stowing it into his storage ring. "Thanks for giving me my contract, by the way, Lam."

"You're welcome, Victor," Lam smiled at him warmly, then continued, "Tomorrow we have a meeting with a jurist. After we make our case and you indicate your willingness to fight to defend your innocence, the jurist will go before a magistrate and plead our case. We'll be there, but only to watch at that point. Once that's done, and ap'Yensha does the same, you'll find out who your opponent will be and when the bout will take place. The Imperial Magistrate will most likely want to use your duel as an excuse for a gala of some sort."

"Huh. All right. Well, Thayla and I rented a villa nearby—do you guys want to stay with us?"

"No, you'll need to come to my estate. If you're going to be under my care, we better look the part, right?" Victor and Thayla couldn't argue with that, so after they all ate some breakfast, they went by Yasha's shop to turn in their keys to the villa.

The young woman was disappointed that she couldn't sell them any more time in the comfortable home, but she was pleased when they didn't ask for any of their rental fee back. Lam softened the blow of their leaving by offering to tell her friends about the rental, and they parted ways on friendly enough terms. Lam's home wasn't in the city proper but north of the walls in a park-like setting of green meadows and wooded copses cleared of underbrush, giving them a manicured feel.

"It took me twenty-four years to get my hands on a place in these woods," Lam said as they strolled down a cobbled lane between tall, arching bows.

"Why? Wouldn't you rather be inside the walls?"

"Oh, just because we went out a gate doesn't mean we aren't inside the walls—there's another wall about ten miles farther north. You should know that, Thayla; I thought you did work in Gelica before you, um, retired."

"I guess I never got around to these estates." Thayla shrugged.

"Anyway, they're very exclusive, and the families that own them are old. They don't sell—I had to wait for Lord ap'Vebra to make a particularly bad investment, and then I had to give him an out that was too good to be true. It was a purchase decades in the planning." Victor and Thayla looked at each other, and Victor guessed Thayla was thinking the same as he was: this side of Lam was wildly different from the fortune seeker in the mines.

"Captain Lam's been building her influence, you guys. You can't get into politics if you don't play all the aspects of the game," Edeya said, scoffing at their shared glance.

"Why do you want to be in politics, Lam?" Victor asked.

"We've spoken about how important it is to keep gaining in power, haven't we, Victor? I think it might have been in regard to me helping Edeya or maybe not helping her enough for your taste, hmm? Well, when you get near Tier Five, like me, you'll find that raw power increases come slowly. Very slowly. You start to look for other ways to grow your power base, like accumulating wealth. You know I've done that as well, yes? Well, one thing you do with wealth is to increase your political clout. So, you see, there are three ways I'm still working to gain strength—literal power, through levels and artifacts, accumulating wealth, and gaining political influence."

"How much will Victor winning his duel help you politically?" Thayla asked suddenly.

"Oh, very good, Thayla! You caught me—I'm not altruistic. I stand to gain something from helping you and Victor. Is that what you want to hear? Roots! Don't be so difficult!"

"It's fine," Victor said, reaching out and putting a hand on Thayla's shoulder. "Right, Thayla? We're grateful, Lam; don't sweat it."

"Yeah, of course. I'm sorry, I'm still in shock, I think. I'm free, with the axe off my neck, but still, I'm worried about Victor. These lords are vindictive—I can't imagine it's going to go as smoothly as we all hope."

"We'll see what the jurist has to say tomorrow," Lam said. "Let it go for now, though—I haven't been home for a while, and I'd like to enjoy a day here before all the business. Here we are!" She gestured down the lane, and Victor saw that an ivy-covered gate had come into view with a stone guardhouse built into the wall at one end. As they approached, a soldier came out of the guardhouse wearing a livery that matched the banner Edeya had been flying for Lam—black pants, a gold top, and a surcoat emblazoned with a broken, silver crown over a clutch of black feathers.

"Lady Lam, welcome home!" he said, bowing deeply and then moving to open the gate.

Thayla looked at Victor and mouthed, "Lady Lam?" He shrugged and followed Lam and Edeya through the gate, then up the cobbled road that bent to the left and climbed a gentle hill. When they came around the bend,

Lam's estate came into view, and suddenly Victor realized he'd been vastly underestimating the captain's wealth.

The manor and grounds covered the entire hilltop, and it wasn't a small hill. Hedgerows bordered the cobbled road, and Victor could see manicured gardens falling away to the right and left, but directly ahead was the manor, and it looked big enough to house hundreds of people. The central building was several stories high. The wings were long, with imposing, peaked roofs covered with ceramic tile. Ivy grew along the building's walls, and tall arched windows gleamed and glittered in the sunlight, painting the picture of an idyllic, stately old manor in the woods—a place for ancient bloodlines to gather and contemplate their rulership of the world.

As Lam and the trio of her former mine workers strode up the lane to the front door, a dull horn could be heard from within the structure, and then a flurry of activity began to take place—shutters were thrown open all over the building, the front door opened, and uniformed staff came pouring out to line up in a double row. The men and women that worked in Lam's manor fidgeted and stole glances at her as she approached, awaiting her inspection.

"*¿Qué es esto?*" Victor said softly, utterly flabbergasted by the show of wealth and power.

"I know . . ." Thayla said, also looking around wide-eyed, as the four of them started up the final stretch of the drive to the front door, and the servants arrayed bowed deeply to Captain Lam. When they came to the short flight of steps leading to the front door, and the gray-haired old Ardeni with perfectly trimmed mustaches bowed, Lam smiled and cleared her throat.

"Thank you, everyone. It's good to be home. Darn, see that my guests are given quarters in the east wing and that Edeya here is given the Adjutant's rooms near my suite."

"Of course, ma'am," the gray Ardeni said. "Follow me, please," he said to Victor and Thayla. Edeya looked at Lam with a questioning look, and when Lam nodded, she followed along. They shadowed the seneschal into the house, and Victor marveled at the home, both because of its impressive construction and because of the rich appointments, from masterwork furniture to ancient, precious artifacts. Had Lam been plumbing the depths of Greatbone so that she could fill this manor with rare discoveries?

"You seem different, Edeya," Thayla said as they followed Darn deeper into the manor.

"I am different! I've been through a lot of training, and Lam's given me a lot of responsibility. I wish I could be carefree and silly, guys, but the captain has a lot going on right now, and I'm in charge of keeping track of a lot of meetings and strategies. I did miss you guys, though! I'm so happy you're alive and well."

"Excuse me, Miss Edeya, the Adjutant's quarters are up these stairs and down the central hallway. Your quarters are right before the captain's."

"All right. That's me, then, Victor and Thayla! I'll see you tomorrow for our meeting with the jurist."

"Okay, Edeya. See you tomorrow." Victor watched his old friend climb up the stairs and had to admit Thayla was right—Edeya had changed quite a bit. She was taller, stronger, and more sure in her movements, and that uniform with the weird banner sticking up over her shoulder definitely made her seem more . . . impressive somehow.

"Now, if you'll follow me, I'll lead you to your quarters. Do you mind if I ask your names? It will make tending to your needs much easier while you're here," Darn said, continuing down the wide hallway.

"I'm Victor, and this is Thayla. Darn, are we allowed to explore the grounds a bit after you show us our rooms? It's awfully early to shut ourselves away until tomorrow."

"Of course. Perhaps you'd like to visit the captain's gymnasium? She has sparring fields and obstacle courses that many of the local nobles come to practice upon."

"Yeah, that sounds cool." Victor saw Thayla's pointed stare and corrected himself, "That sounds great; thanks, Darn."

"Of course, sir." Darn led them into the east wing of Lam's manor and showed them each to a separate suite. The rooms were nice, with comfortable furniture and plush appointments, but nothing otherworldly. After they'd both seen their rooms, Darn led them into the gardens and then into a large rectangular building with very high walls and a bank of windows near the roof that allowed in the late morning sun. Inside, the floor was very much like a basketball gym—pale wooden planks and rows of wooden bleachers built against the long walls.

"Sparring?" Thayla asked.

"That's right, Miss Thayla. Do you see those double doors?" He paused to make sure they saw the doors he indicated. "Through those doors, you'll find a staircase leading down, and then you'll be in a similar room beneath this one. That's where the obstacle course is."

"All right, we've got it from here, Darn."

"Are you certain you can find your way back to your quarters?"

"Yes, we're good." Victor nodded. He probably would have struggled to find their rooms again, but Gorz would have no trouble.

"Simply flag down any servants you see if you need anything. They all know how to find me." Darn bowed low, sweeping one hand almost to the floor, then he turned and strode away.

"I mean, do you feel like practicing? I was just thinking we'd be bored sitting in our rooms all afternoon," Victor said to Thayla as the little gray-haired man walked away.

"Not really, to be honest. Let's check out the obstacle course, though." Thayla started toward the double doors, and Victor followed after. The stairs down were similarly clad in pale wooden planks, and when they came out on the lower level, Victor saw that the big rectangular room was filled with things that reminded him a great deal of wrestling practice. He saw a peg board built into one wall that was clearly meant to be climbed upward and then sideways. He figured he could do it, but it would be hard—there were nearly a hundred holes going up and just as many to the sides. He imagined trying to climb that many holes back in his old body, and he snorted in laughter.

"What?" Thayla asked.

"The peg boards. That shit would be hard without some monster stats."

"What do you do with them?" Thayla looked at the wall covered with boards drilled with holes.

"You hold those wooden pegs and jam them into the holes, pulling yourself up to the next set of holes. It's like climbing a rope and doing pull-ups at once."

"Oh, I see." Thayla nodded, looking around at some of the other things in the room—swinging ropes, walls, pits, contraptions you had to crawl through, others you had to balance upon. A slow smile began to spread on her face, "Let's try some of these out!"

"Ha, all right!" Victor laughed, and that's what they did, spending most of the afternoon putting Lam's obstacle course through its paces. A few other people came in to work out on the course while they were there, but they all kept to themselves, though they frequently cast annoyed glares at Thayla and Victor as they taunted and laughed at each other, attempting one obstacle or another.

Their fun was cut short sometime toward evening, though, when Seneschal Darn made a reappearance and called for them to come down from their ropes to speak with him. Victor and Thayla, still feeling quite competitive, raced down to him, and Victor cheated, using Sovereign Will to boost his agility. He laughed as he basically fell down the rope and then tore over the ground, leaping a high wall to slide to a stop in front of Darn. Thayla, a good thirty seconds behind him, laughed breathlessly as she careened into him, and the two of them fell to the ground in a fit.

"Please! Sir and Madam! Lady Lam needs to see you both urgently! There's been a development." Those words sobered Victor and Thayla rather quickly, as the smiles fell from their faces and Victor straightened up, brushing his clothes smooth.

"What kind of development?" Thayla asked.

"Please follow me to the east parlor. The lady will explain everything."

The east parlor turned out to be a comfortable room with a fully stocked and staffed bar, a dozen couches, an alcove full of bookcases, and a small ivory-colored stage where a weird instrument that looked like a sideways piano sat, unplayed. Lam was pacing back and forth in front of a pudgy Shadeni man with thick, swooping horns that sprouted out of his forehead and curved backward over his ears. When Lam saw Victor and Thayla come in behind Darn, she said, "Good, thank you, Darn! Now hurry and make that delivery. I need to know what magistrate our case will come before."

"Yes, Lady," Darn said with a bow, turning to hurry back the way they'd come. Lam looked at Victor and frowned, then sighed. She started to speak, then glanced at the thick Shadeni and shook her head as if not sure what words to use. She glared at him again, then motioned for Victor and Thayla to sit on the couch nearby.

"Victor, I think I've made a huge mistake."

"No, Lady!" the Shadeni said, aghast.

"Yes! No arse-licking right now, Chal-dak. You sit there and be quiet while I explain things to Victor and Thayla."

"Yes, Lady," the red-faced man said, self-consciously preening one of his long, thick horns.

"Victor, you remember how we discussed the rules for choosing champions?"

"Yeah, it was only a few hours ago—champions have to be the same tier or lower."

"Right, and the rule for challenging someone?"

"You can't challenge someone that's a lower tier."

"Right. Well, I really erred when it came to evaluating Lady ap'Yensha's sanity." Lam lifted her diadem with one finger and rubbed at the red line on her forehead where it had been sitting.

"What do you mean, Lam?" Thayla asked, her face looking strangely blanched.

"Lady ap'Yensha isn't using a champion."

"So, what?" Victor asked. "She's fighting me herself?"

"Exactly."

"Well, how's that a problem?"

"She's high Tier Four, Victor."

"But, how? You just said she can't challenge someone who's lower tier . . ."

"She didn't challenge," Thayla said, her voice hushed.

"Exactly," Lam said. Her affect seemed off, and it took Victor a minute to realize it was because she was refusing to make eye contact with him.

"What do you mean?" Victor wasn't trying to act dense, but he still wasn't getting it.

"When I bought your contract, Victor, you became my ward, so to speak. I became your agent. I issued the challenge on your behalf, assuming the lady would shy away from a direct conflict—I was sure she'd pick a champion. She hasn't fought in person in half a century."

"Huh. Well, this kinda sucks, I guess. Almost Tier Five, you say? *Chingado . . .*"

"I've got Darn looking into the magistrate that will be seeing our case. I'll find a way to get you out of this, Victor."

"No," Victor said, smiling at Lam and then turning to Thayla, making sure the smile was still in place. "I gotta do this, Lam. I have to beat this *bruja* so she'll get off my ass, and I can move on to bigger and better things. I'm sick of this problem plaguing me. I don't want to deal with more assassins or bounty hunters. I want to finish this."

"Victor, there will be other opportunities if we just bide our time. Hear me on this: I haven't seen Lady ap'Yensha fight, but there are stories from the Beneset War—I'm not sure I could beat her."

"Well," Victor said, standing up to his full height and resting his hand on Lifedrinker's head. He took a very deep breath and slowly blew it out his nose, looking at Lam right in the eyes, and then he said, "She may be a tough, dangerous woman, but I'm the descendent of Quinametzin giants, and I can promise you, she's never met a motherfucker like me."

27

AXE WORK

Victor sat in a comfortable leather chair facing the window that overlooked Lam's rear garden. He'd never experienced such comfort in his life. Even back in Tucson, he'd had a small room that barely left room for a folding table next to his twin-sized bed. He remembered sitting in the rickety old folding chair, typing away on his school-provided tablet, trying to get assignments done at the last minute.

It seemed as if he was always hot in that bedroom, but no matter the hour, he could count on his *abuela* to bring him snacks. Sometimes it was a taste of whatever she was cooking, but sometimes it was something just for him—orange slices or a warm tortilla smeared with butter and sugar and cinnamon. "God, but I wish you'd come through that door right now. I could use some advice, *Abuelita*."

He didn't know what he expected her to tell him. What could she possibly say about his situation? In just a few days, he'd have to fight for his life against a woman who was supposedly a lot stronger and more deadly than anything he'd encountered so far. First of all, his granny wouldn't like the idea that he was fighting a woman—she was old-fashioned that way, and she didn't know a thing about Energy or levels. Secondly, she'd tell him to get his head straight and do what his coach had taught him. "Yeah, she'd treat this just like a wrestling match."

The thought of explaining that he was about to fight to the death, and that it wasn't the first time, to his *abuela* filled him with strange emotions. He felt guilty, he felt alone, and he felt lost. He thought about trying to talk to Thayla, but how could he explain his weird emotions to her? She'd tried to hide her feelings when Victor had insisted on going through with the fight, but he'd seen the shadows in her eyes. He knew she was worried and half expected him to fail. It hurt, seeing that doubt in her expression, but what hurt more was that she didn't say anything—she was free now, and her main concern was getting to her daughter. It drove home how alone he was in this world.

Lam had offered to train with him over the next few days before the fight, and Victor had enthusiastically taken her up on the offer. That was two days ago, though, and the captain had been busy with one meeting after another, making it clear to Victor that his situation was just one of the many irons she had in the fire. What was the deal with Lam, anyway? She'd given him his contract and tried to help him out of his trouble, but was she that much better than the powers he was struggling against? It almost seemed as if he was just a pawn in her political games, and Thayla had been right when she brought up the fact that Victor's duel would help her in that regard.

"Don't look a gift horse in the mouth," Victor said, trying to mimic his *abuelo's* scratchy old voice with his thick Spanish accent. Lam had taken the time to meet with the Imperial Jurist and then gone to the hearing with the magistrate, confirming her inside information that Lady ap'Yensha was going to face Victor herself. Lam's contacts had gained a bit more insight into the matter—apparently, the man Victor had killed, her nephew, Bez, while being a colossal fuckup, happened to be a favorite of hers. She felt she had to see his killer destroyed personally. "Lucky me." Victor sighed and kicked his feet out, staring up at the plaster ceiling of his bedroom.

The magistrate had scheduled the duel for some sort of Harvest Fest and insisted it be fought at his estate in the country. Lam hadn't been surprised—such an event would provide a lot of political clout to the host, and magistrates were notorious for capitalizing on such opportunities. A knock at his door interrupted his bout of self-pity, and Victor stood up, moving quickly to open it.

He'd hoped it was Thayla, Edeya, or even Captain Lam, and he was sure some of the disappointment showed on his face when he saw that it was one of Lam's household servants holding a sealed envelope. "Apologies for the intrusion, sir, but the lady has asked that I deliver this envelope to you."

"Uh, thanks," Victor said, taking the thick cardstock.

"Will you be coming down for breakfast, sir, or would you like me to have something brought up?"

"Well, I don't know. I haven't spoken to Lam, er, the lady yet today."

"Very good; please let Binna know. She's at the station at the end of your hall." Victor knew who Binna was—one of Lam's servants that seemed to be posted at the end of his hallway at all hours of the day and night, waiting for him to need something. He couldn't decide if it was cool having someone ready to help him with anything at a moment's notice or if it was just a way for Lam to keep tabs on him. He supposed it was a bit of both, though he felt guilty, wondering how the girl ever got any rest.

"Right, thanks," Victor said, pushing his door closed and opening the envelope. A handwritten note was within:

Victor,

I'm sorry I've been so busy with meetings and arrangements. I promised you some sparring time and intend to make good on it. I'm called away again, but I've sent word to one of my old adventuring friends. Polo Vosh is a great warrior who has spent the years since we delved into dungeons building his strength. He owes me a favor or two, and I've called him to collect: He'll be here this afternoon to train with you.

Thayla has borrowed my driver and coach to collect her daughter. She wanted to talk to you, but I think it's best you keep your head focused on your fight. She's safe, and they'll be back well before Harvest Fest.

– Lam

"What the fuck?" Victor threw the note and its envelope on the table that sat inside the door of his suite, irritated but not sure why. He supposed he had wanted to be there to see Thayla reunited with her daughter, but he couldn't really blame her for not wanting to wait until his situation with the duel was done. Then there was the business of Lam's old friend. Who was Polo Vosh, and why was Lam so damn busy all the time? Was she going back to the mines? Was she trying to make some political moves before the fight?

"Too many questions," he sighed. He supposed he should be grateful—Lam didn't have to find him someone to practice with. She didn't have to do anything. Hopefully, she was right about her friend, and he'd be able to teach Victor a thing or two.

Victor opened the door and walked down the hallway to the servant's station. Sure enough, Binna was there, and the strange little Bogoli jumped to her feet at his approach. She was only about four feet tall, had a shock of long white hair that grew down the center of her scalp, and painted her face and scalp a dark shade of blue with weird silvery designs on her cheeks and forehead. Victor couldn't tell if the designs were the same every day or if she painted something different based on circumstances he wasn't aware of. "Hi, Binna. I'm going down to breakfast."

"Excellent, Mr. Sandoval. I'll see that your room is cleaned while you're out."

"Sounds good," Victor said with a wave. He'd given up trying to get the Bogoli to relax, and there was no way she'd be talked out of straightening his suite. He'd tried on the first day, but it seemed almost to cause her physical discomfort not to do her job. Victor made his way through the hallways and down the stairs to the dining hall adjacent to the manor's kitchens. None of the place settings were out, and no one sat at the long, polished tables. Victor walked through into the kitchens, and there he was met with a more appropriate level of bustle.

Pots simmered and steamed on the big stovetops, and the long wooden picnic-style table that sat along the far wall near the windows was occupied by several staff members eating their morning meal. Victor approached, and one of the cooks, a portly Ardeni woman with curly gray hair, said, "Victor! I was wondering if I'd gotten too much bacon out today—was afraid I wouldn't be seeing you!"

"No, Mrs. ap'Edda, I'm here, and I'm hungry as ever," Victor laughed and walked through the steamy room to the table, sitting on the bench with his back to the windows so he could watch the cooks bustling around the kitchen—he found their activities endlessly fascinating. He loved the kitchens. He loved the smell of them. He loved the carefree fun the cooks had while they worked, and of course, he loved the taste of the food they kept giving him.

The kitchen almost always smelled like fresh bread, but during breakfast time, the scent of bacon was the prevailing odor. Victor waited patiently, but it was only a few minutes before the first plate of food was set before him—fresh buttered bread sprinkled with herbed salt. Victor thanked the cook, a sweaty Shadeni man who grunted and returned to his mixing bowl as Victor began to wolf down the warm, delicious treat. By the time he'd finished a piece of bread, another cook had brought over a plate of bacon, and before he could get far into that, yet another deposited some scrambled eggs in front of him.

He knew that if he stayed at that table, they'd keep bringing him food, so he ate quickly and made a show of getting up and waving as he moved out of the kitchens and into the gardens that flanked the windows. Lam's home had beautiful grounds, and Victor had spent much of the last two days exploring the gardens and groves. He'd kept hoping Lam would find him, take him to her gymnasium, and spar with him, but he found himself left to his own devices, and, though he knew he should be trying to get stronger somehow, he found the slow exploration of the grounds therapeutic.

Victor walked through the herb gardens near the kitchens until he came to a stone fountain with a built-in bench around the water. He sat there, letting his mind wander for a while. Of course, his thoughts kept returning to the fight. For some reason, he couldn't seem to muster the emotions everyone, including himself, thought he should have. He didn't feel fearful or even nervous. He knew, abstractly, that this woman, Rellia ap'Yensha, was powerful. He was pretty sure the Dungeon Lord he'd fought had been Tier Four, and she was supposed to be Tier Five or almost so—no one was really sure. Still, he couldn't seem to grasp the predicament he was in properly.

So she was tough. That just meant he'd have to go all out, right? How could a person, regardless of their level, be more dangerous than a massive, undead snake with acidic fangs? The Dungeon Lord had turned the very shadows against him, driving fear before it. How could any person be more of a challenge than that? He knew he was being stupid—Energy made all logic moot, but that didn't mean he could suddenly conceptualize what he was going to be up against.

Lam, Thayla, and Edeya had all encouraged him to keep cultivating while waiting for the fight. Thayla thought there was a good chance he could make it to Level Thirty through cultivation. He supposed she was probably right—he'd been twenty-nine for a while now and hadn't leveled his Core in quite some time. He'd worked on it half-heartedly but resolved to spend some hours on it tonight. Only needing to sleep a few hours a day really had a way of adding time to his plate.

"Gorz," he said suddenly, "Did you say Reevus's master was something like Tier Six?"

"Reevus often boasted that his master was Tier Seven, though it's possible he was exaggerating to inflate his own importance."

"So what's the difference between a Tier Four and a Tier Seven in terms of power? Is it like the difference between a Tier One and a Tier Three?"

"It's hard to quantify, Victor. Many factors can create a huge disparity between people of the same rank. One factor is the rarity of a person's class. If you reach Tier Seven with an Epic or Legendary Class, your raw attribute scores would be much higher than someone who leveled so high with a simple Basic or Advanced Class. Energy affinity can play a role in a person's overall power, as can racial

advancements and skill mastery. Don't underestimate the importance of artifacts, either. Your axe is an extraordinary item, and you're much stronger with it than you would be with a typical artificed weapon."

"Really? Do you think Lam regrets giving Lifedrinker to me?"

"No, I don't think so. The odds of heartsilver gaining consciousness are very low. Your relationship with Lifedrinker is rather unique—when I review the conversation Lam had with you about the axe, it seems she had given up long ago in her attempts to awaken the weapon."

"She definitely looks better than when Lam gave her to me." Victor reached down and loosened the axe at his belt, lifting it out into his hands. "How about it, beautiful? Feel like talking to me today?" He'd tried every day since he'd heard her voice in his head to get her to speak again, but so far, she'd been quiet, though her handle felt warm, and she buzzed more than ever in his grip, so he knew she was fine. He pushed her cold metal against his forehead and felt her vibrate, but no words were forthcoming. "Don't worry; I know you'll speak when you're ready."

Victor spent the morning walking around the grounds, visiting with the manor's staff, and basically just killing time, waiting for something to happen. It felt as if there were an amorphous weight hanging over his head but that he couldn't do anything about it, which was sort of true—the Harvest Fest and his duel were marching toward him, and no matter what actions he took, he'd be facing Rellia ap'Yensha in just a few days. He supposed he could make a run for it or beg the captain to petition the Magistrate to put off the duel, but he'd already refused such actions, and nothing had changed between then and now. There was no way he would live out his life in this new world, always on the run, looking over his shoulder.

He was saved from his own inaction and boredom by the arrival of Lam's old adventuring friend. It was Binna who tracked Victor down in the dimly lit grove of nut trees at the back of Lam's property. Victor saw her running up and down the irrigation ditches, and he watched her for a while, wondering why the little white-gloved figure was in such a tizzy before it dawned on him that she might be looking for him. He stood out from behind the big tree he'd been poking around, collecting fallen nuts, and called out, "Binna?"

"Mister Sandoval!" She called breathlessly, running down the row toward him. "You have a visitor! He's waiting at the gymnasium!"

"Oh, shit, Binna. I'm sorry you had to hunt me down. Thanks! I'll head over there right now." The poor Bogoli leaned over her knees, breathing deeply, her dark makeup running in rivulets of sweat down onto her white robes. Victor tried to think of a way to make her take a break but couldn't think of anything clever. He decided just to try being direct. "Binna, will you please go and take a break? I insist. I know the way to the gymnasium, and I won't need your services until tonight. I'll look for you near my quarters around dinnertime."

"Yes, sir. I will await you near your quarters." She sounded relieved, and Victor waved cheerfully to her, hurrying off through the grove toward the big rectangular building that housed Lam's practice facilities.

When he strolled through the garden path and up the cobbled lane to the building, he saw a dark-furred Vodkin leaning against the structure. He was huge, dwarfing even Ponda from the Wagon Wheel, and probably a hundred pounds heavier than Victor. He wore an armored vest, bronze-colored and scaled, and a massive axe handle jutted over his shoulder. When he saw Victor approaching, he stepped forward, his thick slabs of muscle rippling with his leonine movements. Victor had never seen a Vodkin that didn't boast a layer of blubber, but there was nothing blubbery about Polo Vosh.

"Victor?" His voice rumbled over the cobbles, and Victor nodded, waving as he came closer. Polo held out a hand, and Victor reached out to shake it. The meaty paw was easily a match for his own grip, and as often happened with competitive men, Victor found himself straining to respond to the Vodkin's tight grip—he imagined they could have smashed walnuts to dust between their palms as they both squeezed.

"Polo, I guess?" Victor asked, noting that, up close, he could see flecks of gold in the Vodkin's big black eyes. His dark fur was longer along the center of his head, running down his back almost like a mane, and when the big warrior smiled, he saw that he had three long canines but was missing the one on the lower left of his mouth.

"Right! Good grip, lad. Now, come inside, I've only got a few days to work with you, and Lam tells me you need to learn a lot when it comes to axe work."

"What? Really? I thought my axe fighting was getting pretty good!" Victor self-consciously put his hand on Lifedrinker's metal head.

"Oh? What's your skill up to? Advanced?"

"Um, improved."

"And you're fighting the old raptor? By the Bearded Turtle, boy! We've got work to do!" Polo turned and walked through the archway into the gymnasium, and Victor followed after, worrying about his ability with an axe for the first time. When Polo pushed the interior doors open and stepped onto the practice floor, he looked around at the liveried house guards practicing, some dozen different bouts going on around the wide, open space, and he let loose a bellow that bounced off the walls and rattled the high windows. "Clear out! Lam's orders! Anyone still here in thirty seconds better be ready to fight me!"

His order had the desired effect—weapons were lowered, and though there were some grumbles, one look at the enormous Vodkin got people moving, and soon Victor and Polo Vosh stood alone in the big gymnasium. "Well, pupil, unlimber that pretty axe of yours, and we'll see what you've got," he rumbled, reaching up and unhooking his own weapon from his shoulder. Victor admired the weapon, from its polished, dark wood haft to the massive crescent blade. The blade had to be the size of a forty-five-pound plate at his old school's weight room. Lifedrinker looked positively petite in comparison.

Victor pulled her out of the loop at his belt, held her crossways in front of himself, and asked, "Should I use any abilities?"

"Not yet, berserker! Let's just see what kind of axe work you can do." Polo whipped his massive weapon through the air, thick curtains of air chasing the blade in a whoosh as it cleaved the space in front of him. "Just try to cut me—don't hold back."

Victor did as he was told, leaping forward and swinging Lifedrinker at the huge target the Vodkin presented, but was stunned to find nothing but air every time his blade cut toward the big man. Polo seemed hardly to move, but still, his body, his clothes, his armor, and his axe were never where they appeared to be when Victor launched his assaults. He'd been afraid to give his swings everything he had when he started, holding back slightly for fear of hurting Lam's friend. Still, as he continued to miss and his frustration mounted, Victor put everything he had into the attacks, even feinting and switching up the direction of his cleaves mid-swing.

Nothing worked, though, and after a solid five minutes of hacking with all his might and Polo seeming to slip through the air like a seal in water, he lowered his blade, leaning on the axe haft and panting.

"Did I say to stop?" Polo growled. Victor's face reddened, and he lifted his blade, trying again, charging forward and thrusting out with Lifedrinker's metal head, trying to catch the Vodkin by surprise. He might as well have written out his plan ahead of time, for all the effect it had. Polo simply danced back, gauging the extent of Victor's reach down to the millimeter.

"All right, now, if you have some way to do it, let's see you move faster. Use Energy."

"Right," Victor said, casting Sovereign Will and boosting his agility. Suddenly his liquid attacks became more like the flickers of a snake's tongue, and Lifedrinker ripped through the air, carving toward Polo with deadly grace. Polo's eyes widened, and for the first time, he seemed to have to concentrate a little on Victor's weapon to dodge it. Still, he did dodge it, and though Victor came closer with each swing, and Polo had to interpose his own axe between Lifedrinker and his flesh a few times, Victor still never managed to touch the man's armor, let alone his skin.

Anyone watching the exchange might have been impressed by the speed with which the two giant men moved. They certainly would have been leery of the whipcrack slices in the air that the axes made as they went through their motions. It was clear that Victor had raw talent and speed but lacked refinement. On the other hand, Polo was a master of economy, only moving the absolute minimum amount to avoid cuts or to place his weapon into a perfect parry. Victor might have wondered what the difference between a skilled axe fighter and a master of the axe was before this session, but he wouldn't wonder that anymore—Polo's skill made it very clear that Victor had a lot left to learn.

"At least you have some stamina," Polo said, finally making the effort to pin Victor's axe to the ground with his huge crescent blade. "Take a breather."

"Do you mind me asking what tier you're in, Polo?"

"While we're on the practice field, you'll call me First Axe. I earned the title at Storm Garden when I trained the Queen's Honor Guard. Clear?"

"Yes." Victor paused, took a deep breath, then finished, "First Axe."

"Good. I'm Tier Five, lad. It's why the captain asked me to come to help you. She's a great fighter but hasn't touched the axe in decades. She was never much good with one, truth be told. I think I recognize that blade, though. That isn't Lifedrinker, is it?" He nodded to the gleaming edge of heartsilver, resting on the springy practice flooring.

"Yeah, this is Lifedrinker. Captain Lam gave her to me a while back, but she's grown a bit since then."

"And you got her a new handle? Or did Lam do that?"

"No, that was me." Victor saw the big Vodkin scowl, and he cleared his throat and added, "Um, First Axe."

"What about those heartsilver veins? Is she waking up?"

"Yes, First Axe. She even spoke to me the other night."

"Really? You know how many new warriors buy heartsilver weapons hoping to wake them up?"

"Um, no, First Axe." Victor was starting to feel kind of stupid saying the Vodkin's title with each sentence, but it seemed to be what the huge warrior wanted.

"If I had a bead for every youngster that wasted his savings on an inert heartsilver weapon, I'd be a very rich Vodkin. Well, I'm rich anyway, but I'd be even richer! Ha. I think I've seen two actually conscious heartsilver weapons in all my days. You've got quite a treasure there, lad, and an axe, no less! At least it's not some frilly, snooty sword. Hah, the captain must be green with envy! She did everything to wake that axe up back in the day! Spoke to it for hours and hours, slaughtered hundreds, no thousands of monsters, letting it drink its fill. She even fought with it in the Beneset War."

"Guess I got lucky." Victor shrugged. "First Axe."

"Well, you must have a strong spirit. Something that struck a harmony within Lifedrinker. Let's see if we can keep you alive to finish your work with her, hmm? You're going to need more skill to face Rellia."

"You think I can improve enough in just a few days?"

"You can improve. Enough? I don't know. You forgot to call me First Axe, which means you're out of warnings. Next time, I'll exact payment! Now get that axe up and get ready to defend yourself!" Polo Vosh grinned, his missing canine conspicuous in the ferocity of his expression. Victor lifted Lifedrinker and watched, with every fiber of his being, trying to figure out how a man so huge and heavy could move so damn gracefully.

28

PREPARATIONS

"That's it, Victor! You got him now!" Edeya yelled from the sidelines. She'd shown up a few hours into his session with Polo and was enthusiastic in her support for him, though it seemed to make Polo want to thrash him even more soundly every time she cheered. Still, Victor appreciated the encouragement and pressed his attack, using everything Polo had deemed "okay for sparring."

Sovereign Will pumped up his agility, Inspiring Presence guided his axe, and Channel Spirit flooded Lifedrinker and his arms with inspiration-attuned Energy. Polo had told him not to use any rage Energy, saying it would make it harder to learn rather than help. He'd been enthusiastically in favor of Victor using inspiration Energy, though, and it seemed to be paying off—Victor was getting noticeably faster and more graceful in his axe movements as the afternoon stretched on.

"Go! Push him!" Edeya cheered as Victor drove forward, whipping Lifedrinker through the air in glittering silver-gold arcs, her blade sizzling with inspiration Energy as it sliced the wind. Polo backed up, dodging with an economy of movement that left Victor bewildered. As Victor's fourth cleave in his lightning combo arced dangerously close to his shoulder, the big Vodkin seemed to shrug, and then his colossal axe blade was there, taking the blow in a shower of golden sparks. Still, Polo whistled for him to stop, backing up a step.

"That was the first time I had to block or be cut. You're learning, novice!"

"Thank you, First Axe," Victor said, the honorific coming more easily to his tongue after several hours of enforced usage.

"C'mon, don't stop now!" Edeya called, and Polo grinned, his big, whiskered jowls bouncing with the movement.

"Your vicious little friend is right. Now's the time to push it!" Polo thrust his axe forward, suddenly smashing the blunt top into Victor's armored chest, knocking him back a few steps. Victor grinned and lifted Lifedrinker, then renewed his efforts to take a slice out of Polo's mountainous body.

Polo was an expert instructor, seeming to always be just out of Victor's reach, yet never so far that Victor gave up. It was as if he knew exactly how close to let Victor get, so he'd keep thinking he almost had him. With each narrow miss or parried blow, Victor gained new insights into how the huge Vodkin moved, and he began to subconsciously anticipate the big warrior's maneuvers.

It was just such a moment when Victor had a true breakthrough, running through a combo, knowing how Polo would respond, and changing up the arc of the final cleave at the last second. Polo's eyes widened, and, again, he moved his shoulders in an almost shrug, seeming to flip his axe through space somehow, so the big, flat blade was suddenly in front of his neck, catching Lifedrinker's edge as she arced in a gleaming slice. A shower of hot sparks sizzled around the two combatants, and a System message appeared in Victor's eyes.

Congratulations! You've learned the skill: Axe Mastery, Advanced.

"Fuck yes!" Victor shouted as sudden understanding flooded into his mind. Suddenly, many of Polo's movements that had seemed like mysterious magic made sense to him, and he knew their counters. What's more, he felt his muscles flex with sudden memories—knowledge of how to flick his blade into parry positions and adjust his momentum a hair's breadth to turn the angle of his attack, catching his opponent off guard. These and a thousand other sparks of insight flooded through his mind and body, and Victor dropped to a knee as he processed all the information.

He was just starting to wrap his head around his new skill level when hundreds of little balls of golden Energy began to form in the air around him. He took a deep breath, bracing himself, and then they surged toward him, bursting like little, golden fireworks as they crashed into him. He held his breath, hoping for another System message, but nothing came, and he sighed, letting out his air in a heavy sigh, "Damn!"

"What?" Edeya asked, having run up to clap him on the shoulder.

"Was hoping I'd get a level off that, but no such luck."

"Ha, the impatience of youth," Polo said, lifting his huge axe and dropping it on the ground with a thud to add inflection to his words. "I think you must have been close to improving your axe skill on your own because I've never seen someone go so quickly from improved to advanced."

"What's your axe skill at, First Axe?" Edeya asked, saving Victor the trouble.

"Legendary, pup. One of only three on this continent. Unless some axe master is hiding out there that doesn't want me to know about it."

"Legendary . . ." Edeya breathed, her eyes unfocusing as she visualized it.

"That's right. I was nearly two decades moving past Epic. I didn't have Inspiration Energy cheating for me, though. You'd be smart to practice with this one." Polo gave Victor a slap on the shoulder. "Assuming Rellia doesn't cut him up in a few days."

"Victor will win. You haven't seen him lose his temper." Edeya reached out and gave Victor's trap a squeeze. "You got this, Victor."

"Thanks, Edeya."

"Rage might help. If you weren't a berserker, I'd tell you to keep your cool, but I've seen what a rager can do—if you're going to win against Rellia, it will be because of your rage. We need to practice more, though—she's going to know about your berserking, and she'll have a plan for it. Trust me—it's all anyone's talking about in the city right now."

"What? Seriously?" Victor stood up and slipped Lifedrinker into her belt loop.

"Well, among certain circles, at least. I'd heard of you even before Lam's messenger came for me. It's not often you get a Tier Five old razor beak coming out of retirement to fight some nobody at the Harvest Fest."

"Is it true Rellia had more kills than Asyr-dak in the Beneset Wars?" Edeya asked, her eyes still distant while she pictured some imaginary battlefield.

"Ha! If you heard that, you can be sure the rumor started with Rellia. Asyr-dak was already a legend before that war even began, and he left this world shortly after. I can assure you that Rellia's not so much as a shadow to his flame."

"Left this world?" Victor asked, having no idea who they were even talking about. "As in died?"

"No, lad, he traveled off world, seeking greater challenges. In the scheme of things, Fanwath is new. I don't know many Energy users at my level, and I'd be considered a novice on some of the older worlds."

"He just, uh, traveled off world? Like in a spaceship?"

"Through the Settlement Stone, you goof," Edeya said, rolling her eyes.

"Oh, yeah, right." Victor nodded, and he supposed he did vaguely remember people talking about how you could pay for teleportation through the Settlement Stones if you had enough money.

"Enough chitchat. Girl, go stand aside; I'm going to see what Victor can do now."

"Yes, First Axe!" Edeya said sharply and scurried off to stand by the door.

"Well, lad, I told Lam I'd give you a thorough evaluation, and I can't do that if I make you hold back all your skills. You ready to show me what you've got?"

"Um, yes, First Axe, but do you mean I can use Berserk? I've been working on my control while I do it, but I can't promise I won't hurt you."

"Ha! By the Turtle's beard! I'll give you one of my old artifacts if you can hurt me. How's that sound?"

"If you're sure . . ." Victor said, unslinging Lifedrinker from his belt. He decided not to leap into a rage but to work his way into it as he might in any old fight. He boosted his agility, channeled inspiration-attuned Energy into Lifedrinker, and cast Inspiring Presence, then he launched a flurry of attacks, immediately driving Polo back with his much-improved axe skills.

Polo grunted and, in Victor's opinion, struggled to dodge and parry all of his attacks, but only just barely. He avoided most of the attacks with subtle shifts of his shoulders and twists of his hips, but he had to intercede with his huge axe blade a few times, dancing away from Victor's cleaves in showers of sparks and the squeal of metal on metal.

"Well? Come on, boy, let's have it!" Polo growled after a minute or two of dodging and parrying, then he launched an offensive, and Victor was forced back, his turn to dodge and parry as the enormous crescent blade flicked ever closer to his flesh. He saved himself losing a slice of his cheekbone by the barest of margins, and, as he stumbled back, he released his hold on the roiling, surging furnace of his rage-attuned Energy.

Edeya, standing on the edge of the practice floor near the open double doors, saw Victor barely save himself from a cut to his face, and then she felt a vortex of Energy pull at her, standing her hair on its ends and raising the hackles on the back of her neck. Victor's lanky, muscle-corded frame was suddenly limned in blazing red Energy, and then he stepped forward with a barked growl, slapping his foot down with a crash and whipping Lifedrinker through the air at Polo's shoulder. The chop was so savage and fast that Polo barely got his gigantic axe blade up in time to block it. A terrific bell tolled in the air as the two blades clashed, and Polo was sent sliding over the practice floor, reeling from the impact. Then things really went sideways.

The explosion of red Energy had happened in an instant, and Victor's attack had taken Edeya's focus for a moment, but as she glanced back at him, she caught her breath and moved toward the door—Victor towered over Polo, his massive, corded muscles standing out like airship cables, and Lifedrinker flicked through the air in one enormous fist, more like a hatchet than a great bearded axe. Victor roared and launched a rampaging, berserking attack against Polo, swinging Lifedrinker in whipping, arcing cleaves with such force that each time Polo blocked the attacks on the flat of his great axe, he was sent stumbling, only his incredible skill keeping him from being smashed to pieces.

The fury of Victor's attacks was such that it took Polo a dozen heartbeats to finally recover enough poise to attempt to turn the tables, using his own Energy abilities to thwart Victor's onslaught. His blade, still parrying the frenetic, devastating hacks Victor was delivering, began to glow with a deep blue-black Energy. Where he rebuked Victor's hacks, azure barriers hung in the air, stationary shields he could seek cover behind. As the barriers stacked up and Polo found himself able to breathe, he began to launch attacks from behind his fortified Energy shields, landing cuts on Victor's arms and legs and smashing his giant axe into Victor's armor.

None of the blows seemed to bother the massive berserker, though, and Victor only roared and smashed Lifedrinker all the harder into Polo's barriers, utterly shattering each of them in just a few swings. Polo was sweating now, and his eyes began to widen with the strain of his defense. That's when red waves of Energy started to emanate from Victor, wrapping around Polo's Energy barriers and seeping into his body. Polo screamed. He began to froth at the mouth, and his eyes lost all semblance of sanity. He threw his axe aside and charged at Victor, smashing into him like a cannonball. Victor, for his part, laughed like a complete maniac. Edeya turned to the double doors, panic in her eyes, and ran out of the room, shouting for help.

When she returned just a few minutes later with several of Captain Lam's house guards in tow, she found Polo and Victor sitting on the ground, laughing and talking loudly. Polo's dark fur was matted with blood. His heavy bronze-scale armor was ragged, torn at the neck, and hanging loosely over one shoulder. Victor, his pale skin no good at hiding his blood, was an even more disturbing sight—his skin and hair were soaked with a thick sheen of bloody sweat. Worse, there were great smears of blood all over the wooden planks of the practice floor. It looked as if a calf had been slaughtered in the room.

Victor saw Edeya come running in with the guards, and he smiled and called out, "Hey, where'd you go? How are we supposed to know who won?"

"You asshole!" she cried, running toward the two sprawled warriors.

"No need for her to testify—of course, I won," Polo said with a deep wet chuckle that turned into a cough halfway through. Victor didn't argue, just leaned back on his bloody palms and watched Polo cough with a raised eyebrow.

"I thought you guys were going to kill each other! Victor, when did you start to grow when you go berserk?"

"Something that happened when I advanced my race in the dungeon." He shrugged, then hoisted himself to his feet using Lifedrinker as a crutch. Looking inward to his Core, he saw that he still had more than half of his rage-attuned Energy to draw on—he must have ended his rage on purpose, which was enough evidence for him that he could hold his own against Polo, regardless of their level disparity.

"That's a hell of a combination with your type of Core, Victor," Polo said. "A bloodline that complements your rage ability like that . . . by the Bearded Turtle, you'd turn the tide on a battlefield."

"Yeah, I guess I got pretty lucky with my skill set," Victor replied, reaching out to help Polo to his feet. The big Vodkin clasped his fist and allowed him to haul him up with a grunt and a wince.

"I'll be taking the evening off. Meet me here at dawn for more axe work. I have an artifact in mind for you, but it'll take some time to get it to you. I left it with the Second Axe back home," he grunted, turning toward the door.

"Thank you, First Axe," Victor called to his back, and Polo raised a hand to wave acknowledgment and then ponderously trudged toward the double doors. The house guards that Edeya had fetched were still staring at the practice floor and Victor with wan faces, but they jumped when Polo walked by and growled at them.

"Well, make yourselves useful—fetch some staff to clean this mess and replace that cracked plank in the center!"

"That was crazy, Victor," Edeya said. "I can't believe you fought Polo Vosh like that. He's a legend."

"Well, if I didn't berserk, and if my bloodline didn't turn me into a fucking giant, he would clean the floor with me."

"True, but that's like saying, 'well, if I didn't use my axe,' or, 'well, if I didn't use Energy abilities.' You know we aren't just the sum of our parts, right? Sure, you got lucky with some of your abilities, but you've been through a lot to get to where you are. Thayla told me about what you went through in the dungeon."

She walked toward the exit, Victor in tow, and continued, "Nobody makes it to a high level without some luck. You think Polo Vosh doesn't have a strong class? You think he didn't find some artifacts early on that made him tougher than the next Vodkin warrior? You think Rellia ap'Yensha hasn't leveraged her family's wealth to help her gain power? Don't sell yourself short, is all I'm saying, Victor."

"Huh, thanks, Edeya." They'd reached the courtyard outside the practice hall, and Victor squinted up between the tall trees at the fading brightness of the pale blue sky. "I'm pretty damn hungry. Wanna hit the kitchens with me?"

"Yeah, I don't have anything else to do. Captain Lam won't be back until morning."

"Where'd she go, anyway?"

"Back to the mine. She's hired a crew to set up a base camp at the deep entrance to the dungeon you found."

"Why not go in from the top? Up near Steampool?"

"I dunno. Knowing Lam, it's because she wants to keep things secret as long as she can. Trust me, the crew she's hired probably have no clue why they're doing what they're doing."

"She's pretty damn smart, isn't she? Always thinking a few moves ahead."

"Yep, I'm learning a lot by working with her."

"Do you . . ." Victor paused and looked at his friend. She was much healthier and cleaner than when he'd known her in the mine. Her uniform looked sharp, her hair was clean and short, and she sported a brace of pearl-handled knives on a bandolier-style strap. Quite the difference from the scrappy little delver that he'd rescued from a cage. Could he trust her to be honest with him anymore? He pushed on with his question. "Do you think I can fully trust Lam?"

"What? Of course!" Edeya looked at him as if he'd sprouted a third eye on his forehead.

"Think about it before you answer so quickly. I'm not saying she isn't trying to help me, but you know she's always got plans within plans. Don't you think she's probably going to gain something from my fight with Rellia, whether I win or not?" He watched as the gears turned behind Edeya's eyes. She opened her mouth to speak, closed it, and opened it again.

"Lam will come out on top, no matter what. You're right. That doesn't mean she doesn't want you to succeed, though. I've heard her talk about how much she wants you to win. She won't betray you, Victor."

"All right, thanks, Edeya." They continued into the kitchens, where Victor performed like a paid act, eating more than any single person had a right to do in one sitting. He polished off a full loaf of bread, slices of cold leftover steak, a bowl of fruit, and when he didn't seem to be slowing down, a platter of cheese, cured meats, crackers, and some sort of thick, fruity jam. Edeya picked at her food, here and there, laughing at his bottomless stomach. When he finally seemed to be slowing down, she gestured toward the doors leading into the manor proper.

"You should go clean up and then do some cultivating. If you can hit thirty, you might gain a new skill or two with your class refinement. I'm sure Rellia has intel about your berserking, but she won't know what sort of refinement you'll get—it could make all the difference."

"Yeah, I must be getting close, don't you think? I'll try to level my Core again, and hopefully, that'll do it."

"I have no idea how close you are—Lam's the only person I've spent any time with that's higher than Tier Two. I've heard that it gets slower and slower to level as you gain power, though. It makes sense, I suppose; each level requires more Energy to improve your attributes and build up your pathways to handle the surges of your skills. You're lucky you've improved your race so much. If I ever want to see Tier Three, I'll need quite a few racial advancements to handle all that Energy."

"Yeah, Thayla told me something similar. All right, well, I'm going to head to my room, Edeya. Thanks for hanging out with me today. See you in the morning?"

"Of course. See you then, Victor." She smiled and waved as he scooted back the bench and stood.

On his way back to his room, he saw that Binna was sitting at her station, and he stopped to say, "Binna, I'm going to spend the evening cultivating. Please make sure no one, well, no one other than Lam or Thayla or Edeya, bothers me. I mean, I won't need any maid service or food or anything, okay?"

"Understood, Mr. Sandoval." Binna bowed, managing to look as though she'd just received an important quest.

Victor went into his rooms, noting that they were clean and that his bed had been made. It crossed his mind that he could get used to that kind of service, and he instantly felt guilty. He wasn't sure why, but the idea of people having to go around cleaning up his mess filled him with a desire to get his shit together. Maybe it was his *abuela* talking, but he felt like he should be able to make his own bed.

He went around the two rooms, closed all the blinds, then sat in the middle of the bedroom's carpet and looked at his attribute points, not wanting to waste any time.

Strength:	**127**	**Vitality:**	**90**
Dexterity:	**40**	**Agility:**	**63**
Intelligence:	**32**	**Will:**	**203**
Points Available:	**10**		

He wasn't sure why he hadn't spent his available points yet. He supposed that, on some level, he'd wanted to get some advice, and he'd been hoping to have more one-on-one time with Lam. He could have asked Polo Vosh about it, but they'd been so busy with actual sparring that Victor hadn't thought about it. Now he was about to try to push his way into another level, and he felt that he should distribute his available points first. What if it made a difference with regard to his class refinement?

One thing was certain: he'd learned that none of his attributes were pointless. Even intelligence seemed to play a factor in how he performed in combat. He'd learned that all of his physical attributes were related in one way or another, but he seemed to be doing fine balancing them. So far, his lower dexterity hadn't negatively impacted his strength. Even when he cast Berserk and his Titanic Rage kicked in, pushing his strength up around five hundred, he hadn't noticed a problem. "Would I notice when I'm raging out, though?" he asked the shadows in the room.

Victor couldn't deny that his high will had served him very well. It helped him to avoid fear, avoid mind control, and allowed him to dominate others with his Project Spirit ability. More than that, he could boost his other attributes with it. "Fuck it," he said, pushing ten points into will.

He hadn't tried to make any new constructs for rage in a very long time, and he didn't know if he wanted to. He decided to stick with what worked, going through his cultivation cycle several times, working through each of the rage constructs he'd made so long ago, sitting in the cage at the Wagon Wheel. Like always, they worked, allowing him to cycle red, pulsing rage through his pathways and slowly build its intensity as he pushed it along until he felt his body was brimming, vibrating with the fury. Then he slowly pulled it back, compressing it into his Core. Each time he did it, he could see the red, throbbing heart of his rage attunement get just a little brighter.

When the disparity between his rage Core and his inspiration Core became apparent, he switched, cultivating the inspiration constructs he'd made while hiding away deep in the crevices of the Greatbone Mine. The discomfort and irritation that had lingered with his rage cultivation faded away, and he built up the white-gold Energy of inspiration in his pathways, over and over, filling himself to bursting and then pulling it in, pushing it into the shimmering sun of his inspiration attunement.

The hours faded away as he continued to cultivate. When his inspiration Energy was built up to the equivalent of his rage Energy, he started again, running through the whole process for each of his attunements dozens of times.

When he felt the click of his two attunements breaching some sort of invisible barrier, he knew that if he looked away from his Core, he'd see the System message telling him his Core had leveled. He didn't look right away, though, hoping that he'd have messages waiting to tell him that the growth of his Core had been enough to edge him over the threshold of Level Thirty. He sat there for several minutes, staring at his Core, at the two orbiting suns of his attunements, and waited, steadying himself.

Finally, utterly calm, his heart barely beating, Victor opened his eyes and looked out, away from his Core, and read what the System had to say.

*****Congratulations! Your Spirit Class Core has advanced to: Base Seven.*****

*****Congratulations! You have achieved Level 30 Herald of Carnage, gained 10 will and 8 strength, and have 10 attribute points to allocate.*****

*****Level 30 Class refinement is available. Class refinement is permanent. Human Energy cultivators will next be offered a Class refinement selection at Level 40. To view your options and make your selection, access the menu through your status page.*****

"Fuck yes!" Victor hissed between his teeth. "Time to see what kind of surprise I can pull out for Lady ap'Yensha!"

29

TOTEMS

Victor sat cross-legged in his dark bedroom, reading through his class refinement options for the hundredth time:

*****Class refinement option 1: Titanic Warrior, Epic. Prerequisite: The strong presence of a titanic bloodline originating from an Elder race. You've begun to unlock the secrets of your ancestry. By leveraging your bloodline to form class abilities, you will continue to build on the synergy between your class and your race. Class attributes: Strength, Vitality, Will.*****

*****Class refinement option 2: Battle Caller, Epic. Prerequisites: Inspiration affinity. You exemplify excellence on the battlefield, inspiring your comrades and turning the tide with powerful tactical boons. Class attributes: Will, Intelligence, Agility, Unbound.*****

*****Class refinement option 3: Spirit Carver, Epic. Prerequisites: Spirit Core, one of several Elder bloodlines. Your mastery of the spirit continues to grow, unlocking ancient abilities that lay dormant in your bloodline. Class attributes: Will, Vitality, Unbound.*****

*****Class refinement option 4: No Refinement. You are pleased with the path on which you find yourself and choose to continue until your next refinement option.*****

Victor only had three options, four if you counted the option of not doing anything, but he felt that this decision was the hardest he'd ever faced. He decided to ignore the second option, Battle Caller. He'd already decided a while ago that he liked his current class more than that, so why would he change now? "I guess if I felt like I made a mistake back at Level Twenty?"

That left two choices, and both tempted Victor for different reasons. The first one, Titanic Warrior, sounded as if it was meant to help him continue kicking ass the way he had been. He'd continue to change to be more like his Quinametzin bloodline, even gaining new class abilities that called forth its benefits.

Right now, whenever he cast Berserk, he gained a massive boost because of his Quinametizin blood. He struggled to imagine what it would be like if more of his abilities had a similar synergy. He felt this option was the obvious, clear "power-up." If he wanted the best chance of beating Rellia, it was the choice—who would want to fight a Titanic Warrior?

Each time Victor started to reach for that little selection button, though, he paused and reread the description for Spirit Carver. This one had something to do with his bloodline also, and it seemed that it was talking about waking up more abilities from his bloodline, not necessarily just the giant-sized aspect of his ancestors. What could they be? Something to do with his Spirit Core, that was clear. "How did I earn this option? Learning to spirit walk and advancing my race?" He wasn't sure it had anything at all to do with Spirit Walk, if he were being honest.

As he vacillated, he looked at the other factors. Both classes were Epic, so they'd be similar in their difficulty to level and increase his attributes an equivalent amount. He liked that he'd still get some unbound points with the Spirit Carver Class, though. "Ahh, fuck! Maybe I should just keep Herald of Carnage. It's not like it hasn't been great so far . . ."

He was purposefully not asking Gorz for advice because the spirit in the amulet had only seemed to muddy the waters in the past. On a whim, he picked up Lifedrinker and held her cool metal to his forehead. "What do you think, *chica*? Titanic Warrior or Spirit Carver?"

At first, nothing happened, but then the axe started to vibrate, and though Victor didn't hear any words in his head, he kept seeing the image of a heart beating, blood whooshing through thick, wide arteries with each pump. "What the . . . he opened his eyes, but he could still hear the heart beating, and when he closed them, he saw it again. It took him longer than he would ever admit to realize it was his own heart. Lifedrinker was showing him his heart. Why?

As he sat there, axe to his forehead, contemplating his heart, a soft, sibilant whisper drifted into his mind, *"Your heart is strong, Victor. Follow it!"*

Lifedrinker had spoken, and apparently, that was all she had to say on the matter because nothing more was forthcoming from the recalcitrant blade. Still, she'd given him good advice, as far as Victor was concerned. She was basically telling him to go with his feelings, and for some reason, he wanted to pick Spirit Carver.

Victor tried to examine his feelings, tried to figure out what it was about Spirit Carver that called to him, or maybe it was something about Titanic Warrior that was pushing him away. He thought about that, about how he wanted to see himself, and though he enjoyed the power that came from his Quinametzin bloodline and his Berserk ability, he didn't know if he wanted to be defined by those things. The idea of a Spirit Carver seemed more nuanced. What even was a Spirit Carver? Would he be shaping his spirit or the spirits of his enemies? Would he be slicing spirits? It seemed kind of ambiguous, and that mystery was intriguing to him.

"Ahh hell," he said, stretching and cracking his neck. "Gorz, wake up."

"I'm here, Victor."

"I have a new class refinement option. Have you ever heard of a Spirit Carver?"

"Let me see." Gorz paused for a few seconds and then continued, *"No, Victor. I have a record of a class called a Flesh Carver, though. It's an Epic Class with several known abilities, one of which is the Flesh Carver's ability to change his or her physical shape."*

"Oh really? Anything else?"

"Another known ability of the Flesh Carver is the ability to craft simulacrum from specially processed tissue taken from conquered enemies."

"*Pinche* fuck! That sounds creepy."

"Just because the word 'carver' is shared between the two classes doesn't mean they'll share anything in common. It's a rather broadly defined term."

"Gah." Victor shook his head, wanting to slap himself for asking Gorz. As he'd feared, the spirit had, indeed, muddied the waters. One thing was clear—something was pulling him either away from Titanic Warrior or toward Spirit Carver, and Lifedrinker had encouraged him to go with his heart. He liked Lifedrinker, and she'd never let him down, so he decided to go for it. Pushing aside his doubts and worries, Victor flipped to the correct menu item in his System UI, then he selected the "accept" option for Spirit Carver.

*****Congratulations! You have refined your class: Spirit Carver. Class spell gained: Manifest Spirit, Basic. Class spell gained: Shape Spirit, Basic.*****

*****Manifest Spirit, Basic: With a tremendous effort of will, you can split off a shard of your spirit for a short while, allowing it to take form as a construct of Energy. Your spirit shard will retain the driving impetus you impart upon it for the duration of its existence, acting autonomously to fulfill that motivation. Your manifested spirit shard will return to you should it be destroyed or at the end of the spell's duration. Energy cost: 500. Cooldown: Medium.*****

*****Shape Spirit, Basic: You are able to impart your will upon your spirit, molding it to take the shape of a totemic beast or object that has special meaning to you. The first time you cast this spell, you will experience a spirit walk, during which you will encounter totems and make a selection for your shaping spell. Energy cost: 1000. Cooldown: Long.*****

"That's pretty fucking badass," Victor said, reading the descriptions for his new spells. He hopped to his feet, excited to figure out his new abilities but unsure where to begin. It seemed as if he needed to cast Shape Spirit before he could cast Manifest Spirit. No, that was wrong—it didn't seem that way; it was that way. He knew instinctively that he needed to complete the Shape Spirit spell before he could first manifest his spirit. "Which means I'll need to do a spirit walk, and I'll be helpless."

Victor pulled out his watch and looked at the time—three in the morning. He strode to the door of his suite and walked into the hallway, padding through the dim corridor to the station where Binna had been biding her time, waiting for the moment he'd need her. Just as he'd hoped, she was there, leaning back in her chair, a towel rolled up behind her head so she could rest it against the wall with her eyes closed. "Binna," Victor hissed in a hoarse whisper, louder than he meant to.

Her eyes snapped open, and she flailed her arms, nearly falling backward in her chair. As the feet of the chair settled and she straightened up, she said, "Gemstones! I'm sorry I was dozing, Mr. Sandoval! Did you need something?"

"Yes, I need you to fetch Edeya and bring her to my room. Tell her it's very important, but don't let anyone else know, okay?"

"You can count on me, Mr. Sandoval!" Binna said, jumping up and snapping a stiff salute before scurrying away down the hallway. Victor chuckled, then went back to his room to wait for Edeya. It wasn't long before there was a tap at his door, and he opened it to find Edeya, two house guards, and Binna standing in the hallway, bright glow lamps hanging from the guards' necks and all but Binna brandishing weapons.

"Damn, Binna. I said to keep it quiet!"

"She tried! I insisted on bringing my guards—too much talk of sabotage in the hallways," Edeya said, peering through the doorway as though to see if someone was hiding behind Victor.

"Sabotage? I haven't heard anything!"

"You've been busy. Anyway, is everything all right?"

"Yes, damn it, I just needed your help with something. You guys can head back to your, I dunno, stations," Victor said to the guards and Binna, then he stood back from the door so that Edeya could come in. She gave her two guards a pointed look, then nodded and stepped inside, closing the door behind her. "They're not going anywhere, are they?"

"No. Sorry, but my training is very explicit about situations like this."

"Damn, Edeya! I just needed someone to watch my back while I cast a spell." Victor sighed and moved past Edeya to throw the bolt on his door. "I was half tempted to try it alone, but the thought of me sitting here, a helpless vegetable, kind of creeped me out."

"Well, look at it this way: now you have me to watch your back, and I have some guards to watch mine. What kind of spell are you going to cast? Why will you become a vegetable?" Edeya loosened the collar of her uniform and produced a spear from some storage device, sheathing her pearl-handled knife.

"It's a kind of spirit walk. My spirit will be leaving my body for a while, and that means I'll be a sitting duck. Um, it means I won't be able to fight anything or even move. I need you to keep my body safe. You good with that, *chica*?"

"Yes, of course. I'm not promising I won't draw something on you, you know, as a reminder to stop calling me girl!" She pulled a chair out from the table, turned it toward the center of the room, and continued, "I'll watch you carefully, don't worry." She sat down, her spear planted on the floor before her, pointing up. "Why the urgency, by the way? I was in the middle of quite a nice dream when your servant started tapping on my door."

"Well, I just leveled and gained a refinement that might give me an edge in my duel. I don't want to waste time figuring it out. Speaking of which . . ." Victor concentrated on his status page and saw that he had ten points to distribute. He stacked them into will, figuring it was more important than ever, what with both his new class skills mentioning it.

With his will up over two hundred thirty, Victor's maximum Energy level was more than twenty-four hundred. While that number seemed high to him, he knew it was far more than it seemed; his regeneration rate was growing steadily with his will score. These days, when he cast one of his bigger spells, like Berserk or Inspiring Presence, his Energy levels had nearly recovered before their duration ran out.

"What are you doing?" Edeya asked, scowling at him from her impromptu guard post.

"Sorry, I had some attribute points to spend. All right, here goes. Don't let someone come and slit my throat, Edeya!" Victor sat down on the rug at the center of the room and closed his eyes, taking several deep breaths to steady himself. When he felt calm, and the only sounds in his ears were his own heartbeat and Edeya's quiet breathing, he instinctively cast Shape Spirit. He felt Energy pour out of his Core, both inspiration and rage-attuned. It flooded his pathways, and then he felt himself lift away from the ground, and when he opened his eyes, he was standing on the spirit plane.

Things seemed slightly different than the last time he'd walked on the spirit plane. The sky and stars were brighter, but there were trees and undergrowth around him, not just grasslands stretching as far as he could see. The trees were tall and thin, with silvery trunks and great canopies of shimmering silver-purple leaves. The undergrowth took on myriad shapes and twilight colors, from blue with orange highlights to deep purple, darker than the shadows under the leaves. Victor felt his bare toes sink into the rich, soft soil, and when he looked down at himself, he saw that he was naked.

His unclothed state felt perfectly natural for some reason, and he didn't bother trying to examine that feeling. Instead, he stretched, enjoying the rich Energy in the air and how his body buzzed with potential. Not sure what pulled him, he started walking in a seemingly random direction, moving between the trees and plant life as though he belonged there, silent and comfortable. He reached out a hand and drew his fingers along the bole of a mighty tree, smiling at the tingle of electricity that tickled his fingertips.

When he came around the tree and walked into a small clearing, he saw a stump with a silvery axe embedded in the top of it. He smiled at the weapon, no, in this case, a tool. It was familiar and called to him, but he didn't think it was the right choice for him. He had an axe with a strong spirit; why would he try to shape his own spirit shard into such a thing? He walked by the stump, still smiling at the feelings the axe had evoked but happy to carry on.

Victor walked through the twilight woods for a while, and soon he came to a downward slope, where he heard the babbling of a stream traversing stones and roots. As he stepped out from the tree line and saw the silvery water splashing along its stony bed, his heart felt calmed by the sight and sound of it.

He followed the ribbon of water with his eyes, and then he saw a great black shape splashing in its shallows. A colossal bear waded in the water, and Victor's heart started beating faster when he saw its mighty, bulging shoulders and snout snuffling and dipping beneath the surface. He ducked behind a nearby tree and watched the massive beast, awed by how it imposed its physical presence on its surroundings.

Something about the bear called to Victor, but he shook his head. No, he admired the bear and thought it was a remarkable creature, but he didn't feel drawn to it. He was like that bear, standing out in his surroundings, an imposing figure, especially when he went berserk, but did that mean he could only identify with a similar totem? Victor shook his head and wandered up the river away from the great beast, listening to the songs of the wind through the trees and the river's counterpoint.

He came to realize he was following a narrow game trail and that it was leading him uphill, away from the river. Victor leaned into the climb, his lungs pumping like bellows, and soon he stepped out of the woods and into a narrow canyon, devoid of trees but with thorny scrubs growing along its sides.

Victor looked up into the endless expanse of stars that shimmered over the spirit plane, and his eyes began to mist at the potential that lay up there. He was so small, his struggles such a tiny part of the tapestry—the enormity of it almost overwhelmed him. Sometime later, a distant sound brought him back to himself, and he realized he'd sat down on a smooth boulder.

Victor shook his head and focused on the sound, and a smile spread on his face. Now, these were familiar voices! The yipping cries of coyotes were echoing up the canyon, and Victor stood, stalking down the dry riverbed under the blanket of stars. When he rounded the corner and saw the pack darting all around, some up on the high canyon walls, others down in the sand, and still more playfully nipping and growling as they romped through the scrub, he broke into a laugh of pure joy.

Coyotes had sung him to sleep countless nights at his *abuela's* house, and Victor knew they were tricksters and scavengers, but he also knew they valued their pack and survived situations that would prove the ruination of greater beasts. They were brave and resourceful, and Victor admired their tenacity.

This was a totem that he could take into his heart. This was a totem he had a connection to. He stared at the romping pack, and one of them turned her silvery muzzle toward him, making eye contact. Victor felt the coyote imprint somewhere on his soul, then the spirit plane faded away, and he opened his eyes to see Edeya pacing back and forth in front of him, her spear held ready.

"Was I out long?" His voice cracked hoarsely.

"Yes!" Edeya whirled around at the sound of his voice. "I was starting to get worried! You were barely breathing and completely ignored me when I tried to wake you! Lam came back, and we have to leave today."

"What? Lam was here? What about Thayla?"

"No, Captain Lam sent word to my quarters, and one of my guards brought the message here. I didn't open the door because I promised I'd keep you safe, and it all seemed suspicious to me! I haven't heard anything about Thayla."

"Well, shit. Thanks. What time is it, anyway?" Victor stood, groaning at how his knees and ankles seemed to be stuck in their bent positions.

"It's after seven. Let's get breakfast and then find out what's going on, hmm?" Edeya moved over to the door and tapped a foot in agitation.

"All right, chill." Victor arched his back, stretching out stiff muscles, then pulled each knee to his chest. "My spell was a success, in case you were wondering."

"That's good. Don't tell me what it did, and that goes for everyone. Rellia is looking for information about your skills, and I'm pretty sure the idiot house guards were telling everyone in town about your fight with Polo Vosh yesterday."

"Fuck, seriously?" Victor hadn't even thought about that. Not many people had known about his bloodline's effect on his raging. He stopped at that thought and laughed. "I don't think anyone but you and Polo saw me berserk, right? I mean, the guards didn't get to the gym until Polo and I were already done, sitting on the floor. What are they telling everyone? That we fought and made a mess?"

"Hopefully," Edeya said, nodding. "Hopefully, Polo kept quiet, too. I'm sure he did—he's no idiot."

They'd been walking while they spoke, Edeya's two guards following a few paces behind, and they arrived at the kitchens just a few minutes later. While they ate, and Victor impressed the cooks yet again, Edeya sent one of her guards to find Captain Lam. They were just finishing up when he returned, red-faced from the exertion of hurrying, and announced that Lam was waiting for them in the front parlor. Victor didn't know the difference between the front parlor or any other parlor, and he certainly didn't know the way, but he just wiped the bacon grease off his face and followed Edeya.

A short while later, they walked into a well-lit room with high windows and several comfortable seating arrangements. Captain Lam was sitting with her legs crossed, reading from a sheaf of papers, and when they walked in, she beckoned them over, gesturing to nearby chairs. "Victor, I hope things have been going okay while I was gone. I spoke with Polo this morning—you impressed him."

"He's a pretty cool guy. I learned a lot from him in just a day. Do you think I can practice with him some more?"

"That had been my plan, but the fates conspire against us. No, not the fates—Rellia ap'Yensha. She's spread some rumors that you're going to back out of the fight. In fact, word around town is that you've already fled the city. Magistrate Thiv-dak has sent his clerk here with soldiers to transport you to his manor. He intends to keep you under lock and key, so you don't ruin his Harvest Fest gala."

"So, if I wanted out of this, I'm screwed, huh?"

"At this point, yes. We could have bargained for a reprieve a few days ago, but the magistrate has a lot of political clout invested in this gala now. Rellia's been leveraging her return from 'retirement' as well. A lot of pieces are moving in the shadows, and I'm afraid your fight has become a fulcrum point."

"It's fine. I wasn't going to back out, anyway. Well, where is this asshole? I might as well get going. Oh, hey, what about Thayla? Any word?"

"Thayla has successfully retrieved her daughter and is en route. I'll see that she knows where you're going. Edeya and some of my house guards will go with you today."

"I will?" Edeya raised an eyebrow, and when Victor looked at her, she smiled and said, "Of course, I will. You think we'd let you go sit in some cell without a friendly face nearby?"

Lam chuckled, then looked around the parlor at the nearby guards and said, "Leave the room and close the doors." To their credit, the guards moved quickly when Lam spoke, vacating the room and closing the heavy doors behind them. "Did you manage to reach Level Thirty, Victor?" Lam asked as soon as they were alone.

"Yes. Last night," Victor replied, not elaborating.

"Learn anything new? Anything that might help you surprise Rellia?"

"Yeah." Victor paused and narrowed his eyes. "Are you trying to decide if you should bet on me or not?"

"I've already 'bet' quite a lot on you, Victor. I'm trying to decide how thorough my contingencies need to be."

"Well, listen, Captain: I know I'm way under this *bruja's* level, but I'm not going to go down easy. My skills are like a fucking cheat mode in this world, and anyone who thinks I'm going out without a big *pinche* mess, better think again." Victor squeezed his two hands into fists, so tight that his knuckles popped. "I'll do my best, all right?"

30

LIFEDRINKER

Victor sat on a wooden bench, watching the metal bars of the portcullis that would raise to give him access to the magistrate's arena. Victor had been brought to the estate two days ago and given a reasonably comfortable room. Edeya had tried to make good on her word, fighting with the magistrate's house guards to allow her entry into Victor's quarters, but they'd been unwilling to bend their employer's orders, so Victor had spent the last two days completely alone.

Early in the morning, after the usual servants brought him breakfast, some guards had come to bring him to this chamber. He'd gotten a good look at the magistrate's villa and grounds on his walk to the fighting pit, and Victor had concluded that, much like on Earth, the people in power here made too much money. The house was extensive, rivaling Lam's for square footage, and the grounds were well manicured and festively decorated.

He'd seen brightly colored, temporary pavilions set up on the lawns, firepits loaded with wood and ready to be ignited, and servants bustling to and fro, setting up tables and loading stations with hors d'oeuvres and crystal decanters filled with liquor. The magistrate was planning an impressive gala, and Victor would be the main entertainment. He didn't like it one bit.

Victor hadn't been mistreated in his days of captivity, that was for sure. They'd fed him well, and he'd even had servants come to his room offering him massages, a haircut, and laundry service. He'd chased them all away, too self-conscious and aware that many of the servants weren't working there by choice. He wasn't sure why he thought that—none of them wore collars or acted in any way other than overly polite. Still, Victor couldn't get the feeling out of his gut that he was fighting for his own freedom while people were forced to serve him.

So Victor sat in the underground chamber attached to Magistrate Thivdak's impressive and quite permanent fighting pit, and he brooded. He couldn't help thinking that he'd be in a better state of mind if he'd been allowed to spend the last two days with his friends or at least training with Polo, which gave him the idea that maybe the magistrate was working with Rellia. Maybe he wanted to make sure Victor didn't have any more chances to improve his skills by working with the master warrior. Was that paranoid? "Not considering all the bullshit I've seen from these people," he growled to the empty room.

He could watch the shadows shift in the tunnel to see that the sun was slowly moving through the sky. He didn't know what time the fight would be; he'd asked the guards that led him here, but they'd all acted as though they knew only about as much as he did. One of them had wished him good luck, though, which Victor took as a good sign. It wasn't as if he was being held and treated like some sort of criminal scum. Many of the servants and guards he'd interacted with had given him a kind of deference, almost as if he was a celebrity.

While he sat there, trying to guess the hour and thinking about how he wanted to get this fight over with, he saw a shadow approaching down the tunnel. A moment later, it resolved into two shadows. He stood and walked to the bars, a feeling in his gut telling him he wanted to see these visitors. A moment later, he heard her exclamation, and then Thayla was jogging down the tunnel toward him, towing a much smaller figure behind. "Victor!"

"Thayla! Hell yes! I was afraid I wouldn't see you before the fight!"

"Not a chance! That magistrate is treating you like a prize hen, afraid everyone will steal you or something, but Captain Lam has her ways. She insisted that someone be allowed to check on your welfare, and Deyni and I were lucky enough to get the job!"

Victor squatted down, looking at the diminutive figure hiding behind Thayla's legs. "So, this is Deyni? I've heard a lot about you, *chica*," he said softly. "Come on, let me get a look at you."

"She's been so shy," Thayla said, turning and gently nudging the little girl forward. "She barely recognized me, Victor. Thank the Ancestors, Rhessa had been showing her pictures and telling her stories about me while I was gone. Come here, sweetie; this is the man I told you about."

Deyni took a step forward into the light of the glow lamps behind Victor, and he saw that her skin was more purple than red and that her hair was a bright teal color that matched her eyes. He almost said something about it but didn't know if it was considered rude. Instead, he reached through the bars and gently tousled her hair.

"*¡Qué bonita!*" He laughed at her giggle, then said, "I'm Victor, and your mommy is my best friend in the world. That means you're my friend too, got it?"

She nodded, suddenly solemn-faced, and then she spoke, her voice small but steady, "Why are you in prison, Victor?"

"I'm not in prison! I'm just resting here before I have to perform later. Those bars are to keep all my fans away!"

"Victor's silly, sweetie, but he's not in prison, don't worry," Thayla said, squatting down to be more on a level with Victor and her daughter. She rested a hand on Deyni's shoulder and smiled at him. "You're going to do fine tonight, Victor. We'll all be watching, and Lam will make sure everything is aboveboard."

"Thanks, Thayla. Do you know how long I have? The *pendejos* that brought me here didn't have a clue."

"About three hours. The guests are starting to arrive, but most of the important ones won't be here for another couple of hours, and then the magistrate will want to give everyone a chance to get drunk and make wagers."

"So, everyone's getting a chance to get rich off my performance, huh? What do you think of that, sweetie? Pretty lame, huh?" Victor poked her cheek playfully with one of his thick fingers and made a stricken face when she pulled away. "What? Do I smell?"

"You smell like flowers! Have they been pampering you?" Thayla answered for the little girl.

"Well, I got bored and took a few baths while I was locked up in my fancy bedroom."

"How am I not surprised?" Thayla laughed. "Back to your other point, though—nothing's stopping us from making a bet. You want me to put some Energy beads down on you? Think you'll win, or should I bet on Rellia?" She smiled, but Victor thought it looked a little forced. He reached out and took Thayla's hand, doing his best to look confident.

"I'll be fine. Thanks for coming to visit me; it means a hell of a lot. Do me a favor, though, and go somewhere safe and relaxing tonight with Deyni.

She shouldn't see this thing, and there's no way you should be apart from her. Here." He reached into his storage ring and pulled out one of the large sacks of Energy beads he'd accumulated. "This is like a thousand Energy beads. Put it all on me. I hope the odds are really against me because it will help us get you set up when this is all over."

"Nice try, but I've already made arrangements for Deyni. My friend Rhessa is here, too. She'll watch her during your . . . event." She took the sack of Energy beads, making them disappear into her ring. Then she leaned forward, pressing her head against two bars, reached through, pulled Victor close, and kissed him soundly on the forehead. "You better win," she said softly.

"Hey, I'm planning on it . . ."

Thayla put a hand over his mouth and said, "I'm sorry, Victor. I'm sorry I left to get Deyni, but when Lam offered her coach and driver, and said I should hurry, I jumped at it. I should have spoken to you first. You know"—she squeezed Deyni against her chest, eliciting a squeal—"we're only together because of you. I'll never forget it."

She stood, taking Deyni's hand and said, "C'mon, girlie. Let's go find something sweet to eat while we wait for this dumb party to get over."

"Deyni!" Victor called after the girl. When she turned to look at him, he said, "Eat something sweet for me too, okay?"

"I will, Victor!"

Victor smiled as he watched them walk away up the hallway, and then he moved back to his bench. In the back of his mind, he knew there was a very real possibility that he'd die in the match tonight. On some level, he knew that's why he'd been feeling down before Thayla came. Her visit and the sight of her back together with her daughter had filled him with a sort of peaceful, relaxed energy, and he knew it was because, in his mind, she'd been telling the truth—he was responsible for their reunion. "If I die tonight, at least I did one fucking good thing with my life."

He whiled away the hours by moving through his axe forms. He knew a lot more of them now that his skill level had gone up to advanced. While working through them, from hooks to parries to cleaves to thrusts, he marveled again at how the System just seemed able to plant knowledge into his head.

While he had the clarity of focus that came from good clean exercise, a thought occurred to him, though. The System didn't *just* plant knowledge in his head—he had to earn it. He had to gain levels and practice and build up his Energy. He wondered what would happen if the System tried to plant advanced skills into the head of a Level Zero, normal human. Would their brain explode?

"It's your time, warrior," a rough voice said from the portcullis. Victor hadn't heard the man approach, so engrossed had he been in his exercise and musings about the System.

"All right," he said, slipping Lifedrinker into the loop on his belt. He moved over to the gate and saw that the man that had come to collect him wore a black robe and hood that completely obscured his face. "Are you, like, an executioner or something?"

"No. This is traditional garb for an arbiter at a trial by combat. I'm supposed to be the faceless embodiment of justice. Don't worry, fighter; I'm impartial because only the court knows who I am. Now, follow me—I've already fetched your opponent, and she waits rather impatiently, furious, in fact, that I brought her up first." A hint of amusement might have colored the arbiter's words, but Victor couldn't be entirely sure.

"Right." He nodded and started up the long, sloping hallway, walking just a half step behind the hooded figure. He could hear the crowd before he could see them. He knew the magistrate's fighting pit was large, and he'd seen the rows of stands around it, but his brain hadn't drawn the connection that they'd all be full of people during the fight. Some part of him had hoped the magistrate would keep the event rather exclusive and that only a few dozen people would show. Judging by the hum and murmur of the crowd, though, his hopes had been fruitless.

When he stepped out of the tunnel into the sand of the pit, the bright lights made him squint, and he held a hand up to shield his eyes. At the sight of him, the crowd went wild, cheering, screaming, jeering, and booing. As his eyes adjusted and he looked around, he saw hundreds, no thousands of faces jammed into the stands around the big circular arena, and standing thirty yards in front of him, Rellia ap'Yensha watched him as a cat watches a mouse.

She wore a glittering silvery chain shirt, a silver diadem held back her bright red hair, and sleek black leather leggings completed her look. She was tall and lithe and paced in her black boots, one hand flicking a rapier about, making it flicker with electric pulses of Energy with each movement. Victor saw she held a short-bladed, single-edged knife in her other hand, and though it was no axe or sword, it looked heavy enough to carve a pig carcass.

The hooded arbiter motioned for Victor to stop then he walked to the center of the pit, directly between the two combatants. He turned toward the tallest stand of bleachers, where a box had been set up for the guests of honor. Victor saw a dozen people he didn't recognize in the box, along with Lam and Thayla.

The arbiter held up a hand and stood there, like a specter, unmoving until the crowd took notice and began to quiet. As silence took command of the spectacle, the arbiter called out with a loud, deep voice, "Per the standard rules of combat trials, the combatants will be allowed their armor and a choice of weapons. All other items, magical or not, will be held by me."

The arbiter turned sharply and walked over to Rellia. He held out a hand and waited while she divested herself of rings and an amulet. He remained still while she stood there looking irritated. After several moments of waiting, he gestured quickly to the diadem on Rellia's head. She shook her head sharply and said something in a waspish hiss. The arbiter stared at her for a moment more, then nodded and turned to walk over to Victor. He held out his hands, empty, and Victor got the hint. He took off Gorz, his rings, and the pouch at his belt, placing them all into the arbiter's hands.

"No other dimensional containers or hidden weapons?"

"No. My belt is enchanted, but I think it's sort of part of my armor, isn't it?" Victor said, patting his ringed armor as if to show there wasn't any room for deception. The links jingled with his efforts, and the arbiter nodded, stowing Victor's items in one of his voluminous pockets, and then he turned and walked back to the center of the arena.

"I am satisfied with the equipment each combatant now holds," he called up to the waiting booth, and the crowd erupted back into a frenzy of cheering, laughing, and talking. The arbiter moved to a ladder built into the arena pit, opposite the box where the VIPs sat. Victor saw that the ladder led to a platform that stood out from the top edge of the ring. It would give anyone standing on it a bird's-eye view of the action.

While he waited for the arbiter to make his slow way up the ladder, he turned his attention to Rellia. She was pacing back and forth, whipping that gleaming, almost liquid-looking rapier back and forth, staring at Victor with a smirk on her face. He hadn't known what to expect when it came to Rellia's looks, but a beautiful, youthful Ardeni hadn't been it. The way people said she hadn't seen any action in fifty years made him think of her as elderly, which he realized now was stupid. In a world where people advanced their race and gained enormous power through the accumulation of Energy, aging wasn't as much of an issue as it had been on Earth. At least not for people that took the risks required to gain power.

"Ready to die, boy?" she called out in a sharp voice that carried over the sand, despite the noise from the stands. Victor had had plenty of opponents trash-talk him, but his coach had always told him to let his skill on the mat do the talking. Victor liked his coach's advice for one reason—he'd seen someone loudly mock his friend Anthony, and then Anthony had taken that fool apart on the mat, winning by points, one takedown after another, utterly humiliating the kid. Victor had seen exactly what his coach had been trying to tell him and determined at that point never to talk shit before a match. "Or a fight," he said, spitting into the sand and ignoring Rellia.

"Combatants! Ready yourselves, then raise your left arm to indicate your ability to fight!" the arbiter called out, having taken his perch. Victor noticed that his voice cut through the crowd's noise as though he was speaking through a megaphone. He looked around but didn't see any such device and figured the man was either using some sort of Energy ability or the stand he was on somehow amplified his voice.

Rellia immediately lifted her left arm, staring at Victor. Victor stretched, then lazily lifted Lifedrinker from the loop on his belt. She was warm and hummed eagerly in his hands. "Ready for some work, *chica*?"

He didn't lift his arm right away. Instead, he turned to the box where Thayla and Lam sat, and he made eye contact with Thayla. Her face was expressionless, and Victor knew she was worried about him, so he smiled and nodded. Then he turned to Rellia and lifted his left arm.

"Let the trial of combat commence!" the arbiter yelled, his voice booming over the arena.

Victor brought his hand back to Lifedrinker, boosted his agility with Sovereign Will, cast Channel Spirit, flooding Lifedrinker with rage-attuned Energy, and then started to cast Inspiring Presence, not wanting to jump straight into a berserking rage. He'd just felt the Energy start to flow into his pathways when a terrible pain erupted in his lower back. He stumbled forward, coughing out a gout of dark, almost black blood, his mind reeling, trying to put two and two together.

He'd been staring at Rellia; the attack couldn't have come from her, half his brain was saying, and the other half said, "She's not there, you dumbass!" He spun madly, whipping Lifedrinker in a brutal cleave, the pain still arcing through him from whatever had happened to his back. He caught a glimpse of her silvery chainmail as she darted around his flank, his cut with Lifedrinker not even coming close.

He continued to spin, trying to get her into his sights, but as he stumble-turned, just from the corner of his eye, he saw another bright flash and then felt pain erupt in his thigh, and when he glanced down, he saw Rellia's rapier withdrawing from a puncture wound that completely pierced his leg.

Blood poured from his wounds like faucets had been turned on, and Victor saw that he was painting the sands red as he stumbled after Rellia. "Fuck this," he growled, backpedaling and finally finishing the casting of Inspiring Presence. The red haze that had begun to cloud his vision faded away as his perception brightened. He saw all the lights around the arena and beyond them the bright moons, and he smiled—this was a glorious place to do battle.

He backed up quickly, putting his back to the arena wall and holding Lifedrinker sideways in front of himself. He panned his vision, locking onto Rellia while she danced back, unable to flank him as she'd been intending. "Ah, ah, *pendeja*," Victor said under his breath. "Time to fight face to face," he said more loudly.

"You've a lot of blood, boy. They'll be washing this sand for days." Rellia angled her advance, her rapier out in front of herself, weaving it in a small circle. Did she want Victor to look at it? He focused his gaze on her hips, another trick his old coach had taught him—if you wanted to see where an opponent was going, don't watch their hands or face.

"Is that a thing? Why would they wash the sand? This place is for fighting," he said, unable to help himself from responding. Just then, Rellia moved into an attack, and it was only pure chance that Victor even saw it coming, she was so fast. Her feet blurred with shadowy Energy, and then she lunged, extending her rapier under his guard and piercing his gut, right through his ringed armor. The liquid, gleaming steel of her rapier rang against the ring it slid through, and then it hung up, the blade growing too broad to slide any further. In fact, she'd thrust so hard, and the metal of her rapier was so fine that it bit into the ring, but not entirely through it, which made it stick.

Despite the horrible pain in his gut, Victor grinned and brought Lifedrinker down in a tremendous hack toward Rellia's arm holding her rapier. Rellia tugged at her blade and, unable to pull it out quickly enough, let go of the hilt so that Victor's axe ripped through nothing but air. Still, he'd disarmed her main weapon, so he grinned as he backed away and gripped the skinny blade, trying to pull it free without slicing off his fingers. Rellia didn't seem perturbed to have lost her rapier. She backed off and watched his struggle with a crooked smile.

When Victor finally got the blade free of his gut and armor, he lifted it as though to throw it out of the arena, and then Rellia laughed. She had a high, trilling laugh, and Victor hated the sound of it because he knew he'd have liked it if he were friends with the woman. Arm back, ready to launch the feather-light blade, he looked at her, and she lifted her left hand to touch her diadem. A second later, Victor stood there, nothing in his hand, and Rellia whipped her rapier back and forth in front of herself.

"Silly oaf," she said, laughing again.

Victor growled and cast Project Spirit, pushing out a wave of inspiration-attuned Energy that had been twisted by the spell into a sickly pulse of discouragement. Rellia's grin faded, and she backed away quickly, almost turning to run, and Victor gave chase. He was fast with his agility boosted, but Rellia was faster. Whatever classes she'd had over the course of her long career must have been ones that increased her agility and dexterity because, even boosted, Victor was unable to catch her when she concentrated on dodging away from her. He kept pushing out waves of discouragement, trying to keep her on the retreat and angling to deliver a hack to her retreating form, sure that with just one well-placed blow of Lifedrinker, he could bring this fight to a close.

At one point during his chase, Victor channeled more inspiration-attuned Energy into his pathways and into Lifedrinker, hoping to give himself the edge he needed to overcome Rellia's speed. Still, she evaded him, and when he tried to renew his Inspiring Presence, he found his inspiration Core had run nearly dry. Finally, frustrated and losing blood by the second, Victor roared and released his rage Core.

As he cast Berserk, letting the spell loose like a terrible hound he'd been just barely keeping on a leash, and the rage began to flood his pathways, he had a final, fleeting thought—why hadn't he tried his new spell? Why hadn't he cast Manifest Spirit? Before he could answer, the red overtook his vision, and he felt his body surge with unbelievable power. The crowd might have cheered, roared, or screamed, but all he heard was the thump of his massive heart, the rushing of blood in his ears, and his own deep, echoing laughter as it rolled out of his gut and into the arena.

If he'd had the presence of mind to register it, Victor might have been disturbed to see that Rellia was also smiling. She stopped her mad dash away from Victor and turned to regard his massive, laughing form. She looked like a child standing before him, and when Victor regarded her tiny form, the only thought in his mind was that this gnat had been trying to bleed him out. She needed to be smashed into the ground. He lifted Lifedrinker with one hand and leaped toward her, launching himself into the air in a miniature dust devil, his momentum pulling sand up in a showering cascade.

Victor's prodigious strength made his enormous frame quick, and when he crashed into the sand near Rellia, whipping his axe through the air, she barely managed to roll back away from the attack. Victor wasn't done, though, and he roared, charging after her, no thought in his mind other than the destruction of this annoying creature. As his lumbering form bore down on her, his wide arms making it difficult for her to try to edge around him, Rellia was forced to backpedal toward the wall.

When Rellia's back touched the wooden planks of the arena wall and Victor was bearing down on her, she didn't look dismayed or lost. In fact, her smile widened. When Victor was just inches away from cleaving her in half, she lifted her arms and screamed. It was a scream to end all screams, and it tore through the air in a cloud of black Energy, engulfing Victor's charging form.

The cone of her attack was rather small, all told, and most of the audience, though they were aware of the power of the scream and could see the strange black cloud that had obscured the area in front of Rellia, didn't suffer the terrible sound of it. On the other hand, Victor was at ground zero, and the echoing terror of it bounced around in his head, and the cloud of black Energy instantly caught him up as if he'd been dropped into a vat of tar. He struggled to keep moving, but he felt his every tendon and muscle being dragged down, as if the cloud was pulling him into the center of the planet.

Victor roared and struggled and pushed more and more rage-attuned Energy into his pathways, trying to break free of the evil sound and its accompanying cloud. Still, he felt the Energy bleeding out of him as though the spell had a way of sapping his power as it held him tight. After what felt like an eternity, the piercing, echoing scream finally faded, and the cloud began to dissipate. Victor found he was on his knees in the arena and that his berserking rage was gone.

Rellia stood before him, and her rapier darted out like a liquid-lightning snake's tongue, and she pierced him several times before he could even begin to lift Lifedrinker. Blood leaked from him like juice from a smashed orange, and Victor realized she'd also been stabbing him while he'd been in the cloud. His vision was already growing dim around the edges, and, though he tried to cast Berserk, boost his Vitality with Sovereign Will—anything—he couldn't find the Energy to make it happen. He slumped down, trying to look at his Core, and, as Rellia backed up a step, giving him a slight reprieve, he saw that he was nearly dry of both types of his Energy.

Rellia lifted her arms, and the crowd roared its approval. She turned back to Victor and said, "You'll never know the trouble I went through to learn that spell. It was the only counter I could get ahold of that I was sure would work on your insane rage. It cost me dearly, and casting it cost me further still, but here we are. I've won, and you're at my mercy, just as I wanted. The crowd would regale me if I cut your throat right now, but I have an offer for you. Are you listening, boy?"

"Ungh," Victor grunted, struggling to lift Lifedrinker, but his body felt so weak, and his mind was so foggy that she flopped, buzzing back down to the sand. He thought she was vibrating more than usual, but it could have been the trembling of his hands and arms.

"Work for me, boy. Do my bidding for ten years, and I'll let you live. I'll hold my boot on your neck and announce my mercy, and then you'll work for my house. Agreed?" Rellia had leaned forward and hissed her offer to him in a way that Victor doubted could be heard by the crowd, even though they'd grown hushed, wondering what she'd do to him.

Victor, foggy though his mind was, thought about her words. He thought about what it felt like to work under the boot of even a benevolent master. He thought about how he and Thayla had escaped the mines and all the things they'd talked about on their journeys. He thought about the Wagon Wheel and Yund and Ponda. He thought about Captain Lam and Edeya and all the wrongs he'd seen in this world. Then he thought of Thayla and Deyni, and he imagined them sitting together with Oynalla and learning about how to cast spirit magic, and he smiled. He smiled a big, bloody, red-toothed smile, and he looked at Rellia and said, "Fuck you, *puta*."

"Idiot," she hissed, then her wicked, lightning-fast rapier flashed out and cut Victor's throat. Victor slapped a hand to the wound, but blood was gushing out faster than he could contain it, and blackness was closing in on his vision like an ever lengthening tunnel. His range of vision narrowed to a small circle, then a pinprick, and with a smile still on his face, he felt his spirit start to lift free of his body. Dimly, very dimly, he knew the crowd was roaring and that Rellia was celebrating, raising her rapier in the air, basking in the crowd's love.

Victor felt his perspective shift; for a moment, he thought he was looking at himself and had a strange, disconnected feeling. *There was Victor Sandoval, and he's dying, but you are something more*, was the thought going through his mind, and he almost embraced it. He almost drifted away completely, but then he felt something in his right hand. Not the hand that had slapped the wound at his neck. No, it was the hand that still held onto Lifedrinker. She was going mad, vibrating and pulsing with Energy, and for a moment, Victor was pulled back into himself, and then he heard something.

"Take from me, Victor. Take what you need! I give it freely. Don't worry about me; we'll meet again." The voice was feminine and lilting, and Victor felt his eyes burst with tears at the sound. He couldn't see, couldn't even open them, but he felt the water running out of them and down his cheeks. *"Your body is strong, Victor. Your heart still works. Don't give up. Take what you need, make yourself great again, and ruin this heartless creature that torments you!"*

Victor tried to speak, and when he couldn't, he tried to just use his mind, his heart, to tell Lifedrinker that he didn't want to live if it hurt her, but he felt her will pushing back, and, more than that, he felt her love. She loved him. *"Take from me! You'll make me strong and alive again. I trust you!"* With her words, Victor felt the pulse of Energy in his hand again, and he broke. He gave in to her demands, and he *took.* Victor pulled Energy out of Lifedrinker into himself. He tugged it up along his pathways and toward his Core and tried to direct it into the dim, weakly pulsing orb of his rage-attuned reservoir.

The Energy Lifedrinker fed him was pure, though, not attuned for rage, and when he pulled it toward that hot, red sun, it diminished as it changed into rage-attuned Energy. Victor knew he'd need to draw more, a lot more, to do what needed doing. Lifedrinker buzzed and thumped in his hand, and Victor knew she was giving him permission, so, with tears flowing down his cheeks, he pulled a massive torrent of Energy out of her, making his rage-attuned Core blaze.

Victor pushed some of the Energy into his pathways, guiding it toward his wounded flesh, and the hot, rage-attuned Energy seared his wounds closed, and, for the first time in over a minute, he took a breath and opened his eyes. He still sat slumped, his head pointed down, and all he saw was blood-drenched sand. His left hand was still clamped around his own throat, held there by the dried blood, no doubt. Lifedrinker lay in front of him, her handle still in his other hand, and Victor was relieved to feel a weak vibration from the weapon—she'd given up a lot for him, but she wasn't dead.

Slowly, Victor lifted his head and took in the arena. The buzzing whoosh that had overwhelmed his ears faded slightly, and he realized that some of the noise was the crowd. Rellia still stood in the sand, waving her rapier around, celebrating her victory. Victor felt a growl start to rumble in his gut, but before he could let his rage overcome him and get him into more trouble, he took a deep breath and focused on his new spell. He cast Manifest Spirit, and when the pattern formed in his pathways, hungry for Energy, he fed it from the rage-attuned Core that Lifedrinker had filled.

An eerie yipping and barking sound began to echo around the arena, and the crowd grew quiet. Rellia lowered her upraised rapier and looked around in puzzlement. She wondered if one of her friends or, more likely, one of her enemies was trying to steal her moment of glory. A flicker of movement caught her attention, and she jerked her head to the right, and sure enough, a skinny red hound stood near the arena wall there, staring at her as it began to pace back and forth, still making that annoying yipping sound.

More yipping cries came from behind her, and Rellia spun to see two more of the hounds. They weren't large—just skinny hounds, but their dusky red fur and glowing red eyes gave them an unearthly, intimidating presence. She turned to the arbiter's platform and yelled, "What is this? Who interferes?"

The arbiter, ever an annoyance, simply boomed out, using his enhanced voice, "There is no interference. Look to yourself for celebrating a premature victory."

"What?" Rellia spun toward the center of the arena where she'd slain the foolish berserker, but he wasn't sitting there, slumped on his knees in a pool of blood. No, he stood now, still in a pool of blood and caked with the stuff from his eyes to the tips of his fingers, but alive.

Victor whistled shrilly, and then Rellia saw movement all around her, and she spun, putting her rapier into a guard position, and readying herself for anything. The red hounds circled her, yipping, barking, and darting forward and back, never quite closing the distance. They were keeping her distracted! Rellia spun again, and this time Victor was closer, and as he stepped toward her again, his mad smile grew and his eyes filled with blood-red fury, and his already tall, muscled form began to grow. "Impossible," Rellia hissed, then she heard a snarl and felt a painful bite on her calf.

Rellia was low on Energy, and there was no way she could cast her spell again. Umbral Shadows of the Harpy had taken far too much out of her—if she tried again so soon, she'd shatter her Core. She'd have to wear the brute down again, bleed him out until this surge of Energy faded, and she could finish him. Again. Another yip and another bite broke her concentration, though, and Rellia whipped her rapier through the air at the hound, only to have it dance back as another came in, nipping at the tendons of her knee. "Ancestors, damn it!" she cried as she tried to drive her knife at the quick little creature.

Just then, Rellia felt, as she often did in combat, that it was time to dodge, and she rolled forward, barely avoiding a heavy cleave from the giant berserker's axe. He laughed and stomped after her. Rellia put out her hand to bound to her feet, only to have one of the hounds come forward to nip at her fingers. She cried out and rolled on her shoulder, trying to drive her rapier into the hound, and she scored a hit on its rear haunch as it darted away. Before she could celebrate, though, the berserker's axe met her outstretched leg, and with horror, Rellia saw her foot parted from her ankle.

Rellia screamed and rolled, only to have several more nipping bites mark her flesh. She pushed herself to her knees and tried to crawl away. She tried to focus enough to cast a movement spell, to fill herself with shadow Energy and streak over the sand, but the hounds were everywhere, nipping and crying, and she was so tired, her Core nearly depleted. Rellia sobbed as she crawled, blood pouring from her ankle and seeping from the dozen little bites all over her arms and legs.

Suddenly she felt a tremendous weight on her lower back, and she was pressed into the sand. The giant berserker was standing on her back, holding her down with one foot. Rellia sobbed again and turned to regard the freak, unable to fathom how this had happened. He was leaning over her, his axe held high in one hand and his big, angry face peering down at her. It looked as if he was grinding his teeth with the effort of holding back the axe, and, as she watched, his face red with effort, he growled out, in a terrible, deep voice, "Do you yield?"

"Yes!" she cried, tears streaming down her cheeks.

The monstrous human, the berserking titan, turned his head to the arbiter and growled, "All witness! She yields!"

"Rellia ap'Yensha has yielded in a trial by combat! All of her grievances are dismissed, and Victor Sandoval is an innocent man!" the petty arbiter bellowed over the crowd, but even his voice was lost after that—the crowd went absolutely insane in celebration. Rellia sobbed into the sand, unwilling to look up and face her "friends" or enemies. Her advanced body had slowed the bleeding of her ankle enough so that she wasn't at risk of death, and she decided to just close her eyes, lie there, and wait for the humiliation to be over.

Victor stood, chest heaving, over the crumpled form of his enemy. He'd wanted to kill her, wanted to smash her into bits and fling them about the arena like dog food. He'd been intent on it, ready to cleave off her other foot, and then her legs at the knees, then the other parts of her, but when he'd advanced, when he'd watched her crawling through the sand, sobbing and bleeding, desperation in her ragged breaths, he'd seen the image of another woman. He'd seen Yrella as she died in a smaller, dirtier pit, and his rage had cooled immensely. It wasn't gone, no, but he knew he couldn't butcher Rellia. Not now, not like this. He didn't know what it might cost him, but he didn't care.

Victor stepped off Rellia's back and turned to the box where Thayla and Lam had been sitting. They weren't there, though, and he ran his eyes over the crowd trying to find them. Everyone was cheering and screaming and clapping each other on the back as though they'd accomplished something great. Seeing their rabid faces, Victor was filled with disgust, and he reached down to pick up the woman he'd just defeated. He was still enraged, still berserk, and he knew he was risking a relapse into violence, but he seemed to have a fairly good grasp on himself. It was almost as if the yipping of his coyote pack helped him to focus.

As he glanced back up, he caught a glimpse of Thayla and Lam moving toward the door that would take them into the ready room. With Rellia, seemingly unconscious under one arm, he moved to the closed portcullis, glaring at the arbiter as he walked. The man's hooded head nodded, then the portcullis was raised, and Victor walked into the tunnel. When he'd made it a dozen steps away from the crowd, he felt his rage begin to fade, and he became more aware of the weight of his defeated opponent. He struggled to shift her into a more normal carrying position, juggling Lifedrinker in one hand.

Rellia stirred then and, with a scratchy, weak voice, said, "Just leave me here. Thank you for getting me away from the crowd."

"All right," Victor said, setting the woman on the ground of the tunnel. He glanced back at his coyotes and saw they'd sat down in the shadows and were regarding him with that questioning look in their eyes that only canines could pull off. He nodded his head and felt the spell begin to fall apart, and his pack dissipated into wispy clouds of red smoke. He looked again at Rellia, but she refused to make eye contact with him, so Victor just grunted again and started down the tunnel, wanting to be away from the arena.

"How'd you do it?" Rellia asked, her voice quiet and weak, chasing after him down the dark corridor.

Victor turned and regarded her for a minute, then he lifted Lifedrinker, her edge bright and shiny, but the lightning veins of heartsilver that had been spreading through the black metal all but faded away, and he said, "Love, I guess."

ABOUT THE AUTHOR

Plum Parrot is the pen name of author Miles Gallup, who grew up in Southern Arizona and spent much of his youth wandering around the Sonoran Desert, hunting imaginary monsters and building forts. He studied creative writing at the University of Arizona and, for a number of years, attempted to teach middle schoolers to love literature and write their own stories. If he's not out enjoying the beach, you can find Gallup writing, reading his favorite authors, or playing *D&D* with friends and family.

Podium

DISCOVER
STORIES UNBOUND

PodiumAudio.com